SCARS OF THE SUNDERING
BOOK 3

SALVATION

Scars of the Sundering
Book 3

Salvation

Hans Cummings

Scars of the Sundering

Book 1 – Malediction
Book 2 – Lament
Book 3 - Salvation

Hans Cummings

ISBN: 1-944999-03-5

Electronic edition available through Amazon.com,
Print edition available through Amazon.com and CreateSpace.

Edited by Cynthia Shepp
https://cynthiashepp.wordpress.com/

Cover design by Eric Hubbel
http://hubbelcreative.deviantart.com/

Cover Art by Lily Yang
http://www.lilyyangart.com/

Heraldy by
Axel Löfving

Cartography by Anna B. Meyer
http://http://ghmaps.net/

World of Calliome Logo by
Gwyneth Ravenscraft of G-Sharp Productions
http://www.g-sharpproductions.com/

ACKNOWLEDGEMENTS

For Tink, without whom this would not have been possible.

To Steven D. Russell, your encouragement and enthusiasm was more helpful and inspirational than you can ever know. R.I.P, my friend.

Thanks to Michael R. Hicks, J.A. Konrath, Chuck Wendig, and Michael A. Stackpole for encouragement, advice, and inspiration. You all help give me the drive to make this possible.

Special thanks to Mike Wolff, Craig Majors, John Adamus, Lillian K, and my readers for all their encouragement and feedback.

Chapter 1

Kale squinted from within the Citadel of Fire and Stone's entrance and peered toward the giants' village across the lake. The giants went about their business, seemingly ignorant of what transpired within. He supposed it was possible they were neither aware towering skeletal warriors attended their king, nor the draks, with the aid of their human friend, killed the king, destroyed the skeletons, and discovered the dead dragon.

He folded his wings and swam to the dock where his sister, his mate, and the human, Katka, along with the dragon egg they recovered from the lair, waited for his report. It was the lone valuable object that remained. Kale suspected whatever caused the ceiling to crush the dragon's head was also responsible for the loss of the rest of the treasure. No legends told of dragons who took vows of poverty. If anything, they were all covetous.

"So, what's going on out there?" His sister and his mate squatted, reaching to help him onto the dock.

"Nothing. It's like they have no idea what happened."

Katka cradled her broken arm. "Maybe they don't. Rock is pretty good at blocking sound."

Delilah shook her head. "Obviously, you've never lived underground. Sound travels through rock."

"Through to the village and across the lake?"

Kale crouched by the dragon egg and ran his hands over its surface. Even to him, it felt warm when he touched it, offering him reassurance that the fetal dragon within was still alive. He tried to ignore the discussion between his sister and the human girl about the auditory transmission properties of rocks.

"So? What are we going to do? If they find out we killed their king, they'll stomp us like bugs." Kali stooped behind Kale, wrapping her arms around him and resting her head on his back between his wings. He allowed himself to relish the feeling of his mate's touch before responding.

"We could try sneaking out at night." He glanced at the sky. It would be dark soon. If they took care crossing the lake after most of the giants were asleep and kept close to the village's perimeter, he believed they could pass unnoticed.

"That might work. I know an enchantment that will help us move more quietly." Katka shifted her weight from one foot to the other and gazed over the lake. "I don't fancy being smashed by angry giants. I'd hoped to make apprentice this year."

"Don't worry. We'll get out of this." Delilah touched Katka's elbow and smiled. "Kale and I got through dozens of oroq invasions back home. Sneaking past a few giants will be easy."

Delilah's exaggerations aside, Kale agreed with his sister. Katka was the largest of them, and even she was small for a human. They were all diminutive compared to the villagers. Kale ushered them into the safety of the citadel. *No point risking detection.*

They spent the afternoon discussing strategies based on half-remembered details of the village. The plan was to swim along the cliff until they reached the near shore and then work their way through the forest until they met the road. Kale decided to explore nearby chambers, hoping to find a passage leading to an upper level. Gliding from the citadel across the lake carrying the egg would be easier than holding it while swimming. The citadel was built down and into the mountain, not up, and his search revealed only the remains of a campsite the previous visitors abandoned.

"The only way out looks to be across the lake; back the way we came." Kale held up a broken stick. "I found this though. It looks like a wand."

Delilah took the stick from him. A crooked and gnarled piece of weathered wood, it bore faded runes carved upon its length; telltale signs of arcane use. "I'll bet this belonged to Manless. It probably broke in the fight against Pyraclannaseous, and he ditched it here."

She tucked it into one of her pouches; more evidence to show the court. After the veil of night descended and the giants settled into their evening slumber, the three draks and the human slipped into the water. The drak twins supported the egg as they swam, keeping it nestled between them in Kale's cloak. Kali pulled Katka with her in the water, helping the young human woman to keep up with the group. The utter lack of sound as they crossed unnerved Kale, but he was glad for Katka's enchantment. He observed guards pacing, illuminated by the dim glow of flickering torches, but all seemed unaware of their crossing.

Songs of night birds serenaded the four as they climbed onto shore. Once they checked their gear, they crept from shadow to shadow, as crickets and buzzing insects droned in accompaniment. The giants' dwellings extended along the line where the beach's soft sand transitioned into firm ground-covering foliage at the edge of the old forest. Their homes dotted the valley lakeshore like stone-and-wood monuments to the god of hearth and home.

Katka's enchantment allowed them to pass beyond the great beasts the giants kept as steeds and slip unnoticed into the cover of the forest. Before the trees obscured his view, Kale noted the location of the road leading out of the village and carefully angled their course to intercept it.

By the time the King and Queen had risen high in the sky, barely visible through the thick canopy of the forest, Kale found the road. The light from the giants' fires, now mere dots, flickered on the horizon. Even though the egg was lighter than it appeared, his arms and back ached from carrying it, and from her grumbles, he surmised Delilah's patience with his groaning grew short.

Katka hummed to herself as they hiked, her enchantment of silence no longer in effect. Kali recognized the tune as a popular ditty sung by minstrels in taverns, and she joined in. Within minutes, they were singing the bawdy lyrics.

"Shh!" Delilah smacked Katka's uninjured shoulder with her free hand. "They'll hear you!"

"We must be a league away, maybe two." Kali glanced over her shoulder in the direction of the village. "No one there is hearing us."

A trumpeting roar from ahead sent them scrambling for the underbrush. Lights flared at the far end of the path, illuminating a row of enormous, grey-skinned beasts. Giant warriors sat atop them, each brandishing a spear.

"You have been seen. Hiding is pointless," one of the giants called out as he dismounted, sliding to the ground with a thud. He planted the butt of his spear in the center of the road and stood spanning its width with his legs.

"You steal away in the cover of darkness like thieves. Face us. Should death be your fate, I promise your honesty and bravery will be rewarded with a swift end."

Delilah bumped into her brother. "That's no comfort."

Kale suppressed a shiver at the thought of what the giants would do to them. *How did they beat us here? How did they even know we left?*

The giant called to them again. Kale's sister tried to pull him deeper into the underbrush, but he shook his head and pushed her away.

"I have an idea, Deli."

Kale gambled the sigil on his chest would protect him. He stepped into the road, ignoring the gasps and protests from his friends. *If they worshipped her, I might have a chance...*

He carried the egg carefully, spreading his wings for additional balance. One of the warriors behind the speaking giant threw his spear into the ground before Kale, blocking his path. The head of the spear was as big as the drak's own head.

"Pyraclannaseous is dead, killed by an earthquake." Kale heard his sister hissing and swearing from within the bushes.

The remaining giants brandished their spears. The one on foot raised his hand to stay their ire. "You are responsible for this? And the theft of her child? Why?"

Kale set down the egg and motioned for Delilah, Kali, and Katka to stay put. "She had been dead for some time when we arrived. There was a great rift in her cavern, terrible heat, and the stink of death."

One of the mounted warriors whispered to the giant alongside him. Kale couldn't understand what he said. The lead giant lowered his hand and nodded.

"I'm taking the egg to her brother, Terrakaptis. He'll know what to do. I am draevyehfehdin. It is his will." Even as he said it, the words sounded silly to Kale's ears. The giant seemed to take them seriously, however.

The warrior picked up his spear and used the butt of it to slide Kale's bandoleer away from the marking on his chest. Delilah rushed out, staff glowing, but stopped at a quick head shake from Kale. Next, Katka emerged from the underbrush. Kali followed her, weapon ready.

"When your archmage last visited, he entered the Citadel of Fire and Stone." The giant stepped away from Kale. "The ground shook with rage as he fled. He took to the sky on a column of twisting air. After, our king demanded the bones of our dead and forbade us from entering the citadel. He told us we had displeased him and were to remain in the valley, never to enter the citadel again."

The mounted warriors shook their spears and shouted, pointing at the human and three draks. Kale guessed their intentions. The lone warrior who stood spun on them and slammed the butt of his spear into the ground, shouting a response that quieted the rest.

He returned his attention to Kale. "They say we should kill you. We should roast you and break our fast when the dawn comes. But… I cannot deny the truth I hear in your words."

"If we don't get back to Muncifer soon, the archmage will send more wizards looking for us." Delilah stepped forward, placing a clawed hand on the egg. Kale placed his hand on her shoulder, pursing his lips and shaking his head as he pushed her toward Kali and Katka.

The giant appeared unmoved, his face like a stone. "Annah Brighteyes will decide your fate. You will return to the village with us"—he and the mounted warriors raised their spears—"or you will die here."

* * *

Pancras staggered across the main deck of the *Maiden of the High Seas* as a wave crashed into her side, sending a spray of salt water across the deck and soaking his robes. He cursed as he wiped the water from his eyes. Every time he ventured topside, he returned as wet as if he had stood in a downpour.

Sailors manning the rigging paused in their tasks to laugh at the minotaur stumbling across the deck toward the railing. Pancras's sides ached as he once again returned his morning meal to the sea. Since coming aboard the ship, he'd managed to keep down only about a third of his sustenance. A flash of black and red in the periphery of his vision caught his attention.

The fiendling, Qaliah, skipped over to his side. She grabbed his arm as a heave of the deck threw him forward, driving the rail into his gut. He retched again.

"Never figured you for such a weak-stomached landlubber, Pancras. I figured you getting dead would've cured you of such ills."

The minotaur wished returning from death brought with it such benefits. As far as he could tell, the only benefit he received from his resurrections was literally not being dead. He spat into the sea, wiping his mouth on his sleeve.

"Where's Blondie?" Qaliah scanned the deck, eyes searching for their other companion, Gisella. She grinned, waving to one of the sailors who stared at her.

"She doesn't like you calling her that." Pancras swallowed, wishing his throat burned less from the bile he struggled to keep at bay.

"She's not around, so she doesn't get a say. Below decks? We're supposed to be sparring." Qaliah jerked her sword from its sheath and danced around Pancras, poking him in the rump with the tip. "She's going to teach me to fight, you know."

"Start by killing me." Pancras leaned against the rail and closed his eyes. "Maybe I'll return to life when we've reached Vlorey."

"Ha! Maybe you'd come back all half-rotted this time, craving flesh and blood." The fiendling sheathed her sword and spun before taking Pancras's arm. She laid her head on his chest and lowered her voice. "Sailors don't like such talk, so you probably shouldn't mention any of that too often. We've a long way to go, yet."

"You're doing it wrong, Minotaur." The voice of Eingvar Salt-Wind, captain of the *Maiden*, was that of a man who chewed on stones for supper and gargled with acid.

"What? Standing?" Pancras shut his eyes again and concentrated on not retching.

"You'll never get your sea legs with your eyes closed. Gotta find a fixed point far away and focus on that." The Watchman slapped Pancras on the side. Despite his size, the human stood more than a head shorter than the minotaur. Pancras cracked an eye and regarded the man. His blond hair whipped around his head in the fierce coastal wind.

"There!" The captain pointed to a spot on the coast. "That rock formation. Focus on something like that while you're topside, and move with the ship."

"He's a minotaur, Captain." Qaliah extracted herself from Pancras's arm. "Might as well be a dwarf when it comes to ships and water."

"Nonsense." Captain Eingvar put his hands on his hips and stared across the ocean at the coast. "Some of the best mariners I've known were minotaurs. Dwarves'll sink, it's true, but minotaurs can sail with the best of them. You just need practice, Bonelord."

The captain left Qaliah and Pancras alone. The minotaur's insides churned with each heave of the deck. Staring across the sea at the rock formation on the coast brought him no relief, but he took solace in the fact that he tended to vomit less on an empty stomach.

* * *

"Are you crazy?" Delilah tugged at her brother's cloak and hissed. "This is exactly what we're trying to avoid." The draks and Katka followed behind the lead warrior's mount as the giants marched them back to their village.

"We can't fight them all, Deli."

The drak sorceress disagreed but kept her thoughts to herself now that they were within earshot of the giants. As much as she disliked the idea of seeing her master, the archmage, again, she disliked the idea of becoming food for giants even less. She doubted she could manage the same death-cheating stunt Pancras did in Almeria.

She heard a sniffle behind her and lagged behind for Katka to catch up. The human wiped her eyes when she noticed Delilah staring at her. "Sorry. I was fine until I started thinking of my parents. It's one thing to be away from them in the city, but it's different when you're being marched to the dinner table."

"Stop it!" Kali pushed her way between Delilah and Katka. "Kale knows what he's doing."

Delilah snorted. *She cannot possibly be talking about my brother.* The lights of the village grew more intense as they approached. Even from a distance, the drak ascertained the village was now roused. She worried about what the giants would do to them, and she was curious to learn how they not only managed to discover their escape, but also how they moved ahead of them so swiftly and without detection.

"I hope so. If we die here, my parents will never know what happened to me." Katka kicked a rock and sighed. "The archmage will never tell them the truth."

"No doubt about that." Delilah took Katka's arm. "We'll figure this out. I promise."

She wished she felt as confident as she tried to sound. *Kale might be right about fighting them, but I would've taken a lot of them with me.*

It was still dark when they reached the village. It appeared that every man, woman, and child turned out for the return of the draks and Katka. All except the smallest children wielded weapons and glared at the four with murderous eyes.

Katka squeezed Delilah's arm as the drak sorceress scanned the crowd. Save for the babies too small to stand, their foes appeared to be deadly opponents. Even the children stood as tall as fully grown humans.

"We should have run for it, Kale."

The warriors slid off their mounts, forming a half-circle behind the four companions as their leader called for the village shaman, muffling Delilah's rebuke. A tall, lithe woman stepped forward, holding a baby on her hip. She was clad in crude armor composed of leather, furs, and bark. Sandy hair peeked out beneath a fur-and-feather headdress. Animal bones dangled from her ears and from a braided rope around her neck. Steel-grey eyes regarded each of the four diminutive companions in turn.

The lead warrior bowed before the shaman. He spoke to her in short, rapid sentences, casting backward glances at the four. Delilah's grasp of the giants' language was incomplete, and she understood only the woman's name: Annah Brighteyes.

When the shaman finally spoke, it took a moment for Delilah to hear past her thick accent. "… vengeance. We must take care to direct our anger at those who have wronged us, and I am not convinced these small ones are they."

She handed her baby to one of the males, taking care to coo at the child and kiss its head before fully relinquishing it. She then sat on the ground in front of the human and three draks, although she still towered over them.

"I recognize the mark of the Firstborne upon you." She bowed her head to Kale. "As we are sworn to the children of Rannos Dragonsire, no harm shall be brought upon you." Annah Brighteyes turned her gaze on Delilah, and then to Kali and Katka in turn. "The rest of you will speak in your defense."

The shaman raised her arms toward the sky and threw back her head. "*Kanfod kelwydda!*" A blue halo of smoky light encircled her and streamed into her steel-grey eyes. When her gaze again met theirs, her eyes glowed the color of blooming periwinkles.

"Striped one, kin of the draevyehfehdin, speak to me your tale of woe."

The drak sorceress felt no compulsion to speak truthfully, as was the case during her interrogation at the hands of the archduke. Ignorant of the magic the shaman used, Delilah decided honesty was the safest bet.

"The archduke wants peace. The archmage wants the dragon. I was sent by both to work against the other." She licked her lips and swallowed, waiting for the shaman's reaction. She heard Kali shuffle behind her, moving to stand beside her mate.

"Why then, did you come?"

"My friends and I do not want war with your people, nor do we seek to control the dragon, as the archmage does. He's insane."

"Hosvir says"—the shaman gestured at the lead warrior—"you were sent by one of the Firstborne to seek his kin."

Delilah inclined her head toward Annah Brighteyes. "Terrakaptis. He seeks to wake his brothers and sisters. He says it's time for them to return to the world."

"The Firstborne are wise. They see much that is hidden from mortal eyes. When we received word of your flight, I sent my husband into the Citadel of Fire and Stone, despite the words of our king. He saw our lady's carcass. She was dead long before you arrived."

A murmur circulated through the assembled villagers. Annah Brighteyes raised her hands to silence them. "You will not be punished for the death of one who left this world before you came to us."

Delilah pulled the broken wand from her pouch. "We found this wand in the citadel, a wizard's implement. I do not know who it belonged to, but I suspect whoever owned it killed Pyraclannaseous."

Shaman Annah Brighteyes closed her eyes and bowed her head. She chanted in the giants' language, softly at first, and then in rising in volume and strength. The assembled giants bowed their heads and joined in, reciting in counterpoint to their shaman.

Katka coughed and shuffled her feet. Kali pulled her mate close. Delilah chewed her lip and adjusted the grip on her staff, assuming that since their weapons were not confiscated, the giants were either confident the four were no threat, or they were in no real danger of being executed.

After what seemed like the better part of an hour, the shaman finished her chant. Next, she turned her glowing eyes to Kali. "Speak, Drak, you of another clan."

"Kale is my mate." Her matter-of-fact tone brooked no other explanation.

Her terse reply satisfied the shaman. Annah Brighteyes bowed her head toward Kali. "Loyalty to one's mate is admirable. And what of you"—she turned her gaze to Katka— "Human?"

Katka winced, fighting to keep her injured arm immobile, as she curtsied. The formality of it seemed pointless to Delilah. "I am Delilah's friend. I wanted to help her and her brother."

"Mates, siblings, friends. True to one another. When your Icebreaking archmage was here, there was no camaraderie among his companions, no bonds of friendship, just the stink of fear and gold." The shaman stood and turned to address the assembled Iron Giants.

"What happened is clear, the Litany of Rannos Dragonsire guides us. Like her father before her, the death of Pyraclannaseous rent the earth. The death of a god cracked the world. The death of a god's child cracked the mountain."

One of the giants behind her shook his spear, pointing at the four. He shouted in anger and drew back, preparing to throw it. The shaman interposed herself between him and his target, responding to his threat in a low, even tone.

The warrior averted his eyes and backed away. Annah Brighteyes turned to face the three draks and Katka. "As a people, we are bonded to our Firstborne, none more closely than King Ragnok. Through him, Pyraclannaseous spoke during her long slumber. They call for you to be punished for his death. You"—she pointed at Kale—"tell me of your encounter with him. What was his appearance? How did he act?"

Kale stroked the bottom of his snout as he thought. "He was old, wizened even. He seemed nice at first, but then ordered his skeletons to kill us. We fought back only in self-defense."

"Skeletons? Old? I believe I understand." The Shaman turned to her people and spoke to them in their language. Delilah assumed she relayed Kale's answer to them.

The giants conversed among themselves for several minutes. Several of the younger warriors threw down their spears. They spat upon them before turning and ambling away. Many of the older ones bowed to Annah Brighteyes before returning with their families to their huts. In the end, all that remained were the riders and Hosvir.

"A decision has been reached. It does not make all happy, but I feel it is just. With Ragnok dead, we will need to convene a moot to choose a new leader. Passions run high. You must leave. You are banished from the Valley of the Iron Giants until the gods themselves say you can return."

Fine by me. I'm not ever coming back here. A weight lifted from Delilah's shoulders. Katka's sigh was audible.

Kale raised his hand and cleared his throat. "Can you explain to us what happened to your king? He seemed—"

"Unbalanced," Delilah interjected as her brother searched for a diplomatic way to say crazy.

"His life was tied to our lady dragon's, much like some of your wizards have a small animal assisting them. He was ancient, but her life-force granted him the benefit of longevity and the appearance of youth." The shaman stood, worrying the bones around her neck. "Her death must have caused his age to catch up to him. It destroyed his mind, but I would never have thought he would be willing to defile the remains of his people."

She waved her hand. "It is not your concern. We will deal with this our way. Please, come with me."

The shaman gestured for them to follow her. Delilah helped her brother with the egg, and they trailed behind the shaman as she led them to a hut. It amused Delilah that the giant's dwelling was as large as a well-appointed human's home in Muncifer.

"You will sleep here tonight. I will see you are fed, and then Hosvir will lead you out of the valley in the morning." She waited until they had entered her hut, and she secured the flap of tanned hide before turning to them and lowering her voice. "In time, they will recognize the debt we owe you. I will see that you are not forgotten when we set the course of our future." She faced Katka. "Come, Human. I will mend your wounds."

Delilah observed as the shaman performed the ritual that healed Katka's broken arm. The words the giantess chanted were unlike any which the drak sorceress encountered in her arcane studies. Travelers to Drak-Anor told of mystics who wielded power that could affect living things in wondrous ways, but this was the first time Delilah had witnessed such abilities. Drak-Anor's healers dealt in poultices, salves, and potions brewed by Pancras and other alchemists.

When Annah was finished, she turned and tended to her child as her husband tossed scraps of fur onto the floor for the draks and human to use as makeshift bedding.

Katka stared at her wounded arm, her jaw hanging slack. She moved it, raising and flexing it several times. "That's amazing. Thank you."

Delilah dodged a scrap of fur thrown by Annah's husband and darted in front of the giantess. "The archduke wants peace. He values the friendship of the Iron Giants. I have an idea about how to deal with the archmage."

"Deli?" Kale tugged at his sister's arm. She faced her brother, who kept shaking his head and hissing.

"No, Kale. I've been thinking about this a long time. I know exactly what to do. I just need time." She returned her attention to the shaman. "I'll tell the archduke not to send emissaries until the archmage is dealt with. I'll further instruct him to send them bearing a flag of truce and to await your warriors at the entrance to the valley; they'll go no farther without your leave. We respect your custom to convene a moot and choose your new leader."

Shaman Annah Brighteyes acknowledged Delilah with a grunt and pointed at the furs on the floor. "Sleep now. Go in peace tomorrow. Gaia will watch over you tonight."

Chapter 2

The Golden Slayer stood on the poop deck alongside Captain Eingvar, regarding the *Maiden*'s wake. Their hair whipped in the cool breeze; Gisella had taken to tying hers back while topside. Dolphins arced through the blue-green water, following the ship as she sailed north along the coast. The broad-leafed trees of Raven's Forest were visible on the horizon to their port side.

"You've adjusted to shipboard life much faster than your minotaur friend." Captain Eingvar gripped the rail with both hands and leaned forward, glancing downward to inspect the rudder.

"I used to fish the lakes of the Southern Watch with my father and sister." Gisella missed those simpler days. She planned to return there after she completed her mission for the goddess Aurora.

"That'll help, for certain. Ah, the irresponsible days of our youth." He clicked his tongue. "Tell your fiendling to watch herself. If she leads the men on too much, they'll get the wrong idea and react poorly if she isn't receptive to those ideas. It's a long voyage, and this ship's too big to keep a watchful eye on every dark corner and hidey-hole."

Qaliah made friends easily with the rowdy sailors of the *Maiden*, and the Golden Slayer understood exactly the sort of trouble to which the captain intimated. Not only arduous in nature, a sailor's job spending months on end at sea enforced celibacy. Fraternization was discouraged among the crew while onboard, as most captains felt it led to a breakdown in crew discipline and undermined the chain of command. An overly flirtatious passenger would likely make things difficult.

"I'll warn her. We don't want any trouble, just a smooth ride to our destination." The quartermaster informed them when they boarded that the *Maiden of the High Seas* sailed only as far as Port-of-Dogs. The overland journey from there to Vlorey was faster than sailing up Verdant Point and down to Vlorey.

"This is a safe route." The captain gestured to the expanse of water to their starboard side. "No coves or islands for pirates. Not like sailing down to the Watches, or across to the Elven Empire. Some have called me coward for avoiding those waters or fool for passing up the gold it could bring." He laughed and patted his belly, which strained at the shirt of tarnished metal scales he wore. "I like my safety and comfort more than the praise of danger-seeking fools."

Gisella appreciated the sentiment. Often those who sought danger for gold and glory died young. She hoped to live long enough to raise a family and perhaps live near her sister so their children could grow up together. It was a dream she did not often allow her thoughts to indulge in, not when so much work remained.

She clapped the captain on the shoulder. "I'll go check on Pancras and make sure Qaliah is staying out of trouble." She left Captain Eingvar to run his ship and descended the stairs to the main deck. Sailors scuttled up the riggings like spiders on a web. Qaliah's laughter rang out like a clarion above barked orders and bawdy sea shanties. Crossing from one end of the ship to the other, the fiendling swung through the rigging.

Each of them was required to work aboard the ship while they traveled. Qaliah, obviously, found her calling as a rigger. Gisella, the most experienced traveler of the three, found helping the sailing master as fulfilling a job as one she didn't want could be. Pancras, however, had no time to find work because he'd been ill since the ship left the harbor.

The *Maiden's* spacious top decks belied a labyrinthine interior. Below deck, lanterns provided sputtering light and dancing shadows that swayed with the bobbing of the ship. Save for the senior officers, the crew slept in hammocks stacked three high, filling one of the holds with snoring, swinging sailors. Those who worked below decks, spoke in hushed whispers, mindful of those whose duties required them to sleep during the day. Gisella made her way to the cabin she, Qaliah, and Pancras shared. Previously, it had been quarters shared by the bo'sun and his two mates. She didn't ask Qaliah what she traded for it.

Pancras lay in his hammock, one hand splayed across his face as he groaned with every heave of the ship. His normally shiny, soft fur appeared dry, dull, and brittle, and the sickly sweet scent of vomit permeated the air in the cabin. Gisella noted the partially full bucket that was the odor's source on the floor alongside Pancras's hammock.

She slid the bucket away from him with her foot and then pulled on his arm. "Up you get!"

"Go away."

Gisella gritted her teeth and pulled, yanking the minotaur from his hammock. He crashed onto the floor. The hammock swung away from him and back, entangling his horns and pulling him backward as the ship crashed into an oncoming wave.

"You're doing yourself no favors by staying down here. It stinks, you stink, and you're going to starve if you can't keep food down." The Golden Slayer untangled the hammock from the minotaur's horns and helped him to his feet. Upon examining his glazed, red-rimmed eyes, she determined he suffered from lack of sleep in addition to seasickness.

Pancras mumbled and stifled a belch. He closed his eyes and clutched his stomach as he braced himself against the wall. "Killing me now would be a kindness."

"And face the Lich Queen on my own? No, thank you!" She grimaced as she picked up the half-full bucket and carried it out, calling over her shoulder, "Change your robes and meet me by the main mast. Bring your gear. You need to train with that new weapon."

Pancras fumbled for the maul he acquired in Curton and now used as his arcane focus and symbol of his new status as a bonelord. Forged from a type of red steel with which Gisella was unfamiliar and too large for her personal taste, it fit the minotaur well. The spike protruding from the back of its head left no doubt the weapon was designed for battle, rather than ceremony.

"Now!"

Gisella didn't bother to confirm whether he followed her. She climbed to the main deck, dumped the bucket's contents over the side, and tossed it to a swabbie to clean and return to storage. By the time she finished, Pancras emerged topside, clinging to one of the ropes by the main mast.

For as long as she had known him, Pancras had never been as burly or as muscular as she observed in others of his kind, but as the wind pressed the minotaur's robes against his body, she noted he now appeared almost gaunt. She shook her head. *Never thought I'd play nursemaid to a seasick minotaur.*

* * *

The next morning, after the four broke their fast with Annah Brighteyes, her husband, and her as-yet-unnamed child, Hosvir led the draks and Katka out of the giants' village. Kale enlisted his sister's help to carry the dragon egg. In addition to wondering how the giants knew to intercept them, he marveled that they allowed him to take the egg with no further arguments or discussion.

When Hosvir left them at the edge of the valley, they gaped as he and his towering mount disappeared into the forest.

After he vanished from sight, Katka threw up her hands. "They captured us just to let us go. What was the point? And how did they know what happened in the citadel anyway?"

"I'm not sure they did." Kali helped her mate and his sister secure the egg on the ground so they could rest. "I think they suspected something happened and sent a group to wait for us on the road in case we made a run for it."

"A good guess on their part, if that's what happened." Delilah sat on a rock and rubbed her neck.

Kale took a seat near Kali and entwined his tail with hers as they leaned on each other. "I don't care why they knew or what. I'm just glad they decided to let us go. How are we going to get this egg to Terrakaptis? He's all the way in Drak-Anor. I don't think carrying this thing for months is a good idea."

He glanced at his sister. *She could send a message to him; maybe he'll come pick it up.*

Delilah suggested that very thing. "Of course, folks in Muncifer will have a fit if a dragon shows up asking for us."

"You could tell him to meet you outside the city at a certain time." The human arched her back before circling the egg and examining it.

"If do that, I'm sure the archmage will send me in the other direction on some pointless errand. I don't dare tell him about the egg." Delilah picked at the skull atop her staff.

"What are you going to tell him?" Kale wasn't concerned about short-term security for the egg. The home he and Kali shared in Muncifer featured a passageway connected to a forgotten cavern. It was already fortified with locks and traps and would be perfectly suited to hiding a dragon egg.

Delilah grunted and stood. She paced as she thought and placed her hand on the egg. "No idea. Not the truth, not willingly, anyway."

It occurred to Kale there might be another option. "We don't have to go back. There must be a village or someplace nearby where we could get a cart to help carry the egg."

Katka's eyes widened. "I'm not abandoning my family."

Shaking her head, the drak sorceress clicked her teeth. "No, we're not running. The archduke put a lot of trust in me. Besides, the archmage will just send the slayers after me if I don't go back. If you and Kali want to head back to Drak-Anor, I won't stop you, but I have to end this."

Kali squeezed Kale's arm. Searching his mate's eyes, Kale realized she would accede, no matter what he decided. "We're not going to leave you, Deli. I was just thinking out loud."

With their course decided, the four continued their trek out of the Iron Gate Mountains toward Muncifer. The return journey would take longer since they turned their mounts loose when the mountain paths became too treacherous for them. Kale hoped that Katka's enchantment allowed the lizards to find their way to her family's farm.

The road out of the mountains was not well traveled. Apart from the giants, Muncifer traded little with what few communities existed in the Western Wastes on the other side of the mountain pass. Ill-suited to caravans, the dirt road in that portion of the mountains doubled back, twisted, and often washed out during the rainy season, unlike the predominantly stone road that led to Ironkrag in the Dragon Spine Mountains near Drak-Anor.

The four companions discussed little of importance for much of the journey, spending most of the time swapping jokes and telling stories of the fun and follies of their childhoods. Neither Kali nor Katka had heard most of Kale and Delilah's stories of survival, having been cast out of their clan as soon as the elders deemed they were old enough to make it on their own.

Because of their shared struggle to survive, Kale felt a bond stronger than blood provided and decided long ago he would never abandon his sister. He appreciated that his mate seemed to understand.

As the outline of Muncifer appeared on the horizon, Kale steered the conversation toward more important subjects. "I doubt they're going to let us just walk into the city carrying a dragon egg."

Katka clicked her fingers. "I've been thinking about that."

They set down the egg while the human outlined her plan. "They'll be looking for trouble at the Iron Gate, so we should go around the city and enter from the opposite side at night."

Kali cocked her head. "Don't they close those gates at night?"

The human sorceress drew her wand and grinned. "Sure, but a little charm here and a little enchantment there, and they won't notice us at all. Those who do won't remember in the morning."

"That seems illegal." Kale rubbed the back of his neck. He and his sister were no strangers to pulling pranks, but messing with minds went a step too far, in his opinion.

Katka pursed her lips and stared at the ground. "It is, but it's the only way to get the dragon egg in unseen. You three are small enough, and the streets will be deserted enough that you should be able to make it to the undercity unseen once we're inside the gates." She put her hand on the egg. "It's not like we're smuggling in anything dangerous. It's a baby!"

"Don't get us wrong, Katka." Delilah touched her friend on the arm. "We're no strangers to bending the rules; we just want all to be aware of what we're getting into."

"If we're all in agreement, let's get going." Kale helped his sister pick up the egg, and they resumed their trek toward Muncifer. Skirting the city added almost a day to their trip. The sun hung low in the sky by the time they reached the hill overlooking the gate. Though it was the same gate by which the three draks entered the city with Pancras just a few months earlier, it seemed like a lifetime ago to Kale.

* * *

"What's taking so long?" Delilah tapped her foot as she stood over Katka. The young woman sat on the ground and dug through her pack. Earlier, they had moved off the road into the meadows surrounding the city. The grasses served to conceal their activities from the watchtowers surrounding the city gates.

"This is great"—Katka waved her wand in the air, while continuing her search with one hand—"but I can give us a little insurance if I can find my grinder. I don't suppose one of you has a small crystal or a gemstone or something like that? Damn, I wish I'd taken some from that dragon's cave."

Kale produced a light-colored gemstone he retrieved from his pouch. "Will this work? What are you going to do with it?"

"Perfect!" She withdrew a small metal box from her pack. Its hinged lid featured a crank handle. Katka opened it, dropped the gem inside, and cranked the handle. Delilah winced at the sound of the gem cracking and pulverizing in the mechanism.

"Hey! I didn't know you were going to crush it." Kale gnashed his teeth.

"Crushed gemstones help with charms of this type. Something about the glittering dust catches the eye and makes people more susceptible." Katka poured the contents of the grinder into her hand and returned the machine to her pack. "It's not needed, per se, but every bit helps when we're trying to avoid the guards, right?"

Delilah patted her brother on the shoulder. "Consider it an investment in the egg."

Kale huffed. "Warn me next time. That was an expensive one. Tourmaline, I think."

"All the better." Katka kept the hand in which she held the gem dust tightly closed and hoisted her pack. "Let's go."

They returned to the road, with Katka and Delilah leading the way. Kale and Kali carried the egg suspended in a cloak between them. Two guards stood on either side of the closed city gates, four in all. Stifling yawns, they crossed their spears as the three draks and young human approached them.

"Hold there! No visitors after dark."

Delilah held up a clawed hand. "We're students of the Arcane University. We were away on business for the arch-duke and the archmage."

Katka chuckled. "Believe us, we don't want to be wandering around after dark." She flung the gemstone dust into the air in front of her as she drew her wand. "*Goe'tia prosopo eimaste kalyteroi filoi.* We'd be daft to be out here like this. Let us in, won't you?"

The guards' weapons drooped as their eyes followed the gem dust sparkling in the amber light cast by their lanterns. As it took on an emerald hue, their eyes widened.

"You'd be daft to be out here in the dark." The guard's voice was a monotone. "Here, you'd best come inside." He reached behind him to knock on the gate, but was too far. One of his comrades shuffled to the oaken doors and pounded on them. Gemstone dust glittered as it drifted about the guards' heads.

"Oy! Your shift ain't up," a muffled reply came from the other side of the gate.

"Let them through, they—"

"We're on an urgent task from the archduke." Delilah nudged the man at the gate.

"These ones have urgent business with the archduke. Let 'em pass."

The gate cracked open, and a bearded man stuck his head out. "Here now…"

Katka puffed, blowing some of the dust in his direction. "It's all right. We don't want to be out here. Let us in and we won't be. There will be no problems at all."

He shook his head and blinked as the glittering dust danced around his head. "Right. No problem. Hey, you shouldn't be out here after dark. Best come in now."

The guard pulled open the gate just wide enough for them to pass, ushering them in. "Hurry now, come on. Get home, young 'uns. I imagine your parents are worried sick."

Kali bowed her head as they passed. "Oh, they are. We'll have a right stern talking to, no doubt. Thank you, sir."

The four shuffled through and picked up their pace as they heard the gate close behind them. Delilah risked a glance backward. When she was sure the guards no longer scrutinized them, she directed her companions into a shadowed alley.

Under cover of darkness, Delilah led Kale, Kali, and Katka through the streets of Muncifer. Dashing from shadow to shadow while carrying a dragon egg nearly as big as an adult drak was no small feat. Sneaking past the guards at the city gates required judicious use of Katka's enchantment magic, a regrettable but necessary choice. Thus far, Delilah and her friends remained undetected by folk wandering the streets, and she intended to ensure it remained that way.

Delilah feared what the archmage would do if he discovered she smuggled a dragon egg from the giants' valley. Despite concerns over her brother's sense of responsibility, she left the egg in the care of him and Kali. Kale promised to keep it safe and under lock and key. The desire to linger and examine the runed circle in the cavern below her brother's house tempted her. Had Katka not already returned to the university, the drak sorceress would have remained behind.

That can wait. It's been there for gods-know how long; it will still be there next week. She chuckled in amusement at her unusual patience, then nodded a greeting to the sleepy guards at the gates of the Arcane University. *You must be getting old, Deli-girl.*

Delilah crept past sleeping students in the barracks. When she reached her bunk, she noticed Katka already fast asleep. As she crawled into bed, she hoped the archmage, or someone, would see fit to move her out of the initiates' barracks in the morning. An apprentice now, and having returned from her first assignment, she felt it fitting she be given a bit more privacy. Where initiates shared what amounted to a glorified bunkhouse, apprentices shared quarters with only one other apprentice. Delilah planned to ask the archmage about it during her meeting in the morning. Worry over the dragon egg, the implications of Pyraclannaseous's death, and what the archmage was up to kept Delilah awake.

The morning arrived far too early for the drak's liking. She felt as though she had barely fallen asleep by the time the wake-up bell rang. She rolled out of bed, and were it not for Katka catching her, would have fallen flat on her face. Delilah balled her fists into her eyes and yawned. The drak sorceress rushed to grab a bite to eat before presenting herself to the Council of Wizardry.

Apart from the requisite guards, only the Red and Blue Wizards attended Archmage Vilkan. They conversed in low voices as Delilah approached, their words drowned out by the clicking of her clawed feet on the stone floor.

"Hmm… my apprentice returns."

The archmage's slow and deliberate pronunciation gave Delilah the impression that he hid his surprise.

"What news have you from the giants?"

"Nothing good, I'm afraid." The drak sorceress considered her words. She didn't want to give the archmage the impression she withheld information from him, but neither was she ready to reveal exactly what transpired when they visited the giant king. "The giants were unwilling negotiate. They were mourning the passing of their king, and no successor had yet been chosen."

The best lies contained a kernel of the truth, and while what Delilah told Archmage Vilkan omitted critical information, it did not contain any outright falsehoods. She suspected many of the giants in the village would mourn their king. Whatever madness held sway over him surely made the lives of the hard-working mountain folk difficult.

The Blue Wizard turned to face the Red Wizard. "Ragnok, King Under the Mountain, is dead."

"King of the Iron Giants no more."

Archmage Vilkan raised his hand and called for silence. "Yes, yes. Good riddance. Tell me of his castle. The one across the lake?"

Delilah swallowed. "We were not permitted entry."

"The dragon." The human clenched his fist. "Tell me of the dragon. Did you see it?"

What was left of it... and a broken wand. Her eyes flicked to the wand tucked into the archmage's belt before returning to meet his gaze. "We saw no signs of a dragon. The mountains were still. If there's one living in the caves near that village, it's either sleeping or dead."

Archmage Vilkan furrowed his brow. "Who accompanied you?"

The human clasped his hands behind his back and stared at her. His eyes bored into hers as though he sought to wrench the knowledge from her thoughts. Delilah tightened her grip on her staff and peered up at him. The longer she waited to answer, the deeper his frown became.

"Novice Katka accompanied me."

His eyes grew wide as his fists clenched and unclenched. He crossed the distance between them in two great strides.

"You said I could take what resources I needed. There's safety in numbers."

The archmage reached forward, as though he intended to grab her collar, but as Delilah wore only a cloak, he clenched his fist before retracting his hand. He lowered his hands to his sides and closed his eyes, taking a deep breath before opening them again.

"What does she know of your mission?"

Delilah cocked her head. "I told her that I was to deliver a message of truce and invitation to peace talks. That's all."

As Archmage Vilkan contemplated her words, Delilah studied the wand tucked into his belt. The archmage's proximity to her provided an excellent vantage with which to memorize its details, her head nearly eye-level to his waist. There was no guarantee, of course, that the archmage replaced his wand with one exactly like the broken one, if that was what transpired, but she noticed similarities between the wand he now wielded and the one her brother recovered from the campsite near the dragon's lair.

You never went there and you found nothing, Deli-girl. You have to believe it while you're on university grounds.

"Very well, Apprentice." The archmage clasped his hands behind his back and returned to his chair. He sat, smoothing the front of his robes as he did so. "Tell me of the giants. How did they behave?"

The drak sorceress scratched her chin. "I wouldn't say they were friendly, but they weren't hostile. I got the sense they didn't want us to be there, but tradition or something demanded they be courteous. You know, like when you're at a clan gathering and you see that cousin you hate, but can't get into a fight with her because it'll cause more trouble than it's worth?"

Delilah wagered Vilkan understood tension that sometimes occurred at family celebrations, and indeed might actually be the object of avoidance, given how he treated anyone he judged to be beneath him. However, she was not familiar enough with human relationships to know how they handled family politics. His nod indicated his understanding. He drummed his fingers on the arm of his chair before leaning forward with a sigh.

"Return to your duties. I shall call on you again tomorrow." He reclined. "Or I won't. I must contemplate this."

Content to leave Archmage Vilkan to his ruminations, she exited the Court of Wizardry. As an apprentice, most of her studies were self-guided, and since she had no other impending responsibilities, she took the opportunity to leave the university grounds and head into the city. She needed to inform her brother about her plan for dealing with the archmage.

* * *

Kale awoke to the sound of the front door slamming shut. A meek "sorry" followed the clatter. Kali glared at him, bleary eyed and shoved him out of their bed to deal with the disturbance. He pulled the fur blankets with him, dumping them in a pile at his side as he grinned at his cursing mate.

He shuffled down the hallway and into the front room that served as a storefront for Ori, their limner tenant. The dark-blue drak, sat behind the counter, hunched over an open codex. He dipped his quill into a vial of ink and glanced up as Kale turned the corner.

"Oh! I thought you might be back but wasn't sure. Did I wake you?"

Rubbing his eyes, Kale yawned and nodded. "We returned late last night."

"Oh. How did you get in the city? Don't they lock the gates at night?"

"It wasn't easy." He peered at the book Ori illuminated. Verses written in flowing script covered the page.

"Oh, just a book of poetry. Some noble wants it embellished to give as a gift for a lady he's courting." He set down his quill and spun the book to give Kale a better look. "He must be desperate; he didn't even haggle over the price I quoted. I always start at double my normal rate."

Ori flipped through the book, showing Kale the work he'd completed so far. The striped drak admitted he knew little about art, but Ori's work appeared intricately ornate, fluid, even to his untrained eyes.

"Good? All right, I'm going back to sleep, Ori. If anyone comes looking for us, we're not back yet. Not until Kali and I get up." He didn't wait for Ori's response or acknowledgement before he shuffled off to bed.

Kali had pulled the pile of furs onto her side, leaving Kale a bare spot on the pelts that covered their bed. The drak flopped alongside her, resting his head on a thick area near his mate's face. Since growing wings and gaining the ability to breathe fire, he found he didn't need the furs wrapped around him to stay warm.

When he awoke again, ambient light streaming from the storefront told him it was mid-morning. Kali's soft, steady breathing indicated she was still asleep. After rolling away from her, he padded down the hallway to the door that led to the cavern below. He unlocked it and entered the staircase, closing and locking the door behind him. Certain the egg was safe—the traps and alarms he and his sister set would wake the dead—he sought only the peace of mind that came with visual confirmation, and he felt he owed it to Terrakaptis to give the egg as much attention as possible.

Chapter 3

Delilah ran through the undercity toward her brother's home, dodging pedestrians, ignoring vendors hawking their wares, and ignoring calls from the guards to slow her pace. She narrowly missed running into a potato cart, and the tawny-furred minotaur pushing it cursed and shook his fist at her as he stopped to pick up potatoes dislodged by his sudden stop.

When she arrived at her brother's home, she stopped short when, through the window, she spied the blue drak, Ori, already at work. She groaned and peered through the dusty glass searching for her brother. He was nowhere to be seen, so she steeled herself, breathed, and pushed the door open.

"Oh, Delilah!" Ori set down his quill, hopped off his stool, and sped around the counter to bow to her. "I'm so pleased you have returned."

Her patience with the overeager drak waned. "Where's my brother?"

"He's"—Ori looked over his shoulder—"he's not back yet."

Delilah's impatience turned to concern. *He should be back... Where in the name of Maris's bloody spear could he be?* Her eyes narrowed as she regarded Ori. "What do you mean? Where is he? We returned together. He should be here."

She pushed past the limner, intending to search every corner of the house before initiating a city-wide search.

He grasped her arm. "No, you can't! Please, he's not back yet. He should be soon, but not yet."

Delilah spun on him, yanking her arm from his hold. She drove her staff into his chest, pushing up his head with the skull. Azure tendrils formed in the air and swirled around the top of her staff.

"What's your game? Where's my brother?"

Ori whimpered and backpedaled, stopping with his back against the counter. At times like this, Delilah wished for a pointier focus on the end of her staff, rather than that old lizard skull. Any destructive forces she channeled through it into the blue drak would certainly kill him, and until she located her brother, that was not an option.

"Where. Is. My. Brother?" She punctuated her words by jabbing the skull into Ori's chin. His eyes widened with fear; the blue drak sputtered and stammered, unable to string together enough words to form a coherent sentence.

The drak sorceress's patience with the fool expired. There were spells that would coerce Ori into talking, but it frustrated her that she knew none of them. As she prepared to bash him under the chin with her staff, she heard the creak of the cellar door and spun to confront this new threat.

Kale stood, staring at her, his mouth agape. She heard Ori scramble and take cover behind a piece of furniture.

"Where have you been?" She dropped her staff and ran to her brother, grabbing him by the shoulders. "Why didn't you come straight home last night?"

"I… we did." Kale spread his wings as he clasped his sister's arms. He looked past her to Ori. "What did you tell her?"

A mewling whimper was Ori's only response.

Kale's eyes widened, and a grin overtook his face. "He… he told you I was not home, right?"

Laughter wracked his body as he squirmed to escape Delilah's grasp. She pushed her brother out of the way and retrieved her staff. Ori scrambled to avoid her as she snarled and stalked him around the room.

"You lied to me."

"Oh. No! I—it—told—"

"Deli!" Kale caught Delilah's arm as she passed and stifled his mirth long enough to explain the situation.

The drak sorceress clenched her teeth. "You told him to tell me you weren't home?"

Her brother shook his head.

I wish he'd shake that stupid grin off his face.

"I didn't think you'd be here straightaway. I told him to tell anyone who came around that we weren't home yet."

"What's going on out there? Can't you all be quiet?" Kali's shouts from the bedchamber silenced them.

Delilah seized the interruption to pull her brother close and whisper in his ear, "I came to see it and talk to you. Where is it?" She hoped Ori was out of earshot.

"Downstairs, Deli."

The drak sorceress left her brother to deal with Ori and proceeded down the stairs toward the cavern. She ran her hand along the bookshelves lining the staircase, disappointed she never seemed to have time to discover what secrets the dusty tomes contained. When she entered the cavern, the sconces flared to life.

Kale had nestled the egg against the wall, shoring it up with hunks of debris and rocks. Delilah knelt alongside it and ran her hands over its pebbly skin. She felt the life within it— the grandchild of a god. The dragon egg itself, albeit much larger, seemed not much different than a drak egg.

Who was the father? Had she been keeping this egg since before The Sundering? I wonder if she even put up a fight or if Manless caught her asleep.

The creak of the cellar door tore her away from her thoughts. Delilah stood and turned to spot her brother descending the steps. She found his lopsided smile irritating.

"You sure gave Ori a scare."

She examined the runed circle in the center of the room rather than face her brother. Deciphering what it all meant and how it all worked required more time than she could spare right now.

"So, what's your plan for the archmage, Deli?"

She traced one of the runes with a claw. "I'm going to challenge him to a duel."

Kale snickered, but it was laughter of disbelief, not of amusement. "You're what?"

"The Rite of Combat, enacted by Gerald the Craven as set down in the third series of essays entitled *Arcane Rules: Civilized Magickry.*" She stood and faced her brother.

"He's an archmage, Deli." Kale took his sister's hands. His smile disappeared, replaced by furrowed brows and a frown. His hands felt hot, but she did not pull away.

"I'm not an apprentice, Kale. I'll bet I was slinging spells in combat when he was still a novice. Back home, I was one of the most powerful sorcerers in Drak-Anor, if not the most." Even now, she felt magic flowing through the world as easily as a farmer smelled honeysuckle on a spring breeze. "And I've learned much since we left."

She withdrew from him and crossed her arms over her chest. "But, not yet. There are a few things I need to take care of first." She ascended toward the shop, glancing at her brother. "Protect the egg while I'm gone. I may not be able to return before this all goes down."

Ori ducked behind the counter when he saw Delilah re-enter the shop. She stood on her tiptoes and then rapped on the counter, peering down at him. "Sorry about earlier. I look out for my brother, you know? And he looks out for me."

"Oh. I understand." Ori popped up, knocking the quill out of a vial of ink but stopping the jar from tipping over only by sticking a claw into it. He frowned and wiped the ink on a nearby cloth.

She decided to throw the drak a bone. "Good work watching the place while we were gone. We appreciate it. I don't know if Kale told you that yet."

"Oh. No, he didn't say anything." Ori scrunched up his face, and then smiled, as if it took a few moments to register that he had been praised. He held up a claw. "Oh! Don't leave yet, please."

Ori turned around and rummaged through one of his small chests of supplies. He returned with several narrow, gold pieces of fabric. "Oh! I noticed the ribbons on your horns look dirty and frayed. I would be most honored if you would accept these to wear."

Delilah, thankful she was unable to blush, touched the ribbons tied to her horns. They were little more than colored strips of cloth she'd torn off a discarded cloak. She couldn't even recall their original color. The ribbons Ori offered were made from finely woven, shimmering fabric. She took them from him and rubbed them between her fingers. They were slick, yet soft.

"Oh. They're silk bookmarks. Printers sometimes bind them into expensive books, but they look like they're about the right size."

The drak sorceress grinned and tore the tattered ribbons off her horns. She knelt before Ori and offered the silk strips to him. "Do you mind? I can't see the top of my head, and I'd like them to be straight."

"Oh! Yes... yes, of course."

She felt him fumble before deciding on the right kind of knot. While he worked, she studied his feet and noted his meticulously trimmed claws. *That's a stupid thing to notice, Deli-girl.*

He stepped away when he'd finished tying the ribbons. She stood and offered the nervous blue drak a smile. "They're perfect. Thank you."

Ori was still sputtering and shuffling his feet when she left.

* * *

When Kali finally awoke, Kale informed her of his sister's plan. If she harbored the same doubt as he, she hid it well. "She knows what she's capable of, Kale. One human wizard should be easy compared to the fiendling and crystal golems we fought in Almeria."

His mate had a point, but he suspected Archmage Vilkan to be a more powerful wizard than the fiendling who ran the salt mines. He set aside his concerns and left with Kali to wander the undercity and shop. They needed to restock their larder, and Kali desired a few knickknacks to add a more personal touch to their home. Kale indulged her. He didn't know how long they would remain in Muncifer, but he figured it wise to make the best of the time they were there.

Together, they continued to clean and repair their home. Though the space was livable, signs of its abandonment were too obvious to anyone who entered it. Furniture needed mending, floors needed sanding and polishing, and more than once, Kale yearned for the smooth stone floors of Drak-Anor.

As he sanded the floor of the hallway on his hands and knees, he voiced his complaints to Ori. "Why even cover the rock with wood? What's the point?" Tempted to tear up the floor and take it down to bare rock, Kale considered the building's underlying construction. Their cellar wasn't directly below their dwelling, so he didn't understand the reason the previous owners utilized wood for flooring.

"Oh, whoever built the place probably wanted a level floor. That's why they build them like this in Maritropa. Plus, having it all connected makes the house more stable. I think."

"A level floor? That's weird." Kale, accustomed to the natural slopes, curves, and dips of the floors in Drak-Anor, could not conceive of a reason to need or desire a level floor.

"Oh, well, not that weird if you keep a lot of things you don't want rolling away."

"Do they have a lot of round decorations in Maritropa? All the draks I know prefer things that remind them of crystals."

Ori chuckled. "Oh, well, you know, there are a lot more elves and humans in Maritropa than draks. We live in the same kinds of homes they do there."

"How strange." Kale cursed the pain in his knees and the builder who seemed to have a vendetta against the natural curvature of stone. *Probably elves. They're always doing things with wood. Do they make elves as small as draks?* He kept his mind occupied with thoughts of tree-dwelling, short elves until he finished sanding the floor.

He heard a customer conversing with Ori and eavesdropped only long enough to determine it was a standard business transaction. Sighing, he felt a familiar twinge in his gut. His mind wandered, nostalgic for the days of fending off dwarf invasions, Kali's companionship being the only factor that muted those feelings of restlessness.

Those days were long gone. Drak-Anor, while not quite allies with the dwarves of Ironkrag, no longer raided their Deep Road caravans. Having grown up during a time of perpetual conflict, Kale found peaceful times boring and often grew restless. He threw down his sanding block and stretched as he walked toward his bedchamber.

His mate had gone wandering the market. From the bedside table, the puzzle box Terrakaptis gifted him beckoned. It had been weeks since he worked with it, and he still couldn't figure out three of its sides. He pulled it onto his lap and lost himself in its clockwork intricacies.

* * *

After a week of intense abuse by Gisella, Pancras could walk the ship unaided and not spew his guts across the decks. Though not actual mistreatment, the pain he incurred during the first few days she forced him out of bed made abuse seem like an apt description.

Food aboard the *Maiden of the High Seas* was only food in the academic sense. It was technically nourishing and would keep one from starving to death, but the bonelord was not convinced living on it was better than the alternative. Once, he found weevils in his hardtack, which put him off eating the rest of the day. To his dismay, he found the bugs typical of grain-based foods on the ship and eventually forced himself to make do.

His daily exercises with Gisella worked muscles he had not used in years, and he often collapsed into his hammock exhausted. Even his withered arm, despite appearing as though all the muscles atrophied beyond use, felt sore and fatigued. The pain and discomfort were necessary, however, if he were to put his maul, Shatterskull, to use. Bonelords fought undead when necessary, and Pancras owed it to the goddess Aita to commit himself fully.

Qaliah called to him from the rigging, and he waved to her before he ducked through the door into the fo'c'sle. When he wasn't training with Gisella, or concentrating to keep his meals down, Pancras assisted the ship's surgeon/carpenter, Stumpy.

Little more than a closet equipped with a desk and a table upon which to operate on wounded sailors, Stumpy's infirmary left a lot to be desired. From the peg-covered walls hung various dual-purpose cutting tools. They sawed through bone and wood.

Stumpy's absence from the infirmary didn't bother Pancras; he had a list of tasks to complete, and he didn't want the man looking over his shoulder. He cobbled together a small alchemy lab on top of Stumpy's desk, and Pancras pulled over a stool from which to work.

Brewing potions on a rolling ship presented difficulties in measuring liquid ingredients and keeping volatile mixtures stable. An explosion in such tight quarters would be catastrophic. For the time being, Pancras limited himself to creating less unpredictable substances like poultices and ointments. The captain requested illumination gems for the lanterns, as well, and although the minotaur could create such minor artifacts, he had yet to convince the captain that irregular lumps of glass were not suitable replacements for properly cut gemstones.

He heard an insistent thump at the door. Pancras yanked it open to greet a grimacing Qaliah.

"Got something for this?" She held up a raw, bloody hand. Against her jet-black skin, he found it difficult to distinguish blood from water, but he followed its distinctive metallic odor. He noted a whiff of sulfur accented hers, as well.

"What happened?" Pancras withdrew a jar of ointment from his pouch. He dabbed away the blood with a cloth before smearing it on.

Qaliah flinched and gritted her teeth. "That stings."

"Hush." He wrapped her wounded hand in clean linen.

"I slipped. Grabbed a rope in time but still slid a bit before stopping." The fiendling flexed her bandaged hand, noting its mobility would be restricted until it healed. "No big deal. Hey, did you ever find out why they call the surgeon Stumpy? He's got both legs and arms, and he's taller than me."

The question had plagued Pancras for a few days after he had been introduced to Stumpy. Fortunately, the surgeon possessed a sense of humor about it. "He told me that on his first day, he had to do three leg amputations."

"Better he be cutting them off than having his own cut off to earn the name, right?" Qaliah hopped onto the table and stretched her legs. She lay down and rolled over, reaching out to Pancras. "Lock the door. Let's have some fun."

He regarded her. The fiendling began to untie her top. He seized her hand to stop her. "That's um… that's…"

Pancras struggled to find a diplomatic way to approach the issue. He felt his skin burn hot under his fur. He made no secret of his desires, but he didn't advertise either.

"Hey, I don't normally go for big folk like you, yeah?" She wiggled underneath Pancras's hand so it rested on top of her breasts. He snatched it away. "I mean, I think you might have girth issues, but Gisella says it's bad for morale if I 'entertain' the sailors. It's been too long, and I know you've not shared anyone's bed since we left."

"She's right."

Qaliah took hold of Pancras's belt. "So, take these off! I can't be gone all afternoon."

The minotaur backed away, bumping into a wall full of saws, acutely aware that one wrong move could become painful and bloody. "You're very nice…"

With groan, Qaliah reclined and slapped her forehead. "Cybele's tits! You're one of those 'only minotaurs' types, aren't you? A little hot-blooded fiendling's not good enough?"

Reaching behind to steady the myriad sharp, pointy tools at his back, Pancras pulled away from them, feeling his robes snag. "Males. I prefer males. It's not that you're not attractive, probably. You're just not attractive *to me*."

The fiendling retied her shirt and rolled off the table. "I should've bedded the dwarf, but no, we abandoned him in Curton." She slammed the door behind her as she left, still complaining about their former companion's absence.

Pancras sat on the stool, resting his face in his hands. *Aita's bloody bones.* He sat silent for a few minutes before following after her. He searched the main deck but saw no sign of her. Crew members he questioned reported not having seen the fiendling since she left to have her hand bandaged.

The minotaur found her in their cabin. She rummaged through her pack.

"Qaliah, I—"

"Save it." She stood up, holding a leather glove. She pulled it over her bandaged hand and clenched her fist. "You made yourself clear. There's nothing more to discuss."

"You seemed upset. I didn't want—"

The fiendling slapped him on the arm. "You turned me down. It happens. I'm over it." She tilted her head. "Unless you're having second thoughts?"

Pancras stared into her ice-blue eyes and shook his head. "No. I just don't want any bad blood. Don't tell the crew?"

"There isn't, and I won't." Qaliah chuckled. "You're nicer than most people are toward me. It's fine. I'm good. You?"

The minotaur nodded and rubbed his horn as she left. His relief at clearing the air lasted the rest of the day, even when Stumpy brought in a screaming sailor with a gaff hook embedded in his chest.

Together, they worked beyond the toll of the next watch bell to remove the hook without further injuring the sailor. The whole time, Stumpy muttered and cursed about "clumsy swabbie" while Pancras handed him the supplies he needed. By the time they finished, the man rested comfortably. Once they washed away all the blood, it was suppertime. Pancras sat to eat with his friends, satisfied with his good work.

* * *

"How are things, Delilah?" Katka greeted her friend as Delilah, seated beneath the university's blood oak, read one of the books the librarian let her borrow. It was a history of the Arcane University, covering a specific period when the guild burned through several archmages as teams of rivals challenged each other to duel after duel under Gerald the Craven's then-new guidelines.

"I hardly see you anymore." The human girl sat next to her friend.

"Been in the library. The archmage left me to charge a bunch of lightning bombs they're going to use for practice and ran off to Dolios-knows where. He's been gone two weeks now, and his tasks for me only took two days." The drak sorceress spent her free time reading history and the guild rules. When she wasn't doing that, she studied Gil-Li's grimoire, trying to make the new techniques second nature. Delilah closed the book and tilted her head at Katka. "And I dragged my feet, too, so to speak."

Katka tapped the book Delilah held. "Anything good in there?"

A slow smile spread across Delilah's face, baring her teeth. "Loads. I'm ready. I just need to find the right time and place."

"Can't you…" The human waited until a group of gossiping students passed. "You can't just challenge him anywhere?"

"Well, yes." Delilah put the book on the bench beside her and stretched. "But it'll look better if I can do it right after he acts belligerent or disrespects me."

She picked up the book and gestured for Katka to follow her. After returning the tome to the library, they headed to the dormitory. Delilah poured two goblets of wine and handed one to Katka.

"When things go down, I want you to lay low, all right?" Delilah kept her voice hushed. She wanted to protect her friend from being caught in the crossfire. If she failed, she didn't want any suspicion of collusion to fall on Katka.

"I want to help."

Delilah shook her head as she drained her goblet. "It has to be one on one. In fact, it would be best if you went to visit your family as soon as you hear about it."

Katka sipped from her goblet and shuffled her feet as she stared at the floor. "I guess I could go home for the Festival of Apellon." The entire city bustled with preparations for the sun god's most holy celebration, held on the summer solstice.

"You should be an apprentice by now." The drak sorceress couldn't understand why Katka had not yet been allowed to take the Novice Trials and advance to apprentice.

"I'm… how did you put it? Dragging my feet." Katka smiled into her goblet.

"For what?" Delilah paced the floor, mentally cataloguing the spells she planned to use to fight Manless.

"Well, when you defeat the archmage, you'll be the archmage. Then you can take me as your apprentice."

Delilah stopped in her tracks. The logical part of her brain comprehended what the consequences of her actions would be, but hearing Katka voice them made them real. Her bed creaked in protest as she sat on its edge.

"Archmage…"

"You knew, right?" Katka joined her friend on the bed and put her arm around her. "If you win, you're going to be archmage. And headmistress, too, I suppose."

The drak bit her bottom lip until the pain was too great to bear. The brief hope she was dreaming proved false when she didn't awaken. "I know, but I never thought about what that meant. I just want to get done with this stupid guild crap and join up with Pancras again so we can all go home."

"The archmage should be able to go wherever she wants, right?"

The revelation changed nothing, but it helped to strengthen her resolve to see her course through to its end. If she defeated Archmage Vilkan, Delilah would become the Mages Guild's first drak archmage since before The Sundering. *I could rescind these penalties, pardon all the renegades, do anything, and go anywhere I want!*

The drak smiled at her human friend. "Well, I guess I have to win, huh?"

Chapter 4

Through fair weather and foul, calm winds and storms, the *Maiden of the High Seas* sailed north along the Andelosian coast. Gisella, Qaliah, and Pancras worked, sang, ate, and laughed alongside the crew for months. The Golden Slayer stood on the fo'c'sle as the ship tacked against the wind and changed course to sail around Verdant Point, the last leg of their voyage.

Gisella traded her southern furs for lighter garb, but found the sun at these latitudes hotter than she preferred. Even with her armor stowed below, her light linen chemise did not provide relief from the heat, yet, without it, her skin would burn under the unrelenting onslaught of the sun. Most of the sailors worked shirtless now, used to the conditions, and even Pancras wore naught but a leather kilt and harness. His withered arm caused some concern for the crew at first, but he explained it away as an old injury caused in a tangle with another wizard and as merely cosmetic.

She observed as he held a railing in place until the ship's surgeon/carpenter lashed it with a rope. Although he had never been fat or flabby prior to her training that honed the minotaur's body, his muscles still lacked chiseled definition—a telltale sign of a sedentary life.

Qaliah scampered through the ship's rigging like a spider at home in its web and struck with her blades faster and deadlier than a spider's venomous fangs. Her skills with her crossbow branded her an expert marksman as well.

I've done well. If we are to meet our end fighting the armies of the Lich Queen, she'll be hard pressed to claim our bodies.

The Lich Queen. The Witch Queen. Bekkhildr the Iron Witch. Her kin. Her grandmother, once. Gisella never knew her, of course. She was defeated before Gisella's mother, Vibeke, ever thought about children or marriage. Nevertheless, the same blood flowed within her veins. Upon her sister, the gods bestowed Alysha the same arcane talent as their grandmother. Gisella understood arcana from an academic standpoint, but she lacked the innate talent to utilize it. Thus, her sister learned wizardry, and Gisella became a slayer.

Behind her, she heard the clopping of hooves on wood. As there was only one minotaur aboard the *Maiden*, she did not need to turn and face him to know it was Pancras. He leaned against the rail beside her as they gazed across the cerulean water at the tree-covered land of Verdant Point.

"A few more days before landfall." The muscles in the minotaur's good arm knotted as he gripped the railing. Though the seas were smooth, dark clouds moved overland in the distance.

"If feels like the calm before the storm." Gisella looked forward to being on land again and riding Moonsilver across the rolling plains of Cardoba toward Vlorey.

"I don't think it's moving this way."

"Not the weather." She looked up at Pancras. The bonelord's fur regained its healthy sheen, and for all the trouble he had endured acclimating to shipboard life, he seemed to be none the worse for the wear, although Gisella noticed some graying of the fur around his muzzle.

"No... who knows what we'll find in Vlorey. Maybe these signs we're chasing will add up to nothing." He rubbed his right horn.

"Any more dreams? Visions? Visitations?"

Pancras shook his head. "Nothing. When I speak to Aita, she remains silent, but I do feel that she's listening. It's calming."

"Aurora, too, has been silent." *Not that she ever answers anyway.* The goddess of love was not known for being talkative; she preferred to let actions speak. They were an odd pair, Aurora and Aita. One devoted to beauty and love, the other to death, yet both working toward a common end to prevent the return of the Lich Queen.

Their love for the world outweighs their ambivalence toward each other. A priest of Aurora might say that "love conquers all," but Gisella understood that to be just a pleasant sentiment.

"We will need a plan once we're settled in Vlorey." Pancras grunted and tapped his hoof against the saxboard.

"We'll have to spend a few days getting the lay of the city. Qaliah and I can do that while you report to the Arcane University."

"Perhaps someone there will be able to give us more information."

"We can hope." Gisella knew little about Vlorey. The only people she'd met from there currently lived in Etrunia and had been uninvolved in Vloreyan politics for decades. She tickled the underside of his chin. "New gray?"

Pancras chuckled and rubbed his muzzle. "I haven't seen a mirror lately. I'm not as young as I used to be. When this is all over"—he sighed—"I hope I can return to a life of quiet contemplation and never be anywhere near the word 'adventure' again."

The Golden Slayer smiled. "If we make it through alive, I think we all deserve some peace and quiet."

* * *

"*Apprentice*," Archmage Vilkan roared from his office. In disgust, Delilah dropped the scrolls she was carrying and trotted in.

Barely back a day and he's already running me ragged.

The human wizard was hunched over a writing desk, scrawling on a long piece of paper. He rolled it up sealed it, and then offered it to Delilah.

"Take this to the archduke. Have you finished sorting those scrolls I brought back?"

Delilah replied through clenched teeth. "I had to stop to come see what you wanted."

"Then continue with that once you've returned with his reply, understood? I want those scrolls sorted before my meeting with the council this afternoon." The archmage bothered to neither glance up nor acknowledge Delilah's response. She stuck out her tongue at him, took the scroll, and left.

As she passed through the outer chamber, she kicked the scrolls on the floor out of her way. When she first starting sorting them, she unrolled a few only to discover they were written in elvish script. She understood a bit of the spoken language, but she never learned to read or write it.

"Apprentice, do this. Do that. Come here. Go there," she grumbled to herself as she left the headmaster's tower and strolled through the halls of the Arcane University's main keep. She observed Katka practicing her charms on a dog as she passed through the university grounds and waved to the human girl.

The city streets were packed with work crews preparing for the Festival of Apellon. Street-spanning banners were being hung, monuments were being restored with fresh coats of paint, and façades were being repaired. As she made her way to Grimstone Keep, Delilah fantasized about summoning a creature of earth and stone, as she'd seen Gil-Li do, and ordering it to crush the archmage like a grape.

All in good time, Deli-girl. All in good time.

The drak sorceress entered the keep and raced through the corridors. The guards, accustomed to her comings and goings, nodded as she passed. When she reached the archduke's chambers, two guards barred her way.

"Their graces are occupied and not to be disturbed."

Delilah presented the scroll from the archmage. "This is from Archmage Vilkan. I'm to await a response."

One of the guards pointed toward a chair. Delilah frowned and climbed into it to wait. It was over an hour before the doors opened and a short, round woman, the archduchess, wearing a yellow-and-green gown, emerged. Her long, brown hair hung in twin braids down her chest.

The drak slid off the chair and bowed to the archduchess as she passed. She was rewarded for her deference with a smile and a head nod. Sweeping past Delilah, she was a woman on a mission. Two small children ran after her, giggling and screeching.

The guard held the door open for Delilah. "The archduke can see you now."

Archduke Fyodar's jovial expression fell when he saw Delilah. She waited for him to be seated behind his rough-hewn oaken desk before handing him the scroll from the archmage. He broke the seal and unrolled it. His sour expression turned hostile before he finished reading it.

"Do you know what this says?" His voice quivered with restrained fury.

"No, Your Grace."

Since returning from the valley of the Iron Giants, the drak met with the archduke on several occasions and found him to be reasonable and honorable. In short, he was not a bad sort, for a human. He regarded her with steel-grey eyes and then tossed the scroll at Delilah.

She caught and unfurled it.

Fyodar,

It has come to my attention that trouble is brewing in the undercity. I thought we had agreed that you would deal with unrest in the city. Now it seems there is some sort of drak messiah down there. One the draks claim will deliver them from their oppressors.

This cannot stand.

If you are unable to do what it takes to keep our city safe, I will eliminate the filth from our fine city myself. I understand how the years can dull one's abilities, particularly for those un-accustomed to the rejuvenating effects of arcane powers.

Draks are little more than vermin, cast-offs from whatever process the gods used to create magnificent creatures such as dragons. Do not trouble yourself with them. After the Festival of Apellon, I will be more than happy to scour the city.

I realize the irony in using one of the little vermin to deliver this message. I had hoped she would be able to assist me in my dealings with the wyrm the giants seem to worship, but as she returned empty-handed, her usefulness is at an end. Deal with her as you will. I suggest sending her to your chef. Lizard is excellent braised in red wine with roots and onions.

Vilkan Icebreaker
Archmage of Muncifer
Headmaster of the Arcane University - Muncifer

By the time Delilah reached the end, her hands trembled, so she tore the parchment. It drifted to the floor, landing against a clawed foot.

It must be a joke. These are the words of a madman. It must be a joke!

"He takes me for a fool." The archduke stood, his chair falling against the wall. He stomped around his desk, patting his round belly. "The years may have softened my body, but not my mind. I know from whence draks come."

The archduke poured himself a goblet of spirits from a crystal decanter, draining it in one gulp before making another. He poured one for Delilah and handed the drink to her. "In my youth, I undertook the Pilgrimage of Tinian. Do you know what that is?"

Delilah sniffed the smoky brown liquid in the glass. The fumes caused her nose to burn. She shook her head, disguising her distaste in her reply before taking a sip. Fiery liquid burned its way down her throat.

"Would-be priests of Tinian are required to visit the temple of the patron of every major city on Andelosia. Traveling from Muncifer to Celtangate, to Maritropa, Ironkrag,

Velzuna, and Vlorey takes years, as you might imagine." He drained his second glass, poured himself a third, and returned to his seat behind his desk.

"The idea is to gain an understanding of each god subordinate to Tinian, while knowing that each is just as important in their own way. It's as much about learning the relationship between the gods as it is a journey to pay homage to all of them. One learns about the various creation myths and other stories."

He held up a finger. "In not one of them are draks called vermin or cast-offs. They are very clearly stated to be descendants of the Firstborne, the six dragon children of Gaia, and"—he clicked his fingers—"a dead god whose name escapes me at the moment."

"Rannos Dragonsire." Delilah heard that part of the story from Terrakaptis. "Wait… six Firstborne? There are six?" The drak scratched her head.

"Ah, yes, Rannos Dragonsire, whose death caused The Sundering."

"Who are the other Firstborne?" In all her time talking with Terrakaptis or listening to Kale talk about him, Delilah heard of only four Firstborne, the Earth Dragon, the Fire Dragon, the Water Dragon, and the Air Dragon.

Archduke Fyodar waved his hand. "I don't recall their names. In addition to the four most people know, there's the Void Dragon and a magic… err… Aether Dragon. Neither dwell on this world, which is why their lores are not widely known. I found dragonlore fascinating as a youth. Still do, but I have little time for such pursuits these days."

"And now one of the Firstborne is dead." Delilah's shoulders slumped. "Killed by a wizard. Probably Manless."

The drak's inquiries over the last several weeks indicated no other wizard accompanied Archmage Vilkan to the giants' village earlier in the year. The archduke insisted they not make any direct accusations until they gathered more proof, however. News of the dragon's death distressed Fyodar, but learning the giants were willing to focus their quest for vengeance softened the blow.

"Yes, and now he turns his sights on your people." Archduke Fyodar ran his fingers through his beard. "For what purpose, I wonder."

Delilah tapped the butt of her staff on the floor and set her jaw. "I don't care. I'm not going to let him kill draks." She considered telling the archduke of her plan to challenge Archmage Vilkan. *No, better to tell him I'm archmage after I've succeeded. That way, he can't try to talk me out of it. If I die, none of it will matter anyway.*

He regarded her with raised eyebrows. Delilah bowed to the archduke. "I await your response."

"I must consult with Theros. Tell the archmage his intervention will not be necessary. I will do what I must."

* * *

Kali flipped through one of the illuminated tomes Ori had completed while he and Kale installed new shelving under the counter. Kale swore as the blue drak smashed his hand with a hammer.

"Aim better."

"Oh! Sorry."

Kale stood, sucking on his knuckles. His mate's eyes were wide as she flipped through the book. "I didn't know humans were this flexible."

The striped drak examined the illustration to which Kali pointed and flipped forward several pages. "Wow, Ori. There are a lot of naked humans in this book."

"Oh, I didn't write it. I just illuminated it. A noble wanted to give it to his wife as a gift. He was very explicit in how he and his wife have been unable to conceive and thought this book might help. Don't tell anyone about that, please? I was paid extra for discretion."

Kale couldn't think of anyone with whom he would discuss Ori's work, except maybe his sister. He didn't consider it a breach of trust to tell her. After all, she was family.

The blue drak yelped and scrambled backward as a glowing boggin passed through the closed shop door and hopped on the counter.

It faced Kale. "Mistress Delilah is on her way for a conference with you and your mate. She expects complete privacy, so if you could send the limner on a pointless errand, she would be most appreciative." The boggin yipped and vanished in a puff of azure aether.

"Oh! I… well… do you…" Ori wrung his hands and paced about the room.

Kali snickered as Kale gripped Ori by the shoulders. "I'm sure she didn't say exactly that. Those messengers she sends never get the message exactly right."

He lied, of course. The messengers Delilah summoned always transmitted the intent of the message, even if they didn't use the exact wording of the conjurer. He steered Ori toward the door.

"Look, she's probably in a bad mood, so it might be best if you did make yourself scarce. You like her, right? You don't want to make her mad?"

"Oh, yes, very much. I mean, no, I don't want to make her mad." He stopped and tapped his chin with a clawed finger. "Should I buy her a gift to cheer her up?"

Kali and Kale answered in unison, "Yes!"

The striped drak fluttered his wings and ushered Ori out of the shop. "Take your time. Kali and I can finish these shelves. We'll see you in the morning."

"Oh, yes. In the morning. See you—"

Kale shut the door and turned to his mate. "I have the feeling some nasty business is about to go down." The drak couldn't explain why he felt that way, but he felt a heavy sensation in the pit of his stomach.

To keep his thoughts from wandering into dark places, Kale continued installing the shelves under the counter with Kali's assistance. They finished just before Delilah entered the shop.

She locked the door behind her. "I think we should go downstairs."

"Ori's not here." Kale took his mate's hand.

"I feel safer talking about this in the cavern." Delilah led them downstairs. Wind whistled through the cavern below the shop, fresh breeze blowing in from the chasm that bisected Muncifer. The sconces flared to life as Delilah passed them, an effect that always fascinated Kale. *I wish they'd light up for me.*

After ensuring the defenses they erected were active, Delilah turned to her brother and his mate. "The archmage has cracked."

"What happened?" Kali squeezed Kale's hand. He glanced at the dragon egg, still safe and sound where he secured it. *I wish she wouldn't say cracked.*

"He sent a letter to the archduke telling him he was going to eradicate all the draks in the city." The drak sorceress leaned her staff against the wall near the egg, clasped her hands behind her back, and paced. Her tail lashed with each step.

"What? Why would he do that? What did we... they do?" Kale scratched his head. Muncifer wasn't the best place for a drak to live, but he sensed the general population didn't want to run them in their entirety out of town.

"I don't know, Kale. But the archduke and I agree—we can't let him do it." She pulled the torn, wadded-up scroll from one of her pouches. "I'm going to confront him about it and challenge him."

Kali put her hand on Delilah's arm. "Are you sure about

this? He's the archmage. Won't the entire Arcane University back him up?"

The drak sorceress shook her head. "It will be nice and legal according to the rules of the Arcane University and Mages Guild. I've been doing a lot of research about it. He'll have no choice but to face me properly."

"I hope you're right, Deli." Kale pulled his wings in tight. "If you fail…"

"If I fail, he'll round up and kill every drak in Muncifer." Delilah picked up her staff and glanced at her brother and his mate as she climbed the stairs. "So, I can't fail. I'll let you know when and where. When you hear from me, go to Grimstone Keep. Tell them who you are; the archduke should keep you safe until I've dealt with Archmage Manless."

Kali rested her head on Kale's shoulder. "I hope she's right."

"I have faith in my sister." Kale took a deep breath. "She's a good fighter, but maybe we should have a plan in case she loses." The drak hated to consider the prospect of his sister losing but needed to consider his mate and the dragon egg's safety. Both Delilah and Terrakaptis counted on him.

* * *

On her way to see Archmage Vilkan, Delilah stopped at the Arcane University's tavern, the Enchanter's Focus, for a dose of liquid courage. For all her talk about the justification for her challenge, she honestly did not know if the high wizards would support her. If they didn't, she stood a chance of being disintegrated right there in the Court of Wizardry.

After quaffing a mug of strong ale, she strode across the common area toward the council chambers. Several students called out to her, but the drak waved to them without stopping.

As always, the university's seneschal, Lyov, manned his podium outside of the Court of Wizardry's chambers. The old seneschal peered over the rims of his spectacles at the drak sorceress. "The court session hasn't started yet." He furrowed his brow. "I don't recall the archmage sending for you, Apprentice."

She held up the scroll she had taken to the archduke. "He didn't. I have urgent news—a response from the archduke."

The seneschal's expression remained unchanged. "And this response merits the interruption of the Court of Wizardry?"

Delilah resisted the urge to roll her eyes at the old man. "Can't interrupt a meeting that hasn't started."

The barest hint of a smile crept onto Lyov's face. "Fair point. Go on in."

The drak sorceress nodded her appreciation and entered the court. To her dismay, most of the wizards were in attendance. Archmage Vilkan was engaged in a quiet, yet heated conversation with the violet-robed wizard. Though she could not see their faces behind their impassive masks, Delilah felt the eyes of several of the high wizards upon her. The gaze of the Brown, Red, and Yellow Wizards in particular followed her as she approached the archmage.

He outstretched his hand when she stopped alongside him. She raised an eyebrow at it and cleared her throat.

"Give me the archduke's response, Apprentice." He presented his hand again and glanced at the paper she carried.

"His response was verbal, and he requested I deliver it to you before the court." That wasn't exactly what the archduke said. Delilah gambled on the fact that the archmage did not have spies or magical scrying devices located in the archduke's private chambers.

"Very well. If the archduke wishes to play games, I will indulge him for now." He motioned to the Violet Wizard, and they took their respective seats on the dais. Delilah moved to the center of the assembly, licking her lips and trying to quell the flutter in her stomach.

"In response to your letter"—Delilah held up the torn scroll—"the archduke has respectfully responded that he will do what he must."

She let the words hang in the air for a moment. The drak opened her mouth to continue.

"That's it?" Archmage Vilkan stood, clenching his fists. "That is all you came to tell me?"

"Not at all, Archmage." Delilah bowed her head. "He shared the contents of the letter with me." She threw the scroll to the ground and impaled it with the butt of her staff. "I will not permit you to exterminate my people."

The archmage threw back his head and laughed. Delilah noted the high wizards in attendance directed their attention toward him, not her. "You will not?"

"Draks are descendants of the Firstborne, the children of Gaia and Rannos Dragonsire. We are not 'little more than vermin.'"

"Be gone, Apprentice." The archmage's hand dropped to the wand at his waist. "I will discipline you in private."

She drew the broken wand from a pouch and cast it on the floor. "Look familiar? We found it in the lair of Pyraclannaseous. A Firstborne. She was dead, but the signs that a wizard had been there were clear. How curious the wand resembles yours."

Strands of aether flowed toward Archmage's Vilkan's wand as he drew it. Delilah raised her staff. "I challenge you, Archmage, to the Rite of Combat as enacted by Archmage Gerald the Craven in *Arcane Rules: Civilized Magickry*. I challenge you for crimes against draks and the murder of a Firstborne dragon!"

"Renegade!" The blast from Archmage Vilkan's wand stopped short, splashing against a shield erected around the drak by several of the high wizards simultaneously. They all stood, holding various arcane foci as they faced the archmage.

"A challenge has been issued."

"Antiquated rules, but still effective and enforceable."

"Your apprentice has adhered to protocol. Will you break that covenant?"

Archmage Vilkan drew himself up and slid his wand into his belt. He clenched his jaw as he glared at the assembled wizards before settling his hate-filled gaze on Delilah.

"The Iron Crossroads. Tomorrow." He gestured toward the door. "Be gone from university grounds. I declare you a renegade and hereby banish you from the Arcane University."

The Violet Wizard turned to Delilah. "You must confine yourself to the city."

The Brown Wizard nodded in concurrence. "Slayers will hunt you down should you now flee."

"Use your time wisely. Prepare… in whatever manner you choose." The Red Wizard stepped down from the dais and approached Delilah. The high wizard picked up the torn scroll and read it.

"This will be archived and entered into evidence." The Red Wizard held aloft the letter. "Should Archmage Vilkan emerge from the challenge victorious, I will call an inquiry into this matter."

From the corner of her eye, Delilah saw the Yellow Wizard gesture to her, encouraging her to leave. Delilah bowed to the Court of Wizardry, turned on her heels, and exited. Once the doors of the court shut behind her, she ran.

As she crossed the university grounds, she scanned for Katka. The girl stood in the practice yard, destroying training dummies with lightning. She put her wand away when she saw the drak sorceress approaching.

"Come to practice with me?"

Delilah panted to catch her breath and shook her head. "I just challenged Manless to the Rite of Combat. Tomorrow at the Iron Crossroads."

Katka covered her mouth with her hands. Her eyes grew wide. "Tomorrow?"

"Make yourself scarce. If I lose…" Delilah suspected Vilkan's wrath would be as widespread as it was merciless.

"I'm scheduled for my Novice Trials tomorrow. I can't leave town." The human's voice trembled. "If I miss it, it could be months before they let me take it again."

"If I win, I'll be archmage, and I'll excuse you." The drak put her hand on Katka's arm. "If I lose, he's going to come after you because you went with me to see the giants. At least make the slayers work for it."

Katka fell to her knees and pulled Delilah into a hug. "Don't lose."

Chapter 5

"I have good news, and I have bad news." Delilah announced her presence as she entered Kale's shop. She swore under her breath when she saw the storefront was empty and strode through it to the rear of the building where Kale and Kali made their home. Seated at the table in the kitchen, they examined Kale's puzzle box. A cauldron sat near the hearth, bubbling and sizzling. The aroma of roasting meat wafted from it.

"You should lock your door when you're back here and that other drak's not around."

"Ori." Kali continued her examination of the box unabated. "Sorry, we forgot. We've gotten used to having him up front watching the store during the day."

"Did you say something when you came in, Deli?" Kale glanced up at his sister.

"I said I have good news and bad news." She pulled over the spare chair with her staff and joined them at the table. Since her last visit to their kitchen, Kale and Kali replaced the old chairs with furniture specifically designed to accommodate draks' tails.

"I issued the challenge." The drak sorceress rested her chin on her hands as she eyed her brother. *Better look at him all I can now; it might be my last chance.* She glanced around the kitchen. *Homey. This is really a home now.* She felt a pang of envy and homesickness for Drak-Anor.

"Is that the good news, or the bad?" Kali eyed Delilah over the top of the puzzle box.

"That's the bad news."

Kale scratched his head. "Well, we knew you were going to do that. What's the good news?"

"They didn't kill me outright." Delilah threw up her hands and smiled. "In fact, the high wizards made him stand down when he tried to murder me right there in front of all the assembled wizards of the Court of Wizardry. It happens tomorrow at the Iron Crossroads"

"Oh, that's… good?" A range of emotions crossed Kale's face, and his sister understood he was confused whether he should be happy for her or worried. The drak sorceress wished she felt the mirth she wore on her face.

"We've been busy while you were away." Kali slid the puzzle box to the side so it didn't block anyone's view. "We scouted the quickest route to Grimstone Keep and to the nearest city gate from there."

"We're packing up everything we can't live without before we go there to watch the duel tomorrow." Kale took his mate's hand. "You know, in case you lose and we have to flee the city."

The orange drak turned her head toward her mate but turned her eyes toward Delilah. "Don't lose. I like him how he is."

Kale's eyes darted back and forth from his mate to his sister. "What do you mean?"

Delilah understood. She reached across the table and took their hands in hers. "I think she's worried about how you'll react if I die, Kale. You know you'll be a wreck."

"I… I wouldn't… I…" Kale stared at the table. "Well, I might be." He stared at his sister, tears welling in his eyes. "Don't lose, Deli."

The drak sorceress squeezed her brother's hand. "Don't worry, Kale. You won't have to have that conversation with Pancras and Sarvesh." She pushed herself away from the table. "I need to prepare. I'll see you after."

* * *

Kale found sorting through his possessions focused his mind away from Delilah's impending peril. He believed his sister could win, but he was not immune to feelings of dread.

Images of her twisted, burned, and dead body intruded into his idle thoughts. In the end, he found his daggers and his puzzle box were all that he really wanted, although Kali insisted he keep his hat with him.

"It makes you look dashing." She adjusted it on his head. "And makes you easy to pick out in a crowd of draks."

Kale spread his wings. "These don't?"

His mate smiled and nuzzled his cheek. "Sure, if you want to be obvious."

"I can't really hide them." To illustrate his point, Kale folded his wings in as close to his body as he could.

Kali stroked his cheek. "Silly." She nuzzled his neck again. "I know you're worried. We'll handle this together. No matter what happens."

"Yes." Overcome with longing for days past, Kale recalled a time when he and his sister enjoyed no responsibilities apart from ensuring Drak-Anor's defenses were maintained. No secret dragon eggs. No wizard duels. No minotaur crime bosses looking over their shoulders.

"I'm ready, love." Kali hugged him.

Kale scanned the home they built. He and his mate put a lot of work into the old house over the last several months, and it felt like a home they built together, even if that wasn't literally true. He found himself hoping that his sister was victorious more so that he wouldn't have to leave behind all he'd built.

The guilt at that thought gnawed at him. His thoughts were interrupted by a pounding at the front door. He glanced down the hallway, but could only discern irregular shapes through the shop window.

When he answered the door, Boss Steelhand bowed in greeting, crossing his steel hand across his chest. "Good afternoon. May I come in?"

The drak furrowed his brow and stepped aside to let the minotaur pass. "What do you want?"

"Can't I stop by for a visit while I'm in the neighborhood?" The black-furred minotaur glanced around the shop. "I'm surprised you're closed."

"Ori…"—Kale stopped himself from lying outright to the minotaur—"my mate and I wanted some privacy, so we told Ori to take the rest of the day off."

"Ah… making little drakling, eh?" Boss Steelhand elbowed Kale in the ribs.

"What? No, that's not—"

"No matter." The minotaur tapped the top of the counter. "I actually have a message for you."

Kali entered from the back rooms. "I find it hard to believe you're a messenger now."

Boss Steelhand spread his arms. "Just because I run the undercity doesn't mean I don't have other responsibilities. People think it's all knocking heads and collecting kickbacks. They're wrong."

Kale crossed his arms over his chest and spread his wings as Kali came to stand beside him. "So, what's the message?"

"Word of your sister's machinations has spread, as well as her reason for challenging the archmage."

Kale's heart sank. *I never told him about Delilah.* "I don't… have—"

"Oh, please." Boss Steelhand tapped his temple with a metal finger. "I have eyes and ears all over town. Furthermore, I don't care that you kept her from me. The ins and outs of your family aren't my concern."

"So, you know about Kale's sister. So, what?" Kali tapped her foot, her claws clicking on the wood floor.

"You may find this hard to believe, but I don't want the draks run out of town. If the humans succeed at that, there is no doubt my folk will be next. We'll all be rooting for your sister."

"That's very nice, thank you." Kale doubted the minotaur came all this way just to deliver that message.

"If she fails, don't do anything hasty." Boss Steelhand clasped Kale and Kali's shoulders. "The archduke won't allow the archmage to have his way with us."

The minotaur winced as Kali gripped his hand. Kale noticed the point of her dagger pressed into the underside of Steelhand's wrist. Her lips curled in a derisive snarl. "What's your game?"

Boss Steelhand's eyes flicked to Kale's mate. "You think a dagger at my wrist is going to kill me?"

"I think I can bleed you enough that you'll be stumbling around while my mate roasts you alive. That's what I think."

The minotaur chuckled and then broke into an uproarious laugh. He lifted his hands away from the draks and kept them in the air as he stepped backward.

Kali stepped forward, brandishing her dagger. "Think we're funny, do you?"

"You misunderstand. As outsiders, you don't know what the undercity was like just five years ago. Crime ran rampant, and the streets ran red with minotaur and drak blood on a daily basis. It was civil war. Vilkan came in and cleaned up. Killed all the old bosses and put me in charge, with the archduke's blessing, of course."

Kale rubbed the sigil on his chest. He pulled Kali toward him, and she lowered her weapon.

The minotaur lowered his hands. "I have a reputation, even though Vilkan was responsible for most of it. Now, I don't agree that draks need to be relegated to the undercity. It was a bad time, for lots of reasons, but those bad apples are gone. Vilkan seems to think he didn't go far enough. I disagree, the archduke disagrees, and your sister disagrees. The archduke and I support her."

"You know the archduke?" Kale couldn't perceive the ruler of a city like Muncifer allying himself with a criminal like Boss Steelhand.

The minotaur chuckled. "Yes, you could say that. Anyway, the archduke sent me down here to head off any potential trouble on the evening of the duel. Just be calm and let events play out. The archduke will fight for the draks here. He gives his word."

"We were told to go to Grimstone Keep and watch the fight from there." Kali sheathed her dagger and placed her hands on her hips.

"Good idea. The battlement affords a good view of the crossroads." He meandered through the shop and opened the front door, pausing to regard the two draks. "I'll see you there."

After he left, Kale turned to his mate. "I don't think he's telling us everything."

"You think?" Kali shook her head. "Let's finish up. I'm hungry."

* * *

On the morning of the duel, fog clung to the lower parts of the city. Delilah broke her fast with a meat pie she purchased from a vendor in the city market and made her way through town. Word spread all over Muncifer that the archmage's apprentice challenged him to the Rite of Combat in accordance with old traditions. Everywhere the drak sorceress went, people stopped, pointed, and whispered. Some made signs to ward off evil as she crossed their path, while others wished her luck.

As a game and method of keeping her mind off the peril, she kept a mental tally of how many people wished her luck versus treated her like a villain or plague carrier. To her surprise, she counted nearly triple the number of well-wishers than detractors. *I guess the archmage isn't that popular... or they just like an underdog. Just wait until they see what I can do.*

She wagered everyone in town underestimated her. They saw her as just an apprentice, a wizard still in school, with the bare minimum of knowledge required to keep from exploding herself. Her status as an apprentice was true in the academic sense, and Delilah counted on her battle experience to give her the upper hand, even if Archmage Vilkan possessed more raw power.

The drak stood before the east gates of the city and offered a prayer to Maris, the goddess of battle. For good measure, she included Selene, the goddess of magic. She stepped through the gates and stopped to add a prayer to Tinian, king of the gods and Gaia, the Earth Mother, and in a way, grandmother of the draks.

I hope you all are watching. Or listening. I don't believe that pap about Children of Destiny, but if it means anything to you, this human killed a Firstborne, and I'm going to avenge that and make sure the egg hatches. So, you know, a little help would be appreciated.

Delilah left Muncifer behind and followed the road east toward the Iron Crossroads. Bursting with meltwater running down from the mountains, the gully extending toward the city filled Muncifer's cisterns. Across the field, Delilah saw Archmage Vilkan Icebreaker. In the distance, the Iron Gate Mountains formed a splendid backdrop, stretching across the horizon like a wall. Rolling farmland flanked the road, creating a funnel that led straight to the crossroads. It was as if Calliome herself said, "This goes no further."

In a way, I suppose Gaia is the world, and the world is Gaia. Maybe it is just I face him like this. The wind whipped her cloak around her legs, threatening to trip her. The drak sorceress unhooked the clasp at her neck, allowing the wind to carry away the garment.

Behind her, Delilah sensed observers lining the walls of Muncifer. She knew in her heart neither her brother nor Katka would stay away, and they likely stood somewhere among the crowds.

Throughout her approach, Vilkan stood, arms crossed, a statue in the crossroads. Were it not for his robes flapping in the wind, one might mistake the archmage for an intricately detailed carving.

His arm twitched.

The drak raised her staff above her head, erecting a shield just in time to intercept the bolt of lightning arcing from Vilkan's wand. The booming roar of thunder rattled Delilah's chest, and she wrinkled her nose at the lingering odor of ozone in the air.

She stood fast and plunged her staff in the ground. Concentrating on what she learned from the grimoire of Gil-Li, the drak envisioned tendrils of azure aether ripping into the earth and pulling forth.

A blast of air hit Delilah in the chest like a giant's fist. She flew backward, skidding across the ground, trailing a cloud of dust. Coughing, the drak rolled over and pushed herself onto her hands and knees just in time for another bolt of lightning to lance toward her. The bolt splashed against her shield, covering her in a coruscating film of dancing electricity.

Out of the corner of her eye, she saw Archmage Vilkan advancing on her, multi-colored tendrils of aether swirling around him. She scrambled to reach her staff, diving forward to avoid another blast of lightning, seizing it and rolling into an upright position.

"Synnefotone shifone!" A ray shot toward the archmage, and where he stood, a whirling cloud of blades appeared. Delilah didn't wait to see their effect as she ran, angling around to flank him. Stabbing pain in her chest kept her pace slow, making every breath feel like fire.

The cloud of blades exploded outward, disappearing in a glittering shower of sparks. She observed a tattered and bloody archmage emerge from the cloud, pointing his wand directly at her.

"Time to end this, Drak." Archmage Vilkan flicked his wand and swirled it. Dark clouds gathered, and thunder heralded an oncoming storm. The sky darkened, and green flashes illuminated clouds laden with rain.

Tiny droplets fell. It rained, at first, but then turned to sleet and ice. Delilah ignored the stinging icy shards and tightened her grip. She tapped the ground with the butt of her staff as azure wisps formed from the vapor around her.

"*Kaléste gi stoicheiaki!*"

The archmage halted his advance as the ground rumbled beneath him. The surface broke, showering him with rocks as a fist punched its way free of its earthly confines. A ten-foot tall, human-shaped stone being climbed to the surface.

The wizard gawked. He dove to the side as the creature brought its fists down in an overhead strike intended to smash the puny human for attacking its master.

Delilah allowed herself a smile and then pointed her staff at Vilkan, following his track as he sped and jumped away from the rock creature. "*Ophayra!*"

A globe of blue fire shot from the eyes of her staff, streaking toward the archmage. Her aim was not true, and it exploded behind him, throwing him forward just as her summoned creature reached to smash him.

"Damn it!"

* * *

Kale hopped up and down, trying to view the battlefield. The merlons were too tall for him to see over, and too many humans crowded at the lower spots. Most of the spectators appeared to be students from the Arcane University, but many nobles mingled among the robed men and women.

"Shove over, will you? That's my sister down there!" He threw himself against one of the guards in an attempt to move the man but succeeded only in receiving a sore shoulder and a dirty glare.

"Look!" Kali gripped his bandoleer and hauled him to his feet. She pointed farther down the battlement near where a black-furred minotaur in blue robes stood near a bearded human wearing a fur-trimmed cloak and a gold crown. "Isn't that Boss Steelhand?"

The two draks made their way through the crowd. The minotaur possessed the same grey-flecked muzzle as Boss Steelhand, although his hands were covered with black leather gloves. His intense stare was fixed on the battlefield. Kale tugged at his robes. "Hey!"

"What…" The minotaur did not seem surprised to see them, but he appeared rather annoyed that they broke his concentration.

"We can't see. That's my sister down there." Kale peered over one of the embrasures in front of the minotaur. He spotted a dot moving in the distance. It moved toward another dot standing at the crossroads.

"Stand here." The human gestured for Kale and Kali to take the spot in front of him and the minotaur. Kali clung to Kale's arm as they shared a space and peered through a crenel.

A bolt of lightning crossed the distance between the two figures, dissipating as it hit a magical shield. The rumble of thunder reached Muncifer at the same time the shielded figure flew backward as if punched by an invisible fist.

"I hope that wasn't your sister." The bearded human frowned.

"Me too." Kale feared it was Delilah. As far as he knew, she trekked to meet the archmage on the field of battle, and it was the figure that had traveled from the city that was thrown.

The magical shield protected the prone figure from a second lightning strike. The figure then dodged forward. A flashing cloud glinted in the sunlight, surrounding the other figure before it flew apart.

Kale felt the wind shift. The two draks glanced up to see the sky, clear and blue just a moment earlier, darken and fill with menacing grey-green clouds. Rain fell, plinking off the armor of the assembled guards before turning to ice. Observers shrieked and ran for cover. Kale spread his wings and huddled with his mate under them. The ice melted as soon as it touched his body; a mere annoyance when faced with the sight of his sister's deadly duel as it unfolded. The bearded man took a shield from a nearby guard to protect his head and face from the stinging ice.

Despite the vast distance that separated them from the combatants, they felt the earth rumble as a stone creature tore itself free and chased after the larger combatant. The minotaur standing behind Kale sucked in his breath.

"Earth magic…"

"Quite impressive." The bearded man, whom Kale suspected was the Archduke of Muncifer, crossed his arms over his chest. "She's just an apprentice?"

Boss Steelhand grunted. "Vilkan never had respect for draks, nor minotaurs. You know he views us as lesser races."

Kale felt eyes on him. He noticed the archduke scrutinizing him and his mate. "I was too lenient with him, Theros. I let him push me too far."

"This drak may be the solution to our problems, Your Grace." Boss Steelhand rested his hand on the archduke's shoulder.

Kale turned just as the remaining crowd gasped. He saw a ball of blue fire narrowly miss the running figure. It was one of his sister's signature attacks, capable of reducing several opponents to ash at once.

And she missed.

* * *

A blast wave hit Delilah in the chest, throwing her to the ground. She rolled and covered her head as bits of dirt and rocks rained upon her. Two stubs that once were legs were all that remained of her summoned creature of earth and stone. The drak felt sharp fragments of rock draw blood as they peppered her legs and back.

Damn, I wish I'd kept my cloak.

She crawled forward toward a depression she found that appeared to give some shelter. *Think, Deli-girl, think! This human is no different than those smelly oroqs you used to fight.* Delilah pulled herself over into the dip, crying out as she felt the impact of a heavy boot on her spine.

"I'm going to break your back and grind you into the dirt." The archmage twisted his foot and pressed down. The drak bit her lip to keep from screaming in pain. "When I'm finished with you, I'm going to scour the rest of your filth from Muncifer."

A bit of rock beneath his boot dug into her spine, slicing through scales. She swung her staff up toward him, hoping she was close enough to knock him off balance. She felt resistance but then almost lost hold of her staff as the archmage yanked upward on it.

Delilah muttered under her breath as she squirmed and fought to extract herself from beneath his boot. *"Kalee'steen enoch leetiké goyna."*

Followed by growls and yips, a succession of pops filled the air. The archmage cursed, and Delilah felt relief as the pressure on her back diminished. She pulled herself forward and rolled into a sitting position. The swarm of boggins she summoned leaped and bit the archmage. She wanted to laugh at the sight of the human running, swearing, and kicking balls of fur and teeth. The pain in her spine radiated around her ribs and made even breathing difficult.

You can still move everything. He doesn't have you beat yet, Deli-girl.

The wind picked up, howling in her ears. She felt the pressure drop before she heard the terrible roar. The clouds above swirled, and a funnel descended, tearing up the ground and sucking up clouds of dirt. Hail the size of Delilah's fist fell from the sky, battering the drak until she erected another shimmering shield.

Debris pelted her as she stumble-crawled toward a nearby boulder. It provided no protection against the hail, but it gave her some cover from the debris. Across a rocky stretch of field, Delilah saw a water-filled depression. The roaring vortex was deafening, closing in on her, and making it difficult to see or even think.

She dashed out from behind the boulder, pointing her staff over her shoulder. "*Ophayra!*"

The sorceress recognized the fireball would likely have no effect, but hoped it might serve as a distraction. A wave of heat washed over her. Whatever it hit was close. As she ran toward the depression, Delilah couldn't tell if it was a water-filled sinkhole, a small pond, or a puddle. In desperation, she dove into it.

Delilah received a mouth and nose-full of watery mud for her effort. The depression housed a puddle that contained so little water, she splashed out most of it on impact. She dared to glance over her shoulder at the advancing funnel of roaring, howling wind. Her fireball set alight some of the drier debris, and flames swirled around the vortex.

The drak felt herself being pulled by her legs, being dragged out of the mud and across the ground. Her claws left deep gouges in the earth as she tried to find some purchase.

It was no use. The whirlwind picked up the drak and flung her through the air. It was all Delilah could do to hold onto her staff as she twisted and flew higher and higher. Swirling dirt blinded her while stinging ice slashed her scales.

Below her, Muncifer receded until it was a child's toy on the tabletop of the world. She tumbled, passing through a small cloud, as though she floated in a dream. Then, as the cloud passed, she viewed the world below her, rushing closer at impossible speed.

She screamed.

Chapter 6

The *Maiden of the High Seas* lurched under a massive wave. Pancras gulped and seized a handful of rigging as his stomach knotted. In celebration of the end of their voyage, he indulged in a larger-than-usual meal with which to break his fast, unaware that Nethuns, god of the sea, planned, as a going-away present, to pummel their ship with a storm.

Thunder crashed, and a resurgence of rain rolled across the deck. He strained to find the land through the sheets of rain, but viewed only an expanse of grey. While the deluge soaked him through, the bonelord solaced himself with the fact that, this far north, the precipitation felt pleasantly warm.

Pancras pulled himself along the rigging until he reached the steps leading to the poop deck. He clung to the bannister as he climbed, reaching the top as a wave crashed over the bow.

"Damned summer squalls!" Captain Eingvar lashed himself to the ship's wheel. The watchman shouted to make himself heard over the gale. "I thought we'd get to port before one of these damned things caught us."

"Are they always this bad?" Pancras stumbled across the deck as the ship listed to one side and then the other.

"Ha! This is nothing. The worst will be behind us soon."

To Pancras's surprise, the captain's words proved true. The storm soon passed, leaving behind upended crates, snapped lines, a torn sail, and many wet sailors. The minotaur wrung his clothes over the side as the captain approached him.

"Storms like that creep up on you here. Damned warm, coastal waters are rough." He pointed across the deck. "See those lights in the distance?"

Pancras noticed flickering points bobbing on the horizon. Or rather, the ship bobbed as he peered at the skyline.

"Port-of-Dogs. I reckon they got a soaking, too, but those landlubbers like it. Helps the crops, they always say."

"Oh? What do they grow?" The minotaur had not heard much about this part of Andelosia. The rain brought with it humidity. The air felt thick, and it required effort for Pancras to breathe. He felt as if he walked in a soup of it.

"Around these parts? Peaberries. A lot of fruit orchards further in. Around Vlorey, you'll find the usual food crops, too, but peaberries are big around the port. They roast the seeds and make a drink out of them." He slapped Pancras on the back. "If you need some quick cash, buy a few bushels to sell in the city. Cybele's tits, you can probably get paid to haul them if they're having a bumper crop."

The first mate ran across the deck, summoning Captain Eingvar to handle another crisis. Pancras remained behind to finish drying his fur and clothes. Afterward, he sought out his companions. Gisella, already below deck, packed their gear. The Golden Slayer's luxurious locks hung stringy and dripping, victims of the summer storm.

"We're nearly there." Pancras stripped off his kilt and pulled on a new one before rolling into his hammock. Months of shipboard necessity erased whatever sense of modesty any of them possessed.

"I don't mind the adventure of a sea voyage, but I'll kiss Gaia herself when we make landfall."

Pancras raised an eyebrow. "Gaia won't notice, but I'll bet Qaliah wouldn't mind a kiss."

Gisella laughed. "She wouldn't at that. She's been particularly forward lately. I think forced celibacy and the closeness of all the men is getting to her."

Pancras nodded. While he usually didn't give humans a second glance, their close proximity, general fitness, and the number of bawdy songs and half-naked bodies provided good fodder for his dreams, the kind of which he had not enjoyed in many years.

"I'm sure there will be plenty of opportunity for that in Vlorey." He laced his fingers behind his head. "I suggest we hasten our departure from Port-of-Dogs and get on the road sooner, rather than tarrying in the port."

"I agree." Gisella climbed into her hammock above Pancras's and lay on her stomach facing the minotaur. "I'm glad I didn't have to fulfill my duties as a slayer and kill you... Renegade."

"I'm glad, too."

* * *

Kale screamed as his sister was sucked upward by the tornado and disappeared into the sky. He charged forward, spread his wings, and leapt, only to be snatched down by the steel grip of Theros Steelhand.

"Stay down!"

"Deli!"

The minotaur pulled Kale off the crenellation. "You can't interfere." He held Kale by the shoulders and knelt before him. "The rest of the high wizards will be watching. They'll ensure the fight remains fair and honorable."

Kale wriggled and squirmed in the minotaur's grip, but Theros held him fast. "I can't let my sister die."

"Look!" Kali pointed toward the sky. A tiny figure tumbled and fell as the tornado dissipated just short of a group of buildings near the eastern city wall. Kale's heart pounded in his chest as his sister plunged toward the unyielding ground.

Suddenly, the sky around Delilah darkened and grew hazy until Kale could no longer make out his sister's form. The effect concentrated around her, and the clouds receded, lightened, and then disappeared.

"Tinian's lance, would you look at that!" The archduke leaned forward on the battlement. A building-sized humanoid shape formed from the condensed clouds and water in the gully below the falling drak. It gathered her in its arms and deposited her on the ground in a clearing behind Arch-mage Vilkan.

Kale could only stare, his mouth agape. *That moldy old book taught her that?*

* * *

Delilah dismissed the creature of water she'd summoned from the rain clouds. Adapting Gil-Li's conjuration while she fell was easier than she expected, once she remembered screaming in abject terror wasn't part of the spell. The drak sorceress leaned on her staff while willing her knees and legs to support her weight.

Breathing still hurt, and her muscles felt like goo. To her dismay, the archmage turned and walked toward her. Vapors of coruscating colors swirled around his head and arm, gathering near the tip of the wand in his outstretched hand.

The drak gripped her staff and took a deep breath. Just as she gathered more power to unleash on the archmage, a beam of crimson light lanced toward her. Delilah threw herself to the side, but was too late. The beam caught her across the flank, slicing her open from the hip up and around to her shoulder. She felt a snap when she hit the ground, and her vision faded from the fiery pain coursing through her body.

She dared to examine the wound and noted gleaming white bone. A fountain of blood spurted rhythmically in time to her heart beat. The drak fought to keep her breathing steady and shut her eyes. She grimaced and angled her staff to point at the advancing archmage.

Arcane power flowed into her, fueled by the magic in her blood. She not only tasted, but also felt it. Drawing upon it required no effort. The eyes of her staff glowed with furious red light.

Time to end this, Manless.

Pain in her muscles and bones turned to pleasure. Her scales tingled, like one who experienced the touch of a new lover. She felt her bones knit and wounds close. A dozen possibilities raced through Delilah's mind. With the power of her blood at her disposal, there was no limit to what she could accomplish. She felt it pooling beneath her ravaged body.

"No."

Delilah released the energy, allowing it to dissipate. Grunting with effort, she used her staff to climb to her feet. Her wounds tore open, and she felt a fresh gush of blood pour from her side and run down her leg. The drak kept her arm tight to her body to keep soft tissues from bulging forth from her wound.

"Not like this. *Dapane phlogone!*"

A stream of fire shot from her staff. She guided it toward the archmage whose reflexes were more than a match for the injured drak. He sidestepped her stream of fire and ducked her clumsy attempt to sweep it across his head.

Delilah ceased channeling the fire and fell forward. She clutched her staff tight to avoid falling toward the crowd. The blood roaring in her ears muted all other sounds, and the edges of her vision darkened.

Archmage Vilkan stood close enough that she recognized his smirk. "You're finished, Drak." He lunged forward and backhanded her, sending the drak sprawling. She felt blood gush from freshly re-opened wounds. "All your power is spent. For what?"

The human pressed his boot against her neck. Delilah wrapped a hand around his ankle and dug in, piercing his leather boot with her claws. She dragged her staff along the ground with her other hand, in a futile effort to bring it to bear. He pressed harder, cutting off her air. Her head twisted as he ground his heel in.

"*Akee...*" Delilah coughed and gagged. She felt flesh beneath her claws and squeezed with the last ounce of her strength. The archmage eased up on her neck as the drak's claws gouged the tender flesh of the human's ankle.

"*Akeeda geiosis.*" Her voice was a hoarse whisper, but sufficient to summon the power she needed. The ground rumbled.

With a spray of bloody dirt, a spike of rock burst from the ground between them. It pushed Delilah in one direction and Vilkan in the next. The human kept his footing and dodged another erupting behind him.

A third spike threw him forward. He managed to avoid landing on his face, but as he teetered on the brink of falling, a fourth erupted beneath him, pushing him upward as it plunged into his gut and exited his spine.

It climbed higher and higher, impaling the archmage on a spike of stone as tall as a house. Delilah watched him writhe and scream. A smile crept to her face as darkness took her.

"Got you, you bastard."

* * *

"Deli!" Kale pulled away from Theros and jumped off the battlement as desperate hands grabbed at him. He spread his wings and caught a draft, propelling himself upward as spikes of stone erupted from the ground in the distance. One of the spikes impaled the archmage but hid his sister from view.

The drak angled his descent and flapped his wings to slow his plummet. Kale still had not mastered flight, and even extended gliding tested his endurance. He passed over Archmage Vilkan. A single glance was enough to confirm the human was quite dead.

He spotted his sister lying in a pool of her own blood. Kale banked again and tucked in his wings to descend beside her. He landed hard enough that he knew he'd regret it in the morning and skidded to a stop next to Delilah.

"Don't be dead, Deli. Don't be dead." He lifted her head and cradled it in his lap. Her eyes fluttered open.

"Hey."

"You won! You beat him, Deli."

Delilah coughed, flecks of blood spattering her lips. "I think I'm dying."

"No, no, no. You can't, Deli. You're archmage now." Kale felt tears roll down his cheeks. He took pains not to look at his sister's wounds, but the quick glances he stole were enough to tell him she was eviscerated and bleeding out.

"… favor?"

Kale leaned in to better hear his sister's weakening voice. "Deli?"

"Go away… get help."

"I'm not leaving you, Deli. You stay with me…"

Delilah pushed away Kale's head with a bloody hand. "Get. Help. Stupid."

The drak fell backward. It was all he could do to not drop his sister's head. He stood and backed away. When he turned to race to Muncifer, he observed several others running toward him. Men and women in robes. He jumped up, shouted, and waved.

A few of the humans broke away from the main group to examine the archmage. His body was high above them, still impaled on the blood-streaked spike of rock. One of them picked up the archmage's wand. The others pushed Kale to the side and surrounded Delilah. He heard them chanting and felt arcane energy crackle through the air.

Delilah and the mages who surrounded her vanished in a burst of light. Kale shouted in alarm and yanked at the robes of the person nearest to him. An older woman wearing mossy robes, her face drawn and her hair woven in silver braids, glanced down at him.

"What happened? Where did they go?" Kale pointed to the spot where his sister had lain only a moment earlier. All that remained was a pool of blood.

"Teleport circle. They took her to a healer." The woman knelt to meet Kale's eyes. "Was Apprentice Delilah your mate?"

Kale drew back his lips in disgust. "My sister."

"I'm Master Agata. I'm rather shocked she was victorious. Your sister is supremely talented." The human regarded the earthen spike while the other mages discussed how best to retrieve Archmage Vilkan's body.

"Deli was only an apprentice because he said so." Kale pointed at the corpse. "She's been fighting with her magic for years in Drak-Anor. We weren't hatched yesterday, you know."

Master Agata pursed her lips. "Yes, well… I will admit I cannot tell a drak's age by looking. And, until now, I was unaware some of you possessed wings."

The drak pointed to the sigil on his chest. "We're dragon-kin."

"Of course." The woman stood, placing her hand on Kale's shoulder. "I will take you to her."

Kale spared no second glances as he passed the former archmage's corpse. Master Agata led him to Muncifer. They passed through the city gates and made their way through bustling streets toward the Arcane University. The drak caught snippets of people chatting about the duel. Most heard of it, but few were afforded the opportunity to watch, so the stories were wildly exaggerated and inaccurate. Apparently, Delilah herself changed into a city-sized mountain giant and impaled Archmage Vilkan with a spear fashioned from a stalactite.

Kali met the pair as they approached the university gates. Archduke Fyodar and Theros Steelhand accompanied her. She enveloped her mate in a hug but then scowled at him.

"Don't do that again."

The human wizard bowed to the archduke. "Your Grace. To what does the Arcane University owe your presence?"

"Don't be coy, Agata. I came to check on your new arch-mage."

"I'm sure our healers are doing everything they can, but for now, you'll have to wait. Her brother has the right of first visitation, I think. Hmm?"

Theros pointed to a building just inside the gates. "We can wait in the Enchanter's Focus, Your Grace. I believe they've recently tapped some fresh kegs of mead."

The archduke and minotaur headed for the tavern. Only after Kale explained to Master Agata that Kali was his mate, did the wizard allow the female drak to accompany him.

When they arrived at the university's infirmary, they were stopped by guards. The two hulking men crossed their halberds, barring the door. "No one is permitted."

"Nonsense." Master Agata gestured to Kale. "He is her brother."

"The high wizards have ordered it."

The woman's lips drew a thin line across her face. "I see. Very well." She sat in a nearby chair.

Kali threw up her hands. "That's it? We just wait now?"

Master Agata glanced at the female drak. "Yes."

"It's okay, Kali. They're trying to heal her." Kale pulled his mate away from the door. "We should let them work."

He helped his mate into a chair that he pulled next to Master Agata and stood near her. The chairs were not made for draks, and although large enough to accommodate a tail, the chairs could not accommodate his wings as well. He withstood the discomfort while he waited for his sister, noting his ankles and feet ached from his rough landing.

Kale sat against the wall and rubbed his feet. Just as he found a comfortable position, the door opened. A masked, brown-robed wizard emerged, closing the door behind him.

The high wizard eyed the trio and gestured to Master Agata. The woman stood and bowed.

"The drak's… the archmage's wounds are quite severe, but they are mending. When the others leave, she will need rest, but she should be able to sustain a brief visit." The wizard regarded Kale and Kali. "Kinfolk?"

Kale stood. "I'm her brother." He approached Kali and took her hand. "Kali is my mate."

"It should not be long. Master Agata, a word."

The woman nodded to Kale and Kali before exiting with the brown-robed wizard. Kale rested his head on his mate's shoulder. She placed her hand on his cheek. The striped-drak stroked his mate's rust-orange arm. He lost himself in their supple feel, the rhythm of her breathing, and the slight odor of brimstone that clung to his own scales ever since he learned to breathe fire.

He could not determine how much time passed before the other wizards left Delilah's room, bowing their heads to him as they passed. After helping his mate down from her chair, Kale and Kali entered Delilah's room. Sitting upright in bed, covered in white linen bandages, her eyes closed, and her breathing slow and steady, she did not appear to be in pain. Her staff lay in bed alongside her, the skull that topped it keeping watch like a sentry.

Kale reached for his sister's hand. Her eyes snapped open. They focused on Kale, and she smiled. "I'm not an apprentice anymore."

* * *

Every inch of Delilah's battered, bruised body throbbed. When visitors asked how she felt, "I hurt" was the only response that adequately summarized her situation. Even her scales and claws ached.

Changing bandages unleashed new waves of pain. Healers closed the largest gashes with their arcane powers and applied potions and ointments to encourage Delilah's body to repair itself. *At least breathing doesn't hurt anymore.*

She threw off her covers and swung her legs over the side of the bed. The drak picked up her staff and used it as a crutch as she slid. Once her feet hit the floor, she was surprised her legs supported her weight. A sense of pride in her accomplishment filled her chest, until she took a step.

The room spun around her as if she were a wagon wheel. Her staff clattered to the floor as she clutched at the bed to prevent herself from falling. The blankets, a poor handhold, slid off the bed, covering her in a heap as she collapsed.

"Damn it."

Delilah heard the door open and the sounds of boots running into the room.

"The archmage? Where's the archmage?" The shrill panic in their voices exacerbated her headache.

"Under here." Delilah thrust up her hand through the blankets. "I'm under here…" She restrained herself from calling the guards insulting names.

Rough hands grabbed her and helped her onto the bed. Once she was sitting upright, they stared at the floor and shuffled their feet.

"You can go now." Delilah shooed them away. "And bring me some food or something."

They shuffled out of the room, closing the door behind them. Delilah sighed and reached for her staff. The guards neglected to pick it up; it was out of reach halfway across the room on the floor.

"Idiot longshanks." She scooted up to rest against the headboard. The room in which she convalesced, an interior chamber, contained no windows, and only two enchanted sconces on the wall provided light. The only other furniture, a chest of drawers, stood in one corner. A silver bowl and pitcher, filled with water Delilah presumed, sat atop it.

She slapped the sheets. "Well, Deli-girl. You run this place now. You probably should make some decrees or something. Maybe stop talking to yourself while you're at it."

The door opened, and a tawny-skinned elf wearing silver-trimmed green robes entered. He tousled his dark, mossy hair before bowing. "May I offer my congratulations, Archmage Delilah? Of course, if that is still what you're calling yourself."

"Master Valyrian." Delilah bowed her head to the elf. He acted as her tutor during her first weeks at the Arcane University, bringing her up to speed on certain basic techniques she lacked, having been self-taught for decades.

"What do you mean? Other archmages don't use their names?" She reached up to scratch her head, but a thick bandage wrapped around her forehead stymied her efforts. *Great, it's probably snagged on my horns. I'll bet they threw away those nice silk ribbons, too.*

"It is a personal choice." The elf wizard steepled his fingers. "Some feel taking a new name as archmage helps them maintain professional detachment when dealing with their subordinates, many of whom may have helped them achieve their new position."

"Well, no one helped me, so I'll just stick with my drak name. I was hatched Delilah, and so I'll stay Delilah." The drak pointed at her staff on the floor. "Would you mind?"

"A fine name, to be sure." Master Valyrian handed the staff to Delilah. She secured it alongside her on the bed. "I would not be too adamant that you had no help, however." He placed his hand on his chest and bowed.

"I guess some of you were nice and tried to teach me things." Delilah scrunched up her face and considered her hasty words. "All right, I had a little help."

"That's not what I mean." The elf smiled and shook his head. He closed the door and reached into his robes, revealing a red mask.

Delilah stared at him while her mind processed the revelation. "You're the Red Wizard?"

"Indeed." Master Valyrian turned the mask over in his hands. "We can choose to reveal ourselves to the archmage. However, many do not. They enjoy the anonymity the mask gives them. Some archmages have a difficult time compartmentalizing the words of a high wizard from the actions of their peers."

"So, basically, I should pretend like you didn't just show me that?" Delilah rubbed her snout. *Oh, good. Secrets already.*

"I thought you should know that, while Vilkan's opinions were not his alone, they were a minority opinion. I should think any reasonable changes you wish to enact will not meet with much resistance." The elf hid the mask under his robes as the guards returned with a tray of fruit, cured meats, and wine. Delilah tore into the food with gusto.

Having little to do while she recovered from her injuries but think, Delilah already had several ideas for changes she planned to institute as soon as she was able. Disinterested in micromanaging either the guild or the Arcane University, she recognized duties that distracted her from studying the runed circle under Kale's home would breed resentment.

Reaching into his robes, the elf withdrew a multifaceted stone and placed it on Delilah's tray. "A Herald Stone, Madame Archmage."

Picking it up, Delilah noted that apart from its facets, it appeared much like an ordinary striped rock one might find lying in a field. Mostly dirty-grey in color, dark green striations banded its circumference.

"What is it for?"

"It will let you communicate with the bearer of another Herald Stone. As archmage, you possess the master, of course. All high wizards possess them, as do the headmasters of other Arcane University campuses the world over… well, at least in Andelosia."

He produced his own Herald Stone from within his robes. It was similar to the one Delilah held, except it was smaller, flatter, and mostly red. "Headmasters can communicate with each other, high wizards with each other and the headmasters, and so on. The master stone can initiate communication with all the others, but it requires at least three student stones to initiate contact with the master."

"So, random wizards can't bother me whenever someone spits in their soup." Delilah turned over the stone in her hands. She sensed latent arcane energies within it, the sensation not dissimilar than that which she used to summon her boggin messengers.

"Precisely. When you're well enough to leave this room, use it to convene a council. There are some formalities that must be observed." Master Valyrian bowed. "In the meantime, I will inform the other high wizards and headmasters that we have a new archmage."

The elf left Delilah to her meal. As she continued examining the stone, she realized she'd forgotten to ask him how to use it. Setting the stone aside, she ate, confident everything would fall into place.

Chapter 7

Pancras stepped off the gangplank onto the sturdy, wooden dock and dodged a laborer hauling a bundle of textiles. Port-of-Dogs bustled; a dozen ships, in addition to the *Maiden of the High Seas*, unloaded trade goods. Gisella, still aboard, bade the captain and crew she'd befriended farewell.

He stood at the bottom of the gangplank, waiting for his companions and their steeds. Qaliah bounded toward him, holding her gear to keep it from bouncing. She hopped off the gangplank and glanced around the docks.

"I need a drink. You buying, big guy?" She slapped Pancras across the chest with the back of her hand.

"Sailor grog not good enough anymore?" Raising his hand, he hailed the sailor leading their mounts across the main gangplank used to offload cargo.

"A girl needs something other than swill now and then."

"We're not staying here. We're heading for Vlorey as soon as Gisella disembarks." Pancras took Stormheart's reins from the sailor. He led the horse to the end of the dock where a pile of their tack and saddlebags waited.

While he and Qaliah prepared Stormheart and Comet, Gisella joined them. She cooed to Moonsilver as she saddled her. The fiendling complained about their immediate departure from Port-of-Dogs throughout the packing of their mounts and saddlebags. Pancras's extensive experience with well-meaning, but irritating, friends in Drak-Anor proved good practice for tuning her out.

Qaliah relentlessly pointed out every tavern and inn they passed on their way from the docks to the city gates. Gisella and Pancras kept her between them to prevent her from wandering off, although Pancras wondered if watching the fiendling that closely was worthwhile. She was part of neither his nor Gisella's plans. Still, they had come to appreciate her company over the last several months.

Pancras breathed a sigh of relief after they passed through the city gates and Qaliah declared she had finished griping. They rode onward under the warmth of the setting sun, bound for Vlorey.

By the time they stopped to make camp for the evening, Port-of-Dogs faded from their sight behind them. After dinner, while Qaliah and Gisella practiced their swordplay, Pancras focused inward and renewed his connection to Aita.

The minotaur found initiating such a communion challenging under normal conditions, and despite his efforts, he found it impossible to sufficiently concentrate while aboard the ship. However, the rolling hills of Cardoba, under the moons and stars, provided a more conducive setting.

In his mind, the world slipped away. He spun through space, marveling at the stars wheeling around him. He passed through the emerald and azure aether surrounding and binding the world and glanced over his shoulder. The globe of Calliome spun in a cosmic dance with the King and Queen, all in perfect, synchronous motion with the sun. He felt a familiar, comforting presence envelop him.

Aita.

The goddess said nothing to him. It was not necessary. She touched him with the smallest part of her essence. The duties of a deity were many, their reach and influence interminable, but not unlimited.

On the correct path now, her very presence exactly filled his need. Another presence joined them in the Outer world. The radiance and warmth of Aurora filled Pancras until he felt he might burst.

Images flashed before him. Delilah, broken and bloody in a field. Her brother carrying an egg almost as large as himself. The Golden Slayer holding a spear, ready to kill. A tall, dark man in gleaming armor brandishing a golden sword. The drak twins again, laughing and embracing. The fiendling skipping down a cobblestone street. Finally, he, himself, standing atop a tower, surrounded by fog.

He knew not what the images meant. The past. The future. They were the same to a mortal basking in the presence of deities. What was and what could be. The warmth and comfort of the goddesses faded, and Pancras was left with what was—himself, sitting near a crackling fire in Cardoba while a human warrior and a fiendling sparred and laughed nearby.

* * *

Delilah entered the Court of Wizardry, her head held high, as she passed Seneschal Lyov. The old man bowed to her as she passed. Guards snapped to attention, and the rainbow of robed wizards seated in their traditional chairs stood and bowed. She fought to keep a grin from overtaking her face. The drak sorceress hated participating in pageantry, except, of course, when she was the center of attention.

The chair formerly occupied by Archmage Vilkan Icebreaker was gone, replaced with a small chair more suited to a drak's anatomy. Pleased it did not affront her dignity by requiring her to climb into it, she sat, careful not to strain her sore muscles.

The Red Wizard sat alongside her on the left, Master Valyrian, though she took care to not make any indication that she recognized the elf. The Brown Wizard sat to her right. The other high wizards did not seem to be arranged in any particular order. Delilah suspected that, apart from her position in the center, seats were up for grabs.

"A new archmage has called us." The Violet Wizard stood. "Apprentice Delilah Windsinger challenged Archmage Vilkan Icebreaker in accordance to the Rite of Combat as set down by Archmage Gerald the Craven, and this action has been found just."

The Green Wizard tapped the arm of their chair. "But a mere apprentice? Surely, we need not stoop to such a low level of leadership."

"It was Vilkan's petty foolishness that placed our new archmage at such a low level." The Yellow Wizard gestured toward Delilah. "As I understand it, she served as one of Drak-Anor's chief battlemages for decades before answering his summons to pay her dues."

"A renegade?" the Green Wizard scoffed and laughed. "We can do better, my peers."

Delilah tapped her staff against the floor. Heads turned to meet the gaze of their archmage. "Do you intend to invoke the Rite of Combat?"

A murmur rippled through the high wizards. The Green Wizard withdrew. "No, Archmage. That was not my intention."

"Good. Then let's move on from this pointless discussion. There are changes I want made, immediately."

Another murmur.

That's it, Deli-girl, keep them on their toes. "We're no longer going to dispatch slayers to deal with guild members who are delinquent in paying their dues. Any self-taught renegades who aren't bothering anyone are also to be ignored."

"Ironic."

"Weren't those the exact decrees that brought you here?"

"Vilkan would still be archmage save his petty consolidations."

Delilah held up her hand to stop the chatter. "I am also separating the post of archmage and headmaster." The drak sorceress had thoughtfully considered that particular decree. She possessed neither the desire to teach, nor did she know the first thing about running a school. Learning to be effective in that capacity would be a serious distraction from her research.

The second decree met with silence. The high wizards first glanced at one another and then at their new archmage.

"You're certain you wish to give up that post?" The Yellow Wizard tented their fingers before their face. "Do you have someone in mind you want to name as headmaster?"

"I don't know anything about running a school, or about teaching." Delilah regarded the Yellow Wizard and the other high wizards. "I want the advice of the court about appointing a new headmaster."

Every high wizard contributed their opinions about what sort of person would be best appointed to the position of headmaster. Even the high wizards who claimed to not hail from Muncifer offered their thoughts on the matter. Delilah made a mental note to ask how they came so quickly after she summoned them.

In the end, after hours of debate, they narrowed it down to two candidates, both of whom were experienced and well-regarded: Masters Agata and Galina. "I will speak to each of them privately and make a decision within a few days."

Delilah tapped her staff on the floor. "I have two more points, and then we can adjourn. First, as one of the few acts I will make as current headmaster, I want to appoint Novice Katka as my apprentice."

The Black Wizard held up their hand. "I believe she re-scheduled her Novice Trials for the day after tomorrow."

The drak sorceress had not seen her friend since before the duel. She nodded. "Excellent. In that case, I can wait a few days. Second, there are two items of research I intend to work on. One is a dragon egg I found when I was in the village of the Iron Giants."

She waited for the hubbub to diminish. As yet, Delilah had not revealed any details about her visit to the giants. "I kept many things from Vilkan when I reported back to him, mostly because I did not trust that he would react in an appropriate fashion."

"You told him their king was dead and you saw no dragon." The Blue Wizard tilted their head.

"I saw no living dragon." Delilah raised a finger. "Pyraclannaseous was killed, probably by a wizard, as I intimated when I threw the broken wand at Vilkan. It is likely he was the cause. Being a Firstborne, her death cracked the earth under the mountain."

"The world cracked when Rannos Dragonsire was killed." Clasping their hands, the White Wizard lowered their head.

"That's what the giants' shaman said. She thought Pyraclannaseous's death drove their king mad, causing him to attack us. They are willing to reopen peace talks now that Vilkan is dead."

"The king of the Iron Giants attacked you?" The Blue Wizard gasped. Sparing no details, Delilah recounted her recent encounter with the giants. She emphasized, using sweeping hand gestures, how their spearheads were drak-sized and how they barely escaped with their lives.

"If I may, Archmage…" The Brown Wizard extended a hand. "What is the nature of your research with this dragon egg?"

Delilah stretched her legs. Sitting in the chair stiffened her muscles, and she still ached from the duel. "My brother and I intend to take the egg to Pyraclannaseous's brother, Terrakaptis, the Earth Dragon. I need to know how to care for it, how to tell when it's ready to hatch, all that sort of thing."

The White Wizard nodded. "I am certain such information can be found in the library."

"A perfect task for an apprentice." The Black Wizard nodded in agreement.

The drak sorceress decided to take a risk. "Do the books in our library also speak of moon gates?"

The high wizards turned their full attention to the archmage and proceeded to speak over each other.

"The moon gates are lost."

"Destroyed in The Sundering."

"I have heard the Frost Queen has one."

"Are they tied to the Fae Nexuses?"

"I believe they are affected by the King and Queen."

Delilah banged the butt of her staff against the floor until the wizards fell silent. *It's amazing they can accomplish anything together.*

"I found one." She figured her brother would understand if she left out the details of their discovery.

She swore she heard the Brown Wizard blink. "Where? With the Iron Giants?"

The drak archmage coughed. "Until I learn more about it, I will keep that to myself. I don't want curious onlookers crowding the area."

"A wise precaution."

"Most wise."

"Take care you do not hoard power solely for your own benefit."

The last came from the Green Wizard. All heads turned to regard the speaker. The wizard raised hands, conciliating. "No insult was intended, of course. Just a general caution."

"I'll keep that in mind." Delilah stood and stretched. "We're adjourned. I'm still sore."

They bowed to her in unison and shuffled out, using the side doors, rather than exiting to the main foyer. The Red, Green, and Brown Wizards lingered. When he noticed the Green and Brown Wizards remained, the Red Wizard bowed again and made a hasty exit.

Delilah rubbed the base of her neck. "This can't wait?"

The two high wizards bowed and removed their masks. Masters Galina the Green and Agata the Brown regarded her.

"Oh." Delilah understood. "You want to talk about this headmaster thing."

Master Galina clasped her hands behind her back. "I do."

"As do I, but first"—Master Galina took to a knee—"I owe you an apology."

Delilah furrowed her brow. "For what?"

"I hope you don't think I was unfair. I was hard on you, more so than the rest of the high wizards. It wasn't personal; I don't know you well enough for it to have been personal. I just want a better archmage than Vilkan." She bowed her head.

Delilah placed her hand on Master Galina's shoulder. "I understand."

Master Agata smiled. "Let's get down to business, Galina. The archmage is still recovering from her injuries. We should not keep her too long."

The younger woman nodded and stood, smoothing her robes as she did so. "Very well, then."

Delilah shifted her staff to her other hand and rubbed her side where a bandage covered the long gash that almost eviscerated her. "So, what do you want?"

"We appreciate your confidence in us, and we have thoughts about the archmage and headmaster positions." Master Agata clasped her hands behind her, assuming the same posture as her peer. Archmage Delilah glanced up at the two women and wished to be taller. She found it a bit humorous that they looked downward to her for answers.

"So, what about them?"

"We have spoken at length about this very subject over the last several years…" Master Agata began.

"And, we agree that the position here would be better served by two, rather than one." Master Galina finished the sentence as though the two women had rehearsed their speech.

"Other Arcane University campuses have a headmaster position, as well as a deputy headmaster." The older woman paced as she spoke.

Master Galina's eyes followed as the other wizard crossed the room before turning her attention to Delilah. "There is no good reason for Muncifer to be different."

The drak sorceress admitted she was unfamiliar with the structure of the Arcane University campuses across Andelosia. Her knowledge began and ended with the understanding they were a part of the Mages Guild. "Why is Muncifer different?"

"That's very simple, really." The younger woman raised her eyebrows. "A succession of archmages based in Muncifer felt they knew better than anyone how to run the Arcane University."

The situation smacked of a set-up to Delilah. "Funny how you both have ideas to reform the university, and you both ended up being the top candidates."

Master Agata spun to face her. "Forgive me for being blunt. You, yourself, said you have neither the knowledge nor the interest to be headmaster. Of course we would push for ourselves."

The Master Galina gestured to Delilah. "You'll notice none of the other high wizards campaigned strongly for any other candidate."

"If you're worried about our intentions"—Master Agata gestured to herself and the younger wizard—"as archmage, you have the authority to remove us from the seat at any time."

"Oh." Although that point had not occurred to Delilah, it made sense. She scratched under her chin—one of the few spots that wasn't still tender. "Very well. Master Agata will be headmaster, and Master Galina will be your deputy"—the drak raised a finger—"after I get my apprentice."

The two women eyed each other and slowly turned their heads toward Delilah. She suspected they expected a longer discussion about the subject. The two women bowed to Delilah.

"Very well. Thank you, Archmage."

Having nothing else to say, the two women left the chamber. The drak exited the court by way of the main doors, taking a moment to speak to Lyov.

"Did you need something, Archmage?"

"I was just curious about something. How did you always know to let people in when Manless was still archmage?" Delilah felt no compunction about using the insult now that Vilkan was dead.

Lyov seemed nonplussed by the insult to his former superior. "Archmage Vilkan enjoyed showing off even the smallest amount of arcane power. No task was too simple, too petty for him to employ magic."

He withdrew a small wooden bust of Vilkan from one of his pockets and placed it on his podium. "This would vibrate whenever he needed me to permit entry to anyone waiting. He possessed a matched one through which I could notify him of someone waiting."

Delilah examined the bust. "An impressive likeness."

"An egotistical affectation. With due respect, I hope you have more sense."

"I won't be giving you a little carving of myself, that's for certain. Thank you." Delilah bowed her head and left the seneschal to his work, making her way to the Enchanter's Focus for a much-needed drink.

* * *

Kale tapped his claws against the sides of the metal puzzle box. He grew tired of wasting time, sitting idly by, while his sister healed. Not being able to see her caused him angst. Somehow, knowing she was recovering and seeing her were two different things, and he preferred the latter.

"I'm sure she'll send for you when she's able." Kali placed a bowl of stew before him. It carried with it the aroma of braised meat, spices, and fresh herbs, steam rising from the dish.

"We should just go see her." Kale stirred his stew to cool it. He did it more out of habit, since having undergone his metamorphosis, no meal Kali cooked would ever be hot enough to burn his mouth.

"Do you think they'll even let us on the university grounds?"

"I don't know. We can try." The first time the two draks successfully entered the compound to see Delilah was when they carried a delivery to one of the masters. Kale suspected it was contraband of some sort, but he didn't care at the time. The second, he and his mate were escorted by one of the wizards after his sister's battle with Vilkan. He hoped, as brother to the archmage, access restrictions would be lifted.

"Let's go tonight, then. If we can't get in, the Festival of Apellon is still underway. We can at least join in the festivities."

The two draks rushed through their dinner and left the cleanup for later. In the front of the shop, Ori hunched over a tome he illuminated. The blue drak glanced up from his work as the mated pair passed by.

"Lock up when you leave, Ori. We're going to try to see my sister and maybe enjoy some of the festivities."

Ori's eyes widened. "Oh! Are they having a party for her?"

"No, it's the Festival of Apellon." Kali clucked her tongue.

Kale chuckled and pulled the door closed as they left. The draks they passed in the street all acknowledged him in some way. A bow of the head. A wave. A "good evening." There was no keeping secret his relation to the new archmage, not after the spectacular way in which Delilah confronted Vilkan Icebreaker. For the draks in Muncifer, it was the dawning of a new era. Although most lived in the undercity, every drak knew one of their own was now the undisputed leader of the Mages Guild.

Even the minotaurs in the undercity seemed to give Kale and Kali warmer acknowledgement than before, although one in particular hastened to push his potato cart out of the way when he noticed them approaching.

The streets of the upper city were more congested than usual. Folks dressed in their best finery crowded around street corners and listened to acolytes of Apellon sing his praises. Although the noise of the crowd drowned out the lyrics, Kale found the tunes quite catchy and caught himself humming along by the time they reached the gates of the Arcane University. The ever-present guards stood at attention. Sunburst-yellow ribbons, tied to their weapons, celebrated Apellon's light in honor of the festival. They crossed their halberds when the draks approached the gates.

"Students and faculty only, Draks. This ain't for sightseers."

The other guard snickered and nodded. "Yeah, go on now."

Kale spread his wings and drew himself up to his full height. The top of his head almost reached the guard's waist. "Don't you recognize me? I'm the archmage's brother. I want to see how she's doing."

"The archmage never said nothing to us about no brother." The first guard scratched his beard and eyed his comrade. "How about it, Nazar?"

The clean-shaven guard rubbed his chin. "No, Wasyl, I don't think so. Did the archmage actually speak to you?"

"Umm… no… no, no, no"—he shook his head with vigor—"no, I don't think so. But if she"—he eyed Nazar and shrugged—"if she or he had a brother welcome here, we would have been told, yes?"

"Yes, definitely. Probably."

Kali kicked Nazar in the shin. Her scaled foot clanked against his mail, eliciting only a raised eyebrow from the man. "You cannot possibly be that stupid."

Wasyl laughed. "All right, all right. You have stripes. She has stripes. You're probably kin. Still can't let you in. Our last orders were to only admit students and faculty, and no one has countermanded that."

Kale spat a ball of fire at the men's feet. They scooted backward and brandished their halberds.

"Aita take you both!" He took his mate's hand and turned to leave. He felt a heavy, mailed hand on his shoulder.

The bearded human looked down at him. "Someday, little drak. But not today. We know better than to disobey a wizard. When we see one of the masters, we will tell them you came looking for your sister."

Kali huffed. "Come on, Kale. Let's see if we can at least enjoy the festival."

"Hey, Draks!" Nazar called after them. Kale and Kali glanced over their shoulders at him.

"The best festivities are by the east gate, where the farmers set up."

Kali and Kale left the guards behind and meandered through the winding city streets. Acolytes of Apellon, resplendent in their golden-yellow tunics, led a procession of revelers down the main street, singing and dancing in praise of their god. The two draks became swept up by the undulating crowd, unable to extricate themselves until the east gate came into view.

As they exited the city through the east gate, they noticed a large tent erected just off the road. Pipe music drew them toward a cluster of market stalls near the tent. From the stalls, vendors sold fruit brandy and all kinds of sun-dried fruits.

The two draks purchased a bottle of mountain berry brandy distilled by one of the local farmers. As Kale paid the vendor, he spied the grey-flecked muzzle of a familiar-looking minotaur enjoying a puppet show.

Kale and Kali stood with the crowd and watched the show for a while. The puppets portrayed the story of how a kind duke was beaten and abused by a cruel wizard and how a crude and hastily constructed miniature puppet resembling a drak came and killed the evil wizard.

"It sure didn't take them long, did it?" Kali took her mate's arm.

"When Sarvesh killed the longshanks who killed the Twilight Overlord, the fiendlings in Drak-Anor began singing songs about it practically the next day." Kale leaned close to Kali's head to make himself heard over the cheers and jeers of the crowd. "Of course, they all gave him credit for freeing the city. He was pretty quick to set them straight."

"Enjoying the show?"

Kale glanced up to see Boss Steelhand looming over them. Smiling, the minotaur seemed to sway from side to side a bit.

"That was fast. She's still healing from the fight."

"Indeed." The minotaur nodded and glanced at the puppet stage. "The minstrels are quick to latch onto thrilling heroics like a wizard fight outside the city gates."

He put his arms around the two draks and led them toward one of the many tables set up near the food pits. "Vilkan was not a popular archmage, and there were many who questioned how he gained so much influence over the archduke."

Kali sat next to Kale as Boss Steelhand slid onto the bench on the opposite side of the table and faced them. "So, I'm sure you're wondering how he came to be such a big influence."

The minotaur waved over one of the men serving ale and took a mug. He offered some to the two draks, but they decided to open their brandy instead. Boss Steelhand sent the young man to retrieve empty cups.

"He weaseled his way in over the course of many years. By the time I came to advise the archduke, Vilkan was already manipulating the man. It's hard to turn a man like Fyodar, who prizes loyalty above almost all else, away from someone who'd been true in the past."

"He just took more and more, a little bit at a time." Kali squeezed Kale's hand as she searched Boss Steelhand's eyes for confirmation. "By the time anyone noticed how much he took, he was already entrenched. Like wood ants in an oak."

"Exactly." The minotaur eyed at the bottle of brandy as they waited for the mugs. "Galperin Estate, vintage 750AS. Nice. Northern, family, I think. North of here, I mean. South-central Etrunia."

"What's going to happen now that Deli is archmage?" Kale, not as interested in the history behind the brandy as the minotaur, wanted to know how soon he and his sister could return home to Drak-Anor.

Boss Steelhand watched the crowd over his shoulder. "That depends on her. I'm sure it will take a while for her to get a handle on her new responsibilities. Maybe she has a plan to institute sweeping changes across the Mages Guild."

The minotaur regarded Kale as though he expected an answer. When Kale remained silent, he continued, "Some changes she might suggest will likely be debated by the Council of Wizardry. There's nothing some of those wizards like better than an argument."

Kali opened and poured the brandy after the server returned with three mugs. She shrugged and poured some for Boss Steelhand as well. Kale sniffed it, wrinkling his nose at the floral overtones and tingling alcohol scent. The brandy was sweet and glided down his throat like honey.

"How's that drak working out in your shop?" The minotaur sipped the brandy and smacked his lips. "The limner?"

"Ori?" Kali tossed her brandy down like a shot of whiskey, and her eyes bulged. She coughed, laughed, and then poured herself more. "He's fine. Clean and quiet."

"Good, good." Boss Steelhand took the bottle from Kali and topped off his mug. "Now that Vilkan is gone, I'm going to push for the archduke to relax the restrictions on draks and minotaurs in the upper city. The minotaurs don't get hassled much, but I'm sure you've noticed how few draks intermingle openly up here."

Kale had noticed. He sipped his brandy. "A lot of the draks in the undercity treat my sister and I like we're something special, because of our stripes"—he opened his wings by reflex—"and my wings."

"Are you?" The minotaur leaned forward.

"Not really. We're just draks, like them. Draks help run Drak-Anor, though, so maybe we act different."

"They'll need community leaders. Maybe you and your mate can help."

"Maybe." Kale watched a fire-eating dancer spin past them. Her multicolored, diaphanous gown twirled and swirled around her as she spun and jumped, and great gouts of flame burst from her mouth into the night sky.

Kale observed the dancers while Kali conversed with the minotaur, their conversation fading into the background of the revelry that surrounded them. The three made short work of the bottle of brandy, and when it was gone, Kali dragged her mate away from the table and they bade good night to Boss Steelhand. As they fell into bed, Kali reminded Kale of the work that waited for them in the morning. He dreamed of home repairs as an alcohol-fueled slumber overtook him.

Chapter 8

As Pancras and his companions traveled from Port-of-Dogs farther inland toward Vlorey, neither the heat nor the humidity abated. A cool breeze blowing inward from the coast brought with it the scent of blooming flowers from nearby orchards, making the air less oppressive.

The rolling hills of Cardoba limited visibility ahead of them, but Pancras enjoyed the changing scenery each time they crested a hill. After several days of travel, the terrain flattened, and they descended toward the Bay of Vlorey. Not long afterward, the city appeared before them. *At last. Perhaps I can sleep in a proper bed tonight.* Vlorey sat situated at the mouth of a river, constructed on the many islands that formed its delta, referred to as both the Jewel of the North and Andelosia's Cesspool.

From his vantage as he gazed at the city, Pancras liked what he saw. The city featured a variety of architectures, owing its origins to the ornate designs of Cardoban artisans, incorporating Etrunian influences from settlers moving to the coast, as well as influences from the nations across the Sea of Lost Hope. He was still far enough away from Vlorey, high enough in elevation, that he noticed a castle beyond the city to the north, near the forest of Verdant Point. The city itself covered the delta and sprawled onto the rolling plains to the south

Gisella and Qaliah rode up to him. The fiendling whistled. "Big city. Looks bigger than Muncifer. Nice to see it's not as blocky."

The fiendling referred to the dwarven legacy of Muncifer's architecture, as many of the buildings there pre-dated The Sundering. Pancras spurred Stormheart onward. The road from Port-of-Dogs wound through several outlying orchards and past a few livestock farms scattered along the way.

From above, the sun beat down on them. Pancras, unaccustomed to the sweltering heat, wiped sweat away from his eyes and glanced at Gisella. The slayer adapted her dress for the warmer weather onboard the *Maiden of the High Seas*, yet despite her lighter garb, he noticed her discomfort. Her fair skin flushed, and perspiration matted her golden locks to her head.

Qaliah rode, garbed in only that required for modesty, and Pancras suspected she did that only to avoid a lecture about appropriate garb from Gisella. Smiling and producing not a drop of sweat, the fiendling enjoyed the heat.

The three arrived at the eastern gates of the city as the sun set. A line of empty wagons and carts waited to pass as guards inspected them. One of the guards waved the three on horseback around to the front of the line. He took hold of Stormheart's reins as he leaned on his halberd. Sweat beaded on his dark skin as he took stock of the three companions.

"What's your business in Vlorey?"

Pancras dismounted in order to speak eye to eye; looking down at the guard from horseback made him feel like a giant. Even though he stood well over a head taller than the man while dismounted, he favored it over feeling as though he would tumble if he leaned over to converse with him while in the saddle.

"Arcane University business. I have been appointed the new defenses master."

The guard's expression remained a stony glare. His gaze dropped to Pancras's withered arm. "What manner of affliction is that? Plague?"

At the mention of plague, nearby guards interrupted their inspections and turned. They brought their weapons to bear on the minotaur.

"Be calm." As he raised his blackened hand and flexed his fingers, Pancras wished he hadn't removed the leather gauntlet. "It's an old battle injury. Like a burn, but less painful, thank Apellon." Confident the lie was preferable to disclosing the story of how he had been demon-possessed during a mysterious resurrection, Pancras nodded to punctuate his statement.

The guard gestured to his compatriots. They lowered their weapons and returned to their business. He shifted his eyes to Gisella and Qaliah. "Entourage? Harem?" His eyes narrowed as his gaze returned Pancras. "Slavery is illegal in Vlorey."

Gisella snorted. "I am a slayer of the Arcane University. My business here is my own."

"I'm not a slave! I'm not his whore, either." Qaliah jumped off Comet and strode up to the guard, digging a nail into his chin and forcing him to meet her stare.

He cocked an eyebrow and released Stormheart to move her hand away from his face. "Apologies. Most fiendlings here are employed on the streets, if you take my meaning, and what few minotaurs we have don't seem to associate with them. Humans neither."

"If I wanted people to assume the worst of me, I'd have stayed in Muncifer." Qaliah huffed and returned to her steed.

"Do you have a trade permit?" The guard returned his blank-eyed stare to Pancras.

"No, why would I need that?" Pancras took Stormheart's reins as his mount wandered to introduce himself to a passing merchant's mare. The stallion snorted and whickered in protest.

"There's an entry tax if you don't have a permit." The guard gestured at the line of people standing alongside empty carts and wagons.

"They're traders?" Qaliah motioned toward the waiting folk and pulled herself up on Comet. "In what? Air?

"They get a permit to keep from paying the tax every time they make a delivery to one of the farms. One talon each." The guard held out his hand.

Uncertain of the guard's veracity, Pancras concluded from the man's nonchalance this was not a new con for him. The minotaur fished in his pouch for three silver coins and dropped them in the man's palm. The guard slipped them into his money purse and waved them on.

"Let these three pass."

Pancras, Gisella, and Qaliah rode into Vlorey. The guards defending the city gates gave them only cursory glances as they rode past. The hard-packed dirt of the road gave way to worn cobblestones just as the clean, fresh air of the countryside gave way to the unmistakable odors of a city packed with people. Not for the first time, Pancras cursed a nose more sensitive than those of humans.

Pedestrians clad in lightweight, loose-fitting clothing hurried from shop to shop, avoiding the cart laden with horse dung parked just inside the city gates. A cloud of flies swarmed around it like a maelstrom. Pancras spurred Stormheart on with hope that it was not representative of the odors he would have to live with. A sign up the street caught his eye: *Trader Gate Livery*.

As he dismounted, Qaliah rode up to him. "You're not thinking we should walk this entire city?"

The minotaur regarded the darkening sky. "It's getting late. We need to get our bearings and find a place to stay for the night. There's sure to be an inn nearby. We can take our horses to the Arcane University, wherever that is, in the morning."

Assuming the university was known to most of the city dwellers, Pancras asked the stableboy about it as they collected their belongings from their mounts.

"Never been there myself," The boy spoke around a mouthful of sticky brown substance, spitting residue on the straw-covered floor. "I think it's on Selene's Isle, about three in from the harbor."

Pancras assumed it made sense in the context of the city's geography and tipped the boy a talon. The youth grinned as he pocketed the coin. "You'll want to visit Pacha's Den, over yonder." He nodded to a garishly painted building across the street. "They'll service any one, they will."

He winked to Pancras as he led Stormheart away. When Pancras met up with Qaliah and Gisella on the street in front of the livery, he relayed the location of the Arcane University to them.

"Selene is the goddess of magic." Gisella fanned her hair in a futile attempt to dry it. "At least that much makes sense. Did he recommend an inn?"

The minotaur pointed to Pacha's Den. "He mentioned that place, but I think that's a brothel."

Qaliah's eyes lit up. "You don't say." She examined the building as a man in fancy dress stopped outside the door, glanced up and down the street, and then lowered his head and entered. "Did he say how much they charge?"

Gisella clucked her tongue. "You can do better than that. If you're that desperate, I'll take you to the Temple of Aurora."

"I want release, woman, not a spiritual experience."

Pancras shifted his weight and coughed. Qaliah continued unabated as he led them down the street.

"I've not spent the night in sweaty pleasure since before we left Muncifer. Curton jailed me, you rejected me, the minotaur's not interested, and everyone said it was bad for ship morale." Qaliah ticked off each point on her fingers.

"The priests and priestesses understand the need for release. It's just safer, that's all."

"I'll bet it's not as much fun." Qaliah stopped at the corner. She nodded toward a sign hanging above a doorway just down the side street. "The Brass Bull. Sounds like an inn to me."

"Or a tavern." Gisella pulled her hair away from her neck to avail herself of a cool breeze.

Pancras rubbed his right horn. "I'm guessing they don't accommodate minotaurs, not with that name." Being equated with any kind of bovine irritated him, though it was a type of bigotry he didn't encounter often.

"No harm in asking." Qaliah patted his arm and skipped ahead. She ducked into the doorway. Shortly thereafter, Pancras heard shouting, followed by the clatter of thrown cookware. Ducking a flying frying pan, Qaliah raced out.

The fiendling rubbed her arm as she approached Pancras and Gisella. "Turns out, they're not overly fond of fiendlings, either."

Pancras cocked an eyebrow as he noticed Gisella's hand on her sword. "I'm sure we can find accommodations suitable for all of us. Vlorey is a cosmopolitan city. Certainly, it's not entirely populated with bigoted louts."

As the minotaur led the two women across the street, he hoped he had not misplaced his optimism. The main street turned and led to a bridge, which crossed one of the distributaries. Once they moved away from the city gates, the populace appeared more diverse, and Pancras noticed a number of dwarves, minotaurs, elves, and even draks among the dark-skinned humans.

The half-timbered buildings reminded him of those in Almeria, although their open architectural style allowed better airflow in the buildings. Many neighborhoods featured open gardens and rows of trees and shrubs. In the distance, he noticed a building with multiple towers surrounding a domed central building, the Arcane University.

Gisella stepped behind the minotaur. "Shall we press on? There's still light in the day."

"Not me, I need some hot food and a drink." Qaliah clutched Pancras's arm. "Look, there's a promising place over there. We don't have to get down to business right away, do we?"

Pancras glanced at the tavern to which the fiendling referred. Half of the ground floor sat open to the outside. It appeared the second and third floors contained guest rooms, each featuring large windows that offered views of the surrounding neighborhoods and parks. The sign read: *Screeching Griffon Taphouse & Inn*. "No, I think a final respite is in order. Hopefully, the welcome here will be warmer than at the Brass Bull."

The fiendling stopped abruptly. "Good point. You go first. They'll be less likely to throw cookware at you."

The Screeching Griffon, indeed, welcomed diverse customers, and the three settled in for an evening of food and wine. Their rooms on the third floor afforded them a view overlooking the city in the direction of the Arcane University. Pancras closed the evening studying it from a far, hoping his new life there would not be a sentence of tedium.

* * *

Until Delilah experienced the days-to-day demands of her new position, she didn't have a true appreciation of what being archmage entailed. The first day was light, but once the high wizards sent word there was a new archmage and she would be altering some of the guild's rules, headmasters from all Arcane University campuses, as well as the masters from Muncifer's campus, inundated her with congratulations, requests, and complaints. They ranged from the banal to the outrageous.

Appointing Masters Agata and Galina as headmaster and deputy headmaster in Muncifer alleviated some of Delilah's aggravation. When Galina informed the archmage that Katka passed her Novice Trials, the drak delegated some of the mundane communications to her.

Apprentice Katka proved adept at refusing some of the most outlandish requests in such a way that the petitioners felt their proposals had been given grave consideration, even if Delilah's private response was to collapse in laughter.

She relayed her favorite of these requests to her brother, when, after nearly a week, the archmage finally found time to visit him and his mate at their home. After welcoming her with cheers and hugs, Kali filled mugs of ale and passed them around. While Ori shopped, they sat on stools at his counter to keep an eye on some gold foil he had laid out for his current project.

"The headmaster in Maritropa wanted me to allocate guild funds for a breeding experiment." Delilah laughed. "He wants to cross fish with sheep to create waterproof wool."

Kale cocked his head. "How… would that? Why?"

"Katka thinks he was trying to expose me for a fraud, but Valyrian says he's an old fool and probably thinks he's on to the next greatest invention in the world."

Kali replenished Delilah's mug. "You wizards are a strange lot."

"Have you heard anything from Pancras yet?" Kale returned from the kitchen with a plate of sausages.

"Nothing yet." She retrieved her Herald Stone. Master Valyrian had showed her how to use it. "I left instructions for the headmaster to contact me as soon as he reports in. This thing is great. I can talk to any of the headmasters or high wizards any time I want, and I don't have to wait for those stupid magical messengers to return to me."

"It took you long enough to come visit." Kale stuffed an entire sausage into his toothy maw. "I was afraid you'd forgotten us."

Delilah shook her head and speared a sausage with her fork. "The first couple of days, I could barely walk down the hall without becoming exhausted. Everything hurt. Then meetings, meetings, meetings. No wonder Sarvesh is grumpy all the time if this is what he deals with. It's easier to just stab people you don't like than have to listen to them prattle on and on about things you don't care about."

"We tried to visit." Kali frowned at her mate as grease dripped from his chin onto the counter. "The guards wouldn't let us in."

The drak sorceress frowned. "I'm sorry. The high wizards advised me not to change the 'No Visitors' rule. They said it would be too distracting for the students, and it wouldn't be fair if I was allowed visitors for social calls and no one else was."

"You're not going to stay there, are you?" Kale pushed away his plate. "I mean, you don't have to live at the Arcane University, do you?"

Delilah had not considered living anywhere else. As much as she liked being close to her brother, living with him and his mate seemed wrong. "I don't think it's a requirement, but I probably will. You and Kali need your space, Kale."

Kali bowed her head in thanks to Delilah, but when the archmage glanced at her brother, she noticed Kale frowning. "We've always lived together, Deli."

"Times change." It pained her to admit it. She glanced across the counter at her brother. He picked at a knot in the wood and shrugged. The admission seemed to please his mate; Kali smiled and again bowed her head toward the sorceress.

After they finished their meal, Delilah entered the cavern below to study the runed circle. Kali accompanied her while Kale remained upstairs to sulk and wait for Ori. In the steady light provided by the enchanted sconces, Delilah inspected each rune, brushing away years of accumulated dust and debris. One of the segments possessed a strange indentation. The drak dug into it with her claw and found a hole packed with dirt. When she finished excavating it, she revealed a square cavity, with sloping sides.

While the archmage worked on the runes, Kali swept away dirt from around the circle, pushing it toward the opening to Grannock's Gorge, careful to avoid disturbing the dragon egg. They finished their cleanup close to the same time, and Kali joined Delilah as she stared at the inscribed circle.

"Any ideas?" The orange-scaled drak knelt and traced one of the symbols with a claw.

"I'm not up on my ancient drak runes, but they almost look like numbers. Some aren't"—Delilah pointed to specific runes—"Rannos Dragonsire, Selene, the moons, err... the King and Queen, and these"—Delilah ran her hand along a string of smaller runes near the edge of the stone circle—"the letters are from the Drak alphabet, but I don't know the language. It's gibberish to me, and I don't know what purpose that square hole could serve."

Kali stood and approached the nearest bookcase in the stairwell. "Maybe there's a key or something in one of these books."

"Maybe." The sheer number of volumes that wound their way down the outside wall of the staircase boggled her mind. Delilah had never seen so many tomes outside of the Arcane University's library. She glanced up when she heard the clanking of the door's lock release. Footsteps approached, and her apprentice turned the corner, carrying a heavy, leather-bound codex.

"Archmage!" Katka smiled and raised a hand, staggering under the weight of the book. "I found something."

Delilah's heart leapt, but then she remembered Katka was tasked with researching dragon eggs, not the runed circle. "About dragons?"

Delilah turned the human girl around to face the staircase. "Back up, then. Kale will need to hear this, too."

Katka groaned and tromped up the stairs, followed by the two draks. When they reached the top and returned to the shop, they saw Kale still seated at the counter, his head propped up on one hand as he stared at the door.

"This will cheer you up." Kali hugged her mate from behind. "Your sister's apprentice found some information about dragon eggs."

Kale perked up and regarded Katka with raised eyebrows. "How to take care of them?"

The human girl nodded and opened the codex on the counter. She turned to the middle of the book and flipped past a few pages. "Here it is: 'Eggs can lie dormant for months, even decades, if kept in proper conditions. Without sufficient heat, dragonlings will cease development until such time as high temperatures are regained. Due to their magical nature, or perhaps their close ties with the Earth Mother, dragon eggs will not spoil, as do the eggs of avians.'"

She flipped forward a few pages. "It goes on and on about chickens." She paused and followed along with her finger. "'Though they were unfortunately lost during the Great Harvest Moon Fire, the scrolls of Keeper Branthus the Golden indicate that he revived a thousand-year old dragon egg simply by incubating it in his hearth for a few days. This cannot be verified, of course, since it is widely known that Branthus the Golden was so named for the yellow hue of his skin after he imbibed copious amounts of Heretic's Weed.'"

Delilah furrowed her brow and stared at her apprentice. "So, what does that mean?"

"My parents say people who eat Heretic's Weed see and hear things that aren't there. It also turns your skin yellow. Hogs love it, though." Katka flipped past several more pages. "That's about it. The rest of the book talks about their hoards and mating habits."

Kale scratched under his chin. "So, if we just keep it safe downstairs, we don't have to worry about it hatching?"

The human sorceress nodded and closed the codex. "That's what it sounds like to me. There are two other books

I planned to read on the subject, but this contained such specific information, I needed to share it immediately."

"You did well, Katka." Delilah's praise was cut short by the ringing of the shop bell. Ori pushed his way inside, carrying a box full of ink and sheaves of parchment.

"Oh! I'm not interrupting, am I?"

The drak sorceress hopped off her stool. "No, we were just finishing up."

Kale helped Ori put away his supplies. "Can I hang on to that book?"

Katka looked to her master. Delilah took Kale by the shoulders. "No, I'm sorry. She's not even supposed to have removed it from the university grounds."

"You're the archmage, Deli." Kale brushed his sister's hand off his shoulder. "You can do whatever you want."

The drak wished that were the case. She found being in a leadership position afforded her less freedom to act than she expected. "I really can't, Kale. It looks bad. Besides, if I make too many people angry right now, someone might challenge me."

Delilah's shoulder's slumped. "I don't have another big fight in me so soon after the last one."

Kale turned to his sister. "I'm sorry, Deli. I wasn't thinking about how much fighting that human must've taken out of you. I'm just..." He held up his hands. "You haven't been around much."

"It's okay, Kale. I'll try to return tomorrow. I have to get back to the university now." Delilah did not intend to discuss family issues in front of Katka and Ori. She missed her brother, too, but they were adults, and it seemed to Delilah that their paths were finally diverging as the paths of so many siblings did.

Night had fallen by the time Delilah and Katka returned to the Arcane University. Katka returned the codex to the library while the drak sorceress headed to her quarters. It still bore traces of Vilkan's occupancy, remnants Delilah eradicated a little at a time, as her time and energy permitted. On this night, she couldn't be bothered. She fell asleep thinking of the runes around the stone circle and what they might mean.

* * *

In the morning, after breaking her fast with Pancras and Qaliah, Gisella left the Screeching Griffon to connect with potential allies. Most slayers operated independently, and she was beholden only to Archmage Vilkan until Pancras reported for duty at the Arcane University. She felt confident that the minotaur was, in fact, on his way to do just that.

Logically, Gisella surmised she should start at the Arcane University, but with Pancras already headed there, the Golden Slayer figured he would make his own inquiries regarding the Lich Queen. Instead, she sought out the Temple of Aurora.

A walled temple complex shared by priests of three deities—Cybele, Apellon, and Aurora—the Garden Gallery, so named for the garden at its center, was tended by the priests of Cybele. The temples of Apellon and Aurora that sat at opposite ends of the garden, overlooking blossoming flowers, willows, and babbling streams.

To enter the garden, Gisella passed over a footbridge and through the Gallery of Light, Apellon's temple, filled with painters and musicians practicing their art. Sunshine streamed through stained glass skylights depicting the sun rising over a golden world. She felt both conspicuous and obscene parading through such a serene setting in her scale armor and dirty cloak.

In the garden, the morning sun warmed the air and created a blanketing mist over the flowers that opened their blossoms to greet the day. Perfume-like fragrances mingled in the air, a barrier against unsavory odors of the city. In the center of the garden stood a statue of Cybele, depicted as a voluptuous matron, holding a threshing flail. A stone-lined path wound through the garden, leading to various meditation nooks, and a larger path led directly to Aurora's temple.

Gisella stepped through the temple's open entryway and into the interior courtyard. She admired, as she stepped over it, the mosaic in the center of the foyer floor, depicting the golden seashell of Aurora surrounded by brilliantly colored butterflies. A dark-skinned woman with wavy, light brown hair approached Gisella. She spread her arms wide in a gesture of welcome, but her expression tensed as she eyed the Golden Slayer's armor and weapon.

"Welcome to the Bastion of Bliss, warrior." The woman bowed, spreading her arms. "I am Cressida."

"Blessings of beauty upon you, Cressida." Gisella bowed in the ritual fashion, splaying her arms to the side, her palms facing upward. "May a… spark of love burn… brightly in the flame of your passion." So long had it been since Gisella gave the traditional greeting between priests of the goddess of love, she almost forgot the words.

Cressida's demeanor changed immediately. A smile crossed her face, and a twinkle appeared in her eyes as she took Gisella's arm. "Forgive me. I mistook you for a curious southerner, sister. It makes me sad that you must attire yourself in such ugly, harsh coverings. Is our lady so reviled in the Four Watches?"

That Cressida pegged her as being from the Four Watches so quickly impressed the Golden Slayer, although Gisella supposed her accent probably betrayed her. "Lady Aurora is not widely worshipped, but I'd hardly call her reviled. I wear the armor because I am a slayer of the Arcane University, not a priestess."

Cressida's joyful expression fell, and the priestess turned and led her into the courtyard. They sat on a stone bench beneath a fountain that featured a nude Aurora rising from the sea. Gisella recognized the shell behind the goddess as the traditional visual metaphor for signifying rays of light.

"We harbor no renegades here, Slayer."

Gisella took the woman's hands. Soft and clean, they contrasted the worn and calloused hands that held them. "That's not why I am here." She offered a smile to put the priestess at ease. "I am Gisella the Golden. I have come seeking Renewal and perhaps assistance from my sisters of the faith."

A ritual cleansing performed by the clergy of Aurora, Renewal washed away the stress and grime from a long journey or battle. Because priests and priestesses rarely ventured far from their temples, they rarely required it, unlike the traveling faithful.

"If you have come to us from the Four Watches, then you have completed quite a journey. Renewal is appropriate." Cressida clapped her hands together. Several acolytes garbed in white gowns rushed to her summons.

"Draw a Renewal bath for our sister."

The acolytes bowed and left to do her bidding. She turned to Gisella and smiled. "You will soon feel fully refreshed, though if you continue wearing that heavy armor here, it won't last long."

Although the Golden Slayer appreciated her clothes were unsuited to the warmer northern climes, fashion advice was not the assistance she required. "Have you heard of Bekkhildr, the Iron Witch?"

Cressida closed her eyes for a moment. "The name is familiar, but…" She shook her head. "I don't think I know her."

"The Lich Queen."

The color drained from the priestess's face. She swallowed and took a deep breath. "What of her?"

"I have heard whispers, rumors, that she is trying to reenter this world. A third crusade against the living."

"I have heard nothing." Cressida stood, crossing her arms and staring at the ground. "But, there have been…incidents."

She turned and regarded Gisella. "Why come here, Slayer? The Red Crypt seems more suited to harboring such rumors."

Gisella had not heard of the Red Crypt, but she suspected it to be the temple of Aita. She assumed Pancras would visit it after he checked in at the Arcane University. "I've been traveling with a bonelord. Simple division of labor. Tell me of these incidents."

"The dead are restless in the necropolis." Cressida hugged herself and shivered. "There have been reports of them clawing their way out of their tombs and patrolling the grounds at night. No attacks, though."

"That's very strange." Gisella never encountered undead who didn't attack the living.

"Sometimes, they leave the city, too." The priestess shook her head and gazed at the statue of Aurora. "They just march right out, ignoring any attempts to stop them. The Council of Lords has decreed we are to just leave them be." Cressida spat on the ground. "They're more concerned about the overcrowding of our necropolis than the implications."

Gisella flipped her damp hair off her neck, allowing the breeze to cool her. "They don't think the dead rising and marching out of town is any cause for concern?"

"I believe they see it as our problems getting up and leaving. Our lords are very narrow-minded and shortsighted. After all, they view us as high-class prostitutes."

Gisella snorted, familiar with misconceptions about the priests and priestesses of Aurora. Those misunderstandings extended to a lesser extent to worshippers of the goddess of love. "Optional donations are not a fee for services rendered."

"Few here in Vlorey have the patience to perform our rituals and ceremonies properly, so most men and women looking for those sorts of carnal pleasures find the city's brothels to be more accommodating." Cressida returned to her seat alongside Gisella. She turned the Golden Slayer away from her slightly and held her hair as she bound it with a ribbon she withdrew from a pocket inside her robes.

Gisella closed her eyes as the priestess's hands rubbed her neck.

"Do not worry about such things now, however. Your Renewal will begin shortly. You must put your concerns aside and give yourself over to the glory of our lady."

The priestess's words resonated with Gisella. *It's been too long.* She allowed herself to forget her responsibilities and surrendered herself to the ritual as the priestess massaged her shoulders.

Chapter 9

Kale sat in the cavern alongside a flickering lantern as his only companion and stared at the dragon egg. The lantern provided the only source of illumination this early in the morning, before the sun began its daily journey across the sky. Each time he descended the stairs, he hoped the sconces would flare to life for him as they did for his sister, but each time, he was disappointed.

He contemplated the harness lying alongside the egg, intricate leather straps Kali purchased a few days earlier during one of her trips to the market. She paid Katka to enchant them to decrease the perceived weight and bulk of the egg. Kale tightened the straps around the egg and hefted it, swinging it over his back. Kali had affixed a leather flap to conceal the egg, completing the illusion of a backpack. Carrying the egg still felt awkward, but it was not as unwieldy as transporting it suspended in a cloak. He returned the egg to its makeshift nest and removed the harness before retrieving from his pouch one of the sun-dried fruits he and Kali purchased at the Festival of Apellon. On the one hand, he wanted to breathe on the egg, start a fire, and incubate it. There was plenty of room in the cavern for an infant dragon. On the other hand, he admitted Terrakaptis was better equipped to deal with such a creature.

Little natural light crept into the cavern from Grannock's Gorge as the sun filled the canyon with its brilliance. Deep shadows shrouded all but a small area directly in front of the passage leading to the gorge. Kale stood and stretched, rubbing his aching butt. *I should have brought a chair down here. I don't remember sitting on rocks being so painful.*

The drak paced the floor, staying within the boundary of the lantern's light. Try as he might, he couldn't sense the egg, except by smell, and that was only because he knew what it smelled like. *I need time. I need to talk to Deli about this.*

She's off doing wizard things, and I'm stuck here with this egg. I want to help Terrakaptis and the other dragons, but this feels like wizard stuff.

The door creaked open from above and footsteps descended the stairs. "Kale? Kale, are you down there?"

Kali. He sighed and stretched his wings, picked up the lantern, and met her at the bottom of the stairs. She tilted her head and regarded with him with bleary eyes.

"Is everything all right?"

"Yeah, fine. I'm just trying to figure out what I'm supposed to do now. Delilah's off being an archmage. Pancras is on the other side of the world, and I'm stuck here all by myself with this egg."

Kali embraced her mate and nuzzled his neck. "You're not all alone. I wish you'd stop saying things like that."

A stone formed in the pit of his stomach as he realized he had failed to consider his mate. He turned and wrapped his arms around her. There were many things he thought about saying at that moment, but they all seemed like excuses.

"I'm sorry."

"Don't worry about the egg. It's not going anywhere, and nothing is going to happen to it." Kali held him at arm's length and looked him in the eyes. "The entrance from the gorge is damn near impossible to get to if you can't fly, and it's so well hidden no one else knows it's here. I've waited a long time to be able to live for myself, and it's time we did that."

The drak nodded. "You're right. You're right." He took her by the hand and led her upstairs. Despite the work they still needed to do to their home, Kale's thoughts returned again and again to the egg, his sister, and Pancras. *I'm missing something. There has to be more to my life than this now.*

***

Pancras greeted the day with high hopes but low expectations. His experiences in Muncifer prepared him for an unpleasant assignment at the Arcane University, and although free of the geas placed on him by Archmage Vilkan, the slayer could still force his hand.

The Arcane University occupied an L-shaped island near the center of the river delta. Its towers, among the tallest buildings in Vlorey, provided distinct landmarks from anywhere in the city. Although the waterways served as physical barriers in lieu of walls, one could only access the grounds from a single direction. Pancras supposed someone truly dedicated might swim across the tributary to gain access to the island, but he sensed wards in place to prevent unauthorized access.

Two guards stood watch on the bridge. Watchtowers stood above them, and movement within alerted Pancras that those two guards were not alone. They wore breastplates over light, short-sleeved tunics and kilts. Greaves protected their lower legs. Despite their relatively light armor, sweat glistened on their brows.

Wary, light blue eyes scrutinized Pancras as he approached the guard on the left. The dark-skinned man's hand dropped to the mace on his belt, but he didn't remove the weapon from its harness.

"You have business here?" The guard's deep voice bore a heavy accent, although similar to others Pancras had heard in Vlorey.

I guess I'm really the one with the accent here. "I'm reporting as ordered by Archmage Vilkan."

The other guard approached them and nudged Pancras's maul with his foot. "Do minotaur mages always carry such weapons?"

Pancras lifted it, pulling in just enough arcane energy to cause the head of the red steel weapon to glow with an emerald hue. "I can't speak for others, but I do. I am also a Bonelord of Aita."

"Bonelord, eh? What of that?" The guard pointed to Pancras's withered arm.

"Battle injury." Pancras hoped the guard didn't demand a more detailed explanation.

"I thought you wizards tried to avoid battles." He continued examining Pancras's arm.

"'Try' is the operative word there. Obviously, I am not always successful." Pancras rubbed his shoulder, now self-conscious about his deformity.

The guard grunted and returned to his post. "The headmaster's office is at the top of the central tower, the White Tower." The guard wiped his brow with a dirty rag. "Any of the students can direct you."

Pancras bowed and crossed the bridge, breathing a sigh that he wasn't once again accused of carrying plague. He felt the wards lift as he passed. *I have no idea how to create this effect… and they want me to be defenses master and teach wards?* He laughed at the absurdity of it.

In contrast to Muncifer's squat, blocky structures, the buildings on the grounds of Vlorey's Arcane University were curvaceous, with tall spires. He passed a pair of towers that curved like horns toward one another and another, a spiral, reminiscent of Aurora's Sanctuary in Almeria. Grassy plazas separated the buildings, and stone-lined paths wound through the park-like grounds. Pancras located the central tower without requiring help from any of the students and stood outside it, taking in its architecture.

The White Tower's angular contours appeared almost as though they were chiseled from stone. Windows accented each of three distinct levels, but from the outside, Pancras couldn't tell if more levels nestled in between. He entered the tower and searched for stairs.

A trio of brown-robed students rushed past him in the foyer, bowing their heads as they passed. Another clad in grey robes shook her head at the brown-robed initiates and eyed the tower's central shaft before floating to her desired floor and stepping onto a platform.

Pancras frowned. He'd never learned levitation magic. He approached the central shaft and stepped onto a smooth stone disk, stepping off after it didn't move, and glancing upward.

"You're new here." The statement came from behind him. Pancras turned to face a tawny minotaur with dark brown patches of fur. He cradled a spear in his arms and wore armor similar to that of the Arcane University's guards, but the symbol emblazoned on his chest, a triangle and cross inside a circle, was one with which Pancras was not familiar.

"Yes," Pancras tore his eyes away from the symbol on the minotaur's chest. "I'm trying to get to the headmaster's office, but I never learned how to levitate."

"Huh, a wizard admitting he's not all powerful." A lop-sided grin spread across the minotaur's face. "Are you sure you're in the right place?"

"Quite."

The minotaur led Pancras by the shoulder and guided him onto the stone disk. His hand lingered as he looked upward. "Just speak where you wish to go. That's how we non-magic folk do it." He eyed Pancras's arm. The wizard braced himself for the inevitable.

"Does it pain you?"

Pancras blinked. It was not the question he expected. He flexed his withered hand. "I notice it. It feels different, but no, it doesn't hurt, not exactly."

The armored minotaur stepped backward and tapped the disk with the butt of his spear. "Try it."

Pancras cleared his throat. "Headmaster's office."

The stone disk rose into the air, gliding upward through the central shaft of the tower. He peered over the edge, toward the armored minotaur. "Thank you!"

He soared past landings and portraits of wizards whose facial expressions seemed to warn observers that magic was serious business. Up ahead stood an opening in the ceiling the exact size of the disk, and Pancras double-checked to ensure none of his belongings nor any part of himself hung over the edge. It slid into place inside a semi-circular room. He stepped off the disk, and it fell away.

Seated behind a desk at the far side of the room, a woman sorted through a stack of papers. A silvery globe sat on one corner of her credenza. She glanced at Pancras as he oriented himself. "May I help you?"

Her grey-streaked black hair hung loose around her shoulders, framing her rich, coppery skin. A jeweled stud pierced the side of her wide nose. She adjusted the high collar of her sapphire tunic as Pancras approached.

"I am Pancras of Drak-Anor." He stopped before her desk and bowed. "I've been sent by Archmage Vilkan to fill the master of wards position."

"Have you now?" She picked up the wand from the top of her desk and tapped the silvery orb three times. The wall alongside her desk shimmered, and a portal opened, dilating like the iris of a great eye.

"The headmaster's office is just through there."

Pancras ducked through the opening. Occupying the larger part of the circular area that formed the top of the tower, much of it open to the air, the office beyond featured a cluttered mess of bookshelves, papers, desks, and stacked chairs. A gentle breeze stirred the air without rustling the papers, although Pancras could not detect what mechanism accomplished this.

A thin, balding man whose skin resembled the color of dark amber peered around a stack of chairs. "Yes? Who's that?"

Pancras bowed. "Pancras of Drak-Anor." He told the man of his mandate from Archmage Vilkan. "Are you the head-master?"

"Yes, yes." The man emerged carrying a stack of scrolls. He dumped them on the nearest desk and approached Pancras with an outstretched hand. "Lewin. Headmaster Lewin Stormwind."

The minotaur extended his hand to clasp old man's, half the size of his own. Headmaster Lewin's eyes widened when he noticed Pancras's arm, and he recoiled.

"It's an old injury, not an affliction." Pancras didn't wait for the question this time. The answer seemed to satisfy the headmaster and he grasped Pancras's arm.

"I would like to hear that story someday, when you feel comfortable sharing it." Headmaster Lewin gestured toward a chair near the desk and procured one from another desk for himself. "Come, sit, sit."

"The atmosphere here certainly is different from Munci-fer." Pancras glanced around the room. Apart from the clut-ter, being able to see a clear blue sky above the green-blue sea from a room overlooking the entire city was not what he expected when Archmage Vilkan sent him here.

"Well, you're half a world away." The headmaster raised an eyebrow. "Now, I no longer need a master of wards. I made that request last year."

"Oh." Pancras's stomach knotted up. "I was assigned this post as restitution for being delinquent on my guild dues."

"Yes, the Manless's idea of cleaning up the guild. The new archmage rescinded those decrees right away."

The minotaur blinked. He had not expected a university headmaster to refer to the archmage in such a disrespectful manner. The rest of Lewin's statement hit him like a brick to the head. "Wait, what? A new archmage?"

"Yes. She won the position through the Rite of Combat, if you can believe that." The headmaster leaned forward and smacked Pancras on the knee. "I appreciate that you've come a long way, but that position is no longer available. There is something else, though, if you've the training for it. The alchemy master needs someone to fill in for him. His health is failing, you see, and I've also the need for a deputy—"

Pancras held up his hands. "Wait, when did this happen? With the new archmage? I've been on a ship; I've not heard anything."

"Oh, well, you wouldn't, would you?" Lewin held up a multifaceted crystal, which Pancras recognized as a Herald Stone. "Just three or four days ago, maybe a week? A drak challenged him to the Rite of Combat and won!"

The headmaster cackled. "He worked so hard on the aggrandizement of humans to the exclusion of all others, to move the guild and the university to a more disciplined— crueler, if you ask me—time, only to be undone by rules older than The Sundering."

He hooted and howled with laughter, holding his sides. Pancras rubbed his right horn and stared at the headmaster. *It can't be.* "You said the new archmage was a drak? A… a female drak?"

"Yes, that's—hey, I didn't say she was female."

Pancras felt nauseated. He closed his eyes and swallowed. "You said 'she.' What's her name?"

Headmaster Lewin clicked his fingers. "Oh, it is a pretty name. Something flowery. Delilah. Yes, that's it! Delilah Windsinger, I think it is."

The minotaur's head spun. *Air. Need air.*

He stood and sprinted for one of the archways leading outside… only to slam into an invisible barrier. The impact knocked him backward, and he crashed into a desk, sinking to rest on the floor. Pancras groaned and held his snout.

"There, now. It's not bad. True, we've not had a drak archmage in an age, but the high wizards seem to think highly of her. The first archmage was a drak, you know." The old man offered a hand to help Pancras to his feet. The minotaur gripped it, but he succeeded only in dragging the headmaster to the floor with him.

"Whoo! I'm not as young as I used to be, eh?" He sat alongside Pancras and elbowed him in the ribs. "You really hate draks, eh? Or is it worse?"

"It's worse." Pancras chuckled. "I don't hate draks at all. She… uh… she and I left Drak-Anor together nearly a year ago to deal with this guild business. They sent me here and kept her there." He told Headmaster Lewin about their official status as potential renegades and how, despite Delilah's years of experience, Vilkan deemed her no more skilled than an initiate.

"I never liked him anyway." Lewin sighed and rubbed his neck as he regarded Pancras. "Damn guild politics. Some folk are always meddling in affairs they've no business being in."

"I wonder… strange how events unfold." Pancras shook his head. The shadow demon that had infected him might have been more successful had he not traveled to Almeria and Vlorey. *This whole journey… a waste. I died to get here. I must return to Muncifer.* His mind raced. He felt tremendous pressure at the base of his skull and kneaded the muscles of his neck in an attempt to alleviate the pain. *No. No, death brought me closer to Aita. Gave me purpose. Delilah can take care of herself. Aita wants me to be here, to help Gisella.*

"Hmm?"

"Oh, nothing." Pancras waved his hand. "Idle thoughts. You said you had another position?"

Lewin pulled himself to his feet and approached one of the desks. "Indeed. How are your alchemy skills?"

The minotaur followed the old man as he proceeded from desk to desk, shuffling through papers. "Since I gave up necromancy, it is my preferred discipline."

"Excellent." Lewin held up a stack of papers and thrust them at Pancras. "As I said, our alchemy master's health is failing. You can fill in for him. These should tell you all you need to know about his teaching schedule. Also, I need a deputy headmaster. Someone who knows the current arch-mage might prove quite advantageous." He chuckled and grinned, revealing stained teeth to Pancras.

The minotaur shuffled through the papers the headmaster handed him. "Adjunct alchemy master and deputy headmaster? Yes, I think that will do nicely."

* * *

"Katka, I need you!" Delilah grunted and pulled against the bookcase, but it tilted rather than slid, as was her intention. She noticed the outline of a door behind the bookcase, but she lacked the strength to move the heavy wooden furniture, even after removing all the tomes, treatises, and bric-a-brac.

Her human apprentice sped into the room, tripping over one of the stacks of books. She sprawled onto the floor as she sent books flying.

"Careful."

"Did this guy keep everything?" Katka brushed herself off, wincing as she inspected a fresh abrasion on her elbow. After straightening the sleeve of her robe, she retied the ribbon that kept her hair off her face.

"Everything except Pyraclannaseous's treasure, it seems."

Katka chewed on one of her fingernails. "Maybe she didn't have treasure."

Delilah turned and faced her apprentice. "A dragon with no treasure? Impossible. Come here and help me with this."

Together, they heaved, but the bookcase didn't budge. It moved a fraction more than Delilah had managed alone, and she caught a glint of metal behind the case.

"Hang on, there's something…" She reached behind the bookcase, but felt nothing out of the ordinary.

"Damn it!" Delilah withdrew her arm. She pointed at the gap. "You have long arms… well, longer than mine. There's something back there."

Katka reached behind the bookcase. "I got it." She stuck her tongue between her teeth as she pulled. "I can't…" She stopped and clicked her fingers. "Wait."

The human raced to the opposite side of the bookcase and ran her hands along the side. She whooped in victory when she reached the bottom. She stood and pointed toward the floor. "A latch!" She moved it with her toe. They heard a click, and the wall and bookcase swung toward them, revealing a spiral staircase.

Archmage Delilah stuck her head through the opening. "Huh. I wondered how to access the upper levels."

"What's up there?" Katka held the glowing tip of her wand ahead of her as she advanced into the stairwell. Cobwebs as numerous as the steps corkscrewed upward, like silken buttresses. The two mages left footprints in the thick layer of dust covering each step.

"Do you think the archmage left any traps or anything like that up here?"

Delilah ran a finger through the dust on the steps. "I hoped the treasure was hidden up here, but I don't think Manless entered this level in years. He might not have even known about it."

"He lived in this tower. How could he not know about it?" Katka stopped before a door at the top of the steps. "Maybe he levitated up here so he wouldn't get dust all over him."

"I doubt it." Delilah pulled Katka's illuminated wand closer to the door's handle. She didn't see any sort of locking mechanism. She reached for the handle.

"Master!" Katka caught Delilah's hand. "Perhaps I should—"

The drak sorceress scowled and shook her head. She depressed the lever and pushed open the door.

"You know, Manless probably would have made his apprentice open that."

"Yeah, well, if there's something really dangerous that needs doing, then I'll have you do it." Delilah entered the upper chamber. The dust covering the floor lay just as thick as it had in the stairwell. Beneath a trapdoor set in the ceiling, a ladder leaned against the wall. The drak noticed the floor sloped slightly toward the edges, creating a slight dome over the room below it. Outdoor light entered through thin windows set high on the walls and through small holes near the floor.

To the left of the ladder sat a table covered in broken alchemy equipment. Shards of glass glittered in the light of Katka's wand. Against the opposite wall stood a table upon which sat open-top boxes. Delilah, too short to reach or see into them, directed Katka to investigate.

"Looks like junk." The apprentice pulled the boxes toward her and examined each in turn. "No, wait. Bones, dried leaves… is this tea? Could be divination implements."

"So, this is just some old wizard's laboratory?" Delilah snorted with disgust. *There has to be more here. Why hide the door?*

"Looks like."

The drak continued to examine the room while her apprentice provided light. A third desk had been pushed against the wall near the door through which they entered. Delilah didn't see any chairs in the laboratory, so she pulled open the desk drawers, improvising a stepstool, to inspect the top of the desk, bare, except for a blanket of dust. However, she noticed the depth of the top drawer sat at discord to its front panel. She removed it and set it on the ground.

"Oh, I'll bet it has a secret compartment." Katka leaned in closer with her light.

"I think you're right." Delilah nodded. A quick examination revealed a latch to release the panel covering the hollow underneath it. *All those years building traps with Kale paid off.* She removed the false bottom and discarded it, revealing an object wrapped in dirty, ragged cloth. When she picked it up, the fabric disintegrated, exposing a dark red, truncated square pyramid. The symbol inscribed in the base seemed familiar to Delilah, but the drak couldn't place it.

"Is that a rock?"

Delilah shrugged and held it in the light. "It's made of rock. It seems familiar."

"I've never seen anything like it. Maybe one of the high wizards can identify it."

"Maybe." The archmage glanced around the room one last time. She didn't see anything else of interest, so she gestured for her apprentice to follow her down the stairs. They pushed the bookcase into place behind them. Delilah placed the odd stone in one of her pouches as they resumed sorting through Vilkan's belongings. When she tired of cleaning, Delilah called it a day and followed Katka to the Enchanter's Focus for dinner. The Court of Wizardry convened the next day, and she had a feeling she would appreciate a relaxing evening beforehand.

* * *

Kale lay in bed, wide awake, staring at the ceiling. His mate's arm draped over his chest, and on this night, the steady sound of her breathing did nothing to alleviate his anxiety. After he wiggled out from under her arm, he rolled out of bed and picked up his puzzle box. He took it into the kitchen and set it on the table before he poured himself a mug of ale and sat in front of it. Once situated, he lit a candle to illuminate the workings of the puzzle box.

The drak had unlocked the first two of sides repeatedly, and he could accomplish those in his sleep. With each sequence, the gears whirred, moving the delicate clockwork components inside. With Kali's help, he had solved the remaining sides that stymied him, except for the last.

Once he unlocked the fifth side, Kale turned the box and peered into the sixth. The panel that kept the gears hidden slid away, and through the various cutouts and brass cages, he studied the mechanism. He noticed a tiny lever just inside one of the holes.

Kale poked a claw through and applied pressure to the lever. It clicked, and another panel inside retracted. When he removed his claw, the lever snapped into place and the panel returned to its original position. Again, he pushed down the lever. This time, he held it in place.

Behind the interior panel appeared another clockwork mechanism. Using his free hand, he moved the candle to better illuminate the area he examined. He spotted a second lever behind the interior panel, but he could not reach it with his claw. Keeping pressure on the first lever, Kale fumbled in his pouch until he found one of his lockpicks. He used it to press the second lever. He detected sufficient resistance that he suspected it, too, was spring-loaded.

A globe inside the mechanism spun, revealing a flat disc inside it. He removed his lockpick and his claw, causing the entire apparatus to reset. He removed a second lockpick from his pouch and held it between his teeth as he repeated the sequence. Once the flat disc again revealed itself, Kale pushed the third lockpick through the brass cage, grunting as his snout pressed against the side of the puzzle box and prevented him from reaching the disc.

As he huffed in frustration, he noticed the plate wobble. The drak furrowed his brow and struggled to steady his hands as he withdrew the instrument with his teeth. Kale opened his mouth and allowed it to fall to the table. Then he blew at the disc.

It spun and flashed. Kale jumped backward, dropping his tool and releasing his hold on both levers. With a snap-hiss, the puzzle box shuddered, and the gears and clockwork mechanisms activated. The sides of the box unlocked and unfolded, revealing its center.

A shiny orb hovered above the concave top of a truncated cone. Colors played across its silvery-grey surface as flickering candlelight reflected off it. Stepping around the table, Kale peered at the sphere from all angles. Perfectly smooth, and although it appeared to be composed of metal, it also behaved like a liquid.

After returning to his chair, he picked up his lockpicks and poked the orb. Ripples propagated across its surface, spreading around the globe in ever-diminishing waves. He again pushed against it with the lockpick, deforming the surface, but he could not submerge the thin piece of metal into the orb.

He set the lockpick on the table and reached toward the silvery ball. The head of a snarling dragon flashed before him and vanished as quickly as it appeared. He glanced around the room; his kitchen remained unchanged. Kale reached for the orb a second time. The room vanished, and Kale stood before a cliff. The world rumbled, and the cliff split as a torrent of water rushed through.

Kale yelped and fell backward, overturning his chair as he tumbled to the floor. Again, he found no evidence he'd left his home or that anything unusual occurred anywhere around him. He rubbed the base of his neck as he continued his examination of the strange object. *How does it stay up? Obviously, magic of some sort. What is it? Quicksilver? Deli would know… no. This is mine. Terrakaptis gave it to me. She got her stupid book.*

The drak frowned, climbed to his feet, and put away his tools. Then he moved the candle away from the puzzle box. In the diminished light, the orb took on an unusual sheen that reminded Kale of platinum. He pulled himself forward and rested his head on his hands as he stared at it. The longer he stared, the more the surface of the sphere shimmered, shifted, and undulated. Kale extended a clawed finger.

Another flash. In the scene that flickered before him, the world crumbled. Tens of thousands of deaths occurred in the blink of an eye. A great storm raged between a pair of mile-high cliffs, obscuring their landscape in its roiling black clouds. The drak pushed his claw against the object, finally piercing its surface.

The orb enveloped his hand in a steel grip. He jerked away, but it clung around his hand like a glob of molten metal. Molten, yet cold as ice. A bright flash blinded him, and when his vision cleared, his home was gone.

Chapter 10

That night, the Golden Slayer caught up with Pancras and Qaliah at The Screeching Griffon. Pancras filled her in on his appointment as deputy headmaster and adjunct alchemy master at the Arcane University. Neither needed to ask Qaliah how she spent her day. Her glassy-eyed expression and slurred speech communicated volumes.

"I worked my way out from the inn." She pointed at Gisella and Pancras as she swayed in her seat. "I can tell you which of the ten closest taverns have nothing but swill, which don't serve my kind, and which have the best ale."

"Truly, we are fortunate to have such an attentive information gatherer." Pancras chuckled into his mead. Gisella appreciated the high-quality brew served at The Screeching Griffon, but she missed the mead from back home. She suspected the water gathered from melting snows by the brewers in the Four Watches was purer than that which people in Vlorey obtained.

The Ritual of Renewal occupied most of Gisella's morning and afternoon. Some might say she wasted the day in frivolous pleasure; however, she felt closer to Aurora and more relaxed than since having departed Muncifer. Even the fiendling's prattling about the quality of alcohol and men in the various nearby taverns amused rather than irritated her. She rubbed the golden seashell of Aurora that hung from her neck. It felt appropriate to wear the symbol openly after her Renewal.

"We should get on task tomorrow, if we can." Gisella leaned back to allow the server to place a platter laden with an herb-stuffed fish gazing upward from a bed of wilted greens and colorful vegetables on their table. Qaliah eyed the staring fish, and her ebony skin paled.

Pancras turned her toward the door. "Go outside if you're about to pay Pacha for your excesses."

"How could this be upsetting?" Gisella carved a flank of fish for herself. "This smells and looks better than what we had on the ship."

Qaliah stifled a belch. "I wasn't drunk then."

"I had to explain my arm more times than I cared to today. Tomorrow, I have to teach my first class in the morning and will no doubt have to tell the story again and again. However, I should have most of the afternoon free to make some inquiries. I'll need to move my possessions from here to my quarters at the university anyway." Pancras piled food high on a plate and shoved it in front of Qaliah. The fiendling leaned back in her chair and looked away.

"Ah, yes." Gisella bowed her head and smiled. "Not quite what the archmage had in mind, is it?"

The minotaur laughed. "I got so caught up with our inebriated friend, I almost forgot. Manless is dead."

Holding a forkful of vegetables partway to her mouth, Gisella glanced at Pancras. "What?"

"He was challenged to the Rite of Combat and lost. There's a new archmage. You'll never guess who it is."

"Oh! Oh!" Qaliah shoved the plate of food away from her and waved her hand in the air. "Is it that old bitch? What was her name? You know, Blondie, the one that was always chasing me away from the Blood Oak?"

The memory of the old woman running after Qaliah shouting threats brought a smile to Gisella's face, despite the fiendling's use of the nickname she disliked. "Master Agata. Funny, she'd be my first guess, as well."

Pancras swallowed and shook his head. "No, but she's headmaster now. The new archmage split the positions. She didn't want to run the university and the guild."

Gisella racked her brain, but could not think of any mage at the Arcane University who would choose the guild over academia. *I wonder if Grímar actually brought my sister in?* "Was it a mage from the south? Alysha?"

The minotaur furrowed his brow. "No. It's Delilah."

"Oh." Gisella continued chewing until what Pancras said registered. "Wait… Del… the drak you came with?"

Qaliah hooted with laughter. "Old Manless laid low by a drak? Anetha had a hand in that, I'll bet. Praise the Lady of Justice!"

The Golden Slayer concurred. After all the injustices Vilkan Icebreaker visited upon the draks of Muncifer, it was indeed just that he met his end at one of their hands. "He always lacked respect for self-taught mages."

"I have to say"—Pancras washed down his food with a sip of mead—"I knew she was powerful, but I never foresaw this. And now she's archmage. She rescinded the decrees about self-taught renegades and delinquent dues, by the way."

Gisella's thoughts turned once again to poor Grímar chasing after her sister in the frozen reaches of the Southern Watch. She didn't envy his task and wished there was some way to notify him that his mission was now in vain. *If Alysha decides to play nice and return with him to Muncifer, she's going to be very angry. Her wrath could bring down a mountain.*

"Part of me wishes I could have seen that fight." Gisella chuckled and drained her mead, holding up her mug to call for a refill.

"As I understand it, the high wizards are debating about declaring her an elemental master."

No wizard had held that title since before The Sundering. Gisella was no expert on Arcane Lore, but she learned enough to remember entire disciplines were lost when the world broke. Earth Magic became little more than stories, and most advanced Water Magic dwelt in the realm of fables.

"That seems… unlikely."

"Apparently"—Pancras clucked his tongue—"she learned much from that pre-Sundering grimoire of hers."

The minotaur's arm shot out, catching Qaliah's head before the fiendling bashed it on the table and landed face-first in her plate. He leaned her back in her chair as her head lolled to the side.

Gisella helped herself to the fiendling's mead. "I don't envy her the headache she's going to have tomorrow."

* * *

Kale stood on a grassy cliff, overlooking the sea as it surged and crashed against the rocks below. The sun blazed high in the sky, and the drak noticed how much warmer it felt by the cliff than it did in Muncifer. He spun, searching for a clue, a hint, or a recognizable landmark to tell him where he stood. Although he could no longer see the orb, his hand still felt its cold embrace.

"Deli?" The drak scanned the area for his sister, but he observed only a stone obelisk in the distance and a pale figure standing before it. He ran toward the figure and realized that ropes bound it to the column.

As he drew closer, Kale noticed draconic carvings covered the obelisk. He could not read the words inscribed in an ancient Drak dialect, although he recognized a name: *Rannos Dragonsire.*

The bound woman stared toward the sky and didn't seem distressed. Her alabaster skin and ivory gown stood out like a beacon against the dark stone to which she was bound. Blue and purple flowers blossomed at the base of the monolith.

Wind buffeted Kale as he approached the obelisk. The woman gave no indication she saw him. Her dark hair fluttered in the wind, and Kale heard the unmistakable sound of flapping wings.

A shadow passed over them. The woman looked skyward, eyes wide in wonder, and then she screamed. Kale turned to see a massive reptilian shape approaching. Brilliant green eyes glared from beneath a horned brow. Silver scales the size of breastplates covered the beast, and his wings blotted out the sun, covering the area in darkness. The ground trembled as he landed before the woman.

Kale fell to his knees as a wave of awe overcame him. His legs lacked the strength to support himself in the presence of the dragon's majesty. The wyrm dwarfed even Terrakaptis, and as the dragon circled the obelisk, Kale noticed its smallest teeth were larger than he was.

A small part of the drak's brain reasoned that, logically, he did not know this dragon; yet, in his heart, the creature somehow felt familiar.

The great dragon sniffed the woman, each breath pulling her hair toward him. The creature reached behind the obelisk and snapped the ropes that bound her. She stared at her loose bonds, brow furrowed in confusion. The dragon leapt up and took to the sky. Hesitating, the woman watched him fly away before she fled.

Kale followed her until she disappeared behind a hill. He noticed two additional figures in the distance regarding the sky and pointing. They marched toward the obelisk, and the drak realized they must have seen the events that occurred just moments earlier. As he drew closer to the distant figures, he saw that they were humans. Robed men.

"Hello?"

The humans paid him no mind. Their attention was fixed on the sky. Kale waved to them as he broke into a run. He spread his wings to increase his size, hoping the robed humans would see him.

A roar from behind caused Kale to skid to a stop. He turned and searched for the source. The huge dragon returned, swooping toward the cliff. It required all the drak's effort to keep from once again falling on his knees before the creature's raw magnificence. It was the most beautiful and terrible dragon he'd ever seen, and Kale's very spirit felt drawn toward it. He wanted to bask in the dragon's presence and power.

Twin rays shot from the hands of the humans toward the dragon, who twisted and spun, avoiding the attack. He then dove out of sight. Kale ran to the edge of the precipice, searching for him. The dragon looped around and gripped the edge of the cliff, each of his claws the size of buildings.

"The time of dragons is at an end!" One of the two men held loft a talisman. Another ray shot forth, striking the dragon in the chest while he still clung to the cliff.

The dragon inhaled deeply. Kale noticed a furious glow beneath its scales. The wyrm breathed a torrent of flame at the humans, scorching the ground before them in a whirlwind of fire. The second human braced against the flame as it reached them. Kale shielded himself from the conflagration, squinting to see through the smoke and flames.

When at last the dragon's breath abated, the men stood unscathed. The creature roared in fury and launched itself backward, taking to the air again.

Kale studied the humans as they conferred, shaking their heads and pointing at the dragon as he circled. Both well-tanned and muscular, their robes and lack of armor exposed them as wizards, as if their use of the talisman and conjurations had not already betrayed them. One possessed a tangled nest of jet-black hair, and the other sported sandy-brown dreadlocks.

"Maelor! Kyffin!" The woman of alabaster skin raced toward the men. Kale leapt up and ran toward her, intent on keeping her away from the battle. She paid him no heed. When he stopped in front of her, the woman ran through him.

"Maelor! You must stop this. He released me. Kyffin!" She seized the arm of the dark-haired wizard. He spun on her and pushed her away. She stumbled and fell.

"Away with you, Bronwyn. You've served your purpose."

The dreadlocked wizard pointed toward the dragon. "Maelor, he returns."

"You cannot defeat a god. This is madness!" Bronwyn gathered up her gown and returned to her feet.

The wizard Maelor thrust his talisman toward the dragon and chanted. His language sounded harsh and guttural. Although Kale did not understand the words, he guessed their intent. He turned to watch the dragon.

Clouds gathered in the sky, blotting out the sun. Thunder rumbled in the distance, and the drak noticed a wall of rain advancing on the coast from the sea. The dragon roared and stopped short, hovering instead of landing, flapping its wings and stirring up a maelstrom that buffeted the two wizards and Bronwyn. Kale shielded his eyes until he realized the debris passed through him, just as Bronwyn had.

The dragon jerked to the side as a bolt of lightning struck the ground before the men. Three more followed, each passing through the air where the dragon hovered just a moment before. He growled and snarled as he dodged the electric bolts.

"Your mortal magic is no use. Flee. Flee before me, and I shall have mercy."

"Mercy like your kind showed my Siwan?" Kyffin slashed a wand through the air. Glowing blades spun from the tip. They sliced through the air, striking the dragon. Most bounced off his metallic scales, but one slashed through his wing membrane.

The creature roared in pain and landed, shaking the ground. The three humans clutched one another to remain upright.

"You see? You see, Bronwyn?" Maelor laughed. "He can be hurt."

"Come with me, my love." Bronwyn tugged at Maelor. "Stop this insanity. You cannot blame all dragons for the actions of one. Have you learned nothing?"

"I said away with you!" Maelor shoved Bronwyn. He spun on the dragon, unleashing another ray from his talisman. It, too, splashed harmlessly against the dragon's scales.

"Your mate speaks with wisdom, Human." The dragon slashed at the wizard. Maelor jumped to the side, diving to avoid evisceration.

"You are their father! A father is responsible for his children." Kyffin spun his wand and moved it in a downward slashing motion. The sky flashed as a dozen bolts of lightning struck the ground around them and formed a crackling shield around the two wizards.

A father? Kale glanced at Bronwyn as she crawled toward the shield. He returned his gaze to the dragon. *Rannos Dragonsire!*

The dragon reared and breathed again. The shield absorbed the dragonfire directed toward the wizards, but so great was the fire breath of Rannos that it covered the area beyond the shield, as well. Bronwyn shrieked and screamed as the flames engulfed her. The inferno incinerated the woman, silencing her shrieks of agony. When it ended, nothing remained to mark where the woman once stood.

Again, the wizards stood together, scowling and with burning rage in their eyes for the death of Bronwyn. They clasped hands as they chanted. Rannos leapt forward into the air and snarled. His forelegs bore down on the two wizards, but he bounced off the shield, crashing to the ground, and again shaking the foundation of the land.

Lightning arced down from the storm clouds whirling above, striking the great dragon's back. He rolled on the ground as lightning struck again and again until he plummeted over the cliff. Thunder reverberated as Kale watched the dragon's mighty wings catch an updraft, and he took once more to the sky.

Bright light shone through the clouds. At first, Kale thought the storm might dissipate, but the light grew bright and larger, as shooting stars plunged toward the earth. One of these stars struck Rannos, and the dragon roared in pain as he wheeled out of control. A second meteor continued on its downward trajectory until it crashed into the side of the cliff. Tremors from the impact shook the wizards off their feet.

Kale found himself staggering as the ground shook. The forces did not seem to affect him as violently as they did the humans. He glanced up to see more fiery objects pierce the cloud cover, streaking through the sky and striking Rannos. Some missed, crashing into the landscape and propelling fountains of earth and fire.

The drak ran toward the two men. He leapt toward them, kicking and screaming. His blows passed through them, and when his rage was spent, he collapsed, panting.

"He's wounded, brother. Look!" Maelor helped Kyffin to his feet. Rannos soared overhead, flying in an erratic zigzag as the wizards continued to strike him with lightning and blazing meteors. The dragon circled again, lost altitude, and landed on the other side of a small hill.

Kyffin knelt near the spot where Bronwyn died. "Your wife—"

Maelor waved his hand. "I warned her. It's you and me, brother. We will have justice against all these wyrms. Come! Rannos will fall today." He beckoned for Kyffin to follow.

The two wizards ran toward the spot where Rannos landed. Kale closed his eyes and shook his head. "No, no. I don't want to see this. I don't want to be here."

He felt himself pulled forward. The drak opened his eyes to see himself flying behind the wizard brothers. Whatever magic forced this vision upon him would not be denied.

Rannos hobbled, snarling at the wizards. He held his right foreleg tight against his flank, his shredded and tattered wings unable to provide sufficient lift for him to become airborne again. Maelor drew a glowing, multifaceted orb from his robes. He held it in front of him as the two brothers circled Rannos.

"You see this, wyrm? Do you know what this is?"

The dragon answered by delivering a gout of fire that swirled around the wizards as the orb drew it in. It pulsed with power it gained from absorbing the dragonfire.

"A heartstone."

Kyffin flicked his wand, releasing another spinning blade toward Rannos. It sank deep into his flank, spraying blood across the field. Grass wilted and smoked at its touch. "We ventured deep into the earth to retrieve it. Deep into your mother? Mate?" The human laughed. "It's so hard to keep track of you gods and your incestuous affairs."

Rannos roared in fury. He spat and snarled, lunging forward and snapping his jaws around Maelor. The wizard screamed as one of Rannos's fangs pierced his torso, ripping his body in half as the dragon jerked his head. Maelor's legs collapsed in a heap before Kale.

The drak scrambled backward. Rannos spit, sending the rest of Maelor sailing toward Kyffin. He splattered on the ground, the heartstone tumbling from his bloody, outstretched hand.

"Defilers!" Rannos stomped on Maelor's remains, sending Kyffin falling backward. "I will heal. He will not."

Kyffin dove for the heartstone, rolling forward and clutching it before him as he regained his footing. He drew a ragged breath and pulled a faceted, ink-black stone from his robes.

Rannos's eyes widened. He lunged at Kyffin again, but the wizard moved too quickly. He touched the two stones together just as the mighty dragon's jaws closed around him.

Rannos's head exploded in a shower of gore. The dragon's body reared, then fell, his neck spewing fiery blood, scorching the countryside.

Kale covered his ears as the sound of a thousand earthquakes split the air. It was at once the crumbling of a mountain and the wail of a thousand grieving lovers. The ground shook and tore apart, falling away from the drak.

He flapped his wings to remain aloft but discovered doing so was not necessary. The same force that allowed him to view the events kept him fixed in place as the corpse of Rannos Dragonsire fell into the void. Kale saw no sign of the two wizards. As the world split, great clouds rushed to fill in the gaps, and a violent cacophony so great Kale felt it would crush him became his whole existence.

Fire and lightning danced around Kale. Covering his eyes, he screamed, to no avail. Even without seeing, he witnessed the destruction, and felt it all around him. He sensed it within his core and to the claws on his fingertips and toes.

Calliome sundered.

* * *

Using the top of her staff for light, Delilah crept through the university's library. Even though it was deserted, she felt it appropriate to move as quietly as possible due to the late hour. A voice in the back of her mind reminded her as archmage, she could go anywhere she pleased on the university grounds and no one would challenge her.

Unsure of what she sought, she assumed the library contained books that described magical objects and decided to start her search with those. The stone she found within the deserted laboratory in her tower possessed traces of lingering arcane energies, but so far, Delilah's experiments proved fruitless. Granted, her knowledge of divinations was limited, but even with Katka's help, she learned nothing.

After a few hours of browsing, the archmage's fatigue won, and she returned to her tower. Delilah locked the door to their suite and tiptoed past her sleeping apprentice. She put the stone on her nightstand and crawled into bed.

Sleep came easily to the archmage. She still felt the effects of her battle with Archmage Vilkan, although ministrations of the university's healer mended her wounds faster than she expected. The next morning, she had a servant bring their morning meal to the tower. When they finished eating, Delilah and Katka parted ways.

"In between classes, if you would go to the library and try to find any information on magical stones like the one we found, that would be helpful."

The human nodded as she adjusted her robes. "How long do you think the council meeting will last?"

"I've no idea, really. The high wizards do so love to talk"—Delilah flapped her hand in imitation of a mouth—"and talk and talk."

Katka strode to the practice grounds for her lesson with Master Galina, and Delilah entered the Court of Wizardry. Seneschal Lyov bowed to her as she passed him and wished her a good morning. She reciprocated and steeled herself for the court. She saw only the Violet and Yellow Wizards in attendance.

"Where is everyone else?" She took her seat at the center of the dais.

"Busy."

"Not every meeting is fully attended."

It took only a few minutes for Delilah to discover why not some of the high wizards were in attendance—the wizards had no news and nothing interesting to discuss. The two high wizards present explained that many sessions of the court were formalities only, convened to uphold tradition.

Delilah adjourned the meeting and dismissed them. A page waited for her in the foyer as she left. Seneschal Lyov waved the young man over.

"All right, boy. The archmage is here. Speak!"

The boy stood only a head taller than Delilah. She figured him to be younger than Katka. "The archduke desires a meeting. As soon as possible, if you please." He bowed before the archmage.

"I'll head that way, then." She glanced up at the old seneschal. "See to it my apprentice knows where I've gone."

"Of course." Seneschal Lyov bowed. He tossed a coin to the page, who caught it and ran off.

The drak archmage proceeded on foot to Grimstone Keep, stopping at a nearby tavern to purchase a meat-filled hand pie to eat as she traveled. Halfway there, with meat juices dripping down her chin and crumbs stuck to her chest, Delilah realized her mistake. She cleaned herself with some water from a public fountain to the stares of passersby who no doubt wondered why the new archmage splashed around in public.

The guards ushered Delilah directly to the keep's sitting room where, before a crackling fire, Archduke Fyodar and Theros sat in high-backed chairs facing each other. Each held a snifter of amber liquid. A crystalline chandelier hung above their heads, and the whole room was finished in forest-green drapes and warm oiled-oak panels.

"Ah, Archmage, come in, come in!" Archduke Fyodar beckoned to Delilah and gestured for a guard to bring her a seat.

The drak-sized chair carried by the guard fit between the archduke and the minotaur. A servant offered her a drink as she sat. Delilah sniffed it and wrinkled her nose at the oaky scent.

"The finest brandy in Muncifer." Archduke Fyodar raised his glass.

Delilah tried a sip. Although it burned as it descended her throat, she found the smoky oak and subtle fruit flavors pleasing. "I doubt you requested to see me just to share your brandy with me."

"Right to the point." Theros swirled his snifter. "Fear not, Archmage. These aren't dire tidings. For once."

Archduke Fyodar laughed and raised his glass. "Right you are. And we have you to thank." He nodded to the archmage.

Delilah understood many people were relieved by the passing of Archmage Vilkan, but she didn't expect to be toasted. "I appreciate the toast, but I really do have a lot to do."

"No doubt." Archduke Fyodar called for a refill. "But let us take a time to savor the moment."

"When I finally sort through all the junk Manless left in my quarters, I will."

She stood to leave, but Theros placed his hand on her shoulder. "A message came from the giants today. They witnessed your battle with Vilkan, and they are pleased that justice was done. They're sending emissaries to renew our trade agreements."

"My father established peaceful relations with the Iron Giants before I was born." The archduke sipped his brandy. "It was my greatest shame that I allowed Vilkan to jeopardize that legacy. I owe you a debt, Archmage."

Delilah raised her glass to the archduke. "Glad I could—"

The doors to the sitting room burst open. Guards rushed in, led by their captain. "Your Grace! Dragon sighted coming from the south."

Theros and Archduke Fyodar rose as one. Delilah drained her glass, coughing as the fiery liquid burned its way to her stomach.

"Show me." Archduke Fyodar followed the guard captain. Theros and Delilah hurried after him as he ran upstairs to the battlement.

The south wall of Grimstone Keep overlooked a residential district of Muncifer. As the keep was the tallest building in the city, their vantage afforded them a view toward the spur of the Iron Gate Mountains on the southern horizon beyond the wall of the city.

Archduke Fyodar turned to Delilah. "You said the dragon was dead."

"She is. Her head was split open. She was desiccated and rotting." Delilah climbed into one of the embrasures for a better view, shielding her eyes from the sun with her hand. A shape easily mistaken for a large bird glided toward the city. Its wings were twice as wide as its body was long, and when it turned, the long tail adorned with spines left little room for doubt.

A dragon descended upon Muncifer.

Chapter 11

Pancras found the Alchemy Master's lesson plans and notes a disorganized, jumbled mess. Fortunately, the students, on top of things and eager to continue where they left off, helped him locate the notes he needed. By the end of his first lecture, the minotaur felt certain he could keep up the pace set by the old alchemist.

The minotaur returned to the tower office he shared with Headmaster Lewin. The elderly human, who beat him there, directed a veritable army of novices and initiates as they dusted, carried away boxes, and moved furniture.

"Ah! Deputy Headmaster Pancras. I thought I'd clean up the place. I haven't shared space in so long, I'm afraid I let things become cluttered."

Pancras dodged an initiate carrying a bundle of scrolls piled so tall she couldn't see over them. "That's quite all right. I've been known to let my laboratory in Drak-Anor become somewhat messy."

The minotaur lied in deference to the headmaster's feelings. Back home in Drak-Anor, Pancras had been fastidious and fussy, his workshop never cluttered or messy. To the casual observer, in fact, it was difficult to determine his laboratory was used at all.

"Settling in all right?"

Pancras placed his armful of notes on a clean desktop. "Yes, I suppose so."

"I've arranged for a meal this afternoon." He beckoned Pancras to follow him. "You should meet the other masters and instructors." The headmaster directed one of the novices to disturb neither his desk nor the one Pancras used, and he led Pancras to the faculty dining hall. A humid breeze wafting through the halls did little to diminish the stifling atmosphere.

The faculty dining hall sat in the center of a walled garden behind the headmaster's tower, with its kitchen attached to the far side of the building. Tall date palms dotted the garden, and smaller shrubs lined the paths. Collapsible wooden panels, which composed the walls of the dining hall, allowed versatility; for this gathering, they were folded away, opening the hall to the outside air.

Headmaster Lewin introduced additional staff members as each entered. Save for the elves Vanathiel Falaelwa, master of enchantments, and her sister, Beriwen Falaelwa, adjunct master of enchantments, they all hailed from Cardoba and Vlorey. Pancras noted the former group rolled their *R*s more thoroughly.

The other wizards more than happily swapped rumors about the exact nature of Tybalt Sandalwood's affliction. The popular theory was that the master of alchemy tasted one too many of his experiments.

"I heard he mixed his reagents incorrectly while making a tonic, and it petrified his guts." Master of illusions, Elwyn Grubb, spoke with a slight lisp and gesticulated wildly. More than once, the wizards seated alongside her were forced to dodge her flailing hands.

"Nonsense." Master of abjurations and wards, Albion Bracegirdle, held up his hand to protect his face from errant gestures. "He would have died days ago. I just saw him up and about yesterday."

"It's entirely possible he's just old and feeble and dying of it, as you humans are wont to do." Beriwen poured herself more wine from the silver ewer before her. She and her sister possessed deep green skin and black hair, a stark contrast to the ivory robes worn by both.

"Enough talk of dying humans." Vanathiel turned to Pancras, catching him mid-chew. "Headmaster Lewin tells us you came all the way from Muncifer via ship. He also tells us you practiced the forbidden arts."

He swallowed his mouthful with some dry, tannic wine before answering. "I actually journeyed from Drak-Anor by way of Muncifer, and yes, I was once a necromancer. I have not practiced that in years, however, and I do, in fact, serve Aita."

"Drak-Anor?" Master of evocations, Graeme Longriver, tapped his finger against his chin. "That's in the Dragon Spine Mountains, is it not? Near Celtangate?"

"Closer to Ironkrag, but yes."

"Going through Muncifer is the opposite direction." Master Bracegirdle raised his eyebrows.

"Yes, Remember Archmage Man"—Headmaster Lewin coughed to cover his flub—"Vilkan's decree about delinquent dues?"

"You mean to tell us Manless made you travel all the way to Muncifer, just to send you here because you were behind on your dues?" Master of conjurations, Gilda Brandywood, slammed her goblet on the table hard enough to slosh wine onto the white tablecloth.

"Yes." Pancras chuckled. "I was rather annoyed. He kept one of my drak companions behind, as well. He felt since she was self-taught, she couldn't possibly know anything, and, therefore, he required her to start at the bottom, as an initiate."

Headmaster Lewin winked. "She showed him."

"You're talking about our new archmage?" Master Longriver passed a plate of crispy squid.

"Delilah is a skilled battlemage, but I never expected her to become archmage." Pancras scooped a generous helping of squid onto his plate and shook his head. "I leave her alone for a little while—"

"There has not been a drak archmage since the Age of Legend." Master Vanathiel Falaelwa took the ewer from her sister and refilled her goblet.

The conversation continued until the sun sank low in the sky. Surprised none of the wizards inquired about his arm, Pancras considered the possibility that Lewin had already apprised them. He made a mental note to ask the old man about it the next day. The minotaur bade a good night to the masters as he gathered his things and headed toward the Screeching Griffon. His personal quarters at the university would not be ready for few more days. Walking the streets of an unfamiliar city after a long, exhausting day did not provide Pancras the relaxation he sought before going to bed.

Qaliah and Gisella were dining together when he arrived at the inn. The taproom, full of patrons enjoying the house-specialty mead with their meals, buzzed with the cacophony of dozens of conversations. The fiendling looked none the worse for her overindulgence the night prior and cheered when she saw Pancras.

"Pull up a chair and join us."

Pancras sat between the women. "Please tell me one of you accomplished something today."

"More of the same." Gisella cut through a hunk of roasted pork the size of her forearm. "Chasing down rumors is slow work, particularly when I don't know anyone or where anything is."

"I heard plenty of rumors in the taverns today." Qaliah leaned in close to Pancras. "You'll notice I didn't drink myself into oblivion again."

"I did notice."

The fiendling grinned. "Unfortunately, none of the rumors I heard seemed to have anything to do with the Lich Queen. Mostly rumors about who's sleeping with who and which lady's baby doesn't belong to her husband."

Pancras scratched his chest and waved off a servant carrying plates of food. "Perhaps your time would be better spent getting to know the lay of the city. You're quick and observant. I'll wager you can learn the streets faster than either of us."

They agreed that for the next few days, Qaliah would scout the businesses and neighborhoods while Gisella continued visiting the temples and city watch stations. Pancras, meanwhile, would keep his ears open around the wizards and seek out the Red Crypt. He hoped, now that he was in Vlorey, his goddess would offer more guidance.

* * *

Kale gasped and snapped open his eyes. He sat in his kitchen, in exactly the same spot he occupied before he first touched the silvery sphere. The candle, little more than a flickering nub, cast dancing light on the orb as it hovered over its base. The puzzle box clicked, whirred, and closed. He put his hand on his chest as the pounding of his heart threatened to burst from within it. His breath came in ragged gasps, and he clenched his fists in a futile attempt to stem the tide of tears that threated to flow from his eyes.

He collapsed as his body wracked with sobs. Sweeping his arm across the table, he knocked the puzzle box away, sending it clattering to the floor. Although he recognized that what he just witnessed could not possibly have been real, he felt battered and exhausted from the experience.

Clawed hands held his shoulders, pulling him close. "Kale? Kale, what's wrong?"

The drak sniffled and wiped his eyes as he regarded at his mate. "I saw him die. I saw it all."

"Who? What happened?" Kali pulled a chair near to sit alongside her mate. She glanced around the room. "Kale, your puzzle box."

"Keep that thing away from me!" Kale pulled his mate downward as she stood to retrieve it. "I got it open. It showed me things. I saw him die."

"You opened it?" Kali glanced at the box. It rested against the bricks of their hearth, closed and still. "Who died? Kale!"

He swallowed and took her hand, holding it against his chest. He closed his eyes and slowed the cadence of his breathing before he faced her and explained how he solved the puzzle box and found the silvery orb inside. "Then I touched it, and it transported me to a different place, except no one could see me. I watched as they killed Rannos, and the world broke. I saw The Sundering."

"The Sundering?" His mate regarded the puzzle box again and scooted away from it. She hugged her mate tightly.

He told her about the two brothers and how they conspired to kill Rannos out of some twisted sense of justice for another dragon's attack. "They were mad, not angry, I mean. Insane or something. A woman tried to stop them, but she was killed. Then they used a heartstone and some other rock, and it blew up Rannos. Then the world cracked."

Kali hugged him and nodded. "It was just a dream, Kale. That's all."

"No, no, it was more than that. It was real. I was there; at least, my mind was."

"I don't understand. How could you have seen that? It was almost a thousand years ago."

Kale didn't understand it himself. Mechanical things he could decipher. The puzzle part of the box he had solved, even if it had occupied him the better part of a year to unlock its secrets. The magic within, however, was beyond his understanding or experience.

"Maybe Deli will know something."

His mate cocked her head. "Do you really think so? She's good in a fight, but magical visions seem to be different than what I've seen her do."

"Well, maybe, but I'll bet she knows someone who can help." Kale stood and stepped over to the puzzle box. As far as he could tell, it was inert, just an intricate clockwork puzzle offering no hints as to what was stored within. He picked up it.

"I'm putting this down in the cavern with the egg. Deli can look at it the next time she's here." He hoped she wouldn't have him open it. The last thing Kale wanted was to experience that vision again.

* * *

The dragon roared as it swooped past the city walls. The guards who didn't flee in terror loosed arrows, most of which arced harmlessly past the wyrm. Its roar froze the blood in Delilah's veins, and it was only through sheer force of will that she remained on the battlement.

"Get below, Your Grace." Theros guided Archduke Fyodar to stairs leading inside, but the archduke pushed him away.

"No. No, I won't." The archduke drew his sword and climbed onto the parapet. "The people of Muncifer will not see me flee like a craven beggar."

Delilah did not intend to let the people see the new archmage flee, either. Blue tendrils gathered near the top of her staff as she swung it in the direction of the dragon, aiming ahead of it, anticipating where it would fly next. The sun reflected off its shimmering, opalescent scales.

"*Ophayra!*"

A bolt of azure fire streaked toward the dragon. It banked, and on its back Delilah saw a rider. The fireball exploded prematurely as the rider countered the spell, leaving a sooty, black cloud in its wake.

The dragon dove toward the city gate, opening its maw and breathing a blizzard of frost and snow. It struck the wall below where the archduke and Delilah stood, covering it in a sheet of ice.

"Definitely not Pyraclannaseous." Delilah and the archduke jumped down and took cover behind the merlons.

Theros dove for cover as well, covering his head as the icy blast shot over the wall.

"Could it be seeking revenge for the dragon's death?" The archduke dared peek over the wall. With a cry of alarm, he scrambled backward.

The wall shook as the dragon landed on the battlement and stared at Delilah, its slavering jaws inches from her face. Its hard-edged features were as if chiseled from ice. Blue-tinged white scales covered its neck like armored plates. It snarled and licked its lips.

"Yaamkyrsku, hold!"

The dragon pulled back its head, and Delilah used the opportunity to shimmy from beneath it. She stood and faced the dragon rider.

The woman, clad in white, fur-lined robes, wore a runed breastplate that appeared to have been carved from cloudy ice. Her platinum hair hung in a long, complex braid down her back. She bore a golden, shafted spear whose dark head sparkled as it caught the light of the afternoon sun.

"Where is that mewling cur, Vilkan Icebreaker?"

Theros helped Archduke Fyodar to his feet. Delilah stood before them, her only hope of being seen. She motioned for them to stay back as she addressed the dragon and rider.

"What is the meaning of this attack?"

The woman regarded Delilah and chuckled, as if noticing the drak for the first time. "You attacked us. Answer my question, Drak." She pointed her spear first at Theros and then at the archduke. "Or you, Minotaur. Human? Do you lead these poxy milk-drinkers?"

Archduke Fyodar stepped forward. He held his sword ready but kept it lowered. "I am Archduke Fyodar, ruler of Muncifer."

"Then I am not interested in treating with you." The woman turned her attention to Theros. "Where is the arch-mage?"

Delilah tapped the butt of her staff against the stones. "I am archmage. Vilkan is dead."

"You? A drak?" The woman laughed and slid off the dragon. She patted its cheek and whispered in its ear. The dragon snapped its jaws and launched itself off the city wall. It roared as it took to the sky and circled the city.

The archmage kept her staff pointed at the woman. "Who are you?"

"I have many names, many titles." She waved her hand dismissing the archduke and Theros as she watched her dragon soar. "My own people call me the Frost Queen." She turned and bowed her head to Delilah, her hand on her chest. "I am Alysha Vibekedottir, and I greet you, Archmage."

Archduke Fyodar cleared his throat. "I have heard stories about you. I am curious why you have chosen now to visit Muncifer."

Alysha laid her hand on Delilah's shoulder and guided the drak around the archduke. "I am here on guild business. Yaamkyrsku may circle a while before landing in the countryside. I recommend that your sheep-brained dung farmers not disturb him and just ignore him."

Delilah and Alysha moved away, leaving Archduke Fyodar calling after them. The drak heard Theros calm his liege, advising him to let the slight go.

Alysha opened the door for Delilah as the two descended into Grimstone Keep. "Now, I came here to give that swag-bellied, canker-blossom Vilkan Icebreaker a piece of my mind, but since he's dead, I suppose I should be more civil with you."

"Hold it." Delilah stopped. "I want to stay on the archduke's good side, so why don't you cut to the chase? Why are you here? What do you want?"

"Vilkan sent one of his slayers to retrieve me for being negligent in paying my guild dues. I was feeling charitable so I gave the poor man a warm room in my castle and came to see Vilkan myself." Alysha cradled her spear and leaned with one foot on the wall.

"That's kind of how I ended up here, too." Delilah rubbed the base of her neck. "I rescinded those decrees. You may pay your dues since you're here, but we're not sending slayers out to collect delinquents anymore."

Alysha smacked her leg. "Good! An archmage with sense."

"Follow the stairs all the way down. Then cross the yard to the gate house. The guards can direct you to the Arcane University. I'm sure you can find Seneschal Lyov once you're there." *I'm not going to let this strange woman lead me around.* She turned to return to the battlement.

"You're turning your back on me?"

Delilah faced Alysha. "Your dramatic arrival interrupted a meeting in progress with the archduke. Until I've heard otherwise, you're no more important to me than any other wizard. So, if you want my time, make an appointment." Delilah turned and climbed the stairs without uttering another word, leaving the Frost Queen sputtering in the stairwell.

Theros and Archduke Fyodar still stood on the battlement when Delilah returned to them. The minotaur looked on while the archduke instructed his men to closely observe the dragon but not to disturb it.

"Where's the Frost Queen?" Theros left the archduke to deliver his instructions and strode with Delilah to the battlement overlooking the crossroads. The fields and hills still bore the scars of the drak's battle with Archmage Vilkan.

"I sent her onward to the Arcane University. I told her if she wanted to speak to me in private, she needed to make an appointment like any other wizard."

Theros's eyes bulged, and a strangled noise came from his throat.

"She's just another mage to me." Delilah sniffed and leaned on her staff.

Staring at the archmage, the minotaur shook his head and laughed. "Oh, the stodgy old humans that run the guild are going to love you." He glanced at the archduke, who was walking and talking with several guard captains. "He might be a while. Fyodar wants you present when the giants arrive. We'll send for you."

Delilah turned to protest but reconsidered. The archduke would not likely want her input on crucial negotiations, just her presence. "Fine. If I'm not at the Arcane University, I may be visiting my brother. His home is in the undercity." She described the location for Theros, as best as possible, considering she couldn't recall any of the street names.

"I'm familiar with the area." Theros led her down stairs. "For the record, I think you're going to make a fine archmage. I would be honored to assist you in any way you need."

The minotaur bowed to the drak, dipping his horns low enough that Delilah could touch them if she so chose. He turned, sweeping his robes behind him, and returned to the upper levels. Delilah made her way to the Arcane University with a knot of dread in her stomach. Theros's reaction to her treatment of this so-called Frost Queen caused her to second-guess her actions.

She paused before the university gates. Everything appeared normal. "Well, Deli-girl, it's not the first time you stepped in it. It won't be the last."

* * *

Gisella strapped on her pouches and checked her gear. She didn't anticipate trouble while wandering to the various temples in Vlorey, particularly since they were clustered together in their own walled district, but it never hurt to be prepared. She tossed her cloak onto the bed. Loath as she was to leave it behind, the weather was still too warm for it.

She turned to leave and noticed Qaliah standing in their doorway. The fiendling leaned with one hand over her head, fingering her horns. "Mind if I tag along?"

"No, I suppose not. Why?" Gisella clicked her fingers as she remembered her hair tie. After searching for a few minutes in vain, she stepped past the fiendling and pulled the door shut, pausing to lock it.

"I've had enough of listening to salacious rumors about nobles' social lives. You and Pancras seem to actually have a purpose, and well"—the fiendling chuckled—"I may not be exactly welcome in a lot of the nearby taverns for a few days."

"I don't even want to know." Gisella speculated on the trouble the fiendling caused, but she preferred not to fully contemplate it.

"No, you probably don't."

The two women left the Screeching Griffon together. Gisella, although glad for the company, hoped Qaliah's presence didn't disrupt her plans. The Golden Slayer intended to visit several temples but no taverns. Since her visit to the one temple she was certain could help bore no fruit the day prior, she anticipated the day would be difficult.

Scattered clouds brought patchy relief from the oppressive heat of the sun, and a cool breeze from the bay somewhat mitigated the humidity. The streets leading toward the temple district were not busy this early in the morning, as only Apellon's temple, the Sun Cathedral, held morning services, and those had already completed. From her observations, Gisella determined Vlorey did not venerate only one deity over all the others as was the custom in many of the towns she had visited. Instead, three seemed most prominent: Anetha, Tinian, and Hon.

The Hearth of the Sacred Family, Hon's temple, sat closest to the bridge by which Gisella and Qaliah entered the temple district. Erected on a stepped platform, wider than it was deep, massive columns surrounded the temple. The roof extended to the tops of the columns, and smoke rose from twin chimneys set into the ridgeline. Located in the center of the long wall, a pair of wrought iron gates composed the main entrance. Gisella did not recognize the symbol, a triangle and cross set inside a circle, carved into the keystone above the gates.

The two women entered through the gates, which stood ajar. Gisella felt her palms grow clammy upon crossing the threshold. Hon and Aurora were not exactly allies. Hon, who appreciated structure and discipline, viewed the goddess of love as irresponsible and capricious.

Magical sconces, not unlike those at the Arcane University, lit the inside corridor. It led to a T-intersection, which Gisella judged to sit in about the center of the building. A sign posted on the wall indicated those seeking contract services, including contracts of marriage, should go left while all others should proceed to the right.

Qaliah nudged Gisella as she pointed at the sign and grinned. "Are we getting married?"

The Golden Slayer laughed and turned right. "Not today."

The corridor led to a pair of iron-banded oaken doors, through which the women entered the temple's main gathering space. The hearth room featured a rectangular depression in the floor that ran almost the length of the room. Iron grates covered either end of the fireplace, while the center remained open, allowing priests to tend the hearth.

Several small groups stood in clusters around the room. Gisella determined from their garb they were not priests. She noticed two priests on either side of the fire, stoking it with fresh logs taken from piles at the sides of the room. Although they kept the flames low and steady, the fire added to the heat of the day, and Gisella felt fresh beads of sweat drip down her spine.

A man wearing leather-trimmed black robes approached them with open arms and a smile. His close-cropped curly greying hair framed his face, and his steel-colored eyes sat deep behind a wide nose.

"Welcome to the Hearth of the Sacred Family. Hon's blessings be upon you."

Gisella placed her palm on her chest and bowed, nudging the fiendling to do the same. "Thank you. My friend and I are hoping to find some information."

"I am Hearth Master Nolan. I would be happy to…" His smiled faded when he saw the golden seashell hanging at the base of Gisella's neck. He regarded both women and sneered, "We want nothing to do with your debauchery here."

The fiendling poked him in the chest. "You could use some debauchery."

He stepped backward, pulling a stylized hearth amulet from within his robes. He thrust the symbol in Qaliah's direction. "Back, Fiendling! I'll not fall prey to your corruptions!"

The fiendling grabbed the priest's arm, pulling it downward and twisted it behind his back as she spun him. In a flash, one of her daggers pressed into the soft flesh under his chin.

"It's not nice to go sticking bits of metal in someone's face."

Gisella caught the fiendling's arm and lowered her weapon. Qaliah released Hearth Master Nolan without having to be prompted by Gisella, and the man backpedaled, holding his symbol aloft and calling out for assistance.

"Damn it." Gisella pulled Qaliah along as she retreated toward the hallway. "Obviously, we must look elsewhere for the help we need."

She flung the fiendling into the hallway and bowed to Hearth Master Nolan before she turned and ran. Within moments, the women returned to the street, losing themselves in the crowd.

Chapter 12

Clink, clank, whirr, whirr, whirr.
Clank, buzz, clink, clink, clink.

Kale dreamt of wheels and gears. Motion. Spinning. Locking, unlocking.

Clink, whirr, clink, clink, clink.

Intricate mechanisms, clear as day, sprang into his mind. A box opened, and Kale's eyes snapped wide. His mate slept curled up at his side. Not wishing to disturb her, he rolled out of bed, rubbed the sleep from his eyes, and left the bedchamber.

At least I'm not dreaming of The Sundering. The flickering flame from a passing torch in the hand of a patrolling guard cast dancing shadows on the counter. Without stepping outside to examine the positions of the stars and moons, Kale could not determine how long until dawn broke. He decided instead to open the door to the cellar and acquaint himself with the volumes that lined the shelves along the stairs. The drak ran a clawed finger along the spine of a thick tome bound in faded, red leather. The sweet smell of vanilla and almond assaulted him as he stood with his snout near the books. It reminded him of sweets from a nearby bakery. His stomach rumbled.

Now that his puzzle box was no longer a pressing mystery, the drak needed something to occupy his time. Back home in Drak-Anor, there was no shortage of defenses to tune, but the defense needs of an aboveground city full of bigoted humans were much different, and he wasn't keen on volunteering to help tune siege weapons or build traps.

He hoped to find a diversion in one of the old tomes. Kale figured that since Delilah was out from under the boot of the human archmage, she would spend most of her time investigating the purpose of the runed circle in the cavern beneath his home. However, his sister had come by only once since she defeated Manless. He decided to search through every one of these ancient books and solve the cavern's puzzle himself.

The drak began at the top of the stairs with the volume closest to the door. It was written in a language he couldn't read, so he moved down the line. He perused histories, cookbooks, and personal journals, many of them unintelligible to him, but a few volumes stood out. He pulled out each tome of interest a little farther than the rest on the shelf as he picked through the rows one by one.

A muffled scream interrupted his ruminations. He ran up the stairs and into the shop. Two draks stood at the cloudy shop window, shielding their eyes from the sun's glare as they peered into the street. More screams from outside relieved his anxiety that the earlier scream was his mate's.

"What's going on?"

"Oh! Kale, we were just trying to find that out ourselves." Ori stepped away from the window.

Kali motioned for Kale to join her. "Where were you? I thought you were out. People are running around and looking up. Maybe another giant is falling from the sky?"

Kale opened the shop's door and joined the throngs of draks and minotaurs staring and pointing above them. He searched with his eyes, and then he saw the leathery wings, the ridged spine, and the long, sinuous neck.

A dragon.

Kale's heart leapt until he realized because of the way the sun glinted off the dragon's scales, like packed snow covered with ice, it probably was not Terrakaptis

The dragon circled and flew out of sight toward Grimstone Keep. Kale pushed through the crowd and headed toward the upper city. He heard Kali calling after him and stopped long enough for her to catch up.

"Where do you think you're going?"

Kale pointed to the sky. "I need to find that dragon."

His mate clutched his arm. "Why? What do you think that's going to accomplish?"

He pointed at the sigil on his chest. "If it's attacking the city, I can stop it. Maybe it's looking for the egg."

"Kale"—she pulled him toward her—"it's probably hungry, angry, and looking to do some damage."

Even if that were true, Kale didn't believe the dragon would harm him. After what he saw in the puzzle box, he wasn't sure he cared about its intentions toward the humans.

He tapped the sigil on his chest again. "I know it won't hurt me. Terrakaptis gave me this. He knew something like this would happen."

She released him. "Fine. Then I'm coming with you."

He paused. "Should we bring the egg?"

"That's crazy. The dragon will assume we stole it."

"I'd rather have it and not need it than go all the way out there and have to come all the way back for it."

Kali huffed. "Fine. Wait for me here. I'll go get it." As she left, Kale overheard her muttering herself about how she was going to sneak it past Ori. While she was gone, Kale purchased a few hand pies for them to eat while they traveled. After a short time, Kali returned, carrying the egg on her back within the enchanted harness, and they sped through the streets, ducking under minotaur legs and dodging humans who ran to their families. City guards shouted at people to clear the streets, and many took their posts on the city's battlements.

They couldn't see the dragon, but shouting from the people in the streets guided them toward Grimstone Keep. They had almost reached it when Kale saw the dragon fly overhead again toward the countryside. He led Kali through a side street and continued toward the nearest city gate.

When the two draks arrived at the gate, guards barred their way. They held out their hands, and one sentinel stepped forward. "None shall pass, by order of Captain Tepes."

The gates beyond were barred shut, and the portcullis had been lowered. Kale pleaded to be allowed out of the city to no avail. He turned his back on the guards and searched for alternatives. Guard towers flanked the gate, to the right of which stood a small stable and to the left stood a warehouse. Kale and Kali detoured down an alley that passed between the warehouse and the next building, a burned shell that might once have been someone's home. Behind the warehouse ran another alley, narrow enough he could touch the city wall with one hand and the wall of the warehouse with the other while walking down the center of it. Kali followed behind him.

He glanced up. The battlement hung over the alley far enough that climbing the wall while carrying it risked disaster for the dragon egg. Climbing to the roof of the warehouse appeared easier and safer. Kale jumped up, digging his claws into the mortar between the stones and using the city wall for additional support. Once he had a firm grip, Kali secured the pack with the egg between his wings and followed him, helping him find footing as they climbed.

When they reached the roof of the warehouse, they scrambled up to the peak. At the end, farther from the gate, a section of the city wall extended over the city to go around a watchtower. The peak on which they stood did not quite meet the battlement, but it ran closer than along the other sections. For an adept jumper, it was a dangerous, possibly deadly, jump. Trained jumpers didn't have wings, however.

Kale handed Kali the egg, placed his arms around his mate, and spread his wings. Together, they leaped and he flapped his wings, using all of his strength. Gaining just enough altitude, he grabbed hold of the edge of the battlement, and they scrabbled their legs to gain purchase on the rough stone. The clanking of armor and scraping of boots against the surface of the parapet alerted them to the presence of a passing sentry. They dangled quietly until the he passed before pulling themselves onto the battlement.

Wary guards on either side watching for danger spotted the draks as soon as they mounted the battlement. They shouted and drew their weapons, charging toward Kale and Kali. Wasting no time, Kali pulled his mate forward and sprang off the opposite side, spreading his wings and catching an updraft that allowed them to glide. The shouting guards receded into the distance, and to Kale's relief, they did not shoot them with their bows.

As he struggled to maintain altitude, he searched for the dragon, locating it ahead a few miles, near a farm. It sat near a paddock of cows that sped toward the opposite side of their enclosure, jumping over one another in a desperate attempt to avoid becoming a midday snack.

When they set down in a grassy meadow, Kali shoved her mate away. "You know, one of these days, I'm going to stop going along with your crazy ideas."

He didn't know quite how to respond, adjusting the straps of the egg harness before he donned it. "Come on, let's meet this dragon."

* * *

Gisella didn't stop running until they entered a small plaza near the Garden Gallery.

"Hee! That was fun." Qaliah held her side and giggled. "Still, having people turn me away because of this"—she flicked her tail—"and these"—she pointed to her horns—"is starting to wear thin."

"Things couldn't have been that much better in Muncifer." Gisella had not followed Qaliah's comings and goings in the southern city. Indeed, she had barely interacted with her, despite having spent so much time at the Arcane University.

"They weren't, but at least they liked me at the Enchanter's Focus." The fiendling sheathed her dagger and strode into the grassy area underneath a willow tree. She sighed and picked at some leaves on one of the branches.

"You can remain here, if you like." Gisella laid her hand on the fiendling's shoulder. She understood the trepidation of ignorant folk when dealing with fiendlings. However, despite misgivings about Qaliah's recklessness, she found her likeable enough. "These people fear what they don't understand."

"What's to understand?" The fiendling plucked one of the young green leaves. "I was born a bastard child with demon blood. Obviously, I'm one of the most vile, wicked, and evil people there can be." She stared at the back of her hand. "I was hoping I'd fit in better here."

Gisella took Qaliah's hand. People recognized, intellectually, Qaliah's appearance was superficial, but the stigma of fiendish blood ran through her veins; her horns and tail made that unmistakable.

"I won't abandon you."

"I know." The fiendling turned toward Gisella and hugged her tightly, laying her head against her chest. Gisella fought the urge to wrinkle her nose at the acrid scent of brimstone that lingered on her friend. "I just wish…"

"What?" Gisella looked down and stroked the fiendling's hair.

Qaliah stared into Gisella's icy blue eyes. "I wish you liked women."

The Golden Slayer laughed. "Sorry."

The fiendling released the slayer from her embrace. "Nah, it's all right. I find comfort where I can. Some people can afford to be picky." She put the leaf in her mouth and chewed. Spitting it out, she frowned. "Ugh."

"We should go." Gisella wiped her brow. It was cooler in the shade but no less humid.

"Hey, maybe someone in the temple of Pacha can help. I'll bet there's a bunch of drunks there who no one believes who have tons of weird stories that might fit what…"

Gisella smiled and led Qaliah away from the plaza. The fiendling prattled on about the tales of drunken people. Gisella admitted her companion made a good point. The people who turned to Pacha's temple for help were the exact same people who often saw what others missed and no one believed.

It did not take the women long to discover that the god of mirth, madness, and wine had no temple in Vlorey. The nearest shrine sat at the crossroads near the vineyards outside of town. Gisella returned to the main street that ran through the temple district. She considered each building in turn, thinking about where they should go next, and noticed a minotaur holding a spear and watching them. He covered his mottled tawny and dark brown fur with a kilt and breastplate inscribed with the same symbol she noticed above the gates of the Hearth of the Sacred Family.

As he approached, he adjusted the grip on his spear, a subtle change, but one only those experienced with spears would notice. She touched Qaliah to gain her attention, making sure to keep her free hand away from her weapon.

"I heard of a fiendling and her southern lover causing trouble at the temple of Hon."

Gisella chuckled. "Well, this fiendling is not my lover, so I'd say you have the wrong people. Are you a guard?"

"I am a Justicar. Orion Ironhorn of the Divine Tribunal."

The slayer pulled Qaliah close. She knew of the Justicars by reputation only. Similar to the Arcane University's slayers, instead of hunting down renegade wizards, Justicars hunted down anyone they felt was wicked or a lawbreaker.

"You've heard of us." The minotaur lifted his hoof and tapped it with the butt of his spear. He grunted and stomped the dirt. "I'm certain what you have heard is an exaggeration, just as I am certain Hearth Master Nolan embellished his account."

"It's like she said," Qaliah jerked her head toward Gisella. "We're not lovers."

The minotaur rubbed the end of his snout. "Nolan makes assumptions and jumps to conclusions based on those assumptions." He eyed Gisella, scanning her from head to toe, fixing on the golden seashell around her neck.

"Yes, I see the problem." He pointed to the symbol of Aurora. "Nolan is not the most tolerant priest. In particular, he... dislikes... Aurora. Aurora"—he pointed at Qaliah—"Fiendling, I'm sure you can see where I'm going."

Gisella lowered the minotaur's hand. "And I'm sure stories you've heard about both worshippers of Aurora and fiendlings are likewise exaggerated."

The minotaur chuckled and leaned on his spear. "No doubt. I must ask, however, why did you go to the Hearth of the Sacred Family?"

Qaliah pulled away from Gisella and sat on the grass beneath a willow near the side of the road, stretching out and placing her hands beneath her head. The slayer lifted her hair off her neck, allowing a cool breeze to bring relief.

"You should bind your hair up off your neck."

"I'm not used to the heat here."

The minotaur reached into his pouch and withdrew a red ribbon. He turned to show her his own plaited mane. "Take this. It will help."

"Thank you. I keep losing hair ties." Gisella took the ribbon and braided her hair with it. "My companion and I seek information. We came north following rumors of the Lich Queen."

Orion chuckled and scratched the back of his leg with his hoof. "There are always rumors regarding the Lich Queen. The ignorant invoke her name to explain any ill tidings, particularly as a double-dark night approaches."

"Double-dark, eh?" Qaliah perked up. "Bad things that happen when both moons are dark always get blamed on fiendlings, too, especially when the moons are dark for three consecutive nights."

"It is quicker to make assumptions about the phases of the King and Queen and fix blame based on ignorance and superstitions than it is to seek the truth." Orion snorted.

Gisella rubbed her arms and observed an old woman and what must have been her grandchild stroll across a nearby bridge, stopping to watch ducks swim in the water. "So, there is nothing to the rumors, then?"

"There are strange goings-on." Orion glanced around them, as if searching for eavesdroppers. He leaned in close to Gisella. "I am forbidden to speak of them. In this instance, my duty trumps justice." He spat on the ground and scowled.

"But if I seek the truth…" Gisella touched the minotaur's muscular arm. She noted how soft his fur felt.

"One might learn something at the Red Crypt, but more than that, I cannot say."

Orion picked up his spear and cradled it in his arms. He eyed Qaliah. "Stay out of trouble. Tomorrow night, stay indoors, Fiendling. Find a man or woman, have some wine, do things of which Hearth Master Nolan would disapprove, but stay off the streets." He left the two women to contemplate his words as he joined a crowd of pedestrians moving toward the Temple of the Sky to worship at the altar of Tinian, King of the Gods.

"Well, I hope Pancras can sweet-talk the priests of Aita into revealing something helpful." Qaliah picked herself off the grass and took Gisella's arm. "I think we should follow his suggestion and find some men for tomorrow night."

Gisella resolved not to spend the night in the arms of a strange man, so she strolled with the fiendling out of the temple district, and they headed toward the Screeching Griffon. She hoped Pancras's luck had served him better.

* * *

His schedule mandating no official duties at the university until the afternoon, Pancras seized the opportunity that morning to visit the Red Crypt. Like the other houses of worship in Vlorey, it was located on the temple district island. Despite that, the Red Crypt seemed isolated from the others.

Yew and pomegranate trees surrounded a tall, narrow building constructed of red-veined marble, onto which carved, bas-relief scenes depicted Aita's marriage to Nethuns, Prince of the Sea, and her subsequent descent into the underworld. The building featured neither windows nor doors. Steps led up into a dark mausoleum, lit only by candles. A long, single chamber composed the interior. A few people sat in pews on either side of the center aisle, at the end of which stood an obsidian statue of the Princess of the Underworld. An ebony wood catafalque rested before her. Ravens surrounded Aita's feet. Held aloft in her left hand were the scales with which she weighed one's deeds when they stood before her in the afterlife.

Priests wearing crimson-dyed linen robes tended the candles. As Pancras crossed the threshold into the temple proper, he felt Shatterskull thrum at his side. A bell tolled at the rear of the mausoleum. The priests turned to face him and dropped to their knees.

"Hail, Bonelord! Aita graces this temple with her Chosen."

The adulation stopped Pancras in his tracks. He glanced at his maul and noticed the gleaming, red skull of Aita on its face. He had not expected the temple itself to acknowledge his presence. The people seated in the pews turned and stared at him.

The minotaur cleared his throat. "Good morning."

One of the priests stood and approached Pancras. The others returned to their duties. The priest crossed his arms over his chest, resting his palms on his shoulders, and bowed.

"We are honored, lord."

Pancras waited until the man stood. He was unsure how to respond to the bowing and scraping, so he decided to ignore it. "I'm hoping you can help—"

"Oh yes, of course." The man rubbed his hands together. "We are all at your disposal, lord."

"Please, my name is Pancras." He took the man by the shoulder and walked with him through the pews to the side of the room. "I have been granted visions—"

"By our lady? How marvelous! No one here has been so touched in years—"

The minotaur raised a finger in the man's face. "Stop interrupting, I don't have all day." Pancras hated being rude, but the man's enthusiasm grated on his nerves.

"My apologies." The priest bowed again.

"What is your name?"

"I am Brother Maynard."

"Who is the high priest here?" Pancras decided the best way to obtain what he needed was to ascend the hierarchy.

"I am eldest." Maynard smiled and spread his arms. "But now that you're here—"

"No, no, no." Pancras frowned and held up his hands. "I'm committed to the Arcane University. My duties to our lady are more focused. I'm not here to lead this temple. I seek information."

"I see." Brother Maynard's smile vanished, and he tilted his head downward, while simultaneously glancing up at Pancras like a child unjustly chastised. "What would you like to know, lord?"

Pancras licked his lips and rested his hand on the haft of his maul. Aita's power still flowed through it, unbidden by him. "I've come investigating the Lich Queen."

Brother Maynard's eyes widened, but then he tightened his lips and shook his head. "No. I know nothing."

The minotaur laid his hand on the human's shoulder, his fingers reaching halfway to the man's shoulder blade. "Brother…"

Brother Maynard grasped Pancras's arm. He pulled down, but could not budge it. He ended up lifting himself closer to the minotaur's head and whispered, "Not here. Meet me at Ravenbrier Meadery at dusk tomorrow."

"Where is that, exactly?" Pancras shook the human off his arm.

Brother Maynard fell to the floor, straightening his robes as he regained his footing. He glared daggers at the other priests who turned to regard the commotion. Once they returned to their duties, he motioned for Pancras to accompany him to the entrance.

"Ravenbrier makes the best mead in Vlorey, nay all of Cardoba, but you won't find their sweet nectar in the taverns around town. Oh no, you must leave the city for that." Brother Maynard kept his voice low. "An hour north along the King's Road. It's the only place of import between here and Verdant Palace."

From conversations he overheard during the past few days, Pancras surmised the priest referred to the castle north of the city from which the king of Vlorey ruled what little territory the city-state had carved from Cardoba for its own.

"Very well." Pancras turned to leave and glanced over his shoulder at Brother Maynard. "I hope you're not wasting my time."

"I would not dream of it, lord." Brother Maynard crossed his arms over his chest and bowed. Pancras left the man to his duties and exited the temple. As he crossed the threshold again, he felt Aita's power dissipate from Shatterskull. He glanced down and noticed its unadorned face returned to normal. The minotaur could not determine what exactly bothered him about the human priest. He made his way to the Screeching Griffon, hoping Gisella and Qaliah had discovered something useful.

* * *

Delilah took her seat in the council chambers and waited for the other members of the Court of Wizardry to arrive. Sentinels flanked the doors and the dais upon which all the chairs of the high wizards sat. She didn't know any of the guards' names and wondered if it would be proper to ask. The chamber lay quiet, a welcome contrast to the bickering among assembled wizards when the court was in session. The drak swung her legs back and forth as she waited. They didn't hit the floor, and she contemplated whether it would be worth the trouble of having a footrest added or her chair shortened.

She toyed with the idea of making the Frost Queen wait until the following day, but while Delilah felt the need to assert her authority, she didn't think any good could come of deliberately antagonizing the sorceress from the south.

After a few minutes, The Green and Brown Wizards arrived.

"There will be no others for this session." The Green Wizard took the seat to Delilah's left.

The Brown Wizard took the seat on her right. "They deem this a local matter."

Delilah gestured to the guards by the door. "You can let her in now."

One of the guards opened the door and spoke with Seneschal Lyov. The Frost Queen pushed her way past the old man and the guard.

"It's about time. I did not travel from the Southern Watch to while away my day listening to some old fool prattle on about inconsequential gossip."

The Green Wizard regarded Archmage Delilah. "This seems familiar."

"Alysha has always been rude and impatient." The Brown Wizard nodded.

Delilah held up her hand to silence the high wizards. "What do you want? I already told you the penalties for delinquency have been rescinded."

"I want to see my sister. Where is she?"

The archmage glanced at the two high wizards seated on either side of her and again at the Frost Queen. "Sister? Who is your sister?"

"She refers to The Golden Slayer, Archmage." The Green Wizard leaned against the back of her seat and steepled her fingers in front of her mask.

"The Golden… oh. The one who left with Pancras?" Delilah almost forgot that a slayer had left with her friend. A pang of grief flashed in her heart as she realized she might not see him again. She pushed away the thought and returned her attention to the wizard before her.

"She accompanied another wizard to Vlorey."

The Brown Wizard nodded. "To ensure his arrival."

"Vlorey?" Alysha's jaw fell open. She snapped it shut and clenched her teeth as her knuckles turned white on the shaft of her staff. Blue tendrils swirled around the staff's crown and then dissipated into wispy azure smoke. "Of all the fool-headed…"

Delilah noticed the guards' hands drop to their weapons, and she leaned forward. In the distance, she heard the chime of the university's mealtime bells. "Is there a problem with Vlorey?"

"Not as such, no." Alysha pinched the bridge of her nose. "It's a family matter, one Gisella should not be addressing by herself."

"She's not alone. Pancras is with her." Delilah knew if there were trouble, Pancras would lend a hand, regardless of his personal feelings about the slayer.

"That is not a comfort." Alysha's shoulders slumped. "Archmage, might I request a private audience?"

Delilah glanced at the Green Wizard, her eyebrow raised. The high wizard inclined her head ever so slightly and lowered her voice to a barely perceptible whisper. "That is your choice."

"Very well." Archmage Delilah stood. "I have a task I must assign my apprentice. Meet me in my chambers in an hour."

Alysha bowed. "Thank you, Archmage."

Delilah waited until she exited before clutching her staff and following her.

"Archmage?"

She stopped at the sound of the Brown Wizard's voice. She turned to face the two high wizards. They descended from the dais and stood before Delilah. "We appreciate that you are still uncertain. However, you are archmage. You may do as you wish. Rest assured, if you overstep your bounds, we will warn you."

"I'll try to remember that." In truth, Delilah recognized she was ignorant of how far was too far. In Drak-Anor, she had been responsible for only her brother. The thought that she now possessed authority over all the wizards of Andelosia, possibly Calliome, intimidated her. That the Frost Queen accepted her request to wait an hour encouraged her. Delilah didn't have a momentous task for Katka; she merely wanted her apprentice to fetch sustenance.

She found her pupil in the practice area, setting the training dummies on fire. Delilah watched Katka practice until the young woman noticed her.

"Del… Archmage!" Katka curtsied. "I didn't see you there."

"It's quite all right." Delilah held up a hand to cut off further apologies. "I just have quick favor to ask."

Katka secured her wand in its holster at her waist and smoothed her robes. "Sure. Oh! Did you see that dragon? I think it was attacking Grimstone Keep. Some of the older students—"

The archmage took her apprentice by the arm and led her away from the practice area. "The older students know nothing of what's going on. The dragon is with the Frost Queen. I'm meeting with her in an hour."

"The Frost Queen?" Katka covered her mouth with her hand. "She's here?"

"Yes." Delilah pointed the young woman toward the Enchanter's Focus. "Fetch me something to eat, will you? I won't have time to go and sit; I must prepare for this meeting. Bring it to our chambers?"

"Okay. Anything in particular?"

Delilah shook her head. "No." She caught Katka's arm as her apprentice turned to leave. "No, wait. None of that fish stew. I don't like it."

"Me neither." Katka stuck out her tongue. "I think he makes that to try to cover up the fact that the fish are rotten. I'll be back soon."

The archmage left her apprentice to her task and returned to her chambers. She straightened the outer office, hiding away all the research materials she'd accumulated regarding dragon eggs and runes. She intended to reveal neither Kale's egg nor the runed circle in his cellar to the Frost Queen. By the time she finished tidying, Katka returned with their meals. The drak wasted no time filling her belly. She had a feeling the Frost Queen would arrive early.

She was not disappointed.

Chapter 13

So, basically, all you learned was to ask around the same places I went?" Pancras stared into his bowl of stew as he stirred. Bright floral aromas and sharp spices wafted to his nose. He hadn't thought to ask what sort of meat they served this night and fervently hoped it wasn't beef.

"Yeah, it was a really productive day." Qaliah snorted and drained her mug of ale.

"Unfortunately, everyone we spoke to seemed reluctant to speak of the strange goings-on." Gisella sniffed her mead and sipped it.

"Yes, I experienced that, too." Pancras lifted a spoonful of the stew and tasted it. Pork. He sighed in relief and ate another spoonful. "The priest of Aita said he'd speak to me at Ravenbrier Meadery about it, but not here in town."

The fiendling looked up. "The meadery? I'm coming with you."

"I think we should all go together." The Golden Slayer chuckled. "We spoke to a minotaur who was forthcoming. He suggested we ask at the Red Crypt, in fact. How far away is this meadery?"

Pancras swallowed his food. "An hour north, toward Verdant Palace. We're to meet him at dusk."

"Dusk?" Gisella examined her mug of mead. "Tomorrow is a double-dark night, you know."

"Is it?" Pancras hadn't paid attention to the lunar cycles. "So?"

"The minotaur warned us to stay off the streets."

"What's he going to do to us if we don't?" Qaliah waved her spoon in Gisella's direction. "Is the big bad Justicar going to come hunt us down at the meadery?"

"Justicar?" Pancras had heard stories of the Justicars of the Tribunal. He dismissed them as fabrications, of course.

"The minotaur we met, Orion, I think"—Gisella bit her lip as she recalled his name—"he said he was a Justicar. He was nice enough."

"Well, double-dark nights may be infrequent, but they're nothing to worry about. Most trepidation about them originated in peasant superstitions." Even when he practiced necromancy full time, Pancras never found a double-dark night better or worse conditions in which to practice that type of magic. "Pack your bedrolls. We'll stay out by the meadery if necessary. I don't want to run afoul of the Justicars."

As they resumed their meal, more people shuffled into the inn. The quiet buzz of conversation rose to a roar as merchants complained about their customers and each other. Friends and neighbors swapped gossip over pints of ale and traded barbs and pleasantries as only lifelong friends could.

Through it all, Pancras overheard no mention of disturbances or anxiety over the upcoming double-dark night. He marveled at how they could be so calm. *Or perhaps, their rulers have instilled so much fear into them, they're numb to it.*

"I am going to turn in. I trust the two of you will have everything in order by the time we need to depart tomorrow?"

"We shall." Gisella raised her mug. Pancras nodded his confidence she would keep Qaliah on task, and he headed upstairs.

* * *

The Frost Queen knocked on Delilah's chamber door before they finished tidying up from their meal. Delilah clutched her staff and motioned for Katka to let her in. Alysha swept past the young woman, her robes billowing around her like white smoke.

"Archmage, I must speak to you about my sister"—she cast a glance at Katka—"alone."

Delilah adjusted the grip on her staff. "I trust my apprentice."

"I don't." The sorceress turned and shoved Katka into the hall. "No offense."

She shut the door just as Katka opened her mouth to protest.

Archmage Delilah snarled. "That was uncalled for."

Alysha beat the bottom of her staff against the door. "Take a walk." She leaned her staff against the jamb and clasped her hands behind her back as she paced. "What I have to say is for your ears alone. I'm not keen to trust you, either, but you're the archmage. You have authority that I do not."

"The way you swagger around, who would know?" Delilah scowled as the woman paced before her door. She thought about recalling Katka but remembered she promised herself earlier not to needlessly antagonize a human who traveled on the back of a dragon.

"My sister no doubt realizes this, but she is traveling into grave danger. I need a decree from you to put the resources of the Vlorey Arcane University at my disposal."

"What?" Delilah blinked. She wanted to confirm what Alysha just requested.

"You've heard of the Lich Queen? The Witch Queen? Yes?"

Familiar with the stories, Delilah recalled Lady Milena of Almeria showing them a tapestry depicting the Battle of Badon Hill. Even as isolated as Drak-Anor had been most of her life, word reached them of a rampaging sorceress seeking to dominate the land, being killed, and then rising up even more powerful than before to try again.

"Of course."

"My sister and I have always believed that while her physical body was destroyed at the Battle of Badon Hill nearly thirty years ago, her spirit endured. Weakened, of course, but since then, growing more powerful."

The archmage waved her hand and leaned on her staff. "Yes, there's always stories like that. She died, cursed the land, cursed the victors—"

"They're not just stories. If she's out there still, as a disembodied spirit, she can return."

"How?" Resurrection magic was not a topic Delilah studied, although considering what happened to Pancras in Almeria, she considered devoting some time to it.

"The easiest way would be for her to possess a suitable receptacle. One that would offer little resistance, say her kin."

Delilah narrowed her eyes. "She has kin?"

"Granddaughters, two of them." Alysha tapped her chest with two fingers. "Someone not connected by blood could resist if their will was strong enough, but the bonds of blood are a weakness if the spirit of your kin wishes to possess you."

Realization dawned, and Delilah's eyes widened. "You're the granddaughter of the Lich Queen?"

"Yes, and I'm going to go get to my sister before my grandmother does. I'd like to do it with the Arcane University's help. She is a slayer, after all."

Delilah blew out a breath. "I'll speak to the Council of Wizards."

"No!" Alysha slashed her hand through the air. "They cannot know of this. I was trained only because they didn't know of our connection. Gisella was accepted as a slayer only because of their ignorance. They cannot know."

The drak closed her eyes and tilted back her head. *Great, more secrets.* She inhaled deeply. The aroma of the remnants of their dinner wafted into her nose. *Dinner was good. I could use some more ale, though.*

"Archmage!"

Delilah's attention returned to the Frost Queen. "How do I know this isn't some plot by you to claim the Lich Queen's power as your own?"

Alysha stopped pacing and knelt to bring herself to the drak's eye level. "You don't. I doubt there's any proof I can offer you that my intentions are true."

A smile spread across Delilah's face as an idea blossomed in her head. "Then I'm coming with you. I've never been to Vlorey, but I've fought many difficult battles, and I know where we can recruit another dragon, a Firstborne, to verify your story and blast that Lich Queen back to the Age of Legend."

* * *

Following the road out of Vlorey toward the meadery proved a simple journey. Gisella noted that the hard-packed dirt road was both well traveled and well patrolled. Between the city and Ravenbrier Meadery, they encountered two squads of soldiers clad in the livery of the City Watch of the Free City of Vlorey. As they passed, the guards stepped off the road to allow the travelers room but eyed them, as if searching for signs of malfeasance.

Gisella looked forward to this visit to the meadery. Not only might they learn something to further their investigation, but she was curious about this mead from the north. What she had sampled thus far was not bad, a bit more floral than that to which she was accustomed and lacking in the spice that meaderies in the Four Watches added.

A veritable sea of green extended before them. North of Vlorey lay Verdant Point, so named for its coast-to-coast woodland. The road wound through the forest, past the estates of several nobles, and toward Verdant Palace, official residence of the King of Vlorey.

Trees had been cleared from the immediate area on each side of the road, creating a well-defined lane for travelers to follow. This meant, of course, that the sun beat upon them for most of the day, and the surrounding trees offered no shade.

Gisella offered silent thanks to Orion for her new hair tie. Keeping her golden locks off her neck helped keep her cool, but she still felt as if the sun would bake her.

"How do people here stand this heat? And the sun? It's so intense." She fanned herself with the edge of her cloak.

Qaliah closed her eyes and turned her face toward the sun. "Nice, yeah? None of that bitter cold that flows down from the mountains in Muncifer." Her ebony skin glistened with sweat, but she didn't seem at all bothered by the heat.

"It gets this warm in Drak-Anor, but the air is so heavy here." Pancras wiped sweat from his brow and muzzle. "I feel damp all the time."

"It's oppressive." Gisella shielded her eyes as she searched the sky for clouds. Even with the sun about to set, it promised to be an uncomfortable night.

"Whiners." Qaliah rode ahead before turning Comet around to face them and gesturing to the forest. "Everything is covered with things growing. No bare rocks. No snow. It's beautifully hot. I may never leave."

Pancras snorted. "You almost sound like an elf. Rocks are part of the world, too. They're solid, stable, the foundations of our homes."

The fiendling tucked her hair behind one of her ears. "Fiendling… elf… we all have pointed ears."

Gisella cringed and blinked away a drop of perspiration that ran into her eyes. "They don't have horns. Or hooves. Or a tail. I doubt an elf would appreciate the comparison."

"You're right." Pancras maneuvered Stormheart next to Gisella and her mount, Moonsilver. "I just meant most elves are enamored of trees and the like. The fiendlings in Drak-Anor don't pine for them."

"They're missing out." Qaliah held back Comet and waited for Gisella and Pancras to catch up. "I'd much rather be out here with the sky above than living under a mountain."

The Golden Slayer agreed with that sentiment, although

she preferred the wide open tundra of her home to these woodlands. She liked being able to see to the ends of the world and not have to worry about hidden dangers behind the shrubs and bushes. In the Four Watches, forests were home to many dangers

As they approached Ravenbrier Meadery, they exited the road and traveled down a lane lined with trees bearing curious fan-shaped leaves. Apiaries dotted the clearing, set far enough away from the main road that travelers did not encounter many wandering bees. The meadery itself, a flat, white stone building with a gently sloped roof covered in reddish-brown tiles, sat at the center of a group of fluted columns with unadorned capitals. To one side, a fenced in area with covered stalls and stables waited for visitors.

They left their horses in the care of stable hands and entered the meadery. The air smelled of flowers and sweet honey. A woman stood behind the counter, hammering a tap into a barrel of mead. Her dark hair hung in a long, tight braid down her back. In the corner, while seated on a stool, a man tuned a lute. He glanced up as the three entered.

"Welcome to... Raven... briar... minotaur, fiendling..."

The woman stood and tossed a checkered rag over her shoulder. "Shut your mouth, Alfie. You'll catch bees. We've trouble enough keeping them alive."

She moved around the counter and patted his cheek. He blushed and stared at his lute. "You'll have to excuse my son, here. He's not used to such diverse visitors."

The woman bowed. "I am Tamera Ravenbrier. Welcome to my meadery. I'm surprised to see you all this late. I was considering closing up early."

Pancras led Qaliah to the counter and pulled out a stool for her. Gisella bowed her head to Tamera. "You don't get a lot of visitors at night?" She took a seat alongside Pancras.

Tamera shrugged and smiled. She stepped around the counter and brushed off crumbs from in front of the three.

"On a normal summer night, sure. But it's a double-dark night tonight, and the city folk stop coming out when the King and Queen slumber."

"We're supposed to be meeting someone here." Pancras cleared his throat. "Brother Maynard from… a priest from the city."

"Sure, we know Maynard. Don't we, Mum?" Alfie turned his attention away from his lute. "Haven't seen him in a few weeks."

The dark-skinned woman placed mugs of mead before Gisella, Pancras, and Qaliah. "Well, have a mead while you wait. If you're meeting him, I'm sure he'll be along."

Gisella sniffed at the mug and took a long draught. The floral nose hid a cloying sweetness, and she detected a hint of pepper. It reminded her of the mead from home, although it was just different enough to be memorable. "Oh, that's nice."

"Thank you." Tamera bowed and smiled. "Best mead in the whole of the north, if I do say so myself. Hungry?" She looked past them toward her son. "Alfie, go find your sister."

The young man hopped off his stool and carried his lute to the door. He opened it far enough to stick out his head. "Varina! Varina, get over here!"

"Alfie!" Tamera slapped her rag on the counter. "Go. Get her. Not yell for her. I could've done that myself."

Alfie snorted and shut the door behind him. Tamera clenched her jaw as she shook her head. "My dolt of a son…"

"Do you know anything about the double-dark nights in Vlorey?" Gisella sipped her mead, eyeing the woman over the rim of her mug.

"Everyone seems very secretive about them"—the minotaur drained his mug and wiped his mouth on his sleeve—"fearful, even. I would have thought people in a city like Vlorey would know the phases of the moons are nothing to be feared."

Tamera refilled their mugs. "We get to the city markets a few times a month, but the bees and our sheep keep us pretty busy around here. I don't remember the last time I was in the city at night. We're close, but we don't hear much about goings-on."

"This stuff doesn't get tongues wagging?" Qaliah held up her mug. "It's strong."

"City gossip isn't what brings folks out this way." The woman jerked her thumb behind her. "Most of our regulars come from Verdant Palace or from the fishing villages along the coast."

"The coast? Along Verdant Point?" Pancras loosened his robes and wiped sweat beaded on the fur of his brow with his sleeve.

"Yes. Now they talk of strange things, but you know how fishermen are."

Gisella glanced at her companions. Their blank expressions matched her own ignorance. She shook her head. "We're not from around here. Of what strange things do they speak?"

"Yeah." Qaliah grinned. "What are the men like?"

"They sit around in their little boats all day, or stand in waist-deep water with their nets, hauling in fish, making up stories to pass the time." Tamera rubbed down the countertop. The door opened and a woman who was an image of her mother entered. It was as though they looked back in time at a much younger Tamera.

"You needed me, Mother?"

"Ah, Varina. Put on your apron." Tamera tossed a smock from behind the bar to her daughter. "Bread and cheese for our guests."

"Wow, a minotaur and a... a..." Varina squinted as she looked at Qaliah. Her grey eyes lingered as she eyed the fiendling up and down. "I... perhaps some jam and honey, as well?"

"Of course, girl!" Tamera snapped her rag at her daughter. "Go on."

Varina smiled at Qaliah as she passed, and the fiendling rewarded her with a wink and a grin.

The minotaur cleared his throat. "Now then, you were saying about the fishermen's tales?"

"Oh." Tamera waved her hand in the air. "They're nonsense, of course. Folks walking beneath the waves, strange moans from the forest at night. I don't pay them any mind. When they're here, I'm working. I don't have time for nonsense gossip."

"Hmm…" Pancras lowered his head and rubbed his right horn.

The door opened again. A red-robed, dark-skinned man entered. His face shone with sweat, and what little hair remained atop his head was matted and laid flat against it. Varina nodded at him. "Maynard."

"Bonelord." Maynard took a knee and bowed before Pancras. The minotaur's eyes widened, and he pulled up the man by his robes.

"That's really not necessary."

"Bonelord?" Tamera cocked an eyebrow and regarded Pancras with narrowed eyes. "There's nobody dying around here today."

"Perhaps we, you and I"—Maynard gestured to himself and Pancras—"could step outside to speak?"

The minotaur shook his head and gestured to Gisella and Qaliah. "These are my companions, my friends. Gisella the Golden Slayer, and Qaliah."

"I really need a fancier name around you two." The fiendling frowned.

Pancras continued, "Anything you say to me they can hear."

Tamera's eyes darted from Pancras to Maynard and back. She threw up her hands and approached the door. "I'll just go check on my daughter. Maybe you want some meat with that bread and honey?"

* * *

Brother Maynard wiped his hands on the front of his robes as he watched Tamera leave. Then he returned his attention to Pancras. The minotaur noted that the man's hands trembled, and he seemed out of breath.

"Are you all right? You don't look well."

Maynard waved his hand and shook his head. "I fell behind so I ran to get here before dark. It's hard work running in this heat. I'll be fine."

Pancras pressed his mug into the priest's hands. Maynard drained the mug and set it on the countertop before wiping his mouth with his sleeve.

"Now, what couldn't you tell me in the city?"

"We believe"—Maynard wrung his hands as his eyes darted back and forth, searching the room for eavesdroppers—"recent disturbances are linked to the Lich Queen. Lord Tyron has forbidden anyone to speak of the incidents or interfere, upon pain of death."

The minotaur furrowed his brow and placed his hand on Maynard's shoulder. "Who is Lord Tyron?"

"Minister of the Council of Lords. He rules the city."

Gisella brushed a stray hair out of her face. "And what of the king? Has he no say?"

The priest shook his head and stared into his empty mug. "Lord Tyron controls information going to and from Verdant Palace. The king is preoccupied with the health of Queen Andraste. She's been ill of late."

Pancras scratched his chin. "Could they be related? Perhaps Lord Tyron has something to do with her ill turn?"

"No, no, we don't think so." Brother Maynard shook his head with vigor. "The queen suffers from… well, those of us who are privy swore not to speak of it. The king feels it would undermine the peoples' love and respect for her."

Qaliah snorted. "Sounds like something she caught from a suitor."

"Goodness, no!" Brother Maynard faced the fiendling, his eyes wide. "The king knows all about it and tends to it. He is a good man."

"Then perhaps he could lend aid"—Gisella pursed her lips at Qaliah and gave her a shake of her head—"if we were to get word to him?"

"I doubt you could get word to him. As I said, Lord Tyron controls all information going to Verdant Palace. Without his say, you couldn't even get through the gates."

"I could." Qaliah grinned.

"A fiendling sneaking around the royal palace?" Pancras covered his eyes with his hand and shook his head. "What could possibly go wrong?"

"Bonelord Pancras is correct." Brother Maynard glanced at his empty mug on the counter. "If you're caught, you'd be killed on sight."

Pancras bit his lip and paced. "I would like to avoid involving the royalty, at any rate. I had a bad experience with that in Almeria." He winced as a twinge of remembered pain shot through his stomach and knee. The minotaur turned to the priest. "What makes you think the Lich Queen is involved?"

"Graves in the necropolis have been disturbed. Tombs lie open and empty." Brother Maynard licked his lips. "It started with veterans of the last war, the dead who defeated the Lich Queen."

Qaliah drew one of her daggers and picked her nails with it. "No one noticed these dead stiffs walking around?"

The priest snapped his head around to face her. "There were rumors, of course, when it first started. Those who spoke of the dead leaving the necropolis were rounded up. It only took a few nights before no one saw anything anymore."

"That would certainly explain the attitudes we encountered." Gisella twirled a stray lock of hair around her finger. "The people on the streets don't act as if anything is amiss, though."

"The people of Vlorey"—Brother Maynard clasped his hands together and shifted his weight—"have lost much to the Lich Queen. Almost an entire generation of good folk in the last war. Of course, the Council of Lords has always been fickle and, at times, despotic. These new decrees are different, true, but they're nothing worse than they're used to. King Conner's options are limited at the moment, but he is trying to make changes. Consensus building takes time."

Pancras nodded. A part of life in Drak-Anor, he avoided politics whenever possible. "And it's difficult when those from whom you need consensus feel they're sacrificing without gain."

"Precisely."

"Forget those stodgy, old bastards, then." Qaliah sheathed her dagger. "Let's just be big damned heroes and deal with it all ourselves. Pancras can deal with the undead, right?"

"To a point." Destroying the undead wasn't the problem; rather, whomever was responsible for raising them en masse was, and if the city leaders were involved, it added a delicate complication.

Pancras took a seat and rubbed his forehead. *Why are the politicians always involved?*

The door creaked open. "Finished your sedition yet?" Tamera poked her head into the room. "I'd like to get back to work."

Gisella bowed. "Our apologies." She gestured to the bar. "Please, don't let us interfere with your work."

Tamera led Varina into the room. The young woman carried a tray laden with a variety of white cheeses, breads, and cured meats. She placed the tray on the counter between Pancras and Gisella.

"Refresh your meads?"

The four made small talk while they supped. Pancras contemplated what he learned as he chewed on a piece of herbed bread slathered with butter. *I should like to be in the necropolis during a double-dark night and see what's really going on.*

"You know, I'd like to go up to one of these fishing villages." Gisella took a long draught of mead and wiped her mouth on her sleeve. "See if there's truth in the stories the fisher folk tell."

"That's a good idea." Pancras nodded. "They're less likely to worry about the decrees of the lords of Vlorey. Alas, I cannot go. I have duties at the Arcane University."

Qaliah took Gisella's arm. "I'll keep her company. Maybe we'll find some strapping, lonely men up there."

Tamera snorted. "Don't settle for those louts." She gestured toward Qaliah. "Besides, they're not very welcoming toward your kind."

"I should be off." Brother Maynard straightened his robes. "There's a priory up the road a bit. It's too late to return to the city now."

"Yes, we suspected as much." Pancras smiled at Tamera. "May we impose upon your hospitality and set up a small camp behind the meadery?" He jingled his coin pouch. "I can compensate you."

With payment for their repast rendered and the meadery suitably compensated for the trouble of housing their horses overnight, Pancras, Gisella, and Qaliah bade good night to Brother Maynard and the meadery family and made their camp behind the main building.

They discussed their strategy for the next several days. Gisella and Qaliah would travel up the coast and talk to folk in the nearby fishing villages while Pancras returned to

Vlorey and observed the next double-dark night from within the city. When morning arrived, they purchased more bread, cured meat, and cheese from Tamera and her family, including a small cask of mead for Gisella, and headed out.

Chapter 14

Kale and Kali crept forward, darting between boulders and shrubs as they closed the distance between the city and the dragon. *I wish we had this harness when we brought the egg down out of the mountains.* Kale returned his attention to the dragon, marveling at how the creature's shimmering scales reflected the sunlight as he chased down a buck, pouncing on it like a mammoth cat.

Even from the distance that separated them, Kale heard the cracking of bones and tearing of sinew as the dragon tore into its meal. His mate's face was drawn tight, and she glanced over her shoulder at the city.

"Don't worry." Kale stroked her arm. "At least he won't be hungry when we face him."

Kali slapped away his hand. "I doubt that little buck will fill his belly. Maybe it's just enough to whet his appetite."

He tapped the sigil on his chest. "A Firstborne put this here. He won't eat me."

"Maybe I'm worried about the dragon eating me." Kali's nostrils flared as her eyes flashed in anger.

Kale swallowed and stroked her arm. "I won't let that happen. Kali"—He held her to prevent her from leaving—"please, I need you with me. I won't let him hurt you. Trust me. Please."

The striped drak closed her eyes and nodded. "Fine. If you weren't my mate…"

He didn't want to ponder that at the moment. "Let's go."

They approached the dragon as it hunkered down, chewing on the remains of the buck. Kale motioned for Kali to follow him as he circled the wyrm. A feeling deep inside cautioned that approaching an eating dragon from behind would be one of the more stupid decisions he could ever make in his life.

Cold mountain wind blew across the boulder-covered plain. The dragon angled its wings to keep their fine membranes from catching wind like sails. Kale couldn't help but stare at the dancing colors playing across his glistening, ice-like scales. The dragon tossed back his head, swallowing a man-sized hunk of buck, and growled deep in his chest.

"I can smell you."

Kale froze in place. His mate gasped and seized his arm, digging her claws into his scales.

"You have the stink of the city upon you, little skulkers. Little sneak-thieves." The dragon swung his head around and inhaled. He locked eyes with Kale before unleashing his icy breath at the two draks.

The sigil in the middle of Kale's chest flared with a brilliant light as the blast of snow and ice reached them. A reflex action, he spread his wings to shield himself and his mate. A frozen curtain enveloped them, passing over and to either side, leaving them unscathed even as it turned the surrounding area frosty white.

Kale grimaced as he felt his mate's claws pierce the flesh on his arm. "Ow!"

"How did I let you talk me into this madness?"

The dragon's breath abated, and he roared into the sky, rearing up on his legs and then descending before them. The ground shook as he landed, and the great beast swung his head down to the draks' level. His eyes fixed on the glowing sigil on Kale's chest.

"*Draevyehfehdin!*" He inhaled deeply through his nose and rumbled. "Old magic. Dead magic."

The drak opened his mouth to speak, but the dragon poked him in the chest with a talon longer than a knight's sword. "Who marked you thus?"

"Terrakaptis, the Earth Dragon." *Now I find out if this mark means as much as he said it does.*

"He lives?"

Kale nodded and pried Kali's fingers loose from his arm. "He lairs at the World Tree in Drak-Anor."

The dragon's eyes lingered on Kali. He sniffed the air. "Did his magic grant you wings, as well? Hmm, and yet, you travel with an egg thief. I smell your prize." Like a child playing knucklebones, he snatched up Kali. Kale dove to catch the egg-laden pack as she screamed and dropped it.

"Wait! Stop!" Kale revealed the egg in the pack. "We didn't steal it. We saved it."

The dragon's eyes narrowed, and a long, sinuous tongue snaked from his mouth, dragging along the drak in his hand. Kali squealed.

"If he doesn't eat me, you'll regret this, Kale!"

Kale swallowed and set the egg before the dragon. "We traveled to the lair of Pyraclannaseous. She was already dead, killed by a wizard, but we found this. We couldn't leave it there."

"Terrakaptis's sister." The dragon licked his lips, bringing Kali to them and kissing her before setting her down alongside her mate. She glared at Kale as she wiped off globules of saliva from her face. "Tell me of this dragon-slaying wizard."

"He… he was the…" Kale glanced over at his mate and moved to help her, but she snarled at him and backed away. "He was the archmage of Muncifer."

"I will destroy him." The dragon reared up and spread his wings.

"You can't." Kale stepped forward, holding up his hands. "He's dead already."

"The murder of a Firstborne must be avenged. It is an affront to the gods."

"My sister killed him." Kale puffed out his chest and spread his wings. "She challenged him to answer for his crimes, including the slaying of Pyraclannaseous."

"I am Yaamkyrsku, the Frost Wyrm of the Southern Watch." The dragon bowed his head before he glanced up and smiled at Kali. "Your mate is tasty. Fortunately, I am sated for now. Besides, you have done the *draev* a service, it seems."

"We've kept the egg safe." Kale approached Kali. She stood a few steps behind him with her arms wrapped around herself. He reached for her, but she shook her head and stepped away from him. "We don't know what to do with it."

Yaamkyrsku rolled it with one of his claws and then picked it up. He cradled it close to his breast. "I would be honored to deliver it to a Firstborne. Where is this Drak-Anor?"

Kale pointed in the general direction of the mountains. "Many months north, in the Dragon Spine Mountains, under the volcano Bloodplume."

"I will find it." Yaamkyrsku leapt into the air and spread his wings. The force of the air blasting down threw Kale to the ground as the dragon took flight.

Kale reached toward the dragon. "Wait! I saw The Sundering. I have questions. We should come with…"

Yaamkyrsku ascended higher and higher, far out of range of Kale's pleas. The dragon flew toward the mountains and angled north.

"Damn it." Kale stood and brushed himself off. He glanced over at his mate. Kali pursed her lips, crossed her arms, and turned without a word.

"Kali, wait!" The drak reached for his mate and chased after her.

Ignoring him, she quickened her pace. He followed behind her, calling after her, but he gave up by the time they reached the city gates. When they returned to Muncifer, the guards had withdrawn their alert, and the gates had opened once more. Curious citizens poured out, hoping to catch a glimpse of the departing dragon, and Kale lost her in the crowd.

His wings drooped as he made his way home. A minotaur selling potatoes from a cart chuckled as Kale shuffled past.

"I know that look."

"Just what I need right now, a wiseacre minotaur." Kale made a rude gesture as he passed. Up ahead, he saw Ori struggling with several scrolls and a tome.

"Oh! Kale. Wow, she's mad. I thought it would be safe to call it an early day."

Kale stopped to pick up a scroll the blue drak dropped and placed it on top of the pile Ori held. "Did she say anything?"

"Oh, no, not really. She complained about needing a bath, I think. There was a lot of swearing."

Kale patted Ori on the shoulder. "All right. We'll see you tomorrow, huh? Maybe I'll take you up to the Arcane University, so we can have lunch with my sister."

"Oh. That'd be great. I really like her, Kale. I hope it's okay to tell you that…"

The striped drak nodded and waved to Ori, leaving the blue drak to ramble to himself. He peeked through the cloudy front window, and seeing no one, cracked the door. When he wasn't immediately assaulted with fruit, books, or profanity, Kale entered and locked the door behind him.

He found his mate standing by their washbasin, stripped to her scales. She stiffened when Kale entered the room, and her tail lashed from side to side.

"Kali?"

The female drak turned to face him, her teeth glinting in the light of their lamps. "I used to think you were a dashing hero."

"I…" Kale wasn't sure what to say. He didn't understand why she was so angry. The egg was gone, no longer their responsibility, and they had talked to a dragon.

"Shut up." She stepped forward and poked him in the chest. "You're reckless and irresponsible. We could have been killed. A dragon almost ate me, Kale." She punctuated each word with a poke of her clawed finger. "*A. Dragon.*"

He placed his hand over the sigil on his chest. "Terrakaptis marked me. I knew Yam… Yammas… ker…" Kale found the frost wyrm's name much more difficult to remember than Terrakaptis. "I knew he wouldn't hurt me."

"Exactly. He wouldn't hurt *you*. Did you know that thing on your chest would protect me? That the dragon would automatically extend the same courtesy to me?" She crossed her arms over her chest as she glared at him.

"Well, I thought… uh." He looked at the floor and rubbed his arm where she had dug in her claws. "I guess… no. I guess I didn't."

Gods, she's right. She could've died, and it would have been my fault. Kale felt his legs weaken and tremble. Tears welled in his eyes, and he eyed his mate. "I'm sorry. I was—"

"You *are*"—she pointed to the front of the shop—"sleeping out there tonight. Get out. I won't banish you from our home, but I am banishing you from our bed. Think about it, Kale. Think about what you really want. Are we mates because Pacha's madness took you, or do you really want a life together?"

She gripped him by the shoulders and spun him, pushing him into the hallway. He stumbled forward and grasped the wall to steady himself. Kale felt her judgement on him as he shuffled away.

* * *

"Do you really think this Firstborne of yours will help us?" Alysha stood against the wall of Delilah's chambers, arms crossed beneath her bosom. Katka sat at the table, flipping through a text that described runes from various cultures.

"Terrakaptis loves my brother." Delilah spun her Herald Stone in her hands. She'd spent the previous day outlining her plan with the Frost Queen and convincing the woman that Katka could be of help, even if they kept the details of Alysha and Gisella's family history from her.

The archmage nodded. "He'll help. The challenge"—she held up a finger—"will be in waking him up. It's only been five years since we first woke him, and he'd been sleeping since The Sundering. The Earth Dragon is a drowsy dragon."

"Sounds typical. Yaamkyrsku should be able to carry two humans and two draks." Alysha eyed Katka. "Good thing you're a little scrawny, girl."

"Hm?" Katka glanced up from her book.

"How did you find your dragon, by the way?" Delilah had never heard of a dragon allying itself with a wizard in the manner in which Alysha and Yaamkyrsku seemed to be.

"It's a long story." The woman picked up her staff. "Let's go talk to him, make sure he's amenable to this plan of yours. You might have to bribe him."

Delilah pocketed the stone and picked up her staff. "With what?" She tapped on the table to gain her apprentice's attention and motioned for the young woman to follow them.

"Katka." Alysha laughed.

"What?" Katka's voice rose to a high pitch.

"Are you a virgin, by chance? He says they taste sweeter."

Delilah caught Alysha's arm as Katka made strangled cries. "We're not giving him my apprentice."

Alysha threw back her head and laughed. Leaning toward them, she put a hand on each of their shoulders. "I'm joking! He doesn't eat virgins. Besides, why would a virgin taste any different than anyone else? I doubt he'd be able to differentiate between a man and a woman."

She shook her head and choked back more laughter. "Come on, you two. Relax."

A half dozen times, instructors with requests for Archmage Delilah's time interrupted their journey across the university's grounds. She told them in passing to make appointments with Seneschal Lyov and that she would deal with each of them in turn.

Once they exited the campus, she let Alysha lead the way and fell back to walk alongside her apprentice. "It'll be a miracle if I have any time at all to give you lessons with all these instructors demanding my time."

"I think they all avoided Vilkan. Besides, I'm learning lots from the books you're letting me read." Katka's eyes watched Alysha the way a sheep watches a wolf just outside its pen as they proceeded.

The Frost Queen slowed her pace as they passed through the market. She turned to the archmage. "You know, for having a dragon just outside their gates, everyone seems awfully calm, don't you think?"

Delilah glanced around and shrugged. "Well, maybe they think it's a wizard thing." She hadn't spent enough time around the populace of Muncifer to understand how they handled unusual events.

Alysha nodded and grinned at a nearby guard. "Impressive dragon, eh?"

"Thank Tinian it's gone. We'd have never stood against the beast if it attacked in earnest." The guard shook his head and strode away from them. Alysha's expression fell, and she moved to stop him, catching only his cloak.

"What do you mean, 'it's gone'?"

"You didn't see?" The guard raised an eyebrow and frowned. "It took off and flew away yesterday shortly before dusk."

"No, no, no, no! Why would he do that?" Alysha broke into a sprint, pulling her robes up high to keep her legs from becoming tangled in the fabric. Delilah and Katka chased after her, catching up as she stopped just outside the city gates.

"Where is my dragon? Yaamkyrsku!" Alysha searched the sky.

Delilah waited for the Frost Queen to compose herself. Meanwhile, Katka approached one of the gate guards and spoke to her. When she returned, Alysha still fumed, pacing back and forth while muttering to herself.

"The guard back there"—Katka gestured with her thumb toward the woman—"says she saw two draks walk out there toward the dragon. A little while later, it flew off, and they returned."

"Two draks? What?" Delilah's heart stopped in her chest. "Who?"

"She said it was too far away to see what happened, but one of the draks, an orange one, seemed really mad. The other one had wings and was following the orange one."

Archmage Delilah squeezed her eyes shut. *Kale. What did you do?*

"Tell me what I already suspect isn't true, Archmage." The Frost Queen's voice sounded as icy as her title.

Delilah rubbed her snout and chuckled. "I think we should go talk to my brother."

* * *

As the two women traveled north from Ravenbrier Meadery, the road remained in good repair until they passed the fork that veered off toward Verdant Palace. Beyond that, the hard-packed surface became increasingly uneven and muddy. The trees bearing fan-like leaves gave way to thinner, dark-trunked timber with small blade-like leaves. Insects buzzed about them, and the narrow, twisted trunks of the forest angled toward the thoroughfare, like arms pulling them in.

"That mead woman made it sound like these people were pretty dull." Qaliah gestured up the road. "Do you really think they'll be able to tell us anything useful?"

"I don't know. If there's any truth to their stories, it might give us something to go on." Gisella wiped her brow. The dense foliage trapped the heat, making the muggy day feel even more oppressive. Although she couldn't see far through the trees, she heard the crash of waves upon rocks to their left and wondered if riding up the beach might provide relief.

"And if they're full of beans, then we'll have squandered the double-dark nights. We know interesting things are happening in the city."

"Perhaps." Gisella, unconvinced the more interesting events were necessarily the more informative ones, turned to face Qaliah. "It's possible what's happening in the city is just a diversion."

"Because it'll be seen by more people?"

"Exactly." Gisella glanced again at the path.

Qaliah clicked her teeth together and plucked a bright orange fruit dangling from one of the few trees that bore them in this forest. Juice sprayed as she bit into it. She frowned and spat it out before she threw the rest of the fruit into the underbrush.

"I wouldn't eat those. Sour."

A few hours after passing the fork to Verdant Palace, they noticed a signpost to the side of the road. Hewn from a curious brown-and-black striped wood and adorned with crude lettering that had been filled in with crushed shells, it read:

EBONWICK.

Beyond the sign, Gisella recognized the shape of squat wooden buildings on either side as the path curved toward the sea. "Maybe you should tuck your tail and pull up your hood, Qaliah."

The fiendling did as the slayer requested as they spurred their horses forward.

An old woman watched them as they entered the village. Twisted into long dreadlocks, her grey hair draped over her shoulders and down her back. She chewed on a stick of some sort as she watched them with cloudy eyes set deep into her dark, weathered, pockmarked face.

Half-timbered huts and shacks flanked the road. Midnight-colored timber sharply contrasted the stark white stone that composed the bottom halves of the buildings. Decorations made of various shells dangled from exposed roof joists. Villagers went about their business with slow, deliberate motions. Some sharpened blades, while others chopped wood. Children sat in circles, scratching the dirt with twigs. Crossing their path, a bare-chested man carried a basket of crabs. He glanced up at them and narrowed his dark eyes.

"Don't get many travelers through here. Best turn back. There's nothing here or further on."

Qaliah nudged Gisella. "That means there's something good."

"No." The man dropped his basket of crabs and stepped forward as he clenched his fists. "There's nothing good. Go away."

Gisella laid her hand on the fiendling's arm to silence her before dismounting Moonsilver. She held up her hands. "We're not looking for trouble. We came here hoping to learn about what's going on in your village."

"Morgan!" An older man hobbled out of a nearby shack. He knocked a thick stick against his leg. Gisella noticed the leg was false, a replacement fashioned from the black wood that grew in the area. "Get those crabs to Nyree."

Morgan scowled but picked up his creel and rushed across the road, turning down a path that wound between the huts. The older man approached the two women, dragging his artificial limb.

"Now, here are two young lasses, making trouble."

Gisella bowed to the old man. "That was not our intention."

"I've not seen skin and hair like yours in ages." He smiled at her. "Which Watch?"

She touched her hair. "Southern Watch."

"Ooh." He shivered and laughed. "Too cold for me. I'm Zeb."

"Gisella. This"—she gestured to the still-mounted fiendling—"is Qaliah."

The fiendling waved and smiled, her bone-white teeth a flash across her shadowed black skin.

"Hm. Her skin's darker than mine. North? Across the sea perhaps? Or north coast of the Wastes?"

Qaliah dismounted, holding her hood to keep it in place. "Around. Best if we don't speak of it, I think."

"One of those types, eh?" He gestured to the rest of the village. "Well, we don't have much to offer travelers. If you're looking for friendly hospitality, you'd best turn around and go back the way you came. I hear there's a good meadery less than a day south."

Gisella took the old man's arm. "You're friendly enough. Besides, we've already been to the meadery. It's excellent, by the way."

"Other than you, this place is as cheerful as a graveyard." Qaliah took the reins of their horses and followed behind Gisella and Zeb.

"Well, we're just all waiting around to die, so you're not far off." He shooed away an approaching young woman who carried a bundle of reeds.

"Tell us what's going on. We might be able to help."

"Oh, I doubt that." He patted her hand. "We've been cursed, it seems. Neither of you look like wizards."

"You know what all wizards look like, yeah?" Qaliah clicked her tongue to spur on the horses. The two steeds nickered and whinnied.

Zeb glanced over his shoulder at the fiendling. "Most wizards I know are either fat and slow or skinny twigs. You're both muscular. You've trained, or worked hard."

Gisella regarded the old man. Wrinkles crossed his umber skin, yet his light brown eyes seemed sharp and clear. Fine silver fuzz wrapped around the back of his head where baldness had not yet reached.

"You're very astute."

"I served as a king's scout for many years, lass. Been living out my old age right here, where I was born."

He led them down the main street of the village. The sun burned over the sea to the west, nearing its final descent for the night. Men dragged nets laden with fish up the beach while others stacked wood at the edge of the sand.

Gisella recognized the wood heaps to be pyres, a wall of them. The fishermen dashed through gaps that the other workers filled as soon as they passed.

"Pile that wood high." One of the men called out to the others. "Second double-dark's gonna be worse than the first."

"What happens at night?" Qaliah tied their horses to a post. Moonsilver tossed her head and whinnied.

"The fires keep the dead out." Zeb gestured at the wood heaps and then to the village. "We build them up every night around the whole village."

"The dead?" Gisella glanced at Qaliah. "Dead what?"

Zeb stared into one of the pyres. "Men. Women. Children. Whoever's dead and buried. They've been marching into the sea."

"For how long?"

Gisella's question went unanswered as bells rang across the village. Stragglers on the beach ran across the pyres as men with torches set them ablaze. Villagers in the streets gathered up their belongings and retreated into their huts and shacks. None of them seemed panicked or frightened. To the Golden Slayer, they seemed resigned.

"They're starting. Better get indoors."

"They don't bother you if you're indoors?" Qaliah fingered one of her daggers.

"Never cared to find out one way or another." Zeb pointed at the long building at the end of the street. "The Black Oyster there can put you up for the night. If Cade gives you any lip, just tell him Old Zeb sent you." He removed his arm from Gisella's and hobbled away. "Time to keep my wife company. She doesn't like to spend these nights alone, you know."

Gisella watched him limp away before retrieving her spear from Moonsilver. She unhitched her horse and took the lead. "I guess we're going to the Black Oyster."

* * *

When Pancras returned to Vlorey, it was business as usual in the city. He altered his route to the Arcane University to pass the gates to the necropolis, but he saw nothing amiss. He found the four guards stationed outside the gates to be curious, though. *Who are they keeping out. Or in?* Their expressions did not invite casual conversation, so he passed them and headed to the university.

The day's lessons progressed, and he found his pupils to be eager learners. After a few minutes of basic alchemical theory, he determined his students' proficiency and moved on to more advanced brewing and distilling techniques.

Pupils in his afternoon class proved to be equally astute, and he ended the day energized to create a lesson plan to challenge them all. After dinner, Pancras retired to the office he shared with the headmaster.

The tolling of the university's bell interrupted the minotaur's concentration as he perused the next day's agenda. Another bell from outside the university joined it and then another. Within minutes, it sounded as though all the bells in the city were ringing.

"Headmaster. Headmaster!" Pancras tried to gain the old man's attention but to no avail. He rapped his knuckles on the top of his desk. The headmaster grunted, stood, and shuffled over to Pancras.

Headmaster Lewin stifled a yawn. "Yes, what is it?"

"The bells? For whom do they toll?"

The headmaster listened. "Hm. Sounds like all of them, doesn't it?"

"It certainly does." The minotaur glanced out of the nearby window. Night had fallen across Vlorey. Starlight joined what light escaped through the windows and from around the shutters, insufficient to pierce the shroud of darkness night brought to the city. Flickering points of light moved below; torches carried by patrolling guards.

"Either the king has died, which considering his relative youth and health is unlikely, or it is again a Night of Exodus. How do the King and Queen appear?"

Pancras stepped over to the window. Usually, he viewed Calliome's moons from the chancery windows.

"I cannot see them at all. There are only stars. Double-dark, like last night."

"Oh yes, that's right. I retired early last night. Is it that time again?"

Headmaster Lewin joined the minotaur at the window. The human's head stood even with the minotaur's chest, and he craned his neck to eye Pancras. "Double-dark. Definitely a Night of Exodus."

"I'm not familiar with that celebration." The minotaur rubbed his right horn as he scanned across the university grounds.

The old man wheezed and coughed. "It's not a celebration. Some time ago"—he scratched the patch of scruffy whiskers on his chin—"six lunar cycles? Perhaps seven? The dead started leaving the necropolis. Now, that was on the first double-dark night when the unrest began. Guards tried to stop them the first few times, but they would not be deterred. By their second failure, the Council of Lords chose to sound an alarm across the city on double-dark nights ordering all citizens to vacate the streets and allow the dead to exit unfettered."

Pancras reached for Shatterskull, hanging at his waist. Finding its space empty, he glanced toward his work area and realized he left it leaning against the side of his desk. "Where do they go? For what purpose do they march?"

"The council has not deigned to investigate." Headmaster Lewin pulled over a stool to sit upon. It made him appear even shorter. "We're not even supposed to speak of it."

"That's madness!" Pancras could not conceive of anyone who would consider corpses rising from graves and marching out of the city unworthy of investigation. "What of the king? He agrees with this decision?"

The headmaster pursed his lips and shrugged. "I've never met the king. It is known that the council keeps much from him. They're old aristocrats and don't care for the king's common origins, you see."

"Regardless, they don't feel walking corpses are a cause for concern?"

"It is a forbidden subject." Headmaster Lewin glanced around the room, as though checking to ensure they were still alone. "When it was discovered the dead were leaving the city, inadvertently solving the problem of the necropolis filling up, well"—he chuckled—"they saw it as a boon."

Pancras pulled over a chair and sat, covering his face with his hands. "How have you humans managed to sustain a civilization?"

Headmaster Lewin continued laughing. "It isn't easy. There were objections, of course. Your own temple. The priests of Aita were notably vocal until the council threatened to have them flogged and thrown into the sea for disrupting the peace. That's when the Council of Lords decreed the Night of Exodus was to be given over to the dead, and any talk of disrupting or interfering in any way was criminalized."

The minotaur leaned forward. He placed his hand on Headmaster Lewin's knee. "It is of vital importance that I find out where they're going. Aita has spoken to me, and I believe this is related to the undertaking with which she herself has tasked me."

"You did not learn this from me." Headmaster Lewin pointed a shaking finger at Pancras. "There is one who might be able to help: the Lord Justice."

"Who is that?"

"Oh, um… Lord Justicar Fenwick Blackthorne, head of the Order of Justice." The headmaster chewed his lip. "He answers to the king directly, not the Council of Lords."

"He doesn't have to go through Lord Tyron?"

"Ha! He despises the man. Fenwick is very public about his dislike for the council's shenanigans, especially that twit Tyron. But in the interest of keeping peace, he rarely acts against them openly. I believe he has resources at his disposal which may aid you."

Pancras chewed his lip as he mulled it over. "Thank you, Headmaster." Now, at least, he had more information for Gisella when she and the fiendling returned from their journey.

Chapter 15

B lasted city folk," Cade grumbled under his breath. "Always disrespecting their elders." The fat, hairy man grunted and picked through their coins, holding up a square gold Etrunian talon. "Can't even bring proper money. What manner of scrip is this?"

"It's proper money." Qaliah snatched the coin from his fingers. "It's Etrunian."

"Feh, proper money, my eye. Needs to come from Cardoba to be proper."

Qaliah tapped the bar top with the coin. "Here now, Old Zeb said you'd have beds for us." Qaliah leaned close to the fat man. "You don't want to upset Old Zeb, do you? What difference does it make where the gold comes from? Gold is gold, eh?"

More grumbling. Cade slid a key across the bar top and pointed at a door on the far side, just to the right of the central hearth. "You can both use that room. Hope you brought your own food."

He disappeared into the kitchen area. When it was clear he did not plan to return, Gisella lifted her pack and moved in the direction the barkeep indicated.

"Do you think our horses will be all right? I'd hate to come back in the morning and find Comet all chewed up by dead guys." Qaliah unlocked the door and pushed it open with her foot.

"The stable seemed secure enough. I tipped the lady well."

Qaliah sat on the straw mattress atop their lashed rope-and-wood bed. "So, we're just going to sit here all night while the dead walk around us?"

The Golden Slayer drew her sword and inspected the blade. "Certainly not. I'm going out there, just as soon as the villagers have had time to settle in. We need to figure out what's going on. It might be tied to what's happening in Vlorey."

The fiendling bounced on the mattress, causing the bed-frame to creak in protest. "Or, this village could be cursed, and they're all in on it."

The thought had occurred to Gisella. She sheathed her sword and shook her head. "Unlikely. In my experience, people willingly involved in a curse tend to try to trap others. No one here wanted us to stay and investigate."

"Did you bring in the food?"

Gisella opened her pack and withdrew a loaf of crusty bread and stick of cured meat she acquired at the meadery. She tossed them to the fiendling. "Don't eat it all. I'll want some later, and we don't have anything else."

"Plenty of fish out there; maybe I can grab some while we're out tonight." The fiendling tore the loaf of bread in half and tossed one half to Gisella.

"Leave money when you do."

Qaliah snorted. "Sure, I will."

After they ate, Gisella risked opening the shutters on their window. With no glass, the wooden slats were all that kept intruders and the elements out of the room. She rubbed her hand on the black hardwood; unlike the timber her people used in construction, it felt sturdier than any lumber she encountered in her travels.

Outside, mist covered the ground. The setting of the sun helped cool the air a bit, but the proximity of the ocean kept the humidity high. The absolute black of the double-dark night devoured what little light spilled from their room. Gisella sensed movement in the mist but failed to achieve visual confirmation in the pitch-black conditions.

She checked the straps on her armor, tucked her hair into her helmet, and gripped her spear. Qaliah cocked and loaded her crossbow. She indicated her readiness with a nod.

The two women crept into the hall. The Black Oyster was still. A low fire still burned in the hearth, but Cade was absent, and there were no other patrons in the hall. They made their way across the great hall to the front door, which they found barred shut.

"Looks like they want to keep someone out."

"Or something." Qaliah lifted the bar and set it on the floor. She pulled open the door.

Gisella observed dim light emanating from shuttered windows on buildings across the street. A pall of silence hung heavy over the village, broken only by the shuffling of feet in the darkness. An orange glow from the nearby pyres bathed the streets providing ominous illumination in the absence of the moons.

The two women exited the Black Oyster and shut the door behind them. Gisella stepped carefully, as the mist obscured the uneven and soft village street.

A groan to their right caught Gisella's attention. A man approached them, his skin rotted and flaking off his bones. His eyes burned with an unholy red light. The Golden Slayer leveled her spear. The dead man's head jerked back as a crossbow bolt sank deep into his forehead.

He continued to walk forward, ignoring the two women as he turned toward the sea. Qaliah reloaded her crossbow and aimed again. Gisella pushed it down, shaking her head at the fiendling.

More people appeared from within the mist—men, women, and children, all in various stages of bloat and decay. Like the first man they encountered, the rest of the walking dead, intent on stalking to the beach, passed them.

Gisella motioned for Qaliah to follow her. They dashed across the street and hugged the side of a building, creeping around it toward the beach. Waves lapped at the sand, the only sound, apart from echoing steps from the procession of corpses.

"It'd be nice if the bugs stayed away, huh?" Qaliah glanced around the corner at the beach. In the darkness, the sea was as black as the sky. The two women stared as the zombies shuffled toward and into the water, pressing ever forward against the crash of waves until the sea swallowed them.

More followed—five here, ten there—a steady stream of corpses shuffling inexorably toward the water and then into the drink. After observing for an hour, Gisella pulled Qaliah away, and they returned to their room at the Black Oyster.

"Aita's bloody bones!" Qaliah stripped out of her clothes and tossed them in a pile at the base of the bed. "I knew she was wedded to Nethuns, but I didn't think the way to Aita's Realm lay in the bottom of the bay."

"It doesn't." Gisella removed her armor and placed it on the armchair. "I don't think Aita has anything to do with this."

Before crawling into bed, the fiendling checked the window shutters. In the still of the night, they heard a seemingly endless parade of the dead moving past outside. Neither slept soundly.

* * *

More dreams of metal and turning gears came to Kale in the night. More images of coiled springs, winding and tightening.

Whirr, buzz, clack, clack, clack.

He saw himself hunched over a workbench, constructing some sort of mechanism. He felt desire, a need to create, to build, to use his hands. Kale noticed his dream hands were metal, composed of gears and pulleys. His fingertips were probes and screwdrivers. He felt a sharp pain in his ribs, and Kale's eyes snapped open. He found Ori's clawed foot planted in his side as the blue drak tumbled over him, scattering books and scrolls all over the front room.

"Oh. Kale, I didn't see you there."

The striped drak rolled over, wincing as his wing folded underneath him. He pulled himself up while grasping the leg of a stool and spread his wings to work out the kinks.

"Keep it down in there, you two." Kali's voice sounded less angry than it did the night before. After first helping Ori pick up his belongings, Kale entered the living quarters. He peaked around corners, searching for his mate.

"I'm here." She stood in the bedchamber doorway.

"About yesterday—"

Kali held up her hand. "Not now." She pointed to the front of the shop. "Go to the market and get food. Good food, not a bunch of sweets. Get some ale or mead, too. Maybe wine. I'm not ready to talk to you. I won't be when you return, either."

His mate's words cut deep, and Kale's stomach twisted in knots. He deserved her ire, but not being permitted to apologize felt like she draped a sack of bricks over his shoulders. He nodded and left without uttering another word, stepping past Ori and ignoring the blue drak's inquiries as he exited.

After browsing the market until the deepest shadows of the undercity gave way to the mid-morning sun, Kale returned home with an armful of cured meats, breads, and cheeses. He banged on the door with a pot of curds and whey dangling from his hand. After Ori let him in, he deposited the supplies in the kitchen.

Boss Steelhand was seated at the table across from Kali. The two halted mid-conversation when Kale entered. He set down the goods and then stood alongside his mate.

"This is fine." She gestured to one of the seats by the table. Kale sat.

"I was just talking with Boss Steelhand about opportunities for us to do something good for the drak community here."

"Oh, that's good." Kale couldn't help but wonder what else they discussed while he was away, but the jingling of the bell at the front of the shop distracted him.

"*Kale!*"

His sister's voice filled him with dread. The winged drak closed his eyes and shrank into his chair.

The click-clack of Delilah's clawed feet on the wooden floor and another set of footsteps, the thud of boots, indicated she had not arrived alone. He opened his eyes when he sensed his sister at the kitchen doorway.

Delilah stood in the archway, staff in hand with *that look* on her face. Behind her, stooped over so as not to smack her head, stood a human with platinum hair, dressed in white, fur-lined robes.

"What did you do, Kale?" She noticed the minotaur sitting in their kitchen, and her eyes narrowed. "Theros?"

"Yes, what did you…" The human squinted, her eyes widening as they focused on Kale's wings. She regained her composure and again scowled.

"What do you mean?"

Boss Steelhand cleared his throat. "Perhaps I should leave."

"There's no room. Stay there." Delilah pushed past Kali and leaned on the table, facing Kale. "Tell me about the dragon."

"Oh." Kale chuckled, though he felt no mirth. He tapped the sigil on his chest. "Since Terrakaptis gave me this, I thought I'd go and talk to him."

"The Earth Dragon gave you that?" The human moved into the kitchen and stood next to Delilah, looming over Kale like a hungry giant.

"It's a long story." Delilah held up her hand. "Go on, Kale."

"With the story about Terrakaptis?" Kale scratched his head.

"No!" Delilah slammed her hands on the table. "The dragon two draks went to see after it attacked the city. The one that flew away when you were done."

Kali growled and launched into the tale of how Kale insisted they go investigate this dragon. She told the two wizards everything, including Kale's thought to take the egg to it and how it almost ate her before absconding with the egg, flying off to gods-know-where.

"So, in short"—the human rubbed her forehead—"your brother made my dragon abandon me here."

Kale glanced up at the human. "Your dragon?" He gripped the edge of the table to keep his hands from trembling. "What do you mean?"

"What's Yaamkyrsku going to do with the egg, Kale?"

He dug his claws into the table. "He's taking it to Terrakaptis."

Delilah inhaled, uttering a litany of curses in Drak as she exhaled. "Well, can't blame him for choosing his kin over you, right?"

"I suppose not." The human crossed her arms and glared at Kale. "I still need to get to Vlorey, and I don't have months to travel overland."

"Maybe there's…" Unsure if anyone would listen, Kale wanted to help fix what he messed up.

"There's what? What, Kale? We're doing wizard business now." Delilah turned away from her brother and regarded the human sorceress.

"All the books? Maybe there's a spell or something?" He'd read something about magical transportation when he perused the bookcases in the stairwell.

"What are you on about, Kale?" Kali wormed her way through the crowded kitchen to stand by her mate.

"I saw something about magical transportation, I think, in the books in our stairwell."

Kali covered her eyes with a hand. "In front of the minotaur and the human? We were keeping that to ourselves, remember?"

"Keeping what?" A smile spread across Boss Steelhand's muzzle.

"Show me." Delilah pulled Kale out of his chair. He shook himself free and led the group to the concealed door that hid the downward staircase.

"Clever." Boss Steelhand stroked his chin. "This explains a lot."

"What do you mean?" Kali put a hand on her hip and held the door as Delilah, the human sorceress, and Kale entered the stairwell.

"I remember when the drak who cared for this place died. He was rumored to have quite a treasure trove, but I wasn't able to find it."

"These books were his treasure." Kale pulled out a tome with a cracked yellow cover and handed it to his sister.

Delilah leafed through it until Kale pointed to a page. Her eyes scanned the text and widened at an illustration of a runed circle. She regarded her brother. "When did you find this?"

"Just before the dragon showed up."

"This is it! The Runes of Selene. This is what's in the cellar!" She spun the book around and showed it to the human.

"Runes of Selene? You're joking…" Her jaw dropped. "I found one of these near my castle. I figured it was a calendar of some sort."

Delilah flipped forward a few pages. "It's a portal network. With the right combination of runes, one can travel to any other portal in an instant; you just need to know the right combination. They're all right here."

"So, you're telling me Old Gerah had ancient magic here in the city? And never used it?" The minotaur laughed. "I doubt it very much."

Delilah reached into her pouch and withdrew an angular, dark red stone. "He didn't have this."

* * *

Pancras leaned back in his chair as Gisella finished her tale. "Why would they walk into the sea like that? It makes no sense."

"I checked a map when we returned to the city." Gisella retrieved a rolled sheet of parchment from her pack and spread it on the minotaur's table. She pointed to a spot on Verdant Point and then drew a line with her finger through the bay, past the plains west of Vlorey to a location north of the Celtan Forest. "Zamora."

"Zamora? That's not on the map." Pancras examined the drawing on the parchment. Even with his limited knowledge of northern geography, he recognized the map omitted many noteworthy locations. Not even Verdant Palace was labeled.

"No, but it is there, south of Badon Hill. It's the tower of the Lich Queen. The dead were headed straight for it."

The minotaur rubbed his right horn as he considered Gisella's words. "If they were compelled to travel to a specific location, they would take the most direct route. With no need to breathe, they could travel across the bottom of the bay."

"Exactly. Did you find out what's going on here?"

Pancras threw up his hands. "People are tight-lipped about it. I determined the dead are leaving the necropolis and the city. They keep the university grounds sealed at night, so I couldn't get out. Unlike our fiendling friend, I don't sneak around very well."

Gisella rolled up the map. "The Lich Queen is calling the dead to her. What could an undead sorceress do with so many dead? I can think of only one thing."

The conclusion seemed obvious to Pancras, too. "She's building an army."

Qaliah entered the room carrying a tray of food. "Am I done fetching things for you?"

"We appreciate it." Pancras picked up a turkey leg.

"Making plans without me?" The fiendling opened a bottle of ale.

"We wouldn't dream of it." Gisella stowed her map and transferred slices of meat to her plate. Pancras's quarters at the Arcane University were much nicer than the inn they'd been occupying.

"I did learn of a potential ally: The Lord Justice, Fenwick Blackthorne, head of the Justicars. He's no friend to this Tyron who has been making decrees to keep people away from the undead." Pancras, aware they must put a stop to the Lich Queen's plans, had yet to formulate a strategy for how one minotaur, a fiendling, and a human might accomplish that. Fighting an army of undead seemed like an insurmountable challenge.

"I think we should go see him tomorrow morning." He pointed his turkey leg at Qaliah. "Can you find out where the Palace of Justice is? I don't want to wander around the city aimlessly."

Qaliah laughed as she took a swig of her ale. "That's a switch, me looking for the law."

"What about the wizards here?" Gisella picked at some roasted vegetables on her plate.

"Maybe." Pancras shrugged and shook his head. "They're all academics; I don't think they'd be much use in a fight."

"Want me to 'persuade' this Tyron fellow to let the city watch help us?" Qaliah drew one of her daggers and twirled it by its point on the table.

The minotaur frowned. "I suspect we'll have to deal with him sooner or later, but I want to speak to the Lord Justice first."

"Suit yourself." The fiendling took a second turkey leg and pushed herself away from the table after sheathing her dagger. "I'll see you in the morning. I'll go find that palace."

"Be careful!" Pancras called after her as she left. "Once night falls, they'll want everyone off the streets."

After Qaliah exited, the Golden Slayer chuckled. "Do you think we should have warned her that getting arrested would be a less-than-ideal method for finding the Palace of Justice?"

"Ha! No, I think she knows that." Pancras picked at a notch on the tabletop. "Do you think you might be able to do some digging on Lord Tyron? Perhaps after we see this Lord Fenwick? I'll ask around the university, but my duties keep me from getting out most days."

"Certainly." Gisella tucked a stray golden hair behind her ear. "I'm curious, though, if we do need to travel to Zamora, do you plan to stay here and offer moral support from afar, or will you take the fight to the Lich Queen with us?"

It was a fair question. Feeling guilty he used his duties at the Arcane University a great deal to explain why he couldn't wander about gathering information all day, Pancras shuffled in his chair. He had decided if he kept his nose to the grindstone, as it were, when it came time for him to leave to serve his goddess, the headmaster might be more forgiving. He told Gisella as much.

"I wasn't suggesting that you would shirk your duties, nor should you. You won't have trouble in the morning, will you?"

Pancras shook his head. "I have no classes scheduled for the morning, but I do need to return by the afternoon. I would hope we'll be finished by then."

"Yes, hopefully." Gisella picked up a piece of fruit and stood. She bowed to Pancras. "I will see you in the morning, then. At the Screeching Griffon?"

"I'll see you there. Good night."

After the Golden Slayer left, Pancras tidied up, leaving the tray of food outside his door for one of the apprentices to pick up. He prayed to Aita before going to bed, hoping for further insight, but his goddess remained silent that night. He fell asleep to the peal of bells, tolling for the third and final Night of Exodus.

* * *

Delilah led the group down the stairs, past the myriad bookshelves, and to the cavern in which the rune circle resided. The torch-shaped sconces along the walls erupted with magical flames as she passed. When they reached the bottom, Theros whistled as he surveyed the room.

"All this underneath this abandoned little shop. Gerah was a sneaky one."

Kali raced down the last few steps, catching up to the group. "I've told Ori to tell any visitors we're out, and I barred the door."

Alysha knelt next to the circle, tracing one of the runes with her finger. "These are the same as the ones on the circle in my castle." She pointed to the indentation. "Except that. Mine has a stone in place that I haven't been able to remove."

"I take it that wasn't always your castle." Theros offered Alysha his hand and helped her to her feet.

"A coven of hags led by a pair of nasty cathar occupied it when I arrived. I cleared them out and claimed the castle as my own."

Delilah shivered at the mention of the word, recalling her own battle five years earlier with the cathar warlock outside the gates of Drak-Anor. She tossed the angled stone in her hand and approached the socket.

"Deli?" Kale approached his sister. "Are you sure that's a good idea?"

Delilah glanced at her brother. "If you're scared, leave."

As she said the words, she realized they might have sounded a bit harsh, but she was still irritated that he'd chased away Alysha's dragon. The fact that he was reckless enough to endanger his mate didn't sit well with her, either. It was a topic she decided to broach with him at some point, but not likely this day or the next.

Kali pulled her mate away from the circle. "Stand over here with me. Let the wizards do their thing."

The drak archmage knelt at the runestone and slid the red stone into the socket.

Nothing happened.

Theros tapped a steel finger against his chin. "Perhaps there's an incantation of some sort?"

Alysha leafed through the tome. "I don't see anything in here about that. Maybe whoever wrote this never got one of these working."

"I read about these circles as a student." Theros's hooves clicked on the stone floor as he stepped around the runed circle. "Gil-Li the Graven was the last one known to use one."

Delilah perked up at the mention of the legendary drak archmage's name. "Kale."

"Yes, Deli?"

"Go to the university. Seek out my apprentice and have her bring my grimoire." She wasn't keen on interrupting one of Katka's lessons, but she didn't trust Kale alone with Gil-Li's tome.

"They won't let him in." Theros placed his hand on Kale's shoulder. "I'll go with him."

"Do I need to go to keep you boys out of trouble?" Kali put her hands on her hips and lashed her tail.

Theros cocked an eyebrow. "Certainly not."

The two males left, leaving the three females alone in the cavern.

Delilah stood and cracked her back. She strode around the runed circle, flicking away pebbles with the butt of her staff. "I'm not blind, Kali. And frankly, I don't blame you for being angry with my brother."

"He didn't even think about the fact that the dragon might not extend his protection to me!"

Alysha laughed. "Yaamkyrsku wouldn't have gone through with it. He talks a lot, but doesn't eat anything that talks back."

Delilah regarded her brother's mate. "So, what are you going to do?"

Kali regarded the stairs and threw up her hands. "What can I do? He's my mate now. He's reckless, foolish, and irresponsible. He's not the dashing hero—"

The drak archmage approached her and placed her hands on Kali's shoulders. "He can be. He wants to be. But… you're not wrong. He needs someone like you to keep his head on straight. I can't be, and I won't be, around all the time anymore."

Magnitude of admitting her life was bigger than just herself and Kale hit Delilah at that very moment. She felt very far from home. Deep down, she conceded she would never again see any of her friends in Drak-Anor unless she made it happen. Although Kale's future path had not yet revealed itself, she accepted some time ago that her path diverged from his. Until now, it had not mattered since both their paths had run parallel.

The orange drak glanced at the floor and rubbed the back of one of her legs with the other foot. "I'm just going to stew a few more days, and then I'll talk it out with him. Boss Steelhand… Theros, I guess, he's going to introduce me to some people who work with him. He needs us to help return the draks and minotaurs to the upper city."

"This is all very nice, but we should be trying to figure out how to activate this." Alysha pointed to the runed circle.

"We will." Delilah released Kali and turned to the tall human woman. "I have the Grimoire of Gil-Li. The answers are likely in it."

"Well, Archmage, you certainly are full of surprises, aren't you?"

I hope it doesn't let me down.

Chapter 16

Theros helped Kale locate Delilah's apprentice, and they directed her to retrieve the grimoire. The young human refused to release the book to him, and she insisted on carrying it herself.

"Fine." Kale waved his hand. He didn't feel like arguing. "Come with us, then."

"As fascinated as I am in seeing if these Runes of Selene actually work, the archduke is expecting me." Theros knelt before Kale and rested his steel hand on the drak's shoulder.

"Settle this business with your mate. I need the two of you. I would be very disappointed if your spat disrupted my plans."

The winged drak wondered if he forgot about Theros's plans before he narrowed his eyes. "What are you talking about?"

"Plans I've been discussing with your mate. Frankly, she seems more reliable than you. Now that your sister is archmage, we have an opportunity to change things here in Muncifer for draks and minotaurs. I sat idle for too long under the yoke of the Manless; I'm not going to let anyone further disrupt my plans." He squeezed Kale's shoulder and nodded to Katka before he stood and briskly strode away.

Katka eyed Kale. "What was that about?"

"It's not important." Kale didn't fully understand it himself, and he wasn't prepared to admit that to Katka. He was sure Delilah would tell her all about it soon anyway.

"Oh hey, did that harness I enchanted help with the egg?"

Kale clenched his jaw. "I don't want to talk about that."

Katka pursed her lips. "I'm just curious if my enchantment worked well enough. I'm still learning—"

"Yes, it was fine." The instant Kale snapped, he chided himself for overreacting to her question. The young woman shook her head and said nothing further about it. She cradled

Delilah's grimoire in her arms as if it were a precious child and walked alongside Kale, adjusting her pace to match his. "Your sister is going to make a really good archmage, Kale. I hope you know that."

"Of course she is. Deli's always good at everything." *And I haven't been good at anything since we left home.*

"Your shop looks nice now. I remember what it was like when you first moved in."

"Yeah." He kicked a stone out of the way. *I wish you'd shut up.*

"Have you thought about selling stuff other than that limner's services?" She adjusted her grip on the grimoire. "You could probably do well selling quills and inks and other scribe supplies. There's only one other person in the city selling them, and he's a grumpy old man who hates life."

"What's the point? No one is going to come down to the undercity to buy them."

"You'd be surprised. Maybe not the nobles, but they're all stuffy muffins anyway. Most scribes and priests in the city aren't nobles. They don't mind rubbing elbows with minotaurs and draks. Half my parents' farmhands are minotaurs."

As much as Kale didn't want to contemplate a boring future running a shop in a city months from home, he admitted the idea had merit.

"I guess we can talk about it." *If Kali ever talks to me again. How bad would it be if I just left?* Draks mated for life. A drak who abandoned his mate would be a pariah. *If I go far enough away, no one would know.*

Katka rambled on, her voice fading into the sounds of the bustling city. Kale allowed his mind to wander as they trekked to his home in the undercity. When they arrived, they found Ori still at work, illuminating his latest manuscript. Kale grunted a greeting and opened the door to the cellar for Katka. He shut it behind her and shuffled to the kitchen.

He found Kali seated at the table, a plate of sweet rolls placed in its center along with two steaming goblets, one before her and one opposite her. She gestured to the seat across from hers.

"Join me?"

Kale sat, never taking his eyes off his mate. The flickering light from their kitchen lanterns made her rust-colored scales seem almost iridescent. She gestured at the sweet rolls.

"Help yourself. They're your favorite, right? I just mulled the wine."

The winged drak reached for a sweet roll. "Does this mean you're not mad at me anymore?"

"Kale, why did you mate with me?"

He bit into the pastry. The spices mingled with the sweet honey as he chewed. Kale grunted and shrugged. He really didn't know what she wanted from him.

"It wasn't because you wanted a lifelong commitment, was it? Because you wanted a brood of hatchlings with me? You didn't even think of those things, did you?" She leaned back in her chair and folded together her hands, placing them on the table before her.

"I guess…" He had not thought about it at the time. Any of it.

"You're impulsive and rash. You don't think things through. Am I wrong?"

She wasn't. He was loath to admit it though. Delilah had always been the thinker; most of the time, he cooperated with her.

"No."

"I've done a lot of dishonest things in my life, Kale. I've lied, cheated, stolen, killed. All to survive in Almeria. But when I make a promise, I see it through. Do you know what I'm saying?" She rapped her knuckles on the table. "Hey, look at me."

He met her eyes. To his surprise, she wasn't scowling.

"You're my mate. I take that seriously, Kale. We wouldn't be mates if I didn't want to be with you. To have a family with you." She sipped her wine.

Kale lifted the goblet before him and brought it to his lips. The hot wine eased the nervous gnawing at his belly, and the warmed spices made his nose tingle.

"I'll try to be better." He stared at a knot in the wood tabletop, picking at it with a claw as he shuffled in his seat.

"I know that tone." Kali shook her head. "You just think that's what I want to hear. I know you don't want to be here, that you're bored. It's as plain as those wings you're so proud of. I only want you here if you want to be here."

He eyed her while he chewed. "What are you saying?"

"You're my mate, and this is your home. But, if you feel you need to be somewhere else, I won't stop you. Just don't forget you took a mate and she'll be here in Muncifer waiting for you."

Kali stood and picked up the plate of sweet rolls. She left Kale alone with his thoughts in the kitchen.

* * *

"So? Does it tell you how to work this thing?" Alysha paced the cavern, poking at the runed circle with the butt of her staff. Katka stood with her arms outstretched, holding the grimoire open for Delilah as the drak leafed through the pages.

So far, the drak archmage had been unsuccessful in coaxing the grimoire to reveal any secrets about the circle. Delilah wasn't surprised; the grimoire never showed her what she wanted, only what it thought she needed to learn at the time.

"Nothing yet. I was hoping I might have more control over it."

The arcane script on the pages writhed and danced. Delilah tried to hold them steady in her mind, but her effort yielded no results. She flipped to a new page.

The page flipped back.

"That was interesting. I've never seen a book do that without there being a gust of wind." Alysha licked her finger and held it in the air.

"It's not just a book. I told you, this is the Grimoire of Gil-Li."

"Wait, you were serious about that? *The* grimoire?" Alysha stopped pacing and moved closer to Delilah and Katka. "That was lost before The Sundering, in the Age of Legend."

"Yeah, and Terrakaptis gave it to me."

Alysha moved to touch the edge of the book. A bolt of azure energy arced from the page and struck her in the chest, blasting her across the room. Katka jumped backward and dropped the grimoire on Delilah's feet. The drak yelped, crashing to the floor, her staff clattering away.

The human sorceress groaned and rolled over before pushing herself to her feet. "I guess it doesn't want me touching it. Interesting."

Katka stood at Delilah's side and helped her up. "Are you all right?"

"Fine, fine." The drak steadied herself on her apprentice's arm. In truth, her foot ached where Katka dropped the book.

Delilah noticed a glimmer of motion in the tome and dropped to her knees to gain a closer look. The text swirled and coalesced into a silvery orb before it splashed down onto the page. She ran a claw down the page.

"What is it?" Alysha walked over and peer down at the book.

"I saw something." Delilah looked up at Katka. "Did you see it?"

The young woman shook her head. "Just that dancing text, like always. It still gives me a headache."

Alysha squeezed her eyes shut and backed away. "How can you stand to look at that?"

"It showed me an orb. A silvery orb."

"What… like a ball of silver? What's that got to do with anything?" Alysha retrieved her staff.

Silver didn't seem like the right descriptor. It was silver, and yet not silver. "No, maybe quicksilver? It seemed, fluid."

"An orb of quicksilver?" Katka picked up Delilah's staff and handed it to her. "I think there's an alchemist in town who has quicksilver."

The drak rubbed the back of her head. "It doesn't feel right." She regarded Katka. "I think we need to do some research in the library."

Alysha sighed. "I guess I'll be helping you with that. I can't really do much without Yaamkyrsku."

As they prepared to leave, Delilah heard the door at the top of the stair open, and the telltale sound of clawed feet on wood descending. Kale entered the cavern, carrying his puzzle box.

"What are you doing with that here, Kale?" Delilah tried to keep her tone even. Any disappointment she felt toward him would have to wait until after his mate dealt with him.

He set it on the lowest bookshelf. "I got it open a few days ago, so I don't really want it around anymore. I thought it would be safe down here. I think it might be dangerous."

"Dangerous?" Delilah approached her brother. "What's in it?"

"That thing?" Alysha pointed at the box. "That's just an old puzzle box, isn't it?"

Kale regarded the human sorceress. "Terrakaptis gave it to me. It has this thing in it." He shivered. "It showed me The Sundering, Deli. Like a memory or something. I don't know what it means, but I don't want to bother you with it right now."

"A thing? What did it look like?" Alysha moved forward and lifted the puzzle box off the shelf.

Kale scowled at her. "It was a silvery ball. It was weird, like it was molten, but not really, you know?"

Delilah froze. *That can't be it.*

"Show us." Alysha handed the box to Kale. He took it and backed away, shaking his head.

"I don't know; it was awful. I don't want to see it again. You didn't see what I saw. They had a rock called a heartstone and this other faceted black stone. When they touched them together, it killed Rannos—"

"Yes, yes." Alysha slashed her hand through the air and pointed at the box. "I know the death of Rannos Dragonsire caused The Sundering. Open the box!"

Delilah inhaled and placed her hand on her brother's shoulder. "I need to see the orb, Kale. It's important. Please open the box."

"Okay, Deli." He hung his head and crouched as he removed some tools from his pouch. After a few moments of tinkering with the box, it shuddered, clicked, whirred, and unfolded.

A silvery-grey orb hovered above a base shaped like a truncated cone. Kale stood and backed away, climbing to the third step and sat. He pointed at it. "I just touched it, and it showed me The Sundering."

Kale pulled up his legs and hugged his knees. "I don't understand what I saw, Deli. It felt so real. Like I was really there when those humans murdered Rannos Dragonsire."

Delilah handed her staff to her apprentice and sat in before the sphere. She eyed Alysha and set her jaw. Then she touched the orb.

* * *

Mist clung to the streets of Vlorey as the early morning sun began its journey across the sky. Merchants pushed their carts into place as other vendors prepared their market stalls for the coming day. Couriers ferried their packages along the city's waterways.

Everywhere Pancras went, he found no evidence of people concerned about the walking dead. Folks gossiped about their neighbors, their children, their plans for the day—small, meaningless talk. A team of wizards in green robes prepared to enter the waterways to repair a bit of infrastructure. Pancras learned from one of his chats with Headmaster Lewin that the island delta portion of Vlorey was maintained by teams of wizards who trained for years to learn the powerful, magical rituals.

He met with Gisella and Qaliah at the inn and broke his fast in their company. When they finished eating, they made their way through the city toward the Palace of Justice. According to Qaliah, the building was located in the oldest part of the city, south of the river delta.

Wind picked up as they traversed the streets of a tightly packed residential district. Clouds followed, obscuring the morning sun and making the heavy air feel even denser. Pancras loosened the top of his robes.

"You're sure this is the way?" They stopped to allow a team of horses pulling a textile cart to cross in front of them.

"Have a little faith." Qaliah tapped her chest. "I know my way around a city."

She pointed up the street toward a tall stone building constructed of green-veined white marble. Columns surrounded the entrance above which stood statues of Tinian, Hon, and Anetha, authority, law, and victory, respectively.

As the three neared the building, Pancras noticed a symbol inscribed across the lintel: a cross inside a triangle surrounded by a circle. He'd seen the symbol before but couldn't remember where he saw it.

The Palace of Justice towered above the surrounding buildings. Cauldrons atop short pillars burned with high flames and sat on either side of the stairs leading to the building's entrance. A pair of human guards in gleaming breastplates with embossed sigils stood at the top of the stairs.

The guards crossed their halberds to block their entrance when the three reached the top.

"What is your business with the Justicars?" The guard on the right turned his head to regard Pancras.

"We have business with Lord Fenwick Blackthorne." Pancras hoped he got the name right.

"The Lord Justice? He doesn't see just anyone off the street." As he spoke, the guard's attention turned to Qaliah. She flashed him a bright smile from behind dark lips.

"I am Bonelord Pancras of Drak-Anor and deputy headmaster of the Arcane University of Vlorey." He leaned closer to the guard. "It's official business."

The guard regarded the minotaur looming over him. Then he pulled back his halberd and nodded to his compatriot. "Very well, then. The Lord Justice's chambers are at the top of the grand staircase."

Once inside, the three oriented themselves. The grand staircase rose directly across the foyer from the entrance. Halfway up to the second level, it split and curved around a fountain depicting three gods: Tinian, Anetha, and Hon. Inlaid in gold, black wood parquet surrounded the same symbol Pancras noticed in the lintel a few minutes earlier. Guards posted at doors in the center of the east and west walls stared straight ahead, and two more guards flanked the base of the stairs.

A tawny-furred minotaur, a colossus to the short, bespectacled man with whom he conversed, stood in the center of the foyer. Pancras recognized him as the minotaur he met at the Arcane University. He remembered having seen the same symbol previously on the minotaur's breastplate.

The minotaur glanced up at the sound of Pancras's hooves on the floor, and patted the smaller man on the shoulder before approaching the three. He bowed his head to Gisella and Qaliah.

"Interesting that the three of you should come here together."

Gisella crossed her right arm over her chest and bowed. "Orion, was it?"

Pancras nodded at the Golden Slayer. "You know each other?"

Orion offered his hand to Pancras. "We've met."

The minotaurs clasped arms. His grip was firm, and Pancras felt the muscles of Orion's forearm beneath his fingers. He felt himself flush as he stared into Orion's dark emerald eyes, and Pancras thanked Aita for bestowing him with fur.

"What, erm…" Pancras floundered to hide his discomfort. "What is that symbol on your breastplate? It seems familiar, but my memory fails me."

Orion brushed the symbol with his free hand. "It represents the Divine Tribunal of Anetha, Hon, and Tinian."

"Ah, yes, of course." Pancras knew of the Tribunal, of course, but their agents rarely strayed from the north. *The sculpture of all three along the stairway should have been a clue. I've been out of touch too long, or I'm getting old and forgetful.*

Qaliah peeked over their arms. "If we'd known we were coming here, we would have just asked you the last time we saw you."

"Asked me what?"

Pancras cleared his throat. "Actually, we're here to see the Lord Justice today."

"Ah, Fenwick is up in his office debriefing one of his scouts. I'll escort you."

Orion led them up the grand staircase, pausing at eye level with the top of the fountain to bow his head in deference to the depiction of the Tribunal.

"Getting settled in at the Arcane University..." Orion eyed Pancras expectantly. The minotaur realized they'd never been properly introduced.

"Pancras. Deputy headmaster."

"Don't forget bonelord," Qaliah chimed in from below. Pancras pursed his lips. He had not intended to lead with that.

"Indeed? A bonelord and deputy headmaster of our illustrious Arcane University?" He cocked his head as he regarded Pancras. "Most interesting."

They continued up the stairs until they reached the landing on the second floor. Orion led them behind the top of the fountain to a set of double doors. He pulled them open. "The Lord Justice is right inside."

"Thank you." Pancras bowed his head in thanks. From inside the chambers, he heard a metallic clatter, as if someone in armor had fallen, followed by cursing.

Cloud cover diminished the light which usually streamed in through open windows across from the door in the Lord Justice's chambers. Glowing sconces mounted on the twin rows of columns running the length of the room provided supplemental illumination.

At the far end of the room, a bald, bearded man leaned with both hands atop a desk constructed of striped, ebony-colored wood. His deep russet skin was flushed. A flame-haired dwarf picked herself up from the floor, cursing in Dwarvish as she smoothed her skirt. Her ruddy cheeks were dusted with freckles, and her hair hung in twin braids over her shoulders.

"Apologies." Pancras bowed as the three entered. "I am Bonelord Pancras of Drak-Anor, deputy headmaster of the Arcane University of Vlorey. I assume you're the Lord Justice, and if we're interrupting something"—the minotaur waved his hand toward them—"we can return later."

The Lord Justice laughed as he pushed himself away from the desk. "No need. Come, come!" He waved them in and straightened his blue-and-white checkered tabard, emblazoned with the symbol of the Divine Tribunal. "I was in the middle of debriefing Scout Stonehammer here, but it's merely routine."

"Usually routine." The dwarf retrieved her helmet from the floor. "We'll finish later, Fen… my lord?"

"Yes, later. As always, thank you for your tireless efforts, Scout Stonehammer. Let your captain know the Justicars value your people's commitment."

"Sure. They'll be thrilled." Scout Stonehammer's tone belied her sincerity. She nodded to the three newcomers and exited, adjusting her armor and pulling the doors shut behind her.

The Lord Justice gestured to the chairs near his desk. "Pull up a seat. I assume you and your"—he regarded the two women for the first time since they entered the room—"companions? This is not a social call, I assume."

Qaliah was the first to sit. "Do you get a lot of those?"

Gisella pulled over a chair for herself and Pancras. "We were told that you might be able to assist us."

"With what could I assist a minotaur, a human—a southerner by the look of you—and a fiendling?" He leaned back and rubbed his chin. "Such an unusual company. Normally, a group such as yourselves means trouble."

Pancras spread his hands, palms up. "I assure you, Lord Justice—"

"Fenwick will do."

"Fenwick, we're not looking to cause trouble; rather, we wish to put a stop to it."

Gisella and Pancras outlined their mandate from Aita and Aurora. They told him of their suspicions regarding the Lich Queen and that they believed she was involved in the exoduses of the dead from the city's necropolis. Qaliah interjected with the report from Ebonwick, and Gisella clarified the undead from the peninsula likely traveled under the bay, emerging somewhere west of the city. All signs pointed to the undead converging on Zamora.

"Zamora." Fenwick frowned and rubbed the back of his head. "If what you say is true, it is troubling indeed."

"This whole city seems complacent." Pancras sat forward. "It seems that certain decrees by the Council of Lords, particularly Lord Tyron, are not"—the minotaur chose his words carefully since he was about to implicate one of nobility in a plot—"well, they're not helping the situation."

Fenwick slammed a fist on his desk. "I knew Tyron was up to something. The man is a menace."

"We have no evidence." Gisella laid her hand on the desk and regarded Pancras.

"No, you wouldn't have." Fenwick bit his thumb. "Tyron would be too careful to leave evidence of anything like that. Conspiring with the Lich Queen…" He clenched his jaw and shook his head as embers of rage ignited in his eyes.

"This is all just speculation, my lord. Granted, we both"—Pancras gestured to himself and Gisella—"have received visions from our patrons corroborating the Lich Queen's involvement."

The human waved his hand and stood. "No, I know you believe everything you're telling me. No lie can be uttered in the Palace of Justice."

Pancras blinked and stared at the Lord Justice as he paced, for he had not sensed any such compulsion enchantments when he entered the palace. *The enchantment must be powerful, indeed, and subtle.*

"What, really?" Qaliah tapped her fingers against the arms of the chair. "Then what were you and the dwarf doing just before we entered the room?"

Fenwick stopped in his tracks and chuckled as he raised a finger. "No lie can be uttered. That doesn't mean one is compelled to answer any question. Valora, that is, Scout Stonehammer, and some of her people have been assisting the Justicars with reconnoitering the surrounding countryside. They're part of a larger dwarf contingent from Korbaddan who have settled west of the city on the coast."

Hearing about the dwarves gave Pancras an idea. "Perhaps the scouts could verify our suspicions that the undead travel toward Zamora."

"Yes, I'll have Scout Stonehammer investigate that." Fenwick returned to his seat and clasped his hands together before him. "I'll send a Justicar to see Lord Tyron, as well. The man has refused the last two summons I've sent him about unrelated matters. I have no grounds on which to arrest him, but perhaps he'll be careless."

"Perhaps one or all of us could accompany your Justicar?" Gisella crossed her legs. "We could ask him certain questions under false pretenses and see if he slips up?"

"Provoking someone into incriminating themselves isn't really how we operate."

The Golden Slayer raised her eyebrows. "We're not Justicars."

"Good point." Fenwick smiled and bowed his head.

They agreed on a plan. After first sending Justicar Orion to verify the noble's schedule, the Lord Justice would send the minotaur to meet them at their inn in the morning, and together they would confront Lord Tyron. In the meantime, Fenwick would speak to Scout Stonehammer about changing her patrol to check the shore between Zamora and Ebonwick to determine if evidence of an undead migration in the area existed.

Pancras left the two women and returned to the Arcane University. He was surprised the Lord Justice was amiable; yet, he had no sense that the man had been deceitful. It ran contrary to his prior experiences with humans in positions of authority. He caught up to Headmaster Lewin outside one of the lecture halls.

"Headmaster." Pancras bowed to the old man.

"Deputy Headmaster!" Lewin returned Pancras's greeting. "I'm off to listen Vanathiel's lecture on the resurgence of fey in the world."

"I won't keep you, I just had a question about the Palace of Justice." The minotaur shortened his stride, keeping pace with the human as they walked. "The Lord Justice said no one can tell a lie within the palace, yet I sensed no magical auras at work."

"Ah, yes, you saw him, did you? I hope he gave you a warm welcome. Fenwick is a good sort."

"Yes, he was very helpful."

"Good, good." He held up his hands in a shrug. "It is protected by a divine blessing from the gods of the Tribunal; an ancient magic we with Selene's arcane gifts cannot feel or touch. It's still effective, though."

Although he found the man's explanation unsatisfactory, Pancras did not wish to further delay the headmaster. As well, Pancras wished not to be late to his own class. "Thank you. Perhaps I'll look into it further. Maybe in the library?"

"Oh, possibly." Lewin waved his hand. "Fenwick would be happy to wax poetic on the subject, I'm sure."

He thanked the headmaster again and turned toward the building where his alchemy class gathered. While he prepared his lesson, Pancras contemplated the magical mysteries of the Justicars. He resolved to learn more about them in the coming days.

Chapter 17

The orb engulfed Delilah's claw and flowed up and around her hand. She gasped at its icy embrace as a bright light blinded her. When it faded, she found herself still in the cavern underneath Kale's home.

Subtle differences were her first clues that she no longer stood in Kale's decrepit cellar. The scattered rubble and dust were gone. The sconces still glowed with enchanted light, but the fixtures were shiny and straight.

The sound of footsteps preceded the appearance of a drak descending the stairs. The drak was covered in tattoos.

Gil-Li eyed the spot where Delilah stood. "I recognize you."

Delilah's spine stiffened. She was under the impression what she saw was merely a vision. Kale had been unable to interact with his.

"Relax, I would not harm the inheritor of my legacy. It is through you that I live on. It's about time you showed up."

The drak sorceress flexed her hand in a reflexive attempt to adjust her grip on her staff, but it was not with her. "You can see me?"

"Describe how you… by what mechanism you traveled here." Gil-Li circled Delilah, examining her. "Hm. Stripes. Interesting. A Child of the Gods we would call you."

"There was an orb. Shimmery, like quicksilver…"

"Ah, the Orb of Forgotten Memories. You found that as well as my grimoire? Impressive."

"They were gifts." Delilah shifted her weight as the other drak continued to examine her.

"What sort of fool would gift such prizes?" Gil-Li leaned in close, snout to snout, with Delilah.

"Terrakaptis, the Earth Dragon." Delilah recoiled from the other drak. Gil-Li reeked of moldy herbs. "He thought they might be useful for our journey."

"The Earth Dragon? Interesting. Pity I won't survive to see this world from which you come."

Delilah glanced around the room and cocked her head. "Have I traveled through time?"

"Certainly not!" Gil-Li's tone was that of one who found the very idea preposterous. "The Orb of Forgotten Memories can show many things. What, exactly, depends on who touches it. I bequeathed my legacy to the future, to you, obviously. Tell me, what are you?"

Delilah stepped backward. "A… a drak?"

Gil-Li shut her eyes and took a single, deep breath and then opened them again. "You don't say? I can see you, you know. Title, accolades. What have you accomplished with my knowledge?"

"Oh." Delilah felt herself flush. *That was the kind of dumb mistake Kale would make.* "I am Archmage of the Arcane University, the first drak archmage since, well, you. There is discussion in naming me an Elemental Master, as well. Earth magic was lost until I showed them what I learned from your grimoire. Most water magic, too."

Gil-Li smiled. "That's more like it. There was a time when we draks were the supreme magisters of Calliome. The humans stole our knowledge from us and used it to kill our father."

"Rannos. My brother, that's what the orb showed him—a human killing Rannos by touching a heartstone and some sort of black, faceted stone together. Then The Sundering happened."

Gil-Li hissed, "I died in The Sundering!" She shook her head and spat on the floor. "To think, they hated Rannos so much to bring a heartstone and an Eye of Oblivion together. Humans! Never content with what they're given, always coveting that which others have. Tell me of your brother."

"Kale?" Delilah chuckled. "He's foolish. Brave, but foolish."

"Older? Younger?"

"We hatched from the same egg."

Gil-Li raised her eyebrows. "Brother and sister. Blessed and cursed." She narrowed her eyes. "You haven't mated with him, have you?"

"Ugh. No!" Delilah curled her lip, sneering in disgust at the very thought.

"Good." She glanced down and then shook her head. "Never mind that. Idle curiosity is a waste of this opportunity. You seek answers? What is your question?"

"There are so many…"

Gil-Li patted Delilah on the cheek, her clawed hand carried the same chill as the silvery metal orb. "Why did you use the orb?"

"We're in Muncifer. We're trying to activate the Runes of Selene. The grimoire, your grimoire, showed me a picture of the orb. There are books here, but they don't make much sense."

"Ah, so they are still intact. How long ago was The Sundering, by your reckoning?"

Delilah eyed the ceiling as she made some mental calculations. "It is the year seven hundred sixty-three, as measured after The Sundering."

"So much knowledge must have been lost." Gil-Li shook her head and stepped toward the runed circle. Delilah moved to follow but discovered she stood fixed in place now. She could only turn to watch.

The elder drak approached the circle, and the tattoos on her body flared with azure light. "An influx of arcane energy will activate the portal."

Azure tendrils swirled around the runed circle, pouring into smooth stone at the center. The obsidian rippled. From it sprang an image of the moons. Gil-Li spun the King it until it displayed a waning crescent phase. She did the same for the Queen.

"The moon gates created by the Runes of Selene are keyed to the phases of the King and Queen."

Delilah watched as the elder drak then circled the moon gate, tapping runes on the stone with her foot. "Each moon gate is keyed to a particular sequence of runes. Most of them correspond to constellations in the sky. As long as there are stars, you can find the correct sequence." She turned and winked at Delilah. "Maybe someone wrote them down, though I doubt all the place names endured for nearly a millennium."

A coruscating, shimmering rectangle burst from the obsidian circle. From Delilah's angle, she assessed it to be as thin as a sheet of parchment at the edge, yet as wide as a door from side to side.

"If you look through the moon gate, you will see your destination." She turned and held a finger up. "It is a two-way gate however. Any enemies at the other side will be transported through, even as you attempt to pass through yourself."

"I understand." Delilah chewed her lip. "Tell me about the Eye of Oblivion?"

"Artifacts from another age. Pretty to look at." Gil-Li held out her hand, and a shimmering image of a multifaceted black stone appeared. "Some say they fall from the sky; others say they're found deep in the ground, far from heartstones, of course. Where a heartstone brings life, Eyes of Oblivion bring only death. Brought together, their energies cancel each other out in a spectacular fashion."

Gil-Li smiled. "Or so I've heard." She waved her hand. The stone and the gate vanished, as did the room around them.

Delilah found herself standing in inky blackness with only the vision of Gil-Li before her. "That's it?"

"The gates are meant to be easy to use, at least, for us wizards." Gil-Li smiled and stroked Delilah's cheek. "We draks reigned supreme once. Even the elves were second to us.

Calliome was our world, first. You carry that legacy in your blood. Honor it."

"Wait… what about the Eyes—"

Darkness overtook Delilah, and she felt herself being flung backward. She hit the floor with a grunt. Her brother rushed over to her.

"Deli! Are you all right?"

"… of Oblivion?"

* * *

Pancras took advantage of his light schedule the next morning to again break his fast with Gisella and Qaliah. He did not wish to miss the confrontation with Lord Tyron. A feeling in his gut told him he needed to hear anything the man said to them first hand.

The three did not have to wait long before the Justicar arrived at the Screeching Griffon. Orion entered, his gleaming silver breastplate reflecting the morning sun that shone through the windows. The sight of his bare, muscular legs underneath the leather kilt he wore made Pancras's heart beat a little faster. He looked away and studied the crumbs on his plate.

"Are you all right?" Gisella leaned close to whisper to him.

He held up his hand and nodded. "Fine"

No one had stirred him like that since he and Thanos parted ways. He jumped when the minotaur placed a hand on his shoulder.

"I see you've finished eating." He regarded Pancras. "Ready to depart? I have word that our quarry will be at his estate all morning."

"Yes, I'm ready!" Pancras stood, albeit a bit too fast, and scrambled to keep from spilling his tankard of warm cider.

Qaliah snickered. "We're all going."

"I am curious—what is your stake in all this, Fiendling?" Orion held the door open as Gisella and Pancras exited. The minotaur wizard felt the Justicar's eyes follow him as he passed.

"Got nothing better to do."

"Is that right?" He guided them to the main street and south toward the residential section of Vlorey.

"She's had nothing better to do since we left Muncifer." Gisella adjusted the knot of hair at the top of her head. While she left her helmet at the inn, she nonetheless had tied up her hair to keep it out of the way. She used her spear like a walking stick as they passed through one of the city's markets.

"She won't admit it"—Pancras initially held back but then put his arm around the fiendling—"but I think she's grown fond of us."

Qaliah hugged him. "Stupid, huh? I could be some fat noble's mistress by now, sipping wine and flirting with the stable boys."

"Ha!" Orion clapped the fiendling on the back. "There's still time for that."

"I'm committed now. I told them I wanted to help do something important for once." Qaliah ducked out from behind Pancras and turned to face them as she stepped backward and extended her arms. "And now look at us, walking around Vlorey with a Justicar."

The Justicar clucked his tongue. "Well, if what I was told is true, there may be nothing you can do in your life more important than helping your friends here. I'm too young to have fought against the Lich Queen, but I have no desire to see her return."

"Are you from here?" Pancras dodged Qaliah as she spun and skipped toward Gisella's side. "I've seen other minotaurs, but just here and there. Is there a clan living in Vlorey?"

"Most minotaurs live in the outlying villages, but I was born and raised here in the city. My parents were Justicars. Our family has served the Divine Tribunal for generations."

"Family business, huh?" Qaliah snickered.

"So to speak."

"We don't hear much of the Justicars in Drak-Anor. Nothing, in fact. When I was a lad in Muncifer, my parents told all sorts of stories"—Pancras glanced at Orion and raised an eyebrow—"exaggerated, I'm sure."

Orion touched Pancras's arm. "Share those stories over a tankard of ale later, and I'll tell you if they're exaggerations or not."

The quickening of Pancras's heart was cut mercifully short by a change of subject. The Justicar pointed to a set of wrought-iron gates ahead and to the left. "Lord Tyron's Estate."

When they arrived at the gate, a scruffy guard peered at them from behind the iron bars. His armor was ragged and poorly maintained, and he scratched his unkempt beard before hawking a glob of phlegm to the dirt.

"No visitors!"

Orion rapped on the gates with his spear. "I am Justicar Orion Ironhorn. Open your gates in the name of the Divine Tribunal."

The guard pressed his face against the bars. "And what if I don't, eh? You can't bully me."

He snickered at his pun but hastily jumped backward as Orion slammed his spear against the gate. "Or else, we will break in and use lethal force to defend ourselves."

I guess some of the stories I heard were true—justice at any cost. Pancras lifted Shatterskull and cradled it in his arms. From the corner of his eye, he noticed Gisella shift her stance.

The guard pulled a key from around his neck and unlocked the gates. He pulled them open and stood aside. "I don't get paid enough to fight Justicars."

"Too right." Qaliah tickled him under the chin as she passed.

Lord Tyron's manor house resembled a collection of boxes clad in dusty-rose stucco. The second floor's ornate, curved walls sitting atop the stark, straight-walled first floor caused one to wonder why the architects changed direction partway through construction. The grounds showed signs of once having been covered with meticulously sculptured gardens, but most appeared ill-tended and overgrown, save for the immediate area surrounding the path that led to the manor's doors.

Pancras spotted a few guards patrolling the area, but since no alarm had been raised, they paid the visitors no mind. The path led to an archway, through which sat a small courtyard, featuring a mosaic tile floor. The front door, made from white-washed, iron-banded wood, featured a knocker whose handle had broken off some time ago. Pancras heard music coming from within the manor.

"This man heads the Council of Lords?" Her brows furrowed in confusion, Gisella surveyed their surroundings.

The minotaur wizard agreed with her assessment. He did not expect someone with so much influence to live in such conditions.

"Lord Tyron is notoriously tight-fisted with his money." Orion beat on the door. "Open in the name of the Divine Tribunal!"

"Won't he make a run for it now?" Qaliah positioned herself to keep watch over the manor's grounds.

"He's too arrogant to think anything's amiss, and if he does run, we'll hunt him down."

After a moment, the door opened. A man wearing a formal black-and-red uniform greeted them.

"The Divine Tribunal?" The man sniffed and leaned back his head as he spoke. "Lord Tyron did not tell me he was expecting guests of such import."

Orion pushed the door out of the way and strode past the man. "I'm sure there are a great many things about which your lord does not tell you."

"Indeed." After closing the door quickly, the man rushed to catch up with Orion. "Lord Tyron is in the conservatory at the moment. Shall I announce you?"

"That's not necessary. Just show us the way."

Gisella, Qaliah, and Pancras followed the steward as he directed Orion to the conservatory in the center of the manor. The music the minotaur wizard heard from outside sounded louder now. The steward pushed open the double doors.

A domed glass roof topped the round chamber that composed the conservatory. In the center of the room, sunlight reflected off the pool of crystal blue water surrounded by shrubs and colorful flowers. At the far end, a trio of minstrels played the lyre, horn, and drum. Attired in a tight-fitting emerald jacket, a human male stood, his back facing the door and hands clasped behind him, while he listened to the performance.

"Lord Tyron!" Orion adopted a wide stance, allowing his spear to lean forward. Pancras's concerns as to whether or not the minotaur could make himself heard over the music were laid to rest as the minstrels faltered and stopped playing. The man in green slumped his shoulders and turned, shaking his head.

"Really? Interrupting my sojourn into the wonders of lyrical expression?" His eyes glowed red beneath his heavy brow, like burning embers in a pile of ash.

Darkness flowed from the man, tendrils of shadowy ice extending and engulfing Orion. Pancras felt Shatterskull shift in his hands as the power of Aita flowed through it and into him. Lifting it, he drew the streams of shadow emanating from the noble away from Orion and into the weapon.

"Enough of this." Qaliah fired her crossbow. The bolt caught Lord Tyron in the center of his chest. He grunted and stumbled forward. The darkness retreated, and the fiendling followed her attack with a thrown dagger, her blade catching him across the throat. He fell to his knees, clutching his neck and gagging on the pulsing spray of blood.

"Damn it! We needed him alive." Orion brushed off the lingering remnants of shadowy residue as he scowled at the fiendling.

Pancras raced toward Lord Tyron. He fell to his knees at the man's side, planting the head of Shatterskull in the dirt of a flowerbed next to the dying human. Keeping one hand on his weapon, he grasped Lord Tyron's hand and closed his eyes, allowing the power of Aita to flow through him.

* * *

"Deli?" Grabbing hold under her arms, Kale lifted his sister from the floor. "Are you all right?"

"Get off me!" Delilah flailed her arms and stumbled away from her brother.

"Did you see The Sundering? It was awful, wasn't it?"

The drak sorceress brushed herself off and shook her head. "I saw a vision of Gil-Li using this very moon gate. She spoke to me."

Why did I have to see The Sundering and she got to talk to someone? Kale frowned and scratched his head. He glanced down at the orb just in time to see the puzzle box fold itself up over it.

"Impressive artifact. Maybe you'll let me have a look at it when this is all over." Alysha moved with Delilah to the runed circle. Kale picked up his puzzle box and returned it to the shelf before turning to regard his sister.

"Gil-Li suggested someone may have written down the various combinations of runes that led to specific destinations." Delilah knelt at the circle and traced one of the runes with a claw.

She glanced at her brother. "I asked her about that black stone. It was an Eye of Oblivion. Apparently, bad things happen when they touch heartstones."

"Hm. I've not heard of those." Alysha pursed her lips and eyed Katka. The young woman shook her head.

"It doesn't matter now, anyway." Delilah tapped a claw against the stone. "Kale, did you see anything that looked like a list of these runes in any of the books you searched?"

"No, I didn't see anything like that, but I didn't have a chance to go through all of them yet."

He approached the shelves at the bottom of the stairs. "I pulled out the ones that looked like they might be useful to you, but I only really skimmed them. I couldn't read most of them, so maybe there's something I missed."

Delilah rubbed her hands together. "Okay, we've have a lot of work to do. Katka, Alysha, and I will start looking through books. Kale, you and Kali are responsible for getting us all food, and then you two can help, too. We'll start down here and break when it's time to eat."

Kale wanted to point out that this was his house. He raised a finger and spread his wings. Delilah approached him and clamped his snout with her hand. He grunted and tried to pull away, but she held him fast.

"I'm being bossy, I know. Please, Kale. This is how I need you to help us right now. Please?"

She released him. He stared into his sister's eyes. Gone was the anger he perceived when she asked about the dragon. Still, her expression was that of someone who expected to be obeyed.

He shrugged and nodded. "Okay, Archmage Delilah."

Gisella barely had time to react before Qaliah shot Lord Tyron and then slashed his throat with a thrown dagger. By the time she grabbed hold of the fiendling, the damage was done, and their quarry lay, bleeding out, on the floor of the conservatory. The minstrels shrieked and fled, leaving their instruments behind.

Gisella watched as the bonelord joined with Lord Tyron.

"What's he doing? Can he heal him?" Orion glared at Qaliah. The fiendling ignored him as she reloaded her crossbow.

"No, but he is a bonelord." Gisella shook her head. "He can help him cross over."

"I don't think Lord Tyron will need that sort of help. His eyes, though… he was not a wizard."

"That darkness, those tendrils"—Gisella brushed a bit of residue from Orion's shoulder—"were unlike any magic I've ever dealt with."

The Justicar raised an eyebrow. "I was not aware you had an arcane background."

"I am a slayer of the Arcane University." Gisella leaned on her spear and observed Pancras, a statue as he knelt alongside Lord Tyron. Scarlet blood pulsed through the man's fingers, still clutching his throat as his mouth moved wordlessly.

"A slayer, a minotaur wizard, and a fiendling." Orion chuckled. "Sounds like the start of a bad joke." He eyed Qaliah as she inspected a nearby shrub. "That was very rash, Fiendling."

Qaliah turned and jabbed a thumb into her chest. "Hey! I know demonic energies when I see them." Her voice trembled, and Gisella noticed her shaking. "He wasn't going to talk." She turned away and shivered.

The Golden Slayer approached Qaliah and turned the fiendling to face her. "Demonic? You're sure?"

The fiendling batted her hand away. "Of course, I'm sure." She pointed at her horns. "Where do you think I got these?"

"Hey." Gisella touched Qaliah's arm. The fiendling's skin was burning hot.

"You can't help me; go away." Qaliah pushed past Gisella, moving to the other side of the pool. She squatted and examined the abandoned instruments.

Gisella returned to Orion's side. He raised an eyebrow and nodded toward Pancras. "So we just…"

"We wait."

* * *

Pancras found himself lying on the floor with the shadow's icy hands wrapped around his throat. His own good hand passed through the insubstantial claw. Only his withered hand could touch it.

"You were foolish to enter this man, Bonelord." The shadowy claw squeezed.

The minotaur closed his eyes and concentrated on the reality he knew—that he kneeled on the floor next to Lord Tyron with a hand on Shatterskull. He felt the warmth flowing through it, Aita's power. The demon's grip on his throat weakened.

"Who is your master?" Pancras forced the words past his constricted throat and through clenched teeth.

"Our purpose is beyond your ken." The demon laughed, its voice like a sack of gravel being dragged over cobblestones.

"Whom do you serve?" The bonelord steeled his will and gathered Aita's power, releasing a blast of pure, radiant energy, and blowing the demon backward.

He stood to face his foe. Drawing itself up, the demon towered over him; yet, it was whisper thin, a breath of shadow in Aita's glow. Pancras lifted Shatterskull. The maul's face became the gleaming red skull of his goddess.

"How you've grown. So sweet. Delicious." The demon reached toward him.

Pancras stood on a grassy plain. He was bare chested, and only a kilt covered his lower half. Thanos lay on the ground before him, his chestnut fur slick with sweat. He beckoned to the wizard.

"Come on, then. Ready for another go?"

The minotaur wizard smiled. Seeing Thanos waiting for him always warmed his heart. He fell to his knees and crawled toward his lover. Before him, as he approached Thanos, he saw his withered hand. Bits of grass and dirt clung to it as he touched the ground. He paused and examined his hand, flexing it. It cracked like old, dry leather as his fingers bent.

"Pancras? Don't keep me waiting."

Thanos smiled, but beneath the surface, Pancras felt another presence. He pushed himself to his feet. His lover's smile faded and transformed into a snarl as he launched himself at Pancras.

In midair, Thanos transformed into a winged beast with the decaying, rotten head of rabid dog. Its jaws snapped shut just short of the minotaur's face, its claws dug into his arms as it pushed Pancras to the ground. He gripped the shaft of Shatterskull in his hand and brought the maul around, slamming it into the demon's head.

Its skin sizzled and popped where the sanctified weapon touched it, burning the image of Aita's skull into its flesh. The demon howled in pain, falling backward and clawing at its face as it tried to excise the painful wound.

Pancras the Bonelord stood, holding Shatterskull before him. "I defeated you once, demon. I shall do so again."

Through growling hisses, the demon laughed. "No, no, you have never defeated me."

"Then let this be the first time." Pancras swung his maul.

The demon caught the weapon by the shaft and snarled, "You burn with Aita's power, and so you will win this fight. Have the human. I will be waiting for you, in your world. You know where to find us."

Lord Tyron's ethereal form rubbed the back of his head as he regarded his own body before he turned to face Pancras.

"Damn. Am I dead?" He examined his hand and then scratched his beard. "It doesn't hurt."

"You're not dead, yet, but very nearly so."

Tyron glanced first at the minotaur and then at the two of them on the floor. "Wait, what are you doing there? Here? Are you a wizard of some sort? A mystic? Heal me, you great beast!"

Pancras lifted Shatterskull, showing the skull of Aita to Lord Tyron. "I am a bonelord. I cannot heal you. But you have an opportunity to tell me what is going on. Perhaps Aita will have mercy on you."

"That... thing... I saw you struggle with it." Lord Tyron covered his eyes and groaned. "It was inside me. I saw myself do things. I heard myself say things, but it wasn't me. It wasn't me."

"You were possessed by a demon." Pancras offered the man his hand. He could help him on his journey to the next life.

"I knew that woman who came to me was too good to be true." Lord Tyron shook his head. "Damn. She promised me an heir. Swore by Tinian she wanted nothing more than to provide me with a strong child."

"There isn't much time, Lord Tyron. I need information."

Lord Tyron looked at Pancras. No, he looked through Pancras. "I see the next world. You killed me. You'll get nothing from me."

The human faded from sight. Pancras inhaled sharply and opened his eyes. The bleeding stopped. Lord Tyron was dead.

"Pancras?" Gisella knelt next to him. "What did you learn?"

He let the Golden Slayer help him to his feet. The fiendling sat next to the instruments at the far side of the pool, plucking discordant notes on the lyre.

"There was a demon in him. It seduced him and then took his body."

Orion's knuckles turned white as his grip tightened on his spear. "Are there more? Is the entire Council of Lords compromised?"

"I don't know. He wouldn't give me any more information. I fought with the demon, and it fled"—Pancras reflected on the demon's revelation that he'd know where it went; however, the only place that came to mind, the only place that was a constant in all this—"to Zamora, I think."

The Justicar spat on the floor. "The Lich Queen."

Gisella loosened her hair tie and shook her head, allowing her golden locks to fall around her shoulders. "We need to see if anyone else on the Council of Lords is possessed."

"How?" Orion regarded her. "Ask them to flash us their burning red eyes? Throw salt at them?"

Pancras chuckled. "I wonder if that would actually work."

Gisella pointed across the pool. "Qaliah. She knew in an instant what Lord Tyron was."

At the sound of her name, the fiendling looked up. "Don't go making plans for me without my say-so."

"Then come over here and be part of the conversation." Pancras flipped Shatterskull, whose top no longer glowed as the skull of Aita, and set it head-first on the floor.

The fiendling flicked her tail and set down the lyre. She picked up the horn and joined them on the other side of the pond. "I'm not keen on exposing myself to more demons."

"I thought you were fearless." Pancras noted her trembling.

Qaliah flashed her icy blue eyes at him. "It's not fear." She clenched her teeth. "I could feel it. I wanted it."

She hugged herself and turned away. "I'm not ashamed when I want a man for the night. But this… I needed this like I needed air."

"It calls to you, a primal urge." Orion put his hand on the fiendling's shoulder. "You are strong to have resisted."

Qaliah shivered. "Let's just go. I need to leave this place."

Chapter 18

After a thorough search of the manor house, which turned up nothing of use, Orion waited with Qaliah near the estate's main gate. Gisella and Pancras instructed Lord Tyron's servants to take his body to the Red Crypt, and they departed together. The two women returned to the Palace of Justice to brief Lord Fenwick on the situation at Lord Tyron's estate. Meanwhile, Orion accompanied Pancras to the Arcane University so the minotaur wizard could recuperate from his encounter with the demonic entity that had possessed the human noble.

Lord Fenwick insisted the two women join him in a drink and relax before relaying their tale. Qaliah's hands still trembled as she took the goblet of wine, and it was only after draining two goblets in a row did the visible tension release from her shoulders.

"So, what transpired, exactly? Something terrible by the way our friend was shaking." Fenwick gestured with his goblet toward the fiendling.

Gisella sat in one of the armchairs in Fenwick's chambers and crossed her legs. "Lord Tyron was possessed by a demon. Pancras was able to confront it and drive it from the man after Tyron was mortally wounded."

"Unfortunate that he had to die." Fenwick hid his smile in his goblet. "I'm sure someone will miss him."

Qaliah giggled. "I didn't."

The Golden Slayer frowned and cleared her throat. "We feel it is likely his decrees came from the demon, a way of ensuring the undead could leave the city unhindered."

"Did he say anything? Did you find any evidence?"

Gisella sipped her wine and shook her head. "Nothing to link him or the demon to the Lich Queen."

Fenwick steepled his fingers in front of him. "So, we're left with no hard evidence and more circumstantial evidence that points toward a convergence of sorts at Zamora?"

"So, it seems."

"Damn. I won't be able to convince the king to commit troops without hard evidence. Even if I call in all my favors, and he owes me more than a few."

"Has your scout reported anything yet?" Gisella finished her glass of wine and shook her head when Fenwick offered her more.

"No, I haven't had a chance to speak to Valora yet. I've sent a messenger to the dwarf settlement, so hopefully she knows I have a request for her."

Qaliah accepted another refill. She swirled the wine in her glass. "I need to ask you something, and I'd appreciate a straight answer."

Gisella's heart stopped, and she turned to regard the fiendling as a feeling of dread washed over her.

"Certainly!" Raising his eyebrows, Lord Blackthorne eyed the fiendling.

"Is something going on between the two of you? Because I don't intend to sleep alone tonight after what I just went through."

Gisella felt her cheeks grow hot, and she buried her face in her hands. "What the in the name of Tinian's lance is wrong with you?"

"Hey! I told you how being in proximity to that demon made me feel. The Lord Justice here is a decent sort, so figured if I'm going to bed anyone tonight, it ought to be someone like him, right?" Qaliah tossed back her goblet of wine and stood. Her tail swayed from side to side as she approached Lord Fenwick with a predatory smile on her lips.

Fenwick chuckled and set his own wine goblet on his desk. He took Qaliah's hands as she moved to throw them around his neck and held them down at her sides. "I am truly flattered. Your attentions would be most welcome were I not involved with… someone."

"It's the dwarf, isn't it?" Qaliah winked at him. She leaned in close, dropping her voice to a whisper. "I won't tell. Fine!" Qaliah released Fenwick and spun away, laughing. "I'll find myself another righteous fellow."

She skipped out of Fenwick's chambers, leaving Gisella alone with the Lord Justice. The Golden Slayer stood and bowed, crossing her hand over her heart. "I am truly sorry for that. She had a trying experience with Lord Tyron."

Fenwick laughed and held up his hands. "Think nothing of it." He nodded toward the open door. "I think you should catch up to her though, maybe try to keep her out of trouble."

Gisella grunted an acknowledgement and bade farewell to Fenwick. In truth, Gisella acknowledged the Lord Justice as an attractive man, but for Qaliah to proposition him openly in the company of others was improper, to say the least. Clearly, the fiendling was more shaken than she let on. Gisella found Qaliah wandering down the grand staircase, giggling and skipping about.

She felt a pang of jealousy toward the fiendling's spirit. Usually, Gisella, unopposed to finding comfort in someone's arms, found a night spent in pleasure a good way to celebrate or relax after a trying day, but she deliberately suppressed thoughts of carnal pursuit when she left Muncifer. Whatever surprises this trip held, she intended not to be distracted by involving her emotions where someone else was concerned. Spending time with a lover always carried with it the risk of becoming too attached.

Maybe the fiendling doesn't have that problem. She thought back to the on-again, off-again lovers she left in Muncifer. She hoped they would find that which they sought. Gisella always suspected they viewed her more as a prize than a true partner, anyway.

She caught up with Qaliah as the fiendling left the Palace of Justice. She took her arm just in time to keep her from stumbling down the steps. "Maybe we should return to the Screeching Griffon. You imbibed quite a bit of wine just now."

"Imbided, imbibbed, I wanna be bedded." Qaliah hugged her arm and gazed up at Gisella. "But you aren't going to do that for me, are you, Blondie?"

The odor of wine pervading Qaliah's breath convinced Gisella not to permit anyone to take advantage of the fiendling. She didn't want to find her bleeding out in an alley later that night.

"Let's go to the Bastion of Bliss."

"Oh, sounds good." Qaliah giggled. "What is it?"

Gisella smiled. *The Ritual of Renewal is just what she needs.* "It'll be better than some random man you'll drag in off the street. I promise."

* * *

"How hard can it be to find pictures of runes?" Delilah fought the urge to toss the ancient book to the ground. She inhaled deeply and exhaled slowly as she closed the cover and slid it onto the shelf, spine first.

"I've learned more about boggin mating habits than I ever knew had been studied." Alysha turned another gilded page.

"This one"—Katka held up a book whose frayed cover threatened imminent disintegration—"is about hog husbandry. Maybe I should take it to my parents."

Delilah looked over her shoulder toward the Runes of Selene. "Maybe I should just activate the damn thing and press random sequences."

Alysha cocked an eyebrow. "I think that would be extraordinarily bad. You could open a portal to the Void Realm."

"That does sound bad." Delilah made a mental note to research the Void Realm the next time she visited the library.

"Wasn't your brother supposed to get food?" Katka closed the book and placed it on the shelf, spine first. She rubbed her stomach. "I'm sure it's getting late. My stomach says so."

"I'll check on him." Delilah stomped up the stairs and entered her brother's living quarters. She found neither Kale nor Kali, so she went to the front of the shop. Darkness crept in through the front window, yet Ori hunched over his desk, illuminating, by the light of several candles, the manuscript before him.

"Where's my brother?"

"Oh, Archmage!" Ori gasped and fell off his stool. He jumped to his feet. "I didn't… oh, they went to get more food. Kali said she didn't have enough to feed all of us and two humans, too."

Delilah's stomach grumbled. "Yeah, I guess they do eat more, huh? All right, well, I hope they hurry up. We're hungry."

She returned to the door, noticing, only after she opened the concealed panel, that Ori followed her.

"Oh, would you like help? Kale said you were looking through books."

"Thank you, no." Ori stumbling around on the stairs with all those ancient tomes sounded like an awful idea. "Besides, I think the Frost Queen is tiring of so many draks around here."

Ori did not see through her lie and backed away. "Oh, I don't want to upset the Frost Queen."

"Hey, you can do me a favor, though."

"Oh? Yes? Anything for you, Archmage Delilah." Ori clasped his hands, his eyes growing wide.

"Keep an eye on my brother, huh? He's going to end up on his butt in the street if he doesn't pay more attention to his mate."

"Oh. Yes, I will." From his tone, Delilah surmised it wasn't the kind of favor for which he had hoped. She offered him a quick smile before returning to the two humans below.

Katka looked up when Delilah returned. "Wizard needs food, badly."

"They didn't have enough, so they had to go out." Delilah picked up the next book in sequence. The flowing script immediately identified it as Elvish. Delilah leafed through it, searching for any patterns that resembled the runes on the circle. She saw nothing and handed the book to Alysha.

"Can you read Elvish?"

The Frost Queen opened the book, flipped through the pages, and shook her head. "Never had the opportunity to learn." She returned the text to Delilah. "Not many elves come down to the Southern Watch. They think it's too cold."

"It is."

"I can read Elvish." Katka reached toward Delilah. The archmage handed the tome to her. Her apprentice scanned the first few pages. "Wow, it's a translation of the Chronicles of Bethany the Wise. I didn't know the elves… oh, this is interesting!" She read from the text.

"And so did the scaled people flee the oppression of the Kings of the Seven Kingdoms to dwell under the fiery mountain. Their flight was in vain, as another dwelt there and bound them to his servitude. Toil, blood, and flame awaited them, and thus they dwelt in rivers of lava—"

"Hey, I've heard that." Delilah hopped up a step to peer over Katka's shoulder and into the book. The words still made no sense to her. "That sounds like what the elders used to tell us about how we, the draks, I mean, came to Drak-Anor. Of course, it wasn't called that then."

"Sounds delightful." Alysha picked up another book.

Delilah scratched her head. "Who are the Kings of the Seven Kingdoms?"

"After The Sundering, what civilization remained broke down, and warlords seized power. There were probably more than seven kingdoms, but it's not as poetic to say 'Seven Kingdoms, a Duchy, two empires, and six city-states.'" Katka closed the book and handed it to Delilah to return to the shelf.

"Not to mention, the Chronicles of Bethany the Wise are notorious for only acknowledging the existence of Andelosia, or what remained of it at that time." Alysha chuckled and swapped the tome she perused for another. "All the world's ills, including The Sundering, were blamed on the people across the sea, demons, or the lands beyond the Western Wastes."

"Human wizards caused The Sundering when they killed Rannos Dragonsire." Kale stood at the top of the steps. Delilah hadn't heard him return.

Katka looked up, her eyes wide. "Food? Tell me you have food!"

The winged drak nodded and jerked a clawed thumb behind him. "There's food. Kali was a bit put-out, Archmage Delilah."

The archmage pursed her lips and took his arm as she ascended the stairs. "What's with the formality, Kale?"

"I don't want trouble, Archmage Delilah. You wizards come in here, making demands, telling me what to do in my own house—"

"Get over yourself, Wingy." Alysha patted him on the head as she passed the pair. "Consider our use of your splendid library the price you pay for running off my dragon. At least I didn't flay the flesh from your bones."

Kale stopped and glared at the human woman's back as she proceeded toward the kitchen.

"I don't think she can do that, Kale." Katka smiled at him as she followed Alysha.

"I know you were just trying to help, Kale." Delilah turned her brother to face her. "I was angry, and rightly so. Losing the dragon messed up my plans. We'll figure things out. I appreciate your help. Do I need to talk to Kali?"

"No, I can handle it." He squirmed away from her and spread his wings to block the hallway as he moved, leaving her and Ori to bring up the rear. Ori shoved the door to the cellar stairs shut as he passed.

"Oh, Archmage Delilah! Find anything good down there?"

They found many valuable texts. Delilah wished she had thought to catalogue them as they went. "Plenty, but nothing to solve our current problem." She put her arm around the blue drak. "Say, I don't suppose you've come across any books with rune-like constellation illustrations in them in your work?"

"Oh, no. Nothing like that."

It was worth a try. The kitchen, having been built for a small family of draks, overflowed with the addition of two humans. The room became a jumbled mass of arms, legs, and wings. Katka was short enough to cram herself out of the way in a corner, for the most part, but Alysha's stature reminded Delilah of Annah Brighteyes. That the Southerner had to crouch to move about the house didn't help matters. Kali grumbled as she served everyone but seemed pleased at the gusto with which they all devoured their meal. She noticed Ori partaking and frowned. Delilah caught her eye and shook her head.

When their appetites were sated, she took Kale's mate aside. "I can probably get the Arcane University to reimburse you for the food, maybe some extra for the cleanup." Delilah was unfamiliar with university policies for such compensation, but it sounded like the type of decision that should fall within her authority.

"What else would you command us to do?"

Delilah bit her lips and forced herself not to roll her eyes. "Oh, stop with that. You and Kale, I swear… Look, I got carried away. I should have asked if we could take over your cellar to look through those books and made our own arrangements for food. I was angry at Kale for messing up my plans, and didn't think twice about bossing him around."

Kali crossed her arms over her chest. "Not as angry as I was about almost getting eaten."

"I'm surprised you didn't feed him his own wings." Frankly, Delilah wondered Kali allowed Kale inside the house after that.

"It was tempting." Kali shrugged. "But he's my mate. I have to make it work."

Delilah put her hand on her sister-in-law's shoulder. "He'll come around. He's not used to having to be responsible for, well, anything. Ever."

"I can hear you, you know." Kale worked to clear the kitchen, just a room away.

"So, stop me if I say something that's not true." Disregarding the boorishness of talking about her brother while he was in earshot, Delilah hoped he'd take the cue to sort out his priorities. Taking a mate was a lifelong commitment, and she reminded herself he'd made the decision on a whim.

Kali pulled Delilah into a hug. "Go back to your books. I'll help him clean up. Want some mulled wine for later?"

"Sure, that'd be great."

* * *

"Are you sure you'll be all right?" Orion held the minotaur wizard's arm as he lowered himself into a chair in his quarters at the Arcane University.

Pancras felt his skin burn hot beneath his fur. Though he was flattered by Orion's attention, he was also a little embarrassed by it, particularly because of the way it made him feel. The Justicar stirred up emotions and desires Pancras long ago buried and forgot.

I guess they aren't so forgotten after all.

"Yes, I'll be fine." The chair, covered in burgundy suede with gold rivets, felt firm yet supportive. "Demons are challenging opponents, and this one seemed stronger than the last one I faced."

Orion pulled over the other chair to sit alongside Pancras. "Have you fought many demons?"

"I make it sound like a regular occurrence, don't I?" Pancras chuckled. It seemed frighteningly common since he left Drak-Anor, a trend the minotaur hoped to reverse.

"Perhaps I'll start calling you 'The Demon Hunters Three.'" Orion's grin overtook his face.

Pancras smiled and picked at a loose string on the arm of his chair. "How strange are the paths life takes, eh? A year ago, I wanted nothing more than to tinker in my workshop and advise my friend on how to run Drak-Anor, when he asked for my advice, of course."

"And what is it that you want now?"

"To be back in my workshop, to be honest." Pancras gestured to the room in which he sat. "This is not bad. Teaching here could be fulfilling. But the rest? Tracking down demons, facing off with the Lich Queen, if that's who our nemesis really is? I never wanted that. I hate travel. I hate going into dirty old ruins." He regarded his withered hand and flexed it. The leather gauntlet creaked as his fingers bent. "I hate the pain, the wounds, the discomfort. The things lost that shall never return…"

"Friends?" Orion leaned forward and placed his hand on Pancras's knee.

"Thankfully, no." He looked up and shook his head. "I mean, not recently. Of course, friends in my past have gone. One in particular…"

"Someone to whom you were especially close…"

Pancras found Orion staring at him. No, not staring, exactly. Watching him with eyes filled with a mixture of sympathy and longing. He found it difficult to talk about his feelings with others, especially when he was not certain they would accept his preferences.

"It is difficult." Pancras looked away. "It is not accepted well among our people."

He felt a hand squeeze his knee. "I understand. Believe me, I do."

Pancras's eyes met Orion's. At that moment, he realized the Justicar understood. "How did you know?"

"I didn't, at first." Orion reclined in his chair. Pancras found himself wishing the Justicar had not moved his hand. "I took a chance. Small gestures that could be misinterpreted. Gradually, I came to recognize you were one to whom I could open myself."

The Justicar stood and clasped his hands behind his back as he paced. "I have never understood why we restrict ourselves, why we forbid ourselves from loving a person simply because of the circumstances of our birth. I had a mate once; she was strong, a fine warrior. She died in childbirth." He stopped, his shoulders slumping as he lowered his head.

"I'm sorry to hear that." Pancras shifted in his seat. He never desired a female mate and decided at a young age he did not want offspring.

Orion turned and smiled. "It was tragic, but such is life. I was so certain she and I were the perfect pair, blessed by Aurora, that I turned from my lover. He understood my desire to have children, but he no longer wished to remain where he thought he might encounter me and be reminded of what we once had."

It was not the first time Pancras heard of lovers parting amicably and settling remote from one another to avoid reliving the heartache every day. "What became of him?"

"He joined a trading caravan bound for the south. I'm not sure where. I was so enamored of Sarra that I didn't think to ask." He pulled his chair closer to Pancras and sat again. "It doesn't matter now. I hope you don't think I'm too forward. I have been alone for many years here in Vlorey, ever since Sarra died."

"Forward?" Pancras smiled. "Yes, but it's not unwelcome."

He took Orion's hands and lowered his head. The two minotaurs touched foreheads. Pancras felt his horns slide along Orion's, and the familiarity of the gesture caused his heart to leap. He caught himself smiling as their breath mingled in the warm coastal night.

* * *

"I found it! I found it!" The cry from the cellar stairs disturbed Kale's mental self-flagellation. He found Katka's voice grating, having interrupted his concentration as he catalogued all the ways his life had gone wrong since embarking upon the mission to Ironkrag with Pancras a year prior.

Kali popped her head into the kitchen where Kale still cleaned the mess dinner left behind. "What's that all about?"

"She found it, I guess." Kale tossed his dirty rag onto a pile of similar rags spent from the deep scrubbing he gave the kitchen.

"Great." Kali entered the kitchen and retrieved the dirty rags. "What is *it*, exactly?"

"The symbols they need to get that stupid moon gate in the basement working."

"That's what I thought." She stopped before him. Kale stared at the counter and concentrated on the spot he aimed to erase from it. "Hey, look at me."

Kale suppressed a scowl and forced himself to raise his head. Her dark eyes seemed soft, and she offered him a small smile. "Hey, they'll be out of our scales soon."

"You're not still mad at me?" He continued rubbing the spot on the counter.

"Oh, I'm still angry, but I'll get over it." She nodded at the counter. "You know that's a knot, right? It's never going to come out."

He examined the spot again. She was right. "Yeah, I know. I thought I saw a stain on it. I must have gotten it out." He placed the rag on top of the pile she carried. "What else do you want me to do?"

"Unless you want to check on them in the cellar? Nothing. I'm tired and don't want to work anymore. You?"

Exhausted, but recalling his night of fitful slumber on the floor in the front of the shop the night before, he sighed. "I guess I'll check on them."

His mate rubbed her cheek against his. "Hurry back. I want to go to sleep. I'll keep the bed warm for you."

"Oh, okay." Kale's pace quickened at the thought. The front shop lay deserted; Ori left for his own home as dusk fell across the undercity. He flung open the door that concealed the steps to the cellar and hopped down to where the three women gathered around a black, leather-bound tome, talking over each other and pointing at drawings on the pages.

He cleared his throat until his sister looked at him.

"What, Kale?"

"You found what you need, right? So, Kali and I can get some sleep now?" He braced himself for the inevitable protest.

Delilah closed the book. "Yes, I think this is exactly what we're looking for." She motioned to the two other sorceresses. "We'll study this in my chambers at the Arcane University, so you can enjoy some quiet time."

As she passed him on the stairs, she stopped to touch his arm. "Will it be all right to return tomorrow to do some experiments?"

His sister's polite demeanor gave Kale pause. He could not remember the last time she asked him for permission to do anything. "I guess, sure. Not too early."

Delilah shook her head. "I don't want begin working too early. It will be well after Ori opens shop."

"He has Aurora's fever, you know," Kale blurted. He wasn't sure Ori was ready for Delilah to be quite that aware of his feelings, nor could Kale guess if Delilah held any interest in the blue drak, but for once, he desired her to feel as uncomfortable as she'd made him the last several days. "For you."

The archmage shut her eyes and made a gurgling sound deep in her throat. "I am aware, Kale. But thank you, I'll try not to turn him into a cave lizard." She glanced at the two humans. "Let's go."

Kale let them out, locking the shop door behind them. The enticing lure of his own bed was a siren call he was eager to answer.

Chapter 19

The next morning, while in her chambers, Delilah broke her fast with Katka and the grouchy Frost Queen. Alysha's eyes were puffy, and Delilah counted in the lines on her face the number of hours the southern sorceress spent awake.

"Rough night?" The archmage hoped there would be gold in the Frost Queen's answer.

Alysha stabbed a sausage with her fork, rattling the other dishes on the table. "Maris take them all! Pock-faced, artless, clay-brained, maggot-pies. All of them!" She bit into her sausage with fury, heedless of the stream of hot grease it sent down her chin.

"Ooh." Katka winced. "Your guest quarters are above the elder apprentices, aren't they?"

Delilah concentrated on chewing her sweet roll in an effort to refrain from chortling as Alysha continued her tirade. The drak archmage had not ever heard of sheep-biting skainsmates or unchin-snouted clack-dishes, but the staccato fashion in which Alysha delivered the insults and the way her head bobbed with indignation, caused Delilah to stifle more than one snicker. She would have recorded the various invectives the Frost Queen spewed, but she didn't wish to risk her ire.

"Gorbellied, milk-drinking miscreants!" She threw her fork onto the plate before her. It skipped off it and clattered across the table, embedding itself into the side of a fat sausage. Hot juices dribbled out, blood-like grease spreading in a pool around the slain meat. "You should send them all down to the Southern Watch as punishment. I'll show them how to behave around their betters."

The elder apprentices had, no doubt, been celebrating their upcoming graduation. Delilah was kept informed by Headmaster Agata, but they agreed until it was time for her to confer their newly earned status as guild mages upon the graduates, her involvement in the minutiae of testing or ceremonies was not required.

"Some of them"—Delilah coughed as she choked, suppressing another giggle while she ate—"no doubt, deserve that. We should finish up here and get back to work on the moon gate."

By the time they reached the undercity, the business day was in full swing. Having to wait for merchants to push their carts across streets or for crowds gathered around market stalls to dissipate and allow them to move past made the already-impatient archmage seethe.

The draks, of course, made way for the striped drak, bowing to her and asking for her blessings as she passed. Delilah did so as an afterthought, much to the amusement of Alysha. Their veneration reminded the sorceress why she avoided traveling to her brother's home during mid-morning on market days.

"Would you draks get out of the way!" A minotaur pushing a potato cart snorted and stomped his feet as a deluge of draks crowded around Delilah, blocking his path and trapping him on a rickety bridge spanning the gorge.

Delilah tapped her staff on the walkway and gathered aetherial threads of arcane energy. The lizard skull atop her focus glowed. "You will all have a prosperous day. Now, let the potato-pusher through."

Her proclamation had the desired effect, and the draks parted, like a sea draining into a newly opened chasm in the ocean floor. She motioned to the two humans to follow, and they rushed to cross the bridge before more draks corralled them.

Ori sat at his desk, already hard at work when they arrived. He directed Delilah to the kitchen, where Kale and Kali dined. She instructed Alysha and Katka to wait in the shop, and she announced herself to her brother.

"I'm just letting you know we're here. We'll be in the cellar."

Kale's wings fluttered as he held up a sweet roll. "Want one?"

"Maybe later, I've experiments to run. It might be safer if you stay up here." She glanced over her shoulder into the hallway, lowering her voice. "I don't actually know how this thing will react."

Kali pointed her fork at the archmage. "If you blow up our house, I'm going to haunt you for the rest of your days."

"Hopefully the rock will contain the blast." Delilah ignored Kali's dire warning and led the two humans to the cellar.

Katka sat on the floor with the tome and described each rune to Alysha. The southern sorceress marked the ones she described with a bit of chalk.

"Okay, Archmage," Alysha brushed the chalk off her hands. "The ones I've marked are the rune sequence we think leads to my castle. We know that moon gate is intact."

Delilah channeled arcane energy into the circle. Azure tendrils poured from the skull atop her staff and swirled around the ring. The runes glowed like sapphires in the sun, and an image of two grey globes appeared in the center.

She needed to manipulate the representations of the King and Queen to match their current phases. One was still dark, but the other entered another phase, now that the double-dark period ended. *But was it waxing or waning?*

Delilah hesitated. Alysha pointed at the smaller of the two orbs. "Queen's waxing."

The archmage reached toward the Queen. Her clawed fingers felt as if they touched a warm stone, and she turned it until a slight crescent appeared.

"The other way!"

Oops, that's waning. I should have spent more time studying astronomy with Kale when Terrakaptis offered. She corrected her mistake. When she completed her manipulation of the moons, the King was dark, and the Queen waxed.

Pebbles bounced on the floor as the cavern shook. Dust drifted down from the ceiling. She stepped around the moon gate. Alysha had marked a sequence of seven runes with numbers indicating the order in which they should be pressed. Each one flared with azure flame as she touched them.

The vibrations settled with each activated rune. Her hand hovered above the seventh, a rune that resembled a solid circle, the symbol of Selene, goddess of magic. She touched it.

Sucking the air out of the cavern with a *whoosh-hiss*, a shimmering rectangle sprang from the center of the runed circle. Delilah's eyes widened, and she failed to stifle a squeal of triumph. From the back, it appeared as a swirl of turquoise. The archmage returned the front. Alysha's eyes were wide, and the sorceress nodded.

"I recognize it! I can see the chamber where the Runes of Selene reside."

Through the moon gate, Delilah perceived the edge of the circle. Several runes on the other side glowed, although she couldn't distinguish which from her current angle. Sconces, not unlike the ones in the cellar, illuminated the room, and the translucent blocks which composed the walls glittered as they reflected the light.

"Are your walls made of ice?" Katka, still seated on the floor, squinted at the moon gate.

"My entire castle is ice."

Delilah shivered. "Ugh. Cold."

Alysha took a deep breath. "It's not so bad. Shall I?"

"Do you know the sequence to return?" Delilah took the book from her apprentice and leafed through the pages.

"I think so, but if I don't reactivate it in five minutes, do it from this end." The sorceress nodded at Katka and Delilah before she stepped through. The surface of the door bent as though she pressed against it. Then it rebounded and wobbled before the rectangle retracted and the runes extinguished themselves.

"Wow." Katka hugged her knees. "I wonder what going through that feels like."

Delilah had to admit she was curious herself. "I suppose we'll find out soon enough."

* * *

The next day, after his morning lessons, Pancras went to the Screeching Griffon in search of Gisella and Qaliah. He stopped on one of the arched bridges that spanned the waters of the delta to gaze at some violet flowers growing on one of the small islands.

The warm breeze blowing in from the sea brought with it the smell of salt and fish. He adjusted the front his new robes. They were cut to allow more airflow and uncovered his arms and lower legs, much more appropriate for hot, humid late-summer days in Vlorey.

He spied a fish swimming with the current as water rushed through the delta on its way to the bay. He lost himself in its undulating motions. Behind him, someone giggled. The minotaur turned to see a woman in the arms of a man who leaned close to her and whispered into her ear as she giggled again and blushed. The tight curls of her dark hair remained still, but her aquamarine dress flowed in the wind like the waters below.

Pancras smiled and bowed his head at them before completing his journey across the bridge. His evening with Orion reignited feelings he thought he would never again experience, and now that they had surfaced, he wanted to hold onto them and bask in their warmth and contentment.

He stopped at a cart selling flowers and bought two Aurora Lilies, so named for the brilliant splashes of emerald whose shape resembled the lights in the sky named after the goddess of beauty.

Upon arriving at the Screeching Griffon, he saw neither the fiendling nor the Watchmaiden in the common room, so he tromped up to their room.

Qaliah answered the door when he knocked. "Blondie isn't here."

"Pity." He offered her the flowers. "I brought one for each of you."

The fiendling grinned and took the blossoms. "Ooh, what's the occasion? You know I'm game, but I don't think you're Blondie's type." She winked at him and stood on tiptoes to kiss him on the cheek.

"I just thought I'd brighten your day, that's all."

Qaliah furrowed her brow and licked her lips. Her tailed flicked back and forth. "Yeah? That's… hey, that Justicar took you home yesterday, didn't he? I saw how he was making moon eyes at you. Have you been playing a little prickle-me-tickle-me, the two of you?"

The minotaur felt his face grow hot, and he pursed his lips. "That's really not your business."

"Oh, you found yourself a bull to ride!" Qaliah bounced and giggled, dancing with the flowers and singing a bawdy song filled with euphemisms that Pancras had heard the sailors on the *Maiden of the High Seas* sing.

He covered his face and counted to ten. "Please don't compare my people to cattle."

She stopped mid-hop. "Oh. My apologies! It just slipped out."

"Where is Gisella?"

Qaliah skipped over the bed and sat on the edge. The wood frame creaked in protest. Glancing around the room, Pancras neared the wardrobe, his hooves clopping on the dry, wooden floor, noticing one of the wood shutters had split, and the bureau, covered in a layer of dust, wobbled when he touched it. A pang of guilt stabbed his heart.

"Blondie went to see your friends at the Palace of Justice. She wanted to see if there was an update from that dwarf scout."

He ran his finger along the top of the furniture and held it up "Do you two need money to move to a better inn? I didn't realize this one was so… dirty."

She leaned forward, setting both hands on her knees. "I thought Blondie would want to move for sure after a few days. This place is luxurious compared with what I'm used to. She said she's content, though, so I didn't press the issue."

"All right." Pancras wiped his dirty finger on the edge of his robes. "If you change your minds and need assistance, I brought plenty of funds from Drak-Anor, and my stipend from the Arcane University is more than enough to cover my quarters and expenses there, as well. How are you feeling, by the way?"

The minotaur eyed her, searching for signs of distress. Lord Tyron's demonic possessor unsettled the fiendling in a way Pancras couldn't understand, but he felt sympathy for her.

The fiendling stretched out on the bed, tucking one of her arms behind her head as her tail coiled around her bare leg. "Gisella took me to the temple of Aurora for their Ritual of Renewal. I feel much better now, but it didn't do anything to cure my boredom. I wouldn't complain about a better room, though,"

"I'll keep that in mind." Pancras chuckled. "Let her know I stopped by. I have an afternoon class to teach."

"Thanks for the flowers. Shower me with gifts anytime."

* * *

Kale and Kali crept down the stairs after hearing Delilah's shriek of joy. Before joining the archmage and her apprentice in the cellar, they observed the Frost Queen enter the moon gate and the doorway recede into the floor.

"It worked?" Kale spread his wings to envelope his mate. She wrapped her arm around his waist.

"Looks that way." Delilah gestured to the runed circle. "Now we wait for her to return."

The runed circle appeared no different than the last time Kale saw it, except perhaps it was dustier.

"We thought the house was coming down." Kali squeezed her mate.

"It didn't shake that much." Delilah paced around the circle pointing at runes and speaking softly to herself. "Besides, most of this house is rock. A little shaking won't hurt it. We dealt with stronger tremors all the time in Drak-Anor."

Kale nodded in agreement. The shaking they felt during the moon gate activation would not have awakened him had he been sleeping. Still, after having been buried alive in the Deep Road cave system when Bloodplume erupted for the last time, Kale became a little apprehensive whenever the ground shook.

He raised his foot to scratch his leg. "So, when is she coming back?"

"Any minute now." Delilah regarded her apprentice. Katka, still seated on the floor, held the book in her lap. "How much time?"

The young woman frowned. "It's hard to count with everybody talking. She still has a few minutes, I think."

Allowing Katka to continue counting to herself, the rest of the group remained silent until she finished. By Kale's reckoning, the apprentice gave her more than just a few more minutes.

"She should have returned by now."

Delilah nodded and proceeded to activate the moon gate. Wispy blue tendrils swirled around the top of her staff and poured into the circle. Two grey orbs materialized above the central slab, which the archmage then manipulated.

"Hey, are those the moons?"

His sister answered with a curt nod and made her way around the circle, tapping specific runes with her hand and first, and then trying her foot on one, as Gil-Li had done in her vision. It burst with blue flame like the others.

"Ha! That's much easier." She finished activating the runes, and an azure rectangle sprang from the smooth, dark surface. From where Kale stood, he recognized the shape of a wall that appeared to be constructed from blocks of ice. Just as he was about to have a good look, the Frost Queen stepped through the moon gate, obscuring his view. The azure portal wobbled before it retracted and disappeared.

"Well, that was a dismal failure." She stepped out of the runed circle and knelt next to Katka. "Damn it. I did everything you did. I couldn't even get the moons to appear!"

"That's odd." Delilah joined the two humans. "I didn't channel that much power into it, and you've got to be fairly powerful, right?"

"Powerful enough." Alysha crossed her arms and tapped her foot. "You, girl"—She pointed at Katka—"you try it."

Kali nuzzled Kale's neck. "I'm going back upstairs. Boss Steelhand wants to meet in a little while."

"Oh." Kale folded his wings. "Do I need to come with you?"

"You should, but you can stay and watch a little while longer."

Katka backed away from the two older sorceresses, her hands raised in front of her. "Me? I'm just an apprentice."

"You can do it."—Delilah stepped closer to her pupil and placed a clawed hand on the young woman's shoulder—"just like I did."

The apprentice drew her wand and poured emerald energy into the circle with no effect. After swirling her wand to ensure she covered the entire surface, she stopped.

"Pacha's blue balls!" Delilah stomped her foot. She pointed her staff at the runed circle, and as soon as she concentrated, the circle flared to life again.

"I guess it likes you, Deli."

"Kale, come here." His sister waved him over to her.

"I don't know how to work magic, Deli. You know that." He approached his sister.

"See if you can position the moons." She pointed at the grey orbs floating in a lazy circle within the Runes of Selene.

"Like what?" Kale scratched his head and regarded the orbs. They appeared translucent, mottled grey almost like smoky, glass.

"Touch them, spin, them, whatever."

Kale entered the circle and tried to manipulate one of the moons. His hand passed through it. He tried again and again with the same result.

"That's enough. I figured that's what would happen. You try it, Alysha."

The winged drak stepped aside for the tall human sorceress. Her attempt yielded the same result. Katka tried it again after her before Delilah tried one last time. Only the drak archmage could manipulate the images of the moons.

"Maybe it knows you're the archmage?" Kale sat on the bottom step and rested his elbow on the bookshelf.

"I'm going to try to activate it from the other side." Delilah activated the runes to create the moon gate.

"Wait!" Alysha and Kale shouted at the archmage at the same time.

"What if you can't get it working again, Deli?"

"My thoughts, exactly." Alysha eyed Kale and then his sister. "We don't know that the circle in my castle even works.

It might only accept portals from this location and be unable to initiate them."

"Good point." Delilah gripped Katka's hand and pulled the young woman to her feet. "Hang onto the book." She cradled her staff in the crook of her elbow and took Alysha's hand.

"We'll go through together. Kale, I'm going to try to activate the other side as soon as we're through. If I'm not back in a few minutes, go to the Arcane University and tell them their archmage is in the Southern Watch."

"Wait, Deli…"

Before Kale finished, his sister dragged the other two women through the portal and disappeared.

* * *

When Gisella arrived at the Palace of Justice, she found Lord Fenwick and Scout Stonehammer in his chambers examining a sprawling map that hung over the edges of his desk.

The Justicar glanced up from the map when Gisella entered. "What is it? What's wrong?"

"Nothing. I just wanted to see if you'd spoken to Scout Stonehammer yet." Gisella's long strides covered the floor between the doors and the desk as she spoke. "I have my answer."

The dwarf woman brushed a stray strand of ginger hair out of her face and eyed the Lord Justice. "Impatient, isn't she?"

"A bit."

"My apologies." Gisella bowed her head. "But this is a grave matter… no pun intended. And my personal stake is such that I suppose I am impatient."

Lord Fenwick raised an eyebrow. "Personal, eh?" He grunted and returned his attention to the map. "Well, now that you're here, you can verify what I'm telling Valora here. The undead were last seen entering the sea at Ebonwick, about here."

He pointed to a spot on Verdant Point, which appeared to be the approximate location of the fishing village. He drew a line with his finger to the coast west of the city. "They should emerge there, probably no more than a day's ride out west. There have been no reports from travelers of roving bands of undead, so it's possible they're moving only at night."

Scout Stonehammer climbed into Lord Fenwick's chair and knelt on the table to gain a better view of the map. "Would they even make it across? There's sharks in those waters, I hear."

"I honestly don't know."

"They might not be attracted to the cursed flesh of the dead." Gisella leaned over the map and pointed to the approximate location of Zamora. "We think they're headed here—Zamora."

"Za… hey!" Scout Stonehammer put her hands on her hips and glared at Lord Fenwick. "You want me to go chasing pox-bellied Lich Queen stories?"

"The undead aren't stories. I've seen them."

Lord Fenwick took Scout Stonehammer's hand. Gisella noticed a hint of blush blossom in his cheeks, and his eyes flicked to regard the Golden Slayer before they focused on the dwarf woman. "It's important, Valora. Lord Tyron was possessed by a demon we think is involved."

The dwarf threw up her hands. "A demon! Demons, undead, and the Lich Queen? What year did I wake up in?"

"This slayer and her friends are trying to prevent exactly that—the return of the Lich Queen."

"The things I do for you. Undead make my skin crawl, and I've never even seen a demon before." She jumped off the desk. Her armor clanked and clattered as she hit the floor and paced, gesticulating with wide sweeps of her arms. "What if one of those things gets in me?"

She spun and pointed a stubby finger at the Lord Justice. "And none of your jokes!"

Lord Fenwick held up his hands. "You'll hear no jokes from me. This is a very serious matter. I can ask one of the Justicars to go—"

"Oh, burn that in Hon's hearth. You know I'll do my duty."

"I will accompany you." Gisella approached the dwarf and knelt before her. "My duty to the Arcane University was satisfied when the minotaur took up his post. Qaliah and I—"

"Is that the fiendling?" Scout Stonehammer cocked her head. "Not the fiendling."

Gisella bowed her head. "Very well." She wasn't keen on the idea of leaving Qaliah alone, unsupervised in the city, but it wasn't her responsibility to keep the fiendling out of trouble.

"Are you sure?" Lord Fenwick rolled up the map and handed it to Scout Stonehammer. "Valora is quite the accomplished scout. I have full faith in her abilities."

The Golden Slayer did not miss the wink Lord Fenwick aimed at the dwarf. She stood and crossed her fist over her chest. "And I am an accomplished slayer. I'm confident no adversaries will hinder our efforts."

"Fine then, Blondie." Scout Stonehammer tucked the map in her pack.

Gisella winced.

"Grab whatever you need from wherever you're staying. Got a horse?"

"At the Trader's Gate Livery."

"Ugh." Scout Stonehammer grunted and tightened the straps on her armor. Dark, almost midnight-blue scales, similar to what Gisella wore, but the dwarf's armor had been designed with harder, more geometric lines, as often was the case with dwarven-forged goods. "Get your horse and meet me at the south gate. We leave as soon as you're ready."

The dwarf gestured toward the door. "Get going. I have some more business here, but I don't have any stops once I leave. Don't keep me waiting."

As Gisella exited, she overheard the dwarf as she spoke to the Lord Justice.

"Get down here, Fennie, and say goodbye proper-like."

***

"Pacha's blue balls and Maris's bloody spear!" The cold air surrounding the Runes of Selene in the Frost Queen's castle sucked the air out of Delilah's lungs. She felt as if her toes shriveled, and she clenched her jaw to keep her teeth from chattering.

Alysha laughed and spread her arms. "Welcome to Rime Frost, Bastion of the Frost Queen."

Katka pulled her robes tightly around her. "Don't you believe in fires?"

"Look around you, girl! Fire would melt my magnificent creation."

"How in Selene's name do you stay warm?" Katka rubbed her arms as Delilah began the ritual to reactivate the runed circle. As much as she wanted a guided tour, the bitter cold and her lack of appropriate attire motivated the drak archmage to return to Muncifer as soon as possible.

Alysha held up the hem of her robes. "Enchanted clothing, of course."

The phrase stuck in Delilah's mind as she set the moons to their proper phases and journeyed around the circle, activating runes in sequence. *I need to look into enchanted clothing. That's brilliant.*

When she finished, the moon gate sprang into place. The azure glow from its surface cast dancing blue sparkles on the translucent walls. She extended her hands. "Let's go."

The three women stepped through the portal. The sensation of moving through the surface of the portal, with its slight resistance before giving way, reminded the drak of the time she was swallowed by a dragon. It was the same firm, yet yielding, squish she remembered from inside its esophagus. The experience ended better, however, as she stepped through into her brother's cellar rather than finding herself in a warlock-turned-dragon's stomach.

"You're back!" Kale leapt to his feet, spreading his wings for balance.

"Oh, warmth!" The archmage ran to her brother and wrapped her arms around him. His skin felt burning hot at first, but once she acclimated to the warmer temperature, the cellar felt quite comfortable.

"That's a little dramatic, don't you think?" Alysha clucked her tongue and placed her hands on her hips.

"I actually wouldn't mind going back, once we're properly attired." Katka brought the book to Delilah. "So, why do you think it works only for you?"

The archmage released her brother and took the tome. She leafed through it, sighing before she returned it to Katka. *Right. Elvish.* "I'm not certain. Maybe it only works for the archmage?"

"How would it know?" Kale glanced up the stairs and then at his sister.

"I had a similar thought. What if it *only* activates for an archmage?" Alysha tapped the volume. "Is there anything in there that says who built the circles?"

The apprentice shook her head as scanned the pages. "Not that I've read, but I haven't been through the whole thing."

"Like Kale said, how would it know if I was a random drak wizard or the archmage?" Delilah encircled the circle, examining the runes as if staring at them would unlock a new secret.

"Maybe you have to be a drak archmage?" Kale stretched his wings.

"That seems unlikely." Alysha climbed the steps to the first bookshelf and began to peruse volumes they hadn't yet searched.

"I should go, Deli. Kali is waiting…"

"Go, go. Thanks for sticking around." Delilah waved at him while still examining the runed circle. "I'll talk to you later."

Her brother climbed the stairs and joined his mate. The three women returned to their task of scouring the as-yet-unread treatises on the shelves. *We still have a lot of work to do.*

Chapter 20

Kale's mate awaited him in the shop, chatting with Ori, who showed her the tome he illuminated currently. The winged drak caught glimpses of stylized serpents winding around the outside of the pages as he approached them.

"So, how did it go?" Kali glanced at him as he checked his daggers and pouches.

"The moon gate thing works, but only for Deli. They're trying to figure out why."

"Oh, a moon gate? Is that's what's in the basement."

Kale bit his lips. He forgot they hadn't shared with Ori what lay behind the concealed door. It was impossible to hide their comings and goings from the limner since the door sat in full view of his counter, although he often sat with his back to the hallway into which the door opened.

"Yeah," Kale rubbed the back of his neck. "Don't tell Deli I told you, okay?"

"Oh. Well, I'd love to see it. I illuminated a book about them a couple of years ago. Did you know the Runes of Selene were all built by drak wizards in the Age of Legend?" The limner took the tome he showed Kali and returned it to his stand. He held up one of his brushes and closed one eye as he inspected the tip.

"Really? Did you read the book?" Kale figured if Ori could help, maybe Delilah wouldn't become angry he accidentally revealed their secret to the blue drak.

"Oh, I end up reading just about every book I work on. Sometimes I have to so I can put the right embellishments on the pages. I never could figure out what the gates were supposed to look like, though."

"Kale." Kali tugged on his arm. "We have to get going."

As his mate dragged him away, Kale pointed to the concealed door. "When Deli comes out, tell her what you know."

Once they were away from the shop, Kali's tail entwined with Kale's. "That was mean. Your sister will eat him up if he starts blurting stuff about moon gates."

Kale didn't agree. "She'd be so happy to find someone, a drak especially, who knows about it, she won't think twice." He muttered a quick prayer to Dolios.

They walked through the narrow, shadowy residential streets of the undercity. At this time of day, most draks were out and about, and avoiding crowds was the key to traveling through the undercity in a reasonable amount of time. That the city's draks still believed he had special powers or a special status boggled Kale's mind.

All the residential streets of the undercity led to a stone staircase that climbed up though solid rock and emerged into the predominantly minotaur-populated part of town. Boss Steelhand requested the drak couple meet him at one of his residences.

"It's just up here." Kali pointed ahead, past a crowd of minotaurs assembling a scaffolding around a crumbling building. Kale saw a sign beyond them: *The Wealthy Robber*.

He considered suggesting they stop there on their way home, but his mate stopped before the tavern's door.

"Here? I thought we were going to one of his houses."

Kali stood on her tiptoes and peered through the window next to the door. "Apparently, he owns this place and has some living space upstairs."

"Wow. Living in a tavern? I should have thought of that."

The two draks entered the tavern. A cloud of smoke clung to the beams of the ceiling, wafting up from water pipes on each table. The heads of twoscore minotaurs turned and stared at the draks as they entered. Compared to the human taverns Kale had been in, The Wealthy Robber was built to giant proportions. A log crackled and popped in the hearth, and as if on cue, all the minotaurs returned to their conversations.

They approached the bar and found that the tops of their heads barely reached the counter. Kali climbed onto one of the stools and rapped her knuckles on the bar top to get the minotaur barkeep's attention. "Hey, we're supposed to meet Boss Steelhand here."

Without turning to face them, the barkeep pointed to the stairs. "Downstairs. Door on the left."

"What happens if we go right?"

He shrugged. "Hope you like flour."

Kale moved in the direction indicated. He and Kali descended the stairs and noted oil lanterns illuminated the hallways.

"He's the same minotaur as that wizard Theros, right? I wonder why he doesn't have magical lights."

"Because I try not to flaunt it," Boss Steelhand called from behind the open door on the left.

Three rooms composed the minotaur's suite in the tavern's cellar, all connected by curtained doorways. Boss Steelhand sat in a plush chair before the iron stove located in the center of the room. A plush, ornate rug woven in muted red and gold dyed wool covered most of the floor.

"Have a seat." The minotaur gestured with his steel hand to another armchair that faced the one in which he sat.

Kale spread his wings as they climbed into the chair. With careful positioning, the two draks sat together in the chair sized for a minotaur. Once they were settled, Boss Steelhand leaned back and steepled his hands before him.

"Thank you for coming. I'm glad to see you survived the ire of your sister and mate, Kale."

The winged drak chuckled and studied the patterns of the rug. "Uh, yeah."

"We'll get him straightened out." Kali patted her mate's knee.

"I'll get straight to it. With Vilkan Icebreaker out of the way, the archduke is moving forward with many plans with which he requires my assistance. One of them is removing restrictions on draks and minotaurs here in the upper parts of the city."

"Well, that's good, right?" Kale eyed the minotaur.

"Yes, but our draks have been restricted to the under-city for so long, there's a whole generation who have never been around humans"—he raised his hand—"other than the guards, of course."

"The guards don't do much of anything except stand around and watch the market." Kali shifted and dangled a leg over the arm of the chair.

"Exactly, which is where the two of you come in. I want you to take a leadership role in helping the draks integrate into human society. You're outsiders, and you know what humans are like."

The winged drak frowned. "I don't really. We don't have humans in Drak-Anor."

"I know what you mean." Kali squeezed her mate's knee. "The humans here can't be that different than the ones in Almeria."

"No, not at all. A bit rougher around the edges, perhaps, but that comes from being so close to the mountains. Our winters are harsher than those Almeria experiences."

"Harsher?" Kale's eyes widened. He recalled the drak-high snow drifts in Almeria and shuddered. His exposure to winter from the inside of Drak-Anor had been minimal. Back home, winter snow often blocked the mountain passes and the entrances to the city until springtime, but the weather never affected its interior.

"So, what?" Kali extended her hand toward Boss Steelhand. "You want us to be the mayors of Draktown or something?"

The minotaur threw back his head and laughed. "No! Just community leaders, elders, if you will."

Kale felt as if his eyes might pop out of his head. "Elder? I'm not old enough to be an elder! I don't even have any hatchli—" He snapped his mouth shut and glanced over at his mate. She smiled.

"Whatever you want to call yourselves. I don't care." Boss Steelhand spread his hands. "Just don't go around trying to convince anyone you have any legal authority."

"Okay, fine, so we help the draks figure out how to deal with the humans." Kali leaned forward and tapped her chest with her thumb. "What's in it for us? We've got a good thing going with Ori."

"Whom I set you up with, through Jairo, if you'll remember." He raised his hand. "But I think we can work out something. You help the draks, be my eyes and ears in the undercity, and I'll grant you a modest stipend."

Kale felt his mate stiffen. She cocked her head and stroked her chin. "So, you want us to spy on them, too? There are some shady characters down there."

"No, no, no. Nothing like that." Boss Steelhand shook his head. "I already have people for that. I mean keep me informed about how they're assimilating. If there are any accommodations that aren't being met, that sort of thing. The humans will be resistant to change, but I have the ear of the archduke. You"—the minotaur pointed at Kale—"are the brother of the archmage. Any complaints the humans make about having to share space aren't going to fall on sympathetic ears."

He gestured to the ceiling in a sweeping arc. "Once the dwarves abandoned this city after The Sundering cracked the world, we minotaurs were the first to settle here. We only let the humans join us out of pity. The draks came during the healing, but even more humans came." He brought down his fist on the arm of the chair. "They drove us, well, the draks mostly, into the undercity. It's time they learned their place.

Were it not for the draks, so much of this city would still be in ruins."

"Did the humans enslave the draks?" Kale pondered whether humans subjugating draks was a common theme throughout Andelosia.

"No, but there was some exploitation that occurred. Once the humans were comfortable, they wanted the draks to disappear. The undercity was good enough. Out of sight, out of mind, you know."

"How much is a modest stipend?" Kali was back to business.

"It's negotiable." The minotaur leaned forward. "Look, I'm not talking about revolution or anything violent like that. The wrongdoers have been dead for generations. We all share this city. It's just, some folks need to be reminded of it. I know there'll be bumps, but I think most of the commoners will come around, and believe me, the nobles won't be able to stand alone. They'll cave, and those who can't adjust will leave."

As Kali launched intense negotiations regarding compensation details, Kale tried to keep up, noticing sparring with the minotaur seemed to energize her, a far cry from her earlier protestations that she wanted no involvement with the minotaur or his cronies. Kale, realizing their discussion was over his head, allowed his mind to wander.

Maybe she changed her mind when she discovered he was the archduke's right hand. But what happens if Deli gets that moon gate working? We're going to leave, then, right? She's going to need my help. Pancras needs my help.

If he was honest with himself, Kale did not understand what his sister's plans were or why she needed to go to meet up with Pancras, but he preferred it that way. Making plans was their job, and he helped where and when he was needed.

"Then we'll do a good job for you." Kali patted Kale's knee again, jostling him out of his daydream.

He had the feeling he'd just been volunteered for something he wasn't sure he wanted to be a part of. "I'm sorry, can you summarize? You were talking awfully fast."

Boss Steelhand laughed. "She's quite the negotiator. I think I've been had."

"Don't worry, Kale. We're going to be all right." She offered a hand toward Boss Steelhand as she slid off the chair. They shook on their agreement.

"Starosta Kale and Kali. The humans will like that." Boss Steelhand chuckled. "We'll use their own titles. That'll allow you to talk to community leaders on their own level."

"We're Starostas now?" Kale's tongue stumbled over the word. It sounded like a word he heard the locals use when they weren't speaking in the common trade language, mostly older folk talking among themselves. "What does that mean?"

"It's a title humans around here used to use. Mostly for influential landowners, not quite lords and ladies. When someone is not of the lineage, nobility requires an official position in the peerage. "Both of you are Starosta. Individually, you're Starost Kale and Starost Kali."

"Well, that's weird."

"Human languages don't make a lot of sense, Kale." Kali leaned on her mate. "I learned some Old Etrunian a few years ago, and the words in all the phrases were out of order!"

Boss Steelhand stood. "Find a linguist and figure it out. I have to get back to the archduke." He ushered them out of his suite and up into the tavern. He introduced them to an indifferent minotaur crowd, instructed the barkeep to let them run a tab, and left the two draks alone in a tavern full of minotaurs.

Kale glanced at the minotaurs intently ignoring the two short draks in their midst and then turned to his mate. "Want a drink?"

* * *

True to her word, Scout Stonehammer waited at the city's south gate, formally known as Cardoba Gate. Gisella approached the dwarf woman whose mount resembled a great, fat boar. The hairy creature snorted and squealed at Moonsilver's approach. Gisella paused to determine if Stonehammer's mount was aggressive and then approached them.

"The Golden Slayer atop a white steed. I am not surprised." Scout Stonehammer leaned forward and scratched between her boar's beige-tipped ears. Cream-colored fur near its snout accented its raven-colored coat. Two dirty, white tusks curved up from its lower jaw.

Gisella patted the side of her steed's neck. "Moonsilver has been a good friend for nearly ten years now." The horse tossed its head and whinnied. She glanced at the boar. "Are there any bogs around here?"

"Not where we're going, why?"

"I don't care much for them." Gisella glanced away from the boar and shuddered. "Bad childhood memories."

"Quincy here likes to stomp oroqs in the mountains." Scout Stonehammer put the spurs to her boar and sped through the south gate. Gisella caught up to her on the road. She reined in Moonsilver to keep him from overtaking the boar.

The road turned westward while still within sight of the city's walls. They followed the hard-packed dirt, traveling single file to allow passing caravans the use of ruts worn into the earth from decades of travel. When the city receded from view behind them, Scout Stonehammer guided them off the road and led them north.

"According to the map Fennie showed me, those undead should be coming ashore not too far from here."

"Do you need the map?" Gisella reached around to her pack, but stopped short of opening it when the dwarf shook her head.

"I know this area like my own home. I ride these plains constantly." She pointed ahead. "There's an overlook above the beach. I can't imagine them climbing up the rock cliffs when there's a nice beach they can just wade up onto."

Gisella nodded. "That seems logical. If their instructions are too specific, though, they may have no choice but to scale the cliffs. We should be cautious."

"So, what's your story, Blondie? You come up to Fennie, tell him some wild tales, and suddenly he's all agog, ready to call out the King's Army to help you."

Gisella gritted her teeth at the hated nickname. "Please, call me Gisella."

"I know your name."

Scout Stonehammer's terse reply dripped with jealousy. Gisella spurred Moonsilver forward and faced the dwarf woman. "Then use it, Valora."

The Golden Slayer did not fear the daggers in Scout Stonehammer's eyes, and she maintained eye contact until the dwarf looked away.

"If I've given offense, tell me, and let's be done with it. I don't have time for petty squabbling." Gisella suspected she understood exactly the dwarf's problem. She'd encountered it before, although not since having departed Muncifer. One of the disadvantages of traveling with a minotaur and fiendling was that prejudices against the two of them colored other people's perceptions of Gisella, as well.

"I know your type. You come in, see a tall, handsome man, flash your symbol of Aurora in his face, and flutter your eyelashes—"

"I have not come to seduce Lord Fenwick." Gisella maneuvered Moonsilver in front of Quincy, bringing them to a stop. The boar squealed and snorted in protest. The Golden Slayer slid off Moonsilver to stand eye level with the dwarf.

"He is handsome, I'll grant you that, but that's not why I'm here. I came with Pancras to stop the Lich Queen. That's all. Once my task is accomplished, I plan on returning home. Are we clear?"

"You're in my way." Scout Stonehammer pulled on Quincy's reins and steered him around Gisella and her horse.

"What of that fiendling you're with?"

Gisella laughed. "Qaliah will never consort with a Justicar. Maybe if she were trying to rob him, or her—"

"I overheard Orion talking. He's taken an interest in your minotaur, you know."

"Has he?" It was news to Gisella. She didn't care to keep track of others' relationships unless it affected her missions. "Good for him. Pancras is honorable. Perhaps the two of them will find happiness together."

A bird of prey screeched overhead as it circled some unseen target. Gisella watched as it dove toward the ground, snatched a wriggling creature, and flew away in triumph.

"My clan would string them up. Two males… humph."

Not an uncommon attitude, particularly in the north. Gisella didn't agree with it, herself, and life in the Four Watches could often be harsh and unforgiving. Tolerant of alternative lifestyles, Watchfolk judged others by their actions in battle and how they contributed to their communities. The harsh winters, clan feuds, oroqs, and frost wyrms made certain of that.

"My people have no such restrictions, and Aurora celebrates love in all its forms. Frankly, it's not anyone else's business."

Scout Stonehammer ran her fingers through the fiery fuzz on the side of her face. "Well, I suppose it isn't at that. Answer my question, though, Gisella. What's your story?"

She told Valora of Pancras's assignment and having taken the opportunity to accompany him to pursue her own investigation. "Qaliah joined us because she wanted to leave Muncifer and had no better offer, nowhere else to go."

"And somehow, you and the minotaur just happened to have the same goal, all along?" Valora regarded her, eyes narrowed.

"Not at all. When we departed Muncifer, he believed he was sent here to teach at the Arcane University." She decided not to reveal his subsequent death and resurrection at the Etrunian fort. "There was an... incident... with some death cultists along the way, and Pancras received a vision from Aita. He became a bonelord, en route, and embraced Aita's quest to dispatch the Lich Queen before she regained her power. After the vision, he revealed to me information about my past. Names, relationships, things I had divulged to no one in Muncifer. Only my sister possessed such knowledge, well, and the gods, I suppose."

"Bah! Gods always meddle when they're not wanted." Valora spat on the ground.

"Aurora has never led me astray. Besides, all coincidences look like fate when viewed in hindsight."

"Now, you sound like the clan elders." Valora held up a fist and pulled Quincy to a stop. She and Gisella dismounted. They secured the reins of their steeds to a fallen tree, and Gisella followed Valora up a hill until the dwarf woman dropped to her belly. They crawled to the edge.

Below them, the ground gave way to a sheer rock cliff, stretching downward hundreds of feet to a rocky beach. The waves crashed and hissed against the jagged rocks. Waterlogged tree limbs and a few scuttling crabs were the beach's only occupants.

"It doesn't look like hundreds of shuffling feet have been churning up the beach." Valora pointed to the water's edge.

"You can see an almost unbroken line of that sea moss down there."

Gisella, indeed, observed it. "How long would it take someone to walk across the bottom of the bay from Ebonwick?"

The dwarf rolled over on her back and counted on her fingers. "Good question. It's only been a few days since one of the moons came back, eh?"

"And the dead have been reported to march only on double-dark nights."

"Well"—Valora chewed on her lip—"I don't know what the bottom of the bay is like. It could take a week, maybe more."

"So, we need to make camp and wait." Gisella didn't mind sleeping outdoors. The breeze blowing inland from the sea felt a bit cooler than the stifling humidity of the city.

"Nah, let's go down there and see if there are any old tracks. Undead supposedly march from Vlorey, too. They've got to be tearing up the ground somewhere. There aren't any floaters, right? Just walking undead?"

"As far as I know."

Gisella and Valora crawled away from the edge and returned to their mounts. The dwarf cursed as she swung her leg over Quincy's back.

"Damn, I was hoping this would be a quick and easy job."

* * *

Another day of perusing tome after tome from the shelves in Kale and Kali's cellar brought no answers to Delilah. Her failure to determine why only she could activate the moon gate gnawed at her. Ori's persistence in insisting he possessed some important information served only to irritate her further.

She left Alysha and Katka to scour the volumes while she returned to the Arcane University. Guild business called, and Headmaster Agata requested an audience several days in a row,

Delilah met with the headmaster in the Council of Wizardry chambers. She waited in her center chair, newly outfitted with a raised footrest to keep her short legs from dangling. The elderly woman strode in, her footsteps echoing through the empty, stone-walled chamber, and bowed.

"Archmage."

"Headmaster." Delilah returned the bow with a nod of her head. "I apologize for keeping you waiting. I was engrossed in my research."

"Which? The moon gate or the egg?"

The egg? Maris's bloody spear, I forgot I told them about that. "Well, the dragon took the egg, so I've been concentrating on the moon gate."

"You allowed that dragon to fly off with Pyraclannaseous's egg?" Headmaster Agata's mouth hung agape, her eyes betraying her simultaneous horror and incredulity. Delilah, certain the old woman's eyebrows would merge in the center of her face and remain fixed like that for eternity, threw up her hands.

"Kale did. You can blame my brother. He claimed the dragon was quite eager to meet with Terrakaptis, which is where we wanted the egg to go in the first place." Delilah hoped the dragon told the truth. If Yaamkyrsku lied, she would not allow Kale to forget it. His helping with the moon gate mostly made up for his gaffe of sending the dragon away in the first place, but only barely.

Acting on an idea she had, Delilah leaned forward. "What do you know about the moon gates?"

Headmaster Agata frowned and clasped her hands behind her. "Not much, I'm afraid. Only what I read in history books. They were built in the Age of Legend and thought lost during The Sundering. There were always reports of a suspected site cropping up here and there, but no one took them seriously."

"Why not?"

"No one knew how to make them work."

Except me, apparently. "I see. That's about all I was able to find out, too."

"Fine. Now then, there's some school business to discuss." Analogous to torture, Delilah accepted the mundanities of running the Arcane University as a necessary cost of her new station. Most of the issues Headmaster Agata brought before Delilah did not actually require archmage approval; however, she did it out of deference to an archmage who resided on campus. Delilah felt as if the words "Yes, that's fine," were burned into her brain.

Once she had addressed all of the headmaster's concerns, Delilah strode the grounds as a demonstration of her interest in the students, gave some pointers to a group of novices who practiced on the training dummies their precision to deliver fire to a target, and finally, returned to her brother's house to check on Alysha and Katka's progress. Ori, of course, illuminated his most recent project at his raised desk behind the counter, and Delilah steeled herself to rush past him.

"Oh! Archmage Delilah, please wait."

"No time, Ori. Important things to do!" Delilah trotted through the shop and headed straight for the cellar door.

"Oh. Well, this is important, too. It's about your moon gate."

Delilah stopped, her hand hovering just above the concealed door pull. She growled her brother's name before forcing a smile and turning to face the blue drak.

"Oh, uh, I read about them in one of the books I illuminated."

Her smiled faded. "What about them?"

"Oh, well, they were built in the Age of Legend—"

Blah blah, I've heard all this before. Tell me something new, or I'll turn you into a newt.

"… built by draks. Oh! Did you know draks first formed the Mages Guild?"

"Wait, what? What was built by draks?" Delilah held Ori by the shoulders, and the color drained from his face.

"Oh! The moon gates. The moon gates were built by draks."

"That's it!" Delilah pulled the blue drak into a hug, rubbing the side of her face against his. She turned, barely registering the thud of his body as he hit the floor, and threw open the door to the cellar. Delilah sped down the stairs, clutching at the bookshelves to keep from sliding into Katka and Alysha, both seated on the bottom step reviewing different tomes. Losing hold of her staff during her descent, she allowed it to tumble down the steps and onto the cavern floor.

"What's wrong?" Alysha offered a hand to the archmage.

"Only drak wizards can activate the moon gates because drak wizards built them!" Suddenly, it all made sense to her. Most powerful artifacts, unless specifically constructed for use by anyone, were attuned only to those who built them.

Alysha clicked her fingers. "Because during much of the Age of Legend, there were only drak wizards."

Katka picked up Delilah's staff and handed it to her. "Great. What's that mean for us?"

"Well, I guess it means we're not going anywhere without her." Alysha pursed her lips and pointed to the archmage.

"It also means we can stop fooling around with all these books and try to figure out where the closest moon gate to Vlorey is." Delilah approached the runed circle and activated it. She set the Queen and King to their proper phases and stared at her apprentice.

It took Katka a moment to realize the archmage awaited her response. "Oh! I think we've worked out what a lot of the combinations are, but we couldn't test them without you, of course."

"Without maps from the Age of Legend, we had to makes some guesses." Alysha handed Delilah a piece of parchment on which the two women had drawn a key to possible combinations.

The archmage scanned the paper. Except for Celtangate, all of the locations close to Vlorey included a question mark. "Why, this seems pretty straightforward. I thought when the world was healed, it returned to pretty much the way it was before The Sundering."

"Well, sure, all the landmasses are pretty much the same." Alysha leaned on her staff.

"A lot of the cities changed names." Katka pointed to Velzuna. "Back then, this was just Cardoba, the city, I mean. After the healing of the world, the city expanded its territory, the nation was called Cardoba, and they changed the name of the city to Velzuna."

"Why?" Delilah scratched under her chin. "That makes no sense."

"Who knows?" Katka threw up her hands. "Ask someone in Velzuna. There are probably a dozen different stories."

"I guess we should just go down the list, starting with the ones closest to Vlorey. How will we know if the moon gate opens in the right general area?" Delilah, unfamiliar with the city, knew only that it sat on the northern coast.

"It sits near the water, and it'll look warm." Alysha took the parchment from Delilah. "I'll call out the runes. We'll start with the ones we think are near Vlorey, and move on to Ortuuz if that doesn't work, though I don't fancy we'd find a boat on an island rumored to be uninhabited."

The archmage activated the Runes of Selene, set the moon phases, and worked her way around the runic depictions of the constellations as the Frost Queen announced them.

When she tapped the last rune, the moons vanished, and the azure glow flickered out.

"Damn. I guess it was too much to hope for this to be easy." Delilah activated the circle and tried the next one.

The next three gave the same result—instant deactivation. With the fourth combination—labeled *Faenwar?*—the gate sprang open. Water poured through the moon gate. Delilah dove out of the way as the torrent rushed past her and bowled Katka off her feet. Delilah's staff spun across the room, landing on the far side of the runed circle. Her apprentice was swept away by the flood waters as they continued to pour out of the open moon gate.

"How do I shut it off?" Delilah yelled to Alysha as she ran after Katka. Her apprentice screamed and grunted, bouncing off the walls, as she was flung down the tunnel that led to the chasm outside. The water gushed out of the tunnel like an uncorked keg, and Delilah made a desperate dash, diving to grab Katka's sleeve. She managed to hook a claw on the young woman's robes and then another.

The smooth, stone walls of the tunnel offered little upon which to gain purchase, and the rushing water threatened to knock the drak off her feet. Katka's weight, greater than Delilah's own by a factor of two, didn't help.

Delilah's claws dug into the wall, leaving white gouges as the water pushed her along. The gorge came into view, the precipitous drop beyond the entrance promising a long fall and sudden stop.

Her apprentice twisted against the rush of water and grasped Delilah's arm. Their eyes met as the drak's grip on the wall gave way. They tumbled toward the edge.

Chapter 21

Upon examination of the beach, they found no evidence the undead had marched across the sand. With little to go on other than the assumption the undead traveled in nearly a straight line from Vlorey to Zamora, Scout Stonehammer and the Golden Slayer rode in an arc away from the coast. This afforded them the greatest chance to cross the path the undead used, assuming they had not sprouted wings and flown across the land.

The rocky, scrub-covered plains near the coast gave way to rolling grass and farmlands further south. They covered a good amount of ground by the time the sun set and the moons rose; however, they discovered no evidence to help them determine whether the undead had traveled through the area

Scout Stonehammer built a small, low fire in a shallow pit and piled rocks around the edges to further shield the flames from sight. They found a short shrub on which to secure Moonsilver. Gisella suggested Valora hitch Quincy to a bramble at the other side of camp. Once they completed preparing the area for their overnight stay, Valora sat against her saddle, chewing on a slice of jerky.

"They can't not leave tracks right?" She waved the jerky in the air as she spoke.

"I've never tracked undead before." Gisella sipped some of the Ravenbrier mead she brought along. "I assume if their strides are similar to those of a live person, they would leave traces of their passage. I don't see how they cannot."

"I hope they don't sneak up on us in the night." Valora pulled at her gorget. "I hate sleeping in armor."

"The ones Qaliah and I encountered in Ebonwick didn't seem interested in us at all." Gisella shared Valora's disdain of slumbering fully clad, but out in the open, she was reluctant to risk being unprepared if they needed to act quickly.

"Well, Quincy is a pretty light sleeper, so if anything moves around out there or startles him, he'll squeal, but I'm not taking any chances." She pulled an axe out of the scabbard on her saddle and laid it across her lap.

Gisella gazed at the waxing moons, rising just above the horizon, although the Queen showed more of her face than did the King. "I could keep watch while you sleep. I'll wake you when the moons have completed half of their nightly journey."

"Suit yourself. No one but Quincy keeps watch when I'm out here alone."

Within a few minutes, Gisella heard the dwarf snoring. The warm night air, the mead, and fatigue from riding all day conspired to thwart her plans, causing Gisella's eyes to grow heavy. Determined to keep watch, despite Valora's assurances that Quincy's vigilance was sufficient, she paced to remain alert.

When she finally sat again, sleep overtook her. She awoke to Quincy's grunts and snorts in response to Valora's cooing at him. Her neck ached from falling asleep with her chin resting on her chest, and she found a tender area on her side where her breastplate pinched throughout the night.

Gisella removed her armor and linen shirt to examine the bruise, heedless of the show she'd give the dwarf if Valora turned to face her. The angry, plum-colored contusion followed the contour under her arm.

"I suppose that's a mark of Aurora?" Valora crossed her arms as a crooked smile overtook her face.

"The mark of a fool who fell asleep sitting partially upright." Gisella dressed herself and winced as she donned her breastplate. The dense and oppressive air indicated the day would be even more humid than the last.

"I searched around a bit before you woke up. Some scrub deer came through in the night but nothing else by the looks of it. Eat up and let's get moving."

Gisella washed down some dried fish with mead as Valora doused the fire and scattered the embers. Shortly after setting out, they came upon a farmer's field that lay fallow for the current season. The dark, rich earth was churned up all across the field, as if someone recently plowed while drunk.

"Nothing's planted, which isn't unusual necessarily, but why does it look like someone's been digging?" Valora patted Quincy's neck and urged him forward, but the boar snorted and backed away from the dirt.

Gisella's stomach twisted in knots. She slid off Moonsilver and gripped her spear. "If they didn't plan any crops here this season, grass or weed should have sprouted by now, yes?"

"Something." Valora dismounted and joined Gisella at the field's edge.

The Golden Slayer jabbed her spear into the dirt and dragged it through the soil. Impractical for plowing, it moved enough soil to confirm her suspicions.

A long, white bone lay exposed. Gisella followed it with her spear and uncovered a bony hand. She moved to a different spot and scraped some more, exposing a tuft of hair still attached to the worm-infested flesh of a head.

Scout Stonehammer made a gesture to ward off evil. "If this whole field's like that, there could be thousands of corpses under the dirt."

"They're moving at night and concealing themselves during the day." Gisella cleaned the tip of her spear with the edge of her cloak. "That's why there have been no reports outside the city."

Valora shielded her eyes from the sun, gazing toward the southern horizon. "The homestead isn't too far away. Should we warn them?"

Gisella, already halfway to Moonsilver when she heard Valora's question, intended to do just that.

* * *

The instant Delilah realized she was about to be flung into the gorge to her death, she became most disappointed that no vision of her life, no vision of her past adventures, no vision at all flashed before her. *All my life, and there's nothing worth remembering? That just doesn't seem fair.*

She felt a tug, and a force pressed against her, pushing in all around and lifting her from the rushing water. Katka, still clinging to her arm, was also pulled, sputtering and shrieking, from the flood. As the two passed backward over the torrent and through the tunnel, Delilah observed the deluge diminish to a trickle and cease.

Alysha deposited the two at the edge of the runed circle. She lowered her staff and leaned on it, shaking her head. "I think you should find a better place to stand when we open the next one."

Delilah cursed and removed her cloak, throwing the soggy cloth to the floor. Her feathers and fetishes dripped water wherever she stepped. She helped her apprentice to her feet, and turned her attention to Alysha, as Katka stripped out of her waterlogged robes.

"How did you close it?"

"I know an incantation to block magic. I figured it couldn't hurt to try."

The archmage retrieved her staff. "It won't hurt the moon gate?"

"It shouldn't." Alysha picked up the ruined remains of the tome Katka had been holding. "So much for this old thing."

"Damn." Delilah regarded the soggy remains of the ancient text. "Maybe Ori can fix it."

Katka stood shivering in her smallclothes and held up her dripping robes. "I don't suppose you know an incantation to dry these?"

"We can dry them by the hearth upstairs." Delilah gathered all the wet garments, including Katka's robes. "Bring that parchment with the combinations and the book, if you can."

Kale waited at the top of the stairs. "Hey, I thought I heard running water and screaming."

Delilah held up an armful of wet clothing and squeezed, trickling water down the stairs. "Apparently, someplace called Faenwar is underwater now. Is Ori still here?"

"Yeah, he's packing up for the night." Kale jerked his thumb toward the front of the shop.

"Have him come see me in the kitchen when he's done, please. We need to borrow your hearth to dry our clothes."

Kali stood in the kitchen, roasting a bird of some sort. Delilah arranged the clothes near the edge of the hearth, hoping no grease splattered on them. Katka placed the ruined book on the table. The two sorceresses warmed themselves by the fire and explained to Kali what happened. Alysha excused herself and headed to the upper city to find a tavern.

"Oh, Archmage! Kale said you wanted to see me?" Ori appeared in the doorway, holding an armful of rolled parchments.

"One of our books got a little wet." Delilah pointed to the tome. "Can anything be done to save it?"

"Oh, my. Oh, no!" Ori dropped the supplies he held in his arms, scattering rolls of parchment throughout the hallway and kitchen threshold. Candle flames flickered as Kali sighed, although Delilah suspected that was just a trick of the light, rather than her mighty wind.

The blue drak slid a claw under one of the pages and lifted it with care. He peered under it, muttered to himself, and sighed. "Oh, oh, oh! Perhaps with divine intervention."

"Well, damn." Delilah looked at her apprentice. "You memorized that whole thing, right?"

Katka eyes widened, and she shook her head. The fire sputtered as water flew from her hair into the hearth.

"Oh! I might be able to recopy some of it." Ori flipped the page and turned his head as he tried to decipher the text. "What language is this?"

"Elvish," Delilah and Katka answered in unison before then eyeing each other and giggling.

"Oh. I can't read that. I'll probably get a lot of the words wrong. They're smudging."

"I can." Katka rubbed her arms. "Maybe my mistress will let me work on that with you as a special project for a while?"

"I'm all for that." Delilah removed her harness and laid it on top of her cloak. The feathers were probably ruined, but she hoped to salvage the fetishes. "It's important, right?"

"Oh, Archmage Delilah"—Ori bowed his head and crossed an arm over his chest—"you should know that I'll do anything for you, but this project is too big. I have to… um… I have bills to pay…"

Delilah patted Ori on the cheek. "The Arcane University will compensate you for your work, of course. Thank you. I'd appreciate it if you could start right away, though." She nuzzled the nape of his neck.

The blue drak sputtered and nodded, gathering up the remains of the soggy tome. As he exited the kitchen, he tripped over a chair before slamming into a wall and spinning around the corner into the hallway. Delilah winced as she heard Kale shout when the two collided.

"You know he's smitten with you, right?" Kali pursed her lips as she kicked a stray roll of parchment away from the hearth.

* * *

"You should pick up some extra classes." Orion put his arm around Pancras and guided the wizard's head onto his shoulder.

With everything going on regarding the Lich Queen, Pancras actually wanted fewer classes. He glanced up at the Justicar. "Why? Trying to get rid of me?"

"Ha! No. The nobles are calling for blood. Lord Tyron was unpopular, but still he was influential. His cronies have the ear of most of the noble houses."

Pancras squeezed his eyes shut. *Politics. Why do politics have to come into it?*

"Of course, since a Justicar was involved in the incident, their ability to investigate is limited, and the King has decreed that he has full faith in us. That won't stop the nobles from hiring mercenaries. You and the fiendling should lie low for a few days. They have short attention spans, and we can stir the pot a bit to remind them that they have better things to do."

The afternoon sun crept across the room. Qaliah informed Pancras the day prior of Gisella's spur-of-the-moment adventure with Scout Stonehammer and swore to let him know when she returned. The fiendling promised to seek him out daily.

As if on cue, they heard a knocking at the door. Pancras ducked out from beneath Orion's arm.

"Back in Muncifer, they wouldn't let non-students onto university grounds without the permission of the headmaster." Pancras pulled on his robes and approached the door. He waited for Orion don his loincloth and tunic, leaning with one hand on the door in case Qaliah decided to pick the lock.

"Maybe she sweet-talked the old man?" Orion moved to the armchair near the hearth as he dressed.

"I wouldn't put it past her." Pancras opened the door, and the fiendling bounded in.

"Past who, past what? Do you think I'm a sneaky slut?" She flicked Pancras's ear as she skipped past.

The minotaur reached up to stop the involuntary twitching of his ear and closed the door behind her. The fiendling sat in the chair opposite Orion, Pancras's seat.

"Do you have a reason for slipping into those terrible rhymes? I take it Gisella has not yet returned?" Pancras pulled over one of the chairs from his table and seated himself between her and Orion.

"Nah, not back yet." Qaliah sat up straight, hands on her knees and stared directly at Orion. "So, I didn't interrupt any lovin' time, did I? I can leave if I did."

The Justicar shifted in his chair and focused on the smoldering embers in the hearth. Pancras glared at her and snorted.

"Oh, I interrupted something, that's obvious." The fiendling leaned back in the oversized chair and yanked at her skirt to keep it from bunching up beneath her. "I won't stay long."

Orion, still staring into the fire, waved his hand in dismissal. "I need to be leaving anyway. Duty calls."

Over the last several days, Pancras learned much about the Justicars, although Orion would not reveal details about the responsibilities that took him away just before dusk. After the first night, Orion departed before dusk and returned after dark, explaining it away as "his duties."

"You're very conscientious." Pancras stroked Orion's arm.

"What sort of duties? Do you Justicars all get together at suppertime to beat down illegal gambling dens?" Qaliah leaned toward Pancras. "I heard they come down hard on dens that don't pay Dolios his due."

"Nothing like that. They're just mundane obligations, traditions, mostly."

A smirk appeared on Qaliah's face. "He's got another lover." She crossed her arms over her chest.

Orion gripped the arms of his chair and growled. Pancras scowled at Qaliah. "You're pushing too far."

"Am I? Just a bit of jest… unless it's true."

"It. Is. Not." Orion spoke through clenched teeth. "Fiendling, it would be very easy to tell the nobles that you're the one who killed Lord Tyron. They'd have their scapegoat and leave everyone else alone after they stretched your neck."

"Easy, yes, but that wouldn't be the truth, would it?" Qaliah smirk grew wider.

Relationships were not his forte, but Pancras noticed Qaliah's words aggravated Orion. He put his hand on his lover's leg. "Tell me of these duties. It will change nothing. Perhaps I can help."

"You're wrong. It will change everything."

* * *

While Ori and Katka began the arduous task of separating the soggy pages of the tome, Delilah studied the parchment of possible rune combinations her apprentice and Alysha compiled. Most of the locations were unfamiliar to her, but pre-Sundering geography was not a subject taught in Drak-Anor. One of the notations, scribbled in her apprentice's hand, caught her eye: *Parsembdan = Maritropa*.

She had often heard traders visiting Drak-Anor speak of Maritropa floating high in the sky above the crystal blue waters of a lake, sitting roughly halfway between Almeria and Vlorey along the trade road.

"Hm. I bet a floating city didn't feel much of The Sundering at all."

"What?"

Delilah glanced up. She had forgotten Kali stood behind her in the kitchen while she prepared the evening meal.

"Sorry, I was talking to myself." She rolled up the parchment. "I'll get out of your scales."

After checking on Ori and her apprentice, Delilah returned to the bookshelves that lined the cellar stairs. Something about the Maritropa and Parsembdan notation seemed familiar, but she couldn't summon the memory. She heard her brother in the cavern, breathing fire. Delilah proceeded into the cellar to check on him.

He stood at the far side of the runed circle, exhaling gouts of flame across the puddles on the floor. Kale must have heard her approach, because he turned to face her.

"Hi, Deli. I was just trying to dry things out down here."

"With fire?"

"The rocks won't burn, and I've been careful to keep away from the wood supports by the ceiling."

The archmage admitted his tactic was effective. "Well, thanks. I hope we don't do something like that again."

"You could have been killed, Deli."

Delilah picked through the tomes on the shelf, searching for one which might contain maps or information about Calliome's geography. "That's why there's more than one of us here when we perform these experiments. Hey, you went through a lot of these books, right?"

Kale approached his sister. "I don't know about a lot, maybe half of them."

"Did you notice if any of them were about geography? Did any of them have maps or anything like that in them?"

"I remember one with pictures that looked like the stars Terrakaptis showed me a few years ago." Kale clicked his fingers. "Yeah, there was one with really old maps in it, too. Pre-Sundering."

Delilah's heart pounded. "Show me, please."

Kale climbed the stairs halfway up to the shop. He pulled a thick, leather-bound tome off the shelf, moved to the next shelf up, and removed another similarly bound volume. He handed them to his sister.

The archmage's eyes bulged under the weight of both works. After staggering upstairs, she lugged them to the kitchen table. She skipped the star charts for the moment and flipped through the other tome. A flowing script, similar to

Elvish, adorned the pages, but Delilah recognized the words as a form of the common trade language.

"What are you thinking, Deli?"

"Dinner's ready, Kale." Kali pulled the roasted bird off the spit and shoved aside one of the books.

"I'll be out of your scales in a minute." Delilah held up a finger. "I just need to find one thing…" She found a map from before The Sundering that depicted the eastern edge of the Celtan Forest. The drawing depicted a lake just south and east, and at its center, with bridges clearly illustrated, sat Parsembdan. She scanned the accompanying text. Slight differences in the dialect and syntax of this antiquated version of the language did not obscure its meaning. Parsembdan had once been a city on an island in the middle of the lake.

She jabbed the map with her finger. "Ha! I was right."

"What? What?" Kale peered over her shoulder.

"Parsembdan, you know it as Maritropa, was an island before The Sundering. Now, it floats in the sky, right?"

Kale's blank expression told Delilah all she needed to know about his knowledge of geography. Kali cocked her head. "It didn't always float? Huh. I wonder how they got it in the air."

"It doesn't matter. This confirms that not only did the names change, but also that some places aren't in the same location anymore! Some of the coordinates we've been using are all wrong."

* * *

As Gisella and Valora approached the farmhouse standing at the far end of the field, they detected no evidence of habitation and took note of two other buildings on the property—a barn topped with a slanted roof and what appeared to be a woodshed. The dwelling seemed lifeless; oddly, although most families kept cooking fires lit during the muggy summers of the north, no smoke drifted up from the chimney. They observed tools scattered on the ground, as if abandoned or dropped.

Moonsilver tossed her head and whinnied, resisting Gisella's desire to move closer. After a few minutes, The Golden Slayer relented, dismounting, and tied the horse's reins to a nearby stump. She picked up her spear, and after Valora secured Quincy, they advanced on the homestead. Clouds gathered near the horizon, dark, ominous, and laden with moisture.

Careful to avoid the churned-up dirt, they meandered through the field to gain entry to the building. The air around the house was still, bereft of birdsong. Only the buzzing of insects cut through the heavy aura of dread.

As they moved closer to the house, they noticed the front door askew, hanging on its hinges as if some great force battered it ajar. Gisella took the lead, pushing the door open with her spear. Creaking in protest, it gave way, falling off its hinges, crashing to the floor, and creating a billowing cloud of dirt. A two-room dwelling, once occupied by a hardworking farming family, lay in ruin.

The sickly sweet stench of rot assaulted the two women. A half-eaten roast sat on the table, covered with flies and mold. A jug of wine lay on its side, having disgorged its contents and having left in its wake a wine stain that bled over the edge of the table, soaking the floor below it dark crimson. Around the table, the chairs were upended. Whoever last sat in them leapt up in a hurry, heedless of the mess they caused.

Valora pointed to a splatter of dried blood on the wall and ceiling. A curtain-covered doorway separated the bedchamber from the living area. Gisella moved the curtain aside to find the bed, unkempt, but unoccupied. The crib positioned alongside the bed and the volume of flies crawling on it hinted at what lay within. Whatever happened here had occurred while the family ate.

"Should we check it?" Valora cast half a glance at the crib.

Gisella shook her head. "I haven't the stomach for that. You?"

"I don't like babies." Valora turned again to the living area. "I don't think I'd much like to see a fly-eaten one."

"They came upon this family at night and slaughtered them." Gisella inspected the room one final time and exited the house.

"Why? If they left you and the fiendling alone, why attack these folk?"

Gisella knelt by a discarded hayfork, pointing to its ichor-stained tines. "Good question. These folk fought back, though. Perhaps if they had remained huddled in their home, the dead would have burrowed into their fields and let them be. Or maybe, they killed them so they could use their fields in the first place."

"Shambling dead can't think that way. Can they?" Valora picked up a hoe almost twice as long as she stood tall, examining its shattered shaft and notched, bloodied blade. She threw it to the ground.

"They also can't know to hide during the day."

The distant rumbling of thunder rolled across the fields. Gisella eyed the sky as the clouds moved in their direction.

"We best get moving, don't you think? I don't fancy being around this place when night comes. Is there an inn or another farm where we might find shelter from that?" Gisella pointed at the oncoming storm.

"This is the closest shelter. Maybe the barn is clear, or the woodshed?"

Gisella regarded the two nearby structures. They seemed in better shape than the farmhouse. "Too close to the fields for my taste. I suppose we should make sure the farmer's family isn't holed up in one of them."

Once again, taking care to avoid the field, they first checked the woodshed. The lock on the outside of the door appeared undisturbed, albeit a bit rusty. Gisella banged on the door and called for the farmer. Hearing neither a reply nor movement from within, she glanced at the dwarf.

"I can whack off the lock with my axe." Valora held up her weapon.

"They couldn't have gone inside and locked themselves in."

"Maybe the parents locked their kids in and drew the undead away." Valora raised her axe and brought it down on the lock. The honed dwarven blade sheared clear through the hasp, and lock clattered to the ground. She pulled open the door to reveal a supply shed packed with cords of wood.

"That answers that." Valora closed the door, but without the hasp and lock, it remained slightly ajar. Next, they approached the barn. The stink of decay as they neared the door almost overpowered them.

"I half-expected that stench to form a cloud." Gisella pulled open the doors, holding her spear at the ready.

Two horses and three cows sprawled across the dirt-and-straw floor. Flies buzzed around the maggot-bloated carcasses. A fresh wave of odiferous rot wafted past, and Valora blanched and dashed away. Gisella covered her mouth with her cloak and peered into the dark structure. Rays of light filtered through gaps in the wallboards, providing enough illumination to reveal no one hidden inside.

She found Valora leaning on the woodshed, her face flush.

"So much for having broken my fast. Anyone in there?"

Gisella shook her head. "No one. The carcasses were partially consumed."

"What ate them? Vermin?"

The two women proceeded toward their mounts. More thunder rumbled in the distance; the storm drew closer. "Possibly, but there are undead that feed on flesh. Perhaps some of them lie under the fields, as well."

When they reached Moonsilver and Quincy, Gisella retrieved the map from her saddlebag. She unrolled it on the horse's flank. A quick consultation with Valora confirmed her suspicions—the farm lay directly on the path between Vlorey and Zamora.

"I've seen enough. I think we should head back to the city. I don't fancy riding in that storm, but if we make haste, we will make it by tomorrow, yes?"

"Sooner than that if we push through the night and the storm isn't too bad. It won't be the first time I've ridden in the rain, and won't be the last, I suppose."

Distant clouds flashed. A few seconds later, thunder rumbled again, much closer than the last time. Moonsilver nickered and stamped her feet while Quincy grunted and dug at the earth, searching for roots or tubers. The two women saddled up and turned northeast, riding toward Vlorey.

Chapter 22

Delilah summoned her apprentice and the Frost Queen to her chambers first thing the next morning. She showed them the maps she discovered. "Place names changed, yes, and some places stayed exactly the same." She held out a hand toward Alysha. "Your circle, for example. But Parsembdan was on an island in the lake. Now, it's an island in the sky. Some places physically moved. That's why half our coordinates don't work."

The Frost Queen furrowed her brows and examined the maps. "You're right. The world changed after The Sundering. Not much, but just enough to throw off the coordinates."

"How do we recalculate?" Katka leaned across the table and examined the upside-down map.

"Ah ha!" Delilah placed the book of star maps on top of the other book. "We just need to figure out how much the sky has changed since then."

Alysha shook her head. "The sky doesn't change. Not much, anyway. New stars appear now and then, but they always fade away."

"No, no, but our position relative to the constellations has changed, ever so slightly." Katka opened the book of star maps. "Look here! The spring charts show the Crown of Tinian."

"The Crown of Tinian is a summer... constellation." Alysha's eyes widened as she reached the same conclusion as Katka.

Delilah grinned. "Ladies, we found our answer. We just need to compensate for changes caused by The Sundering, and all these moon gates should function again."

They worked through the morning compiling a new list of potential combinations. Delilah instructed them to concentrate on locations near Vlorey. When they were finished, they rushed back to Kale's home in the undercity and prepared to resume their experiments once more.

Before descending the staircase, the archmage checked on Ori's progress. The drak had separated the entire tome, allowing the pages to dry. She nuzzled his neck for good luck and followed the two humans down to the cellar.

Delilah activated the Runes of Selene. She turned the moons to their proper phases and paused before activating the first constellation. "We've struck Faenwar off the list, right?"

"Right. As far as I can tell, Faenwar is the Elvish name for Maritropa's gate. Since the city is in the air, wherever the gate was must have ended up in the lake." Katka shrugged. "I think."

The drak archmage nodded, taking a deep breath as she activated the runes in sequence. For the first test, they chose Dwegerthon, a location without any nearby bodies of water. If this test worked, it would confirm their theory.

When the archmage touched the last rune, the portal sprang open. Alysha's cursing was enough to tell Delilah the results were not optimal, but she circled to the front of the moon gate to see for herself. The gate had opened into a wall of solid rock. Small pebbles fell through the gate and bounced on the inner circle's surface. After that, the gate shut down.

"Well, it worked." Delilah activated the runed circle again. "I guess that one got buried after The Sundering. Let's try a location closer to Vlorey this time. Do we have one we think is actually Vlorey?"

Katka examined the parchment and shook her head. "Not really. I mean, any of these strangely named ones could be Vlorey. The way the book was organized suggested these gates were in locations in the north."

"They were probably in or near individual wizards' towers." Alysha peered over Katka's shoulder at the parchment. "Maybe Vlorey itself didn't have a moon gate."

"Pick one." Delilah figured one was as good as any other at this point. As they called out the runes, she activated them one by one until the gate sprang open.

"Oh, wow. You should see this." The awe in Katka's voice spurred Delilah to race to the front of the circle. The moon gate led to what appeared to be a bluff or plateau overlooking a lush forest. An endless stretch of cerulean water lay beyond the trees and stretched to the horizon.

"All right, I'm going through. I'll be back in a few minutes." Delilah adjusted the grip on her staff and strode through the moon gate. She felt the familiar resistance to her passage as she passed through. The relative quiet of Kale's cellar was replaced by the cacophony of dozens of jungle birds.

As she surveyed the area, she discovered she stood not on a plateau, but on top of the remains of a ruined tower. A crumbling set of stairs led downward toward the jungle floor. Vines and moss covered the stone walls, the life-force of the jungle reclaiming the rocks from which the tower was built. The sun hung high in the sky, its heat merciless. Delilah breathed in the warm, humid air and imagined it was not that different than trying to breathe water.

Based on the sun's position, she estimated the sea sat to the north. Now that her new surroundings replaced the distorted picture displayed through the moon gate, she noticed land beyond the water, perhaps an island or peninsula. She followed the line of the coast to the east and noted it met with the coast closest to her.

At the point at which the two coasts met, she viewed the outline of a city, no more than a day or two's journey. She whooped in triumph and activated the moon gate once more. When it sprang open, the archmage wasted no time jumping through it.

"That's it! It's got to be Vlorey." She described what she saw, using her hands to draw an imaginary map in the air. "Where's that atlas?"

Katka ran over to the pile of books they'd been referencing and retrieved the atlas. Delilah flipped through the pages and pointed to a peninsula labeled "Verdant Point."

"I was on top of a tower, what was left of it. I saw that across the water. The city I saw was no more than a couple of days away on foot."

"Hot, humid, and on the coast?" Alysha leaned on her staff and nodded. "Either that's Vlorey or Port-of-Dogs. You're sure you got your bearings right?"

"I know how to tell directions." In truth, Delilah was not one hundred percent confident where that was concerned, but she was sure enough that she decided not to show uncertainty in front of the Frost Queen.

"Get your things, ladies." Delilah rubbed her hands together. "We're going to Vlorey, today!"

* * *

"Tell me, Orion." Pancras squeezed the other minotaur's leg and cast a sidelong glance at Qaliah, hoping the fiendling would read his reproach of her glee in his lover's discomfort.

"It's about my marriage."

"Yes, to Sarra." *What could be so bad about that? Aita's bones, please don't let her be a vampire!*

"I still sup with her family. I feel… obligated to them since she died trying to birth my child." Orion's shoulder's slumped, and he placed his head in his heads.

Pancras stifled a chuckle and exhaled. "That's it? Well, that's no trouble at all. I completely understand."

"Yeah, there's nothing wrong with that. At all." As Qaliah leaned against the back of her chair and crossed her legs under her, her smirk transforming into a frown.

Orion turned to Pancras. "You understand?"

"She was your mate. They are family. Even I"—Pancras placed his hand on his chest—"outcast though I am, understand duty to family. I am a minotaur. My parents taught me that before I left home."

"I feel stupid now, but I am relieved."

Pancras gave Orion's knee a reassuring squeeze and eyed Qaliah. "Well, now that you've ruined our fun, is there any other reason you came here?"

The fiendling avoided his eyes. "It gets a little lonely at the inn without Blondie around. I'm trying to stay out of trouble, like you asked, but there's nothing to do."

"Aita's bones… you're as bad as Kale." Pancras rubbed his right horn. He nodded to Orion. "Is there something we can have her do? What are you good at, Qaliah?"

She counted them off on her fingers. "Turning tricks, gambling, dancing, stealing…"

Both minotaurs groaned, simultaneously rubbing the bridges of their noses. Qaliah giggled and slapped her knees. "You're both doing it!"

Pancras cleared his throat. "Is there anything productive you can do? Anything that contributes to society?"

"Those things were plenty productive in Muncifer. Boss Steelhand had plenty of work for me when I wasn't skipping about playing a fool for Manless. I just haven't met the right people around here."

"And you won't with me around." Orion stood. "I must be off. Sarra's family is expecting me tonight. I suppose I should let them know I might need some evenings for myself."

"There's no rush." Pancras accompanied the other minotaur to the door. They embraced and pressed their heads together before Orion departed.

Qaliah's eyes followed Pancras as he poured himself a drink and sat in the chair formerly occupied by Orion. She held out her hand, palm upraised. "I didn't intend for things to be so awkward, you know. I'm sorry."

"Impulse control, Qaliah." Pancras raised his glass of wine. "You must learn impulse control."

"Yeah, well, fiendlings aren't really known for that, you know?" She hopped off the chair and stepped over to his decanter and goblets. "Do you mind?"

Pancras gestured for her to help herself. Heartened that she thought to ask permission, he smiled. Settling into the big chair opposite him, she sipped the wine and nodded in approval.

"So, if Blondie returns and says we were right and all the dead guys are going to Zamora and it turns out it's really the Lich Queen coming back calling all the dead to her to be her new army"—Qaliah took another drink—"do you really think we have a chance of stopping her?"

The minotaur drained his goblet while he pondered her question. It was a subject he wrestled with, and despite what he personally thought their odds of success were, there was only one course of action. "Our chances? It doesn't matter. We have to try."

* * *

"It works? You found the gate to Vlorey?" Kale held his sister's hands, and the two draks jumped up and down laughing. "That's great!"

"Katka and Alysha are getting the rest of our stuff from the university. We're leaving as soon as they return."

Kale's heart soared. Grinning, he spread his wings. "Great! I'll get my stuff." He left his sister in the shop with Ori and raced to the bedchamber.

Daggers, where are my daggers? Need the bandoleer, too. Cloak? Nah, it's warm there. Oh! My hat! He grabbed the hat he acquired during the past winter in Almeria. He chuckled as he adjusted it on his head and noticed Kali standing in the doorway with her arms crossed.

"Oh, hey, Deli got the moon gate working. We're going to Vlorey." He spun past her and sped down the hallway. He heard his sister talking to Ori. The blue drak stammered and seemed to have forgotten how to speak in complete sentences.

"We are?"

"Sure, me and Deli. Pancras will need our help."

He half-ran, half-hopped down the cellar stairs. The cavern was cloaked in darkness; the magic sconces illuminated the area only when a drak wizard was present. Once at the bottom, he buckled his bandoleer and adjusted his pouches. As he checked his daggers, he noticed Kali followed him.

"I don't know how long we'll be gone."

Kali stood, a statue, silhouetted by the light from the top of the stairs, her shoulders slumped. In the darkness, Kale couldn't see her expression. The winged drak gathered his mate in his arms and held her. She stiffened, her arms remaining at her side, while he hugged her and rubbed his cheek against hers.

"Kale!" Delilah descended the cellar stairs. The gems in the sconces burst with light as she approached. Kale glanced up at the sound of her voice.

"I'm ready, Deli!" He released Kali, and the orange drak stepped backward, glaring at Delilah.

"Ready for what, Kale?" Delilah patted Kali's arm as she passed. She tapped the butt of her staff on the floor. He noticed his sister was not smiling.

"We're going to go help Pancras, right?"

"I'm going, and Alysha's going."

"You're not taking your apprentice?" *That makes sense, I guess. She's pretty young.* "All right, so you, me, and the tall human."

Delilah covered her eyes with her hand and exhaled. "Kale, I'm not taking you, either."

The revelation hit him like a hammer to the chest. He staggered backward and spread his wings for balance. "What? Why?"

His sister turned, and studied Kale's mate, before she glared at him. "You really need me to answer that?"

His chest tightened, stifling Kale's breath. His eyes met Kali's, from behind which screamed a silent plea.

He glanced at his sister. Delilah's gaze appeared steady and stern. Her cheeks flexed as she clenched her jaw.

Kale returned his attention to his mate.

"I told him"—Kali drew a ragged breath—"he... he could do whatever he wanted."

"Kale"—Delilah shook her head and laughed—"I can't believe *I'm* the one telling you this. You accepted responsibility here. I'll admit, I was angry at first, and I didn't approve."

She approached Kali and put her arm around the orange drak's shoulders. "But she's my sister now, and I'll be damned if I'm going to let you shirk your responsibility to her."

Kale couldn't breathe. He removed his hat and allowed it to fall to the floor. "Deli... we always do these things together."

His chest heaved, and he bit his lip to take his mind off the flood of emotions he knew he could not control. "Deli... I..."

"No, Kale." A tear glistened in his sister's eye. "You have to stay here."

Unable to stem the flow, Kale sobbed. "It's because I let the dragon go, isn't it?"

Delilah threw her staff to the floor. "It has nothing to do with that damned dragon! This is about your choices. The choice you made when we got here." She poked him in the chest hard enough to make him take a step backward with each jab. "You took a mate. You bought a home. This"—she gestured to the ceiling—"is your place now."

She gripped him by the shoulders as his knees gave out and held him up. He tried to speak, but he couldn't form intelligible words through his sobs.

"I love you, Kale. You're my brother, I will always love you. I hope one day you'll understand why I can't take you with me."

Kale pushed his sister away and ran upstairs, tripping over several of the steps. By the time he reached the top, his knees were battered, bruised, and bloody. Slamming the cellar door behind him, he ran past a bewildered Ori and out onto the street to lose himself in the crowd.

* * *

Delilah watched her brother flee up the staircase, wincing each time she heard his knees bang on the steps. She jumped when he slammed the door.

"Maris's bloody spear, what a disaster."

Kali wrapped her arms around her sister-in-law and glanced toward the door. "I suppose I should thank you."

For what? Delilah took Kali by the shoulders. "Don't thank me yet. He might be hell to live with after this."

"Did I make a mistake?" The orange drak continued to stare up the staircase. She trembled beneath Delilah's grip.

"He'll come around. Kale's only upset because he knows I'm right." The archmage turned Kali's head to look her in the eyes. "I'll be back as soon as I can. As much as I want to return to Drak-Anor, if you and Kale make your home here… then here is where I'll stay."

"No." Kali shook her head and pushed Delilah away. "No, you can't change your life to suit us."

"Hey, look"—Delilah gestured to the Runes of Selene—"if these moon gates keep working, I'll be able to come and go as I please."

"I guess I should go after him." Kali glanced over her shoulder at Delilah as she climbed the stairs.

"I wouldn't." The archmage followed her. "He'll be back, then he'll pout, and then he'll be okay. Like I said, he knows

I'm right, and once he admits it to himself, everything will be fine."

When they entered the shop, Ori made a point of remaining focused on the manuscript he illuminated. Kali quickly searched the living quarters and then stared out the front window.

Delilah approached Ori and licked her lips. The blue drak was hunched over, his snout mere inches from the paper as he traced a thin gold line with a brush that appeared to contain no more than a couple of bristles. She tapped on the floor with the butt of her staff to announce her presence.

Delilah knew if she touched him in any way, it would wreck his concentration. Ori finished drawing the line, laid down his brush, and spun on his stool.

"Oh, Archmage! Are you leaving now?"

"Still waiting for Alysha." She leaned her staff against the back shelf and stepped closer. "I want to be serious for a moment."

"Oh, okay."

Delilah stroked his cheek. "Thank you for all your help. I won't forget what you've done."

Ori averted his eyes and nodded. "It… it was my pleasure."

"When I return…"

The blue drak turned his gaze to her and took Delilah's hand from his cheek. "Oh, please. I want to ask something."

Ori's thoughtful and gentle nature appealed to Delilah. He wasn't quite the opposite of her brother, but he was close. *At least he's responsible.* Her stomach tightened with a twinge of guilt at how she manipulated him.

"Sure." Delilah smiled and kept her hand entwined with his.

"Oh!" His eyebrows shot up as if he had not expected her to agree. "I don't know what it's like for draks from Drak-

Anor, but where I'm from, we have pretty specific ways of courting desirable females—"

Delilah held her finger up to his lips and fought to keep a smile from devouring her face. "When I return, do what you will."

She left the blue drak stammering and fumbling with words as she returned to the cellar. *Well, Deli-girl, you have to come back now.* She packed up the books they'd used to calculate the moon gate coordinates and folded the parchment containing the list of potential destinations Katka and Alysha had compiled before placing it in one of her pouches. By the time she finished, the two women returned.

Katka handed Delilah her grimoire and carried another pack over her shoulder. "I wasn't sure what all to bring."

Delilah took her aside as Alysha double-checked her things. "I've been thinking; if what Alysha says is true, this trip will be dangerous. I'd feel better with you here. Besides, you can't really practice and study while we're on the road."

Her apprentice's face drew tight, and she nodded as she stared at the floor. "I understand, Mistress."

"I want you to keep working with Ori to restore that book and maybe start cataloging this library"—Delilah held up her finger—"only if it doesn't interfere with your studies. I'm very proud of what we've accomplished together. You're a good friend, Katka, and I couldn't have done all this without you."

Katka threw her arms around the drak archmage. "Be careful, please."

Delilah felt a tear well in her eye. She squeezed the human woman as best she could with her arms full and her head pushing into her apprentice's chest. "The Lich Queen herself won't keep me from returning."

Her apprentice smiled and nodded as she stepped aside. She waited by the stairs while Delilah activated the moon gate.

"Look after Kale for me. He's a handful." Delilah glanced up at the Frost Queen. "Let's go. I didn't spend this much time saying goodbye before I left Drak-Anor."

* * *

Gisella and Valora pushed through the storm and the night, riding without rest until midday when Vlorey appeared at the end of the road. Waterlogged and weary, the Golden Slayer wanted nothing more than to have a bath and go to bed. She resisted the urge to indulge her desire and accompanied the dwarf scout to the Palace of Justice, instead.

Lord Fenwick was indisposed when they arrived, in a meeting with a group of Justicars. Valora led Gisella to the lower levels of the Palace of Justice. "They have their own baths. Now, it's up to you, but I'm going use this opportunity to get cleaned up."

Gisella didn't argue. Attendants cleaned their clothes while they bathed, and they even offered to repair and clean their armor. Valora availed herself of their offer, but Gisella declined, preferring to maintain her mail herself.

"They do good work." Valora held out her hand and spread her fingers as she inspected them. "Keeps my fingers from getting callused and busted up, too."

Wafting up from the water, the steam added to the already humid conditions, but Gisella didn't find it unpleasant. If anything, it made Vlorey's stifling climate bearable, at least for the duration of her bath. "A Watchmaiden always maintains her own armor. It's our second skin when we're out in the world."

A lesson drilled into her since she was young enough to lift a spear, Gisella usually followed it to the letter. Although if her mail required extensive repairs, she entrusted it to a skilled armorer.

"Now you sound like my clan leader." Valora pulled herself onto a stool to keep the water from covering her head while she bathed.

Gisella chuckled. "We left Muncifer with a dwarf from Ironkrag. When he learned we were taking a ship from Cliffport to Port-of-Dogs, he complained incessantly and told us to leave him when he was arrested in Curton. He said dwarves and water don't mix."

The fiery-haired dwarf dunked her head underwater. When she surfaced, she slicked back her hair and wrung it out. "It's mixing with me just fine. Did he never bathe? Besides, this isn't nearly as deep as the ocean. I wouldn't go out on a ship if you offered me Nethun's Pearl itself."

When they finished cleaning off the grime accumulated over a couple days of hard riding, the two women dressed in their freshly cleaned clothes. Gisella donned her armor, but Valora did not as it was still being cleaned and adjusted.

Lord Fenwick's meeting adjourned, and he awaited them in his chambers. "Ah, you've returned! Please tell me everything was a misunderstanding, and there is no army of undead amassing in the south?"

Valora laughed and shook her head as she spread the map across his desk. "No such luck, Fennie."

He glanced at Gisella when the dwarf used her pet name for him. "A little informal, don't you think?"

The dwarf glanced first at the Golden Slayer and then at Fenwick. "She already knows. No point being coy anymore."

"All right, then." His attention returned to the map. "So, what did you learn?"

They briefed him on what they discovered at the farm and their theories about the undead moving primarily at night. When they finished, he lowered himself into his chair and scratched his beard.

"It's hard to determine how many undead migrate during each double-dark cycle, but do you think it's safe to say she's gathered thousands of undead at this point?"

"In total, yes." Gisella wished she could determine how many left the city each time. "Probably, they are mostly un-intelligent undead, but the remains we found indicated the presence of ghouls, too. It would only take a couple to cause the deaths we found at the farm."

"You didn't find the farmer, though? Nor his family?"

"There was a baby…" Gisella shuddered at the memory of the fly-covered crib. "The farmer and any family members who could walk likely joined the undead under the field a night after they were killed."

"Yes, that's what occurred during the last war with the Lich Queen." Fenwick rose and approached the windows, clasping his hands behind his back. "Vlorey and Cardoba bore the brunt of the losses. Tales were told across Andelosia of how fallen soldiers who weren't sanctified after they died rose up to join the army of the enemy and fought against their former comrades."

"She's still gathering her strength." Gisella slammed her fist on the table. "A small force should be able to get past the undead and destroy her while she's still weak enough—"

"Past all those?" Valora laughed and rolled up her map. "You're mad."

"They ignored Qaliah and me in the village, and we have a bonelord on our side."

The dwarf woman sat in one of the chairs near the desk, her feet dangling above the floor. "They didn't ignore those farmers. Once you encounter them again at her lair, they won't defend their mistress?"

Gisella chewed her lip. "I'm not certain; it takes effort to control them."

"The bonelord won't turn?" Fenwick returned to his desk. "He won't join the Lich Queen?"

"Why would he? Aita herself tasked him with destroying her." Gisella narrowed her eyes as she watched Fenwick.

The Lord Justice chewed on his lip. "No, I don't suppose he would. It's risky, but apart from mobilizing an army and marching on Zamora, I think you're right."

"You've both gone mad!" Valora threw up her hands. "You want to send some Dolios-cursed fools to Maris's own dark heart?"

"A mad plan for mad times." Fenwick rubbed the bridge of his nose and nodded at each woman in turn. "Thank you both for what you've done. I won't decide anything tonight." He held up his hand to stave off Gisella's retort. "I know you don't need my permission to act, but indulge me."

His acknowledgement of Gisella's autonomy earned him some points in her eyes. "Very well, what would you have of me?"

"I wish to speak to Conner... um, the king. I don't need his permission to commit Justicar resources, but if we do this and fail, he needs to know what sort of hornet nest we're poking."

Perhaps the king will decide to commit his own resources. "A reasonable precaution."

"I'll depart for Verdant Palace tomorrow. There's no guarantee he'll see me right away, but I don't expect to be gone more than three or four days. It's more than a month to the next double-dark, if I'm remembering correctly, so we should be able to spare that much time, yes?"

His estimate sounded right to Gisella. "It will give me time to prepare. Perhaps the Arcane University has information on Zamora."

"Good thinking." Fenwick turned to Valora. "Fancy a trip to see the king?"

The dwarf woman smiled and shook her head. "I should report to my clan leader. Let him know what's going on." She shrugged. "Who knows? Maybe he'll send a couple dozen dwarf warriors."

Valora gazed at Fenwick, her smile growing, as well as the smoldering desire her eyes. Gisella stood and bowed to the Lord Justice. "Then I shall take my leave of you. If I'm not at my inn when you return, look for me at the Arcane University."

"Very well. Again, thank you."

She left Valora to continue her private debriefing with the Lord Justice, closing the doors behind her as she exited. While she and the dwarf brought Lord Fenwick up to date, the sun had set, and the King and Queen had begun their journeys, their bright limbs peeking over the roofs of the city.

In the dark of night, Vlorey became a mysterious, brooding character. Alleys and avenues, shrouded in darkness, waited like cloaked sneak thieves for their marks. Glowing gems placed inside painted parchment lanterns illuminated major intersections, oases of light in the desert of dark. Gisella assumed mages of the Arcane University provided and enchanted the gems and that they illuminated during the day, as well, but were not as noticeable. Guards patrolled the streets carrying torches similarly equipped as the street lights.

As Gisella continued along to the inn she regarded the night sky and smiled. Though, this far north, several unfamiliar constellations filled the sky, and some familiar ones were absent, the King and Queen nevertheless danced their nightly journey across the black sackcloth of the sky, glittering with the light of thousands of jewels. Raucous laughter and singing filled the air as she passed a tavern, fading and becoming part of the background of night as she moved away.

When she arrived at the Screeching Griffon, she discovered on the bed two droopy flowers and a note from Qaliah. The fiendling's handwriting was blocky, almost dwarf-like it its precision.

Gone to the Arcane University to keep the minotaur out of trouble. He wants to know what you discovered if you're not too tired.

-Q

Simultaneously surprised and ashamed, Gisella noted that Qaliah's message was legible and bereft of spelling errors. She had assumed the fiendling was not well educated. *Perhaps she learned while indentured to the university.* The Golden Slayer purchased a hand pie filled with minced meat and headed again into the city to join her friends at the Arcane University.

Chapter 23

As they surveyed their surroundings from atop the ruined tower, Delilah pondered how Alysha stood the heat while wearing her fur-lined robes. "So, those things keep you comfortable in the heat, as well?"

"Of course." Alysha bowed. "You're the archmage. Surely you know magic is good for more than just blasting things you're angry with?"

Delilah narrowed her eyes and growled. "Yes, I'm not stupid." Once again, the drak cursed the limitations of her self-taught skills. "Let's get going. How far do you think it is?"

Alysha shielded her eyes from the sun. It descended toward the western horizon, and a warm breeze blew in from the bay. "If we don't tarry, I think we can reach the city gates by nightfall."

Once on the jungle floor, they could no longer see the city, but Delilah noted the twists and turns of the descending stairs. Within an hour, the trees thinned, and the two sorceresses found a road in the clearing.

They kept a jaunty pace, though the well-traveled avenue was choked with mud from a recent rain. As the gates of Vlorey came into view, the sun touched the western horizon, and the lingering, wispy clouds glowed pink and orange, ushering in the night.

After paying an entry tax Alysha decried as robbery, the guards permitted them entry and kindly provided directions to the Arcane University. Delilah quickened her step and noticed the Frost Queen scrambling to keep up as the drak stepped faster and faster. When the desire to see Pancras again finally overwhelmed her, she ran.

Within sight of the university gates, Alysha caught up with her and grabbed her by the arm. "Archmage! With all due respect, show some dignity."

"Right." Delilah panted as she caught her breath. Running in Vlorey's oppressive humidity took a toll. *I bet it wouldn't have bothered Kale.* "Because I'm the archmage, and it's proper."

She cleared her throat and approached the guards flanking the bridge that led to the university grounds. They crossed halberds and barred her way. "No visitors after dark."

"Stand aside, I am Archmage Delilah Windsinger, just arrived from Muncifer."

The guard snickered before erupting with laughter. "You? The archmage? And I suppose the White Witch there is your loyal steed?"

A green flare from Alysha's staff joined one from Delilah's. She fought the urge to burn the two men to cinders and instead pulled the Herald Stone from her pouch. "Headmaster Lewin."

The balding man's face appeared. "Archmage! This is an unexpected surprise. What can I do for you?"

"Turn around and tell these two louts to let me pass. They're barring my entry to the Arcane University and mocking me."

Though the image lacked detail, Delilah noticed the color drain from the headmaster's face. Dutiful to his archmage, the headmaster's image rotated to face the men.

"You there! This is Headmaster Lewin. Allow the archmage entry at once!"

Their superior's voice was enough to stop the men's laughter. They peered at his image on the Herald Stone and scratched their heads. They had the good sense to fall to their knees as they lowered their halberds and begged forgiveness. Delilah ignored them and strode past with her head held high.

I rather like this archmage thing. I'm going to get used to this. When she reached the other side of the bridge, she stopped a passing student, his arms laden with scrolls. "You there, where's Pancras?"

She wagered his name would be known around the university, since he was supposed to be a teacher.

The young man licked his lips, his eyes, like bright beacons in the night, contrasted the deep yellow-brown of his skin. "The deputy headmaster?" He jerked his head toward the angular, curving building in the center of the grounds. "Probably in his quarters or office in the White Tower."

"Thank you." Delilah shooed him away.

"You're enjoying this too much." Alysha trailed her as she followed the path to the structure. Once inside, the archmage searched for stairs. Finding none, she clenched her jaw and turned to the Frost Queen.

"I don't suppose you know the trick here?"

Alysha smiled and pointed at the stone disk below the tower's central shaft. "Oh, I've heard stories about this place. If you'd rather not levitate yourself, you can take the Neophyte's Lift."

The drak archmage spread her hands. "You want an admission? Fine, I'm not good at levitating stuff. I taught myself, all right? It was easier to figure out how to burn things than how to move them."

She stepped onto the disk and tapped it with her staff. Alysha joined her and chuckled. "Deputy headmaster's quarters."

The disk floated to the second tier. They stepped off and entered the corridor surrounding the central shaft. Alysha pointed at a student walking slowly in the opposite direction, staring at a book she carried.

"Pardon me." Delilah approached the woman. She turned and looked over Delilah's head, but frowned when she noticed the drak peering at her.

"What do you want?" Her dark skin turned ashen, and she backed away, her voice quivering and shrill.

"Calm down." Delilah sighed. *Don't they have draks in this stupid city?* "Where's the deputy headmaster's quarters?"

The young woman pointed a shaking hand at the second door to their left. Delilah mumbled thanks as she pushed past the woman. Without waiting for Alysha to catch up, the drak banged on the door with her fist.

"Oh, for crying out loud." The minotaur's voice was unmistakable. Delilah fought to keep a boggin's grin off her face. The door opened, revealing an annoyed Pancras dressed in loose robes. His brow wrinkled in confusion until he thought to look downward.

His eyes widened, and his mouth moved, but no words came forth. The minotaur gripped the doorframe and peered into the hallway. He squinted at Alysha and stumbled into the room. Delilah followed him inside.

Pancras collapsed into an armchair before the hearth, opposite another well-muscled minotaur. The minotaur wizard pointed at Delilah.

"De… Delilah. The archmage. Bloody bones, how in Selene's name did you get here?"

Unable to hold back her grin a minute longer, Delilah spread her arms as she spun in place. "Magic!"

* * *

Kale ran through the crowds of the undercity, his wings tucked behind him to keep them from becoming a hindrance. By the time he reached the market area, the crowds became thick enough that he could no longer run, and the disappointment and frustration fueling his tears ran dry.

He kicked a rock out of the way, but it was poorly aimed, skittering only a few feet ahead. When he reached it, he kicked it again, this time sending it clattering across the cobblestones, through the railing, and into the gorge. Other draks called out to him as he passed, but lost in his own thoughts, Kale ignored them. He stopped to peer over the railing.

Most of the gorge, as usual, lay deep in shadow. Glancing around, he saw he wasn't far from the spot where he initially fell into the chasm. That accident led him to discover the cavern and the stairs that led to the abandoned shop which later became his home.

Home. It's not Drak-Anor. That's home, or was. Now, Pancras is gone, and Deli's abandoned me. I'm never going to see home again. The thought brought fresh tears to his eyes. He wiped them away. Across the gorge, he saw a pair of draks pushing a cart with wide, spoked wheels. His eyes followed the spokes as they spun round and round.

Wheels. Spokes. Images of teeth and gears came unbidden to his mind. *I used to build stuff all the time. No one needs traps here. I was good at that.*

He spun and stepped face-first into the hind end of a minotaur pushing a potato cart. The impact sent Kale sprawling with stars in his eyes and fresh tears from smashing his snout.

"Hey, watch it!"

Kale rubbed his sore nose as the minotaur helped him to his feet. "Thanks, sorry."

"You're always causing trouble." The minotaur lunged to grab his cart as it rolled away. "Damn thing."

"Don't you have a brake or something for that?" Kale examined the cart's wheels, discovering a patchwork kludge of mismatched parts.

"No. If you think you can convince the wheelwrights in the upper city to take a look at it, be my guest." The minotaur snorted and adjusted his grip on the cart so he could reposition some unstable potatoes.

"I could rig up a hand brake for it."

The minotaur scratched his head. "Really? That'd be something. I'd pay you. Need any potatoes?"

Kale chuckled. "No, we don't eat those. When you get a chance, come by the limner shop near Shadow Bridge, and I'll fix it up for you. Ask for Kale, but don't come too soon." He checked his pouch for money. "I need to buy some parts."

He waved to the minotaur as he sought out a shop. Kale knew just the place; he passed it often while wandering the undercity. One of the drak tinkers not only repaired pots, but also he did minor blacksmithing and clock repair on the side; although Kale suspected not many draks or minotaurs in the undercity actually owned clocks.

The winged drak returned home with two packs filled with gears, wheels, sprockets, springs, plates, and every tool that caught his fancy. He was drawn to them, as if a force inside told him it was right.

Ori glanced up from his book. "Oh, Kale. Welcome back."

"Thanks. Is my sister still here?" He set down his bags in the corner.

"She's gone." Kali entered the shop from the back. Placing her hands on her hips, she glanced at the packs. "What are those?"

Kale rubbed the base of his neck. "I felt compelled to buy these things. Maybe it's the weird clockwork dreams I've been having, but when I was out there, I was talking to a minotaur who needed his cart fixed, and I... don't know. I just need to build stuff again."

His mate approached him and took his hands. "You're staying then?"

"I was upset"—he bowed his head and brought Kali's hands to his lips—"and Deli and I have never been separated on purpose. I'm sorry. I don't know what else to say."

"Oh! What kind of things do you want to build?" Ori peered over the counter at the bags Kale placed on the floor.

"I used to build traps in Drak-Anor." He regarded the blue drak. "I don't think there's much call for that here, but I learned a lot about clockwork mechanisms working with that puzzle box. Maybe I could make boxes, fancy locks, maybe toys."

"You could sell them here. I'll help." Kali smiled and put her head on Kale's shoulder.

"Oh, well, I'm taking up more room than I need, Kale. I can tighten up my area if you need space, unless you want me to leave."

Kale shook his head and put his arm around Kali. "I won't need that much space. We can share the counter, if that's all right." He recognized he didn't need Ori's permission since the blue drak sublet the space from them.

"We can have a good life together here, Kale. I promise."

"I'm going to try, Kali. I swear on Hon's Hearth, I'm going to try." He meant it. Kale didn't invoke the gods often, and he hoped that invoking the name of the god of pacts would help him remember his promise.

"Just… promise me we won't have wizards coming and going at all hours."

"We won't." Kale smiled. "The next time Katka comes by, we'll talk to her about scheduled access to those books."

His mate helped him unpack, sort, and store beneath the counter all the parts and equipment he purchased. Once he was finished, he worked on creating a hand brake for the minotaur's cart.

It felt right.

* * *

Pancras's mind reeled. Of all the people to come knocking on his door at this time of night, he would never have anticipated one of the draks he left behind. If anyone, he expected Qaliah. The two minotaurs sent the fiendling far enough away on an errand to fetch food so that they could steal a few private moments. He caught his breath as he ducked behind a dressing screen and donned proper robes.

"Feeling self-conscious?" Delilah's human companion chuckled and stood with her arms crossed. Pancras noticed a familiarity about the woman.

"I'm sorry, you are?" Pancras tossed Orion the tunic emblazoned with the symbol of the Divine Tribunal.

The tall, platinum-haired woman bowed. "I am known by many names. I am the Frost Queen, Alysha Vibekedottir, and I have come to find my sister."

Sister, sister... Vibekedottir? Pancras furrowed his brow and rubbed his right horn. "Gisella?"

"Yes, the Golden Slayer. Where is she, Minotaur?"

Delilah cleared her throat. "This is Pancras, one of my mentors and now, apparently, deputy headmaster of the Arcane University here in Vlorey." She cocked her head. "Does that mean you're not First Wizard of Drak-Anor anymore?"

"You forgot bonelord." Orion pulled on his shirt.

Archmage Delilah glanced at Orion and eyed Pancras. "Bonelord? Like that fellow from Vlorey who fought at Drak-Anor when we kicked the oroqs out?"

"Yes, Terrick." Pancras had not thought about the human bonelord in years. "Gisella went scouting with one of the Justicar's people. She should be back soon."

"How did you become a bonelord?" The drak archmage climbed into the chair opposite Orion.

"It is an arduous tale, not nearly as fascinating, I'd wager, as how you arrived here so quickly. It seems impossible. Where is your brother?"

Delilah inspected one of her claws. "Oh, the Frost Queen here, my apprentice, and I rediscovered the secret of the moon gates. Kale had to stay home in Muncifer with his mate."

The strength again left Pancras's legs. He stumbled over to Orion's chair and grasped its backrest. He rested his head on the other minotaur's. "Apprentice? You have an apprentice? Kale has a mate, yes, I remember. I feel so very old, Orion."

Orion reached around and patted Pancras on the flank. "Neither one of us is young anymore."

When he was a student, Pancras learned that the moon gates once existed, taught they were all lost during The Sundering. "It seems we both have long stories to tell—"

A knock at the door interrupted him. Pancras recognized the distinctive pattern of Qaliah's rapping and let her in. The Golden Slayer stood alongside her.

"Hey! Look who I found fresh from the Palace of Justice."

"Gisella"—Pancras bowed his head and held the door open for the two ladies—"your sister is here to see you."

* * *

"Alysha?" Gisella pushed past Qaliah and entered Pancras's chambers. The fiendling swore and staggered in attempt not to drop the fare she carried. Gisella arrived at the Arcane University just as Qaliah returned from her errand.

The Frost Queen faced her sister, her platinum locks moving as she turned, as immaculate as ever. She crossed her arms under her bosom in the superior pose she often adopted when around people she didn't know. She still wore her enchanted fur-lined cloak. *Is she never without it?*

Alysha opened her arms and smiled. "Before I call you a fool, come here."

The sisters embraced. A hint of jasmine clung to Alysha's hair, a scent that brought with it familiar memories of home. "I've missed you. It's been too long."

"That it has, but it would have been safer for you to come see me." The Frost Queen held her at arm's length. "Oh, Gisella, you look well." She brushed the Golden Slayer's cheek. "Getting too much sun, though, eh?"

"I've been miserably hot ever since we arrived." Gisella noticed the striped drak sitting in Pancras's chair. "Is that…"

"Delilah, remember? I'm archmage now, Slayer."

Gisella bowed. "Yes, I heard. Congratulations."

"Now, we have family business to discuss." Alysha rested her hand on Gisella's shoulder. "Is there someplace we might speak privately?"

Gisella moved away from Alysha and retrieved chairs from Pancras's table. "Pancras already knows. The rest may as well, since they're all helping." She nodded to Delilah. "Unless you want to dismiss the archmage."

"Oh, I get to hear juicy family gossip? Excellent! May we eat while we do so?" Qaliah held up the covered basket from which the aroma of fresh bread wafted.

"Hey, I remember you." Delilah pointed a clawed finger at Qaliah. "No more rhymes?"

The fiendling aimed a forced smile at the drak. "An affectation your predecessor demanded. Now that my indenturetude is over, I try to avoid it."

Gisella held up her hand. "You can rhyme and jest and catch up on stories later. I've just met with the Lord Justice, and we've come up with a plan that merits your attention." She nodded at Pancras. The minotaur clung to the back of Orion's chair. His slumped shoulders and vacant expression told of one overwhelmed with new developments.

She cleared her throat. "That is, if Pancras agrees everyone here should be involved."

"Hm?" The minotaur blinked and turned his head toward her. "Oh, yes, I would not dream of omitting your sister and Delilah." He smiled at the archmage. "I know she'll be quite helpful."

"I'll always be here to help you, Pancras." The massive chair dwarfed the drak, making her appear child size, even though she stood in it. "Perhaps you'd like this chair, though? It's a little large for me."

Once everyone was seated, Gisella related the discovery she and Valora made at the farm and their discussion with the Lord Justice upon their return.

Orion stroked his chin. "The king will not interfere with any action Lord Fenwick plans to take, but I don't expect he'll send help. Not with the queen having taken ill."

"Yes, I've heard of this mysterious malady from which the queen suffers, but no one will speak of it." Pancras drummed his fingers on the arm of his chair.

"Those who know are sworn to secrecy." Orion raised his eyebrows and shrugged. "The rest of us live in ignorance."

"Which are you, Minotaur?" Alysha glanced at her sister and smiled. "A secret-keeper or ignorant?"

Orion's head turned toward Alysha. "The latter. I am not in the king's confidence."

"Yes, well, we've been assured it has nothing to do with the matter at hand." Gisella waved her hand in dismissal. "All we can do now is wait for Lord Fenwick to return. Then, I believe, it would be best to head to Zamora and destroy the Lich Queen before she regains power."

"Sister." Alysha's curt tone reminded Gisella of their mother's lectures. "You should not go to Zamora. You're too close as it is."

Gisella snapped around to face the Frost Queen. "Aurora herself has charged me—"

"With giving yourself over to her? Is that it? Because you know that's what will happen." Alysha's lips became a thin line, and her eyes narrowed.

"You lost me." Qaliah held up her hand.

"That's because my sister left out an important detail. The Lich Queen is our grandmother."

Gisella pinched the bridge of her nose and sighed. Pancras was the only one who had been privy, and although she spoke previously of revealing the family secret to Orion,

Delilah, and Qaliah, she had hoped to the need would not arise. "That's not relevant. My will—"

"Is insufficient."

The Golden Slayer glared at her sister. She hated when Alysha interrupted her. "Sister—"

"Not against blood magic, Gisella. You know she won't hold back, and you haven't been trained to resist it, not like I have. She will bind her spirit to your form, and then she'll once again have a youthful, strong, beautiful body." Alysha rose, spreading her arms, and spun in place. "A glorious, beautiful, new Witch Queen who can seduce all the rulers and kill all those who resist. She'll run rampant over the north and then set her sights on the south."

"You two"—Qaliah pointed at the sisters—"are related to that moldy bag of bones?"

"Forgive me." Orion tented his fingers before him. "I don't quite understand what you're saying. How is she more vulnerable than you?"

Gisella understood exactly what her sister meant. "If the Lich Queen's goal is to gain a fleshly body again, she needs a blood relative to possess. It is the only way she can return to this world. My sister"—Gisella bowed her head toward Alysha—"believes I am more vulnerable because I'm not a sorceress like she is."

"Because I have been trained to resist blood magic mind enchantments."

"You know, it occurs to me"—Qaliah clicked her fingers to turn everyone's attention to her—"that she has demons under her command, too. I don't know if you noticed…" The fiendling pointed at her horns and held up her tail.

"What?" Alysha spread her hands. "Are you saying you're in league with her? You're a spy, is that it?" She clenched her fists and stepped toward Qaliah. Gisella extended her arm, restraining her sister.

Qaliah jumped out of her chair and backed away. "What? No!"

Pancras stood, holding his hands out in front of him. "She reacts poorly to the presence of demons. It affects her, physically."

The Frost Queen returned to her seat. "Then she's a liability."

"Look, I want to help in any way I can." Qaliah gripped the back of her chair. "It's the whole reason I came north with Blondie and the minotaur. But I don't think I can be surrounded by demons like the one that was in Lord Tyron. It's not a good idea."

Orion stood and placed his hand on the fiendling's shoulder and turned toward the group. "There's no shame in it, Qaliah. Unless I am specifically ordered by Lord Fenwick, I cannot accompany you. I have duties here in the city that are mine alone, obligations for which I am responsible. But I will aid you in any way I can within those limitations."

"I fail to see how remaining in the city can help at all." Alysha returned to her chair and crossed her arms.

Gisella nodded. She put her hand on her sister's arm. "It's fine, Orion and Qaliah. If we fail, someone will need to warn others. We'll make sure you have all the information we have, just in case."

The Justicar met Pancras's gaze. "Believe me, I will pray to the Divine Tribunal for your success."

"Fortunately, we have time to make a solid plan." Gisella regarded the motley group around her. "Lord Fenwick won't be back for several days. We need to equip ourselves and find out as much about Zamora as we can."

She turned to the archmage. "I was hoping the Arcane University could help with that."

"Pancras and I can scour the libraries here. There's bound to be something, right?"

The minotaur wizard nodded. "Surely. Vlorey fought the Lich Queen before. I'll talk to the headmaster, as well. You'll be expected to address the students while you're here, you know. They haven't had an archmage visit in decades."

The drak's teeth clicked as she snapped her mouth shut and then sighed. "Fantastic."

"It's late. Let's reconvene tomorrow and divide our tasks. I'm sure the archmage and Pancras have some catching up to do"—Gisella rose and took her sister's hand—"as do my sister and I."

* * *

After Gisella and her sister exited, the archmage found herself alone with two minotaurs and the fiendling. Qaliah brought plenty of food and ale for all of them, so they spent the rest of the evening trading stories about how Delilah and Pancras spent the months since their separation.

"You died again?" Delilah jaw hung agape. She turned her glare on Qaliah. "You killed him?"

"And you returned again." Orion stared the ceiling. "No wonder you speak with confidence of having a mandate from Aita. She has tasked you personally."

The minotaur wizard flexed his withered hand. "I would have said yes had she just asked in a dream."

Qaliah stripped the meat from a chicken leg. "The story wouldn't be nearly as interesting."

"She's right about that." Delilah sipped her ale. "I put my apprentice to work with the limner reconstructing the book that got water damaged during our tests. She's pretty smart. She'll probably have all kinds of new information about the moon gates for me when I return to Muncifer." With all of her obligations in the southern city, Delilah considered it might be several years before she returned to Drak-Anor.

"After we've dealt with the Lich Queen, I would very much like to see this moon gate you came through. You're certain only draks can activate it?"

"No." Delilah shook her head and sipped her ale. "Humans can't, at least, neither Alysha nor Katka can. We theorized since they were constructed by draks, they were attuned to draks."

Pancras chewed his lip as he nodded. "That makes sense."

"It's getting late." Orion glanced out the window. "We should turn in. We have a lot to accomplish before Lord Fenwick returns."

"Right." Pancras rose from his seat and gestured to Delilah. "I'll take the archmage to her quarters."

Qaliah hopped out of her chair. "Don't have too much fun without me. See you tomorrow."

As Pancras escorted Delilah out of his chambers, the archmage noticed Orion remained behind. The clip-clop of Pancras's hooves, piercing the still of night, echoed in the stone corridors of the White Tower.

"So, you seem close to this other minotaur, Orion?" It was none of her business. Delilah had never given much thought to Pancras's private life, although she understood disapproval for his orientation was one reason he had left Muncifer in the first place.

"Yes. In the short time we've known each other, it seems we fill a void in each other's lives."

"Good. You deserve to find happiness." *First Sarvesh, then Kale, now Pancras. Everybody is settling down. I could do worse than Ori, that's for sure.*

"I was happy in Drak-Anor. Lonely at times, yes, but happy." Pancras stopped outside a door several rooms beyond his own. He knelt before the archmage and took her by the shoulders.

"I don't want to understate how dangerous this confrontation will be."

"We've faced danger before, Pancras." Delilah understood the look in his eyes, his furrowed brow, that distant, yet intense, expression of one resigned to one's fate.

"Not like this. If I don't return, promise me you'll use your influence as archmage to make a better world for draks and minotaurs."

"I've already started." She clasped one of his hands. "And if I don't return, make sure the secret of the moon gates doesn't die with me. I know I can be flippant at times, but I realize how much they can change the world. I can't even imagine what kind of future the people can build together."

Pancras smiled and hugged her. "I think being archmage agrees with you."

Well, it certainly has turned me into a soft fuddy-duddy, hasn't it?

Chapter 24

Pancras awoke the next morning to an empty bed. Rubbing his bleary eyes, he scanned his quarters, discovering himself alone. The Justicar left earlier than the minotaur wizard expected. *Either that, or I slept too long.*

He slid out of bed and clopped over to the windows. Throwing open the curtains allowed the subdued light of a cloudy morning through. Based on the lack of activity on the university grounds, Pancras surmised he had not overslept.

After taking care of his morning ablutions, the minotaur intended to break his fast with Lewin. He pounded on Delilah's door on his way to the headmaster's office.

As she opened the door, Pancras noticed the drak's bloodshot and puffy eyes. "As archmage, I command you to go away."

"We should eat with the headmaster, Archmage." Pancras grinned and spun her as he nudged her into her quarters and followed behind her. "You should have gone to see him last night before finding me."

"You're more important."

"I'm only deputy headmaster."

Delilah coughed. "You're more important to me."

Pancras felt warmth blossom in his heart. "Be that as it may, we have time for official business today, so we should take care of it. I have a class to teach later."

"Yeah, yeah. Give me a minute." She shuffled over to a water pitcher, poured some in a bowl, and dunked her head into it. When she surfaced, she dripped water all over the floor while searching for a towel, but she settled for her cloak. Delilah threw it in the corner.

"It's too hot for that damned thing anyway." She picked up her staff. "Let's go."

Headmaster Lewin sat waiting for Pancras when they arrived. He jumped to his feet at the sight of the archmage.

"I was concerned when you didn't come by last night, but I didn't want to pry in your affairs."

The old man bowed, touching his forehead with his hands. "I am honored by your visit, Archmage Delilah. I must confess, I'm baffled how you arrived here so quickly."

"It's quite the story, Headmaster." Pancras gestured at the table laden with bread, fruit, and dried meat. "I trust there is enough for the archmage to join us?"

"Oh yes, of course!" Lewin pulled a third chair to the table before dashing to his cupboard to retrieve another goblet. "It would be an honor."

Delilah tugged at Pancras's sleeve. He bent down so she could whisper in his ear. "Is he always like this?"

The minotaur nodded. "Very proper and respectful. Nothing like your predecessor." He realized that was the unspoken part of her question.

Diffuse shafts of dreary, grey light danced throughout the room as the sun fought to burn through heavy clouds above the university wall. As Headmaster Lewin returned, he uncovered some lanterns containing glowing, bright, amber gems. Their illumination brought an earthy warmth to the room, pushing back the dreary morning.

The headmaster, full of questions for Delilah, posed several in rapid succession. The drak answered in between bites of their morning meal. Pancras found her inability to keep up with the old man amusing, despite himself. As the archmage's frustration mounted, he decided to show mercy.

"I'm sure there will be time to discuss all the plans Archmage Delilah has once we return."

Lewin's bushy eyebrows leapt away from his eyes like frightened rodents. "You're leaving? So soon?"

"I've previously spoken of my mission from Aita." Pancras sipped from his goblet. Lewin's stocks were without compare, and the wine's berry-filled nose complimented the selection of fresh fruit the headmaster provided. "We're leaving for Zamora in a few days."

"Zamora?" Lewin placed his hand on his chest. "Why in Selene's name would you go to that dreadful place?"

Delilah drained her goblet and helped herself to more wine. "We're going to scour the Lich Queen and her minions from this world. Raze it to the ground, if need be."

"The Lich Queen…" Lewin's eyes grew unfocused as he stared across the table. "You've confirmed it, then? The undead? The Nights of Exodus?"

Delilah tore a hunk of bread from one of the crusty boules near her. "Well, there's something going on there."

"If it is not the Lich Queen, whoever is calling the dead to them at Zamora must still be stopped." Pancras knew in his heart who their foe was, but he lacked hard evidence.

"Yes, indeed." Lewin's attention returned to his guests. "We should speak to the other masters. Perhaps they can lend aid."

"Their aid would be most welcome." Pancras raised his goblet to the headmaster. "We feel a small force will pose the least risk at this time; however, we have a backup plan."

"One of the Justicars and Pancras's pet fiendling are staying behind. If we don't return, they'll need to bring an army." Delilah briefed Lewin on the plans discussed the previous night. "In the meantime, I want to see all the information this university has on Zamora."

"Of course. I'll introduce you to Master Beriwen Falaelwa. In addition to being adjunct master of enchantments, she's also our chief librarian. Whatever knowledge we have on Zamora, she'll find."

* * *

After a restful night, Gisella awakened and joined her sister and Qaliah in the Screeching Griffon's common room.

A large bowl of fruit-laden porridge sat in the center of the table. Dim grey light filtered in through the windows, supplemented by oil lamps at each table.

Alysha ladled a heaping spoonful of grey goo into a bowl and slid it to Gisella as she sat down. "Cold soggy oat on a mucky, dreary day. Eat up!"

Gisella picked up her spoon and stirred the porridge. To her disgust, the concoction supported her spoon when she let go of it. She preferred a bit more cream in her gruel.

The fiendling washed down a mouthful with a mug of steaming cider. "It's not bad once you get past the gloppiness. Fruity."

To her credit, the fiendling was not a bad judge of food. Meal texture was not usually a hurdle for Gisella; one who lived on the road could not afford to be picky.

Alysha gestured to the common room. "You could have picked a nicer inn. This place is dirty."

"I didn't notice." Gisella glanced around the room. Her critical eye noticed the ill-fitted floorboards and set-in stains on the tables. "After months at sea, it appeared luxurious."

Qaliah raised her mug. "Hear, hear. The alley out back is luxurious compared to the ship. Fewer rats, too."

Gisella chuckled. Although rodents weren't really a problem on the *Maiden of the High Seas*, compared with the rest of the crew quarters, the cabin the three shared on the ship was clean and spacious. Still, a swinging hammock on ship couldn't compare to a proper bed.

"When we return from Zamora"—Alysha pointed at herself with her spoon—"I'm picking the accommodations."

"While you're gone, I can look around and obtain some recommendations." Qaliah tapped the tabletop with her finger.

"You?" Alysha's raised eyebrows betrayed her skepticism.

A raucous cry arose from a group of scruffy, leather-clad men playing mumbelty-peg in the far corner. The innkeeper admonished them for throwing knives into his floor but made no move to stop them.

"Hey, I know luxury." Qaliah placed her hand on her chest. "You don't make a living appropriating goods from rich idiots without learning what it looks like."

Gisella glanced over at the fiendling. "Didn't one of those 'rich idiots' indenture you to the Arcane University for theft?"

"Yes." Qaliah pushed out her bottom lip. "I learned not to steal from wizards, so it wasn't a complete waste."

Alysha pointed at her. "If it'd been me, there wouldn't have been enough of you left to indenture."

"It's a good thing I didn't steal from you then, isn't it, Silvery?"

The Frost Queen flicked a lock of her hair. "You have something against hair?"

"I like it. Blondie's there and yours. Silver and gold." Qaliah regarded the ceiling as she chewed on her lip. "Isn't that a song?"

Of least importance on her list of concerns, Gisella intended not to entertain an in-depth discussion about her tresses. She ran her fingers through a dangling clump, snagging it on a knot. "We should go over the supplies we'll need for the journey to Zamora."

Alysha patted her staff, which leaned against her chair. "I have what I need."

"We'll need provisions." Gisella cast a sidelong glance at her sibling. "It's probably a five-day ride, maybe longer. We'll have to procure you a horse, too."

Qaliah waved her spoon at Alysha. "I'll rent you Comet. Five crowns a day. Replace him if you get him killed."

Gisella noticed her sister making mental calculations. Personally, she thought the fiendling priced Comet too low.

"I could almost buy my own horse for that!" Alysha scowled at the fiendling.

"No, you couldn't!" Qaliah laughed and slapped the table.

"If only that stupid drak had not run off Yaamkyrsku. He could have carried all of us there in under a day."

Albeit impressed her sister allied herself with a dragon since they parted ways, Gisella found herself suppressing a giggle when she learned Delilah's brother ran him off right under her sister's nose.

"You should have trained him better." Qaliah helped herself to more porridge, flicking through the goop to remove the raisins.

"Fool! One does not train a dragon." Alysha sniffed and raised her head. "It is a relationship borne of mutual respect and understanding."

"Broken by a drak with an egg." Gisella snickered. She couldn't help but twist the knife a little.

Alysha slumped in her chair. "I hate you both right now."

"Seven crowns a day, Silvery. That's my final offer."

"That's higher than your last offer." Alysha furrowed her brows and glared at the fiendling.

Qaliah shrugged. "It was a limited-time offer, and it's still cheaper than buying your own horse. Sure, you could buy a swayback nag cheaper, but a good horse will run you a hundred, two hundred crowns, easy, especially around here."

Gisella raised her eyebrows and nodded. Unsure of how Qaliah learned so much about horse pricing since their arrival considering she wasn't at all knowledgeable when they purchased Comet, she suspected the fiendling of attempting to con her sister.

"Just take the five crowns a day, Alysha."

"Hey!"

Gisella quelled Qaliah's protest with a glance. "We don't have time to haggle for a horse for you. It's better to borrow a friend's, wouldn't you say?"

"She's not my friend… fine. Take this as a deposit." Alysha dug in her pouch and threw a handful of gold coins across the table at the fiendling. She pointed at her sister. "You're responsible for the provisions, though."

After breaking her fast, Gisella tended to just that. She spent the morning familiarizing herself with the vendors in the market and stopped by the Arcane University to consult with Pancras and Delilah on what provisions they required.

By the time rain arrived in the afternoon, she had purchased much of the supplies they needed. Having completed the task, Gisella retired to her room to clean and check her armor and weapons and await word of Lord Fenwick's return.

* * *

Master Beriwen Falaelwa proved invaluable in helping Delilah locate what information the university possessed on Zamora. The elf seemed abundantly curious about the drak archmage, particularly on the origin and significance of her stripes; however, Delilah convinced her those answers could wait until she returned from her pending journey.

Most of what had been written about Zamora was chronicled in histories of the war in which Vlorey had been at the forefront over twenty years earlier. According to all accounts Delilah read, no battle actually took place at the tower of Zamora itself; rather, the Lich Queen's defeat occurred at the Battle of Badon Hill. Located some distance southwest, Zamora sat at the edge of the area in which the hills bordered the northern portion of Caernoth.

Well, Deli-girl, if she kills us all, you'll be closer to home than you have been in a long while. Further reports from after the war indicated the terrain surrounding Zamora had become rugged, marsh-like, and possessed of unnatural cold. The foliage fell twisted and ill, as though the land itself had become diseased.

This should have been their first clue she wasn't completely destroyed.

After completing her research, Delilah met with Headmaster Lewin and waited for him to assemble the students. She had not prepared an official statement, as she had not intended for her meeting with Pancras to be an official visit to the Arcane University as archmage.

They convened in one of the largest assembly halls within the Iron Tower. The amphitheater, large enough to seat all the students, featured a podium at the bottom of the lecture hall. Tiered seating stretched up and surrounded her on three sides, towering over the diminutive drak. The masters of the university all sat in the front row nearest Delilah. Pancras's presence in the center of the faculty eased her anxiety.

She cleared her throat, the projection of her voice by the enchanted podium startling her. She jumped, gripping the sides of the lectern tightly enough to scratch the finish.

"Assembled students and faculty, I am honored by the warm welcome you have shown me. My visit here was entirely unplanned, and so, I will not keep you long. Frankly, I don't have much to say right now."

The admission caused a mixture of murmurs and chuckles to circulate the room.

"I've not been archmage long enough to have gained a full understanding of all the guild's policies, and I plan to leave the administration of each university campus to its respective headmaster. However, I will ensure that all students are given the same opportunities to learn, regardless of the circumstances of their birth. The former archmage, Vilkan Icebreaker, whom some of you may know better as Manless"—she paused to allow the laughter to abate—"was a cruel and vindictive man.

"It would be easy for me to condemn all humans for his actions, but I will not. I am self-taught and was perfectly happy having had no guild involvement until he forced my hand. You will, no doubt, hear rumors that I invoked the ancient Rite of Combat and in defeating him, succeeded him as archmage."

Another wave of murmurs circulated the room. Observing the number of head nods, she determined that this information had reached many students.

"I did not go to Muncifer with the intention of becoming archmage. I didn't challenge Manless with that intention, either. Frankly, I wanted to scour his stain from Calliome after learning he murdered a Firstborne."

Most students returned blank stares and shrugged at each other. Delilah sighed. "Obviously, draconic lore needs to be added to the curriculum." She eyed Headmaster Lewin as she spoke. "He killed the dragon Pyraclannaseous, a Firstborne, Daughter of Gaia and Rannos Dragonsire. I saw her corpse with my own eyes. I challenged him to mete out justice.

"Further, after becoming archmage, I rediscovered the secret of the moon gates, a pre-Sundering transportation network built by drak wizards. I intend to revitalize this network to make travel between our universities easier, and in time, perhaps to benefit all the peoples of Calliome. This will require us wizards to work more closely with the common folk of the world than we have in an age. I hope you will join with me in this. Together, we can make the world a better place."

There. I laid it out. It's a plan, I guess. Her words met with scattered applause, and the students murmured to one another. Delilah, uncertain her impromptu speech was wise, spoke from her heart. As she stepped down from the podium and exited the assembly hall through the rear faculty entrance, she trembled and clutched her knotted stomach. *Let's not ever do that again, Deli-girl.*

* * *

The weather broke on the third day and brought with it a steamy, sun-filled morning. A messenger from the Palace of Justice interrupted Pancras's meal with Orion.

A wiry, flush-faced lad wearing the tabard of the Justicars greeted Pancras when he answered the door. He handed the bonelord a note. "From the Lord Justice, sir!" He bowed before turning and running off. The minotaur shut the door and broke the seal as he returned to his seat.

"Fenwick has returned and awaits us in his office. As soon as possible, he says." Pancras turned the parchment over. "It says nothing about his meeting with the king."

"It won't." Orion shook his head. "Fenwick keeps his messages short and to the point. He'll tell you in person." The Justicar tossed a meat-filled hand pie to Pancras and took one for himself before standing and picking up his halberd.

"Best not to keep him waiting."

Pancras collected another meat pie for Delilah, and after they roused her, they left together. Eating as they traveled, the minotaurs endured the archmage's complaints about the early hour. Merchants milled about, either setting up their shops and stalls or running errands that needed to be completed before they opened for commerce.

The Golden Slayer and her sister arrived before they did and were waiting for them along the main staircase reminiscing about home.

"Where's Qaliah?" Pancras scanned the area for her.

"She's a crook and a layabout!" Alysha scowled as she leaned against the base of the fountain of the Divine Tribunal.

The drak archmage tapped her staff on the floor. "I knew it!"

Gisella pursed her lips and glared at her sister. "She decided since she's not going with us, there was no reason for her to 'greet Apellon's arse crack,' as she put it."

Pancras rubbed his right horn as he cocked his head toward Alysha. "Crook?"

"She's charging me five crowns a day to rent her flea-bitten horse."

Orion rubbed his jaw. "Hmm, five crowns a day?"

"Comet is not flea-bitten." Pancras glanced at Orion. "At least, he wasn't when we arrived."

"Then it is a good deal." The Justicar nodded at Alysha. "You should be happy she was willing to lend you a steed at that price."

The sorceress remained unconvinced and grunted. "We're saving the world. It should have been free."

"Dolios help me if she ever schemes with Kale." Delilah hissed under her breath. "He'll end up charging me!"

Orion gestured to the stairs. "Shall we? The Lord Justice awaits."

As they climbed the grand staircase, they passed a pair of Justicars clad head to toe in blue-and-gold enameled steel plate armor. The men clanked as they walked, a cacophony of resplendent metal. Pancras admired them as they passed, engaged in conversation.

When they reached the top of the stairs, he took Orion aside. "Why don't you have armor like that?" He gestured to the two humans, now at the bottom of the stairs. "It's elegant."

"Smiths charge too much for armor like that to fit a minotaur." Orion regarded the men as they left the Palace of Justice. "Besides, that type of finery is easily destroyed in combat. They must be attending an official function for one of the nobles."

A gift then, perhaps, once I return. What one considered an exorbitant price, another might feel was fair. For all the time they spent together, Pancras still had much to learn about Orion.

Lord Fenwick and Scout Stonehammer stood at his desk, examining a map. The dwarf woman stood on a chair alongside the Lord Justice. The two greeted the group when they entered.

"Ah, you received my summons." He glanced out the windows. "And made haste, by the look of things. Excellent!" He raised an eyebrow as he regarded the archmage. "Picked up a new companion while I was away?"

Pancras gestured toward Delilah and bowed. "My friend, Archmage Delilah, of the Mage's Guild. She's to lend a hand."

"The archmage, eh? Very good. I'd heard there was a shake-up among the wizards." Lord Fenwick snapped to attention and nodded at her. "I'm pleased you've chosen to join our little crusade."

Lord Fenwick gestured for them to join Scout Stone-hammer and him around the table. "We've just been going over the best route to Zamora. There was a road through the marshes"—he pointed to a spot on the map between Badon Hill and Caernoth—"but its navigability is questionable."

"Shove over, Dwarf." Delilah tapped Valora's ankle and climbed up in the chair on which the dwarf woman stood. Pancras noticed pain in the dwarf's eyes as she bit her tongue.

"Ugh, marshes." Alysha regarded her fur-trimmed white robe. "That road better be passable."

As much as he hated travel, Pancras viewed mucking about knee-deep mud and stagnant water as close to damnation on this world as one could get.

Gisella elbowed her sister in the ribs. "Those enchanted robes aren't self-cleaning?"

"Well, as a matter of fact, they are. But that's beside the point. I hear there are blood-sucking bugs and worse in marshes"—she leaned toward her sister—"trolls and even dreaded Bog Beasts of Ethiopus."

The color drained from Gisella's face, and her jaw twitched as she gritted her teeth.

Lord Fenwick burst out laughing. "Bog Beast of who?"

Scout Stonehammer bit her lip, and her dusky face flushed as the corners of her eyes wrinkled in suppressed mirth.

"Tell them, Gisella." Alysha snickered. "Tell them of your encounter with the dreaded bog beast. Or shall I?" She held out her hand, palm upraised, as if seeking a bribe in exchange for her silence.

The Golden Slayer slapped away her sister's hand. "We don't have time for this."

"Too right." Lord Fenwick nudged Valora. The dwarf woman cleared her throat and forced the smile from her face.

The Lord Justice cleared his throat. "I've spoken to the king. As I suspected, he's unwilling to commit forces at this time but wishes to be kept informed. He also requested two Justicars as an escort."

Pancras nodded in understanding. *Hence the Justicars in the formal armor.*

"He plans to enter the city and meet with the Council of Lords." Lord Fenwick rolled up the map. "He wants everyone in agreement… in case we fail. Valora and I are ready to depart as soon as your preparations are made."

"We are ready, Lord Fenwick." Gisella regarded Pancras and tilted her head, waiting for his confirmation.

"Yes, indeed." Pancras raised Shatterskull. "Gisella was kind enough to purchase provisions while you were away. We can depart immediately."

"Then I shall take my leave." Orion crossed his fist over his chest and bowed to the Lord Justice. "I have duties."

His eyes lingered as they met Pancras's. The bonelord excused himself from the assembled group and followed Orion into the hall. The Justicar took his hands and pressed them to his nose.

"Be safe. Be careful. Return victorious."

The minotaur wizard lowered his head and pressed it against Orion's, cupping his withered hand around the base of the Justicar's left horn. "You've given me a reason to return, and so I shall." They stood motionless, until Orion broke away and marched down the stairs.

Pancras watched him leave. Orion didn't look back.

* * *

Delilah's eyes widened as the dwarf scout mounted her battle boar. "I need one of those. That's way better than those lizards we bought." As she spoke, she remembered Fang, the nailtooth lizard that carried her to Muncifer more than a year earlier. "I wonder what became of them after we set them loose in the mountains."

"Why did you set them loose?" Pancras raised an eyebrow as he regarded the archmage.

"Long story. I'll fill you in later."

Pancras offered her a hand from atop Stormheart. "Fine. You can ride with me, Delilah." He pulled her up and sat her in front of him. She gripped his bare arm and twisted to face him.

"Where's the rest of your robes? I've never seen you not covered from head to hoof." The minotaur wore a linen shirt the color of sapphires and a black leather kilt with gold studs and buckles.

"Too hot for full robes." He patted Shatterskull, secure it its saddle holster. "Besides, they make wielding this awkward."

Lord Fenwick pulled alongside them astride his snorting black stallion, Shadowmane, several hands taller than their modest steed. "We'll follow the road for a day and then turn south."

The Lord Justice spurred Shadowmane and passed through the city gates at a full gallop. The two Watchmaidens followed, and Pancras and Valora brought up the rear. With the sun at their backs throughout the morning, it seemed as if Apellon himself drove them onward on a quest to eradicate darkness.

As the sun passed overhead and began its descent, flooding their faces with oppressive heat and blinding them, Pancras decided Apellon was, indeed, cruel and intended to cause them as much discomfort as possible before allowing them to rest for the night. That evening, Delilah regaled them with the full tale of Pyraclannaseous and her death at the hands of Vilkan Manless, their discovery of the Firstborne's egg, and her fateful duel with the archmage.

The next day, they turned off the road and onto a dirt trail leading south into farmlands. The first of autumn's cool breezes cut across their path as they rode through the lush, rolling fields of western Cardoba.

Apellon's fury returned on the third day, beating down with heat and humidity. Clouds gathered on the horizon, overtaking them by midday, and granted a reprieve from the sun's intense glare as they continued south. A few days later, the clouds darkened, and the lush farmland became sparse, scrub-covered crags.

On the fifth day, they made camp on a jagged overlook. From the edge, Pancras viewed the soggy wetlands into which they would ride the next morning. Mist clung to the trees and bogs, vapor on the water like a dragon's breath in winter. Fenwick climbed the bluff to join Pancras as he regarded the marsh.

"How far into the marsh is Zamora?" Pancras shielded his eyes from the setting sun and peered into the distance, noting only treetops and swampland.

Fenwick unrolled his map. "We should be able to see it from here. Perhaps the ruins have crumbled below the treetops."

Although Pancras agreed that was possible, he pondered a worse alternative. "Or it could be veiled from sight."

"I was hoping you wouldn't say that." Fenwick rolled up his map and stuffed it in his pouch. "It won't stay veiled from the light of the Divine Tribunal, I promise you that."

Chapter 25

On foot, Scout Stonehammer led the way into the swamp, hacking with twin axes at the vines and branches that obstructed the overgrown path. After some initial grumbling, she permitted Delilah to ride Quincy in her stead as the rest followed behind her.

Humidity and odors rising from the stagnant waters in the Witchmoor labored their breathing. Clouds covering the sun did little to stave off the sweltering heat, and steam rose from the soggy ground surrounding them. The drak archmage struggled to keep the battle boar moving forward. He wanted to stop every few feet to gnaw on the cut ends of vines dangling level with his head.

"Damn!" Valora swore and swung her axe, embedding it into the trunk of a twisted, gnarled dogwood tree.

Delilah raised a fist to signal the column behind her to stop before she dismounted. "What's wrong?"

The dwarf gestured to the trail in front of her. "Just look! We can't get through this gods-cursed tangle."

Delilah saw nothing ahead that would obstruct their journey, nothing Valora's axes couldn't hack away, at any rate. She picked her way past the dwarf, handing Quincy's reins to her as she passed. The air grew thick. Pushing her way forward reminded the archmage of the initial plane of the moon gate, except it didn't give way.

She returned to Valora's side. "There's something there, all right."

Valora spat into the swamp. "Of course there is! Did you think those thorn-covered branches would just part for you?"

"What's the holdup?" Lord Fenwick and Gisella approached them. The Golden Slayer glanced at Quincy as she passed and gave the boar a wide berth, slipping off the path and into calf-high water to do so.

"Something is blocking our way." Delilah gestured to the trail.

"I see that. I've never seen brambles grow that thick." He motioned to Gisella. "Can you see any way through down in the water?"

The Watchmaiden grabbed onto an overhead vine. "I dare not go further. It's been getting deeper the farther I go."

Delilah cocked her head. Gisella stood in water only halfway to her knees. The archmage shooed them all away. "Get back. Get Pancras and Alysha up here. There's wizardry at work."

"What do you mean?" Valora yanked her axe out of the tree. "I know an impassible trail when I see one."

"Whatever lay beyond has enchanted you. The trail is clear, a little overgrown, perhaps, but not impassible. I feel a barrier." She waved Pancras and Alysha over. "What do you see? A clear trail or impassible brambles?"

"Is this some inappropriate game?" Alysha frowned and glared at her sister. "It's clear, of course."

"No." Pancras pulled Shatterskull close to his chest. The weapon's head shifted and flowed, transforming into the image of a grinning skull. "There are powerful enchantments on this path. The work of a necromancer."

"Believe me now?" Delilah nodded at Lord Fenwick. "How's that light of the Tribunal?"

The human grunted. "It's not to be taken literally." Lord Fenwick took Quincy's reins from Valora. "We'll tie up the horses. We'll proceed on foot from here. Can you wizards get us through?"

Valora followed the Justicar. "Through what? Are they going to burn down the trees?"

Alysha pulled her sister out of the muck and moved alongside Pancras and Delilah. "We can breech this if we work together."

The archmage tugged at the Frost Queen's white sleeve. She was amazed how pristine it remained throughout their journey and made a mental note to learn those enchantments from Alysha before they parted ways.

"Guess what there isn't time to learn when you grow up blasting dwarves and oroqs?"

"Blasting what?" Valora's voice called from the trail behind them.

Alysha leaned down. "*Dialysee goe'tia.* Just follow my lead."

She stood in the center of the trio and raised her staff. Wispy tendrils of sapphire energy flowed into it. "*Dialysee goe'tia. Dialysee goe'tia.*"

The minotaur stood alongside her, repeating the incantation in unison as he held Shatterskull before him. Azure tendrils flowed through his weapon, swirling through the air as they mixed with the energy from the Frost Queen's staff.

Delilah raised her own staff as the eyes of the lizard skull glowed with cerulean light. Energies from her staff joined with the energies of the Frost Queen and Bonelord of Aita, forming a turquoise sphere that expanded around them until it burst with a blinding flash, obliterating the enchantment in a spray of turquoise fire.

The archmage leaned on her staff as she examined their handiwork. The path was now clear. She glanced over her shoulder at Valora and gestured ahead. "After you."

* * *

Gisella turned away from the magical blast, yet still felt a wave from the dissipation of arcane energy. Pinpricks crawled all over her skin as she leaned against a dogwood and removed her boots, emptying the water that filled them. When no liquid poured out, she sighed. *I hate enchantments.*

She cursed her foolishness in wading into such an illusion. Her training as a slayer was supposed to protect her from succumbing to such arcana, yet she had been deceived by the trickery as easily as Fenwick and Valora had been. The phantasm had appeared perfectly natural and real to her.

Alysha slapped her on the shoulder. "Don't feel bad, sister. I've not seen a more powerful enchantment covering a large area like this."

Everyone checked their weapons and armor once more before proceeding. Valora continued to hack away at vines growing too close to the path. Ahead, Gisella noticed the trees and shrubs appeared more twisted and overgrown than those behind them. Some leaned away from the path, bent away from the direction in which they traveled, as though attempting to flee from what lay ahead, anchored in place by the very roots which gave them life.

More clouds rolled in, completely blocking the setting sun from view. Thunder rumbled in the distance, and the trees grew knobby and warped. A foul odor lingered, permeating the air so thoroughly Gisella tasted it.

Valora held up her hand, signaling the rest to stop. She trotted back. "There's a clearing up there, some sort of structure."

"Zamora." Pancras hefted Shatterskull. "Hold here a moment."

The minotaur trotted forward. He waved for them to join him before crouching and crawling into the brush.

The rest of the companions did likewise, following his path though gnarled vines and branches until they crested a small rise. Gisella heard moans and the shuffling of dead feet before she saw them.

Like an obscenity directed at Calliome itself, Zamora jutted upward through the moor. Curved, twisted spires thrust into the sky like fingers clawing at the heavens and blocking the glare from a fell, pulsating light at the top of the tower. Blackened and withered foliage surrounded the tower, succumbing to the perversion of scores of undead shuffling around it. They infested the surroundings like rats in an old grain mill. Beneath gray, rumbling skies, mist clung to the shrubs and vines covering the ground.

Gisella adjusted the straps on her armor as Scout Stonehammer emerged from a nearby thicket. The dwarf frowned and shook her head. "It's like that all over. This place crawls with undead. I can't get an accurate count since they keep moving, but I'm guessing it's just about everyone who left Vlorey over the last couple of months, all those drowners, too."

She shivered. Lord Fenwick pulled her close, wrapping his arms around her. "It shouldn't be this cold, either, huh?"

"We should have brought an army."

Pancras snorted. "More fodder for her legion. Every one of ours who dies becomes one of hers."

The minotaur crept forward to crouch alongside Gisella. "That unnatural chill is the taint of demons."

"That's what I feel." Delilah hugged her knees to her chest. "It's oppressive, like all the joy has been sucked out of the world."

"All the color, too." Alysha pointed at the sky and the forest in the distance. "They're leeching the life out of everything here."

"Definitely demons." Gisella felt them, too. Being aware of their presence, without seeing them felt almost worse than facing them. "Qaliah will be glad she didn't come."

"Based on what happened last time"—Pancras glanced at the Golden Slayer—"I think we can all be glad of that."

"Well, Wizards." Fenwick cleared his throat. "How do we defeat them? Demons are far beyond anything Valora and I are used to fighting."

"I like the army idea." Scout Stonehammer's eyes flicked to the tower and then to Gisella. "Let's raze the place to the ground. I don't fancy becoming part of her undead legion."

"Nor do I." Pancras lifted Shatterskull. "However, this situation requires a finesse more subtle than brute force, I think."

The Golden Slayer observed the undead shuffling about the tower grounds in the distance. There did not seem to be any pattern to their wanderings and no patrol route that she detected. They behaved as though they awaited a command from their master with no instructions regarding what to do in the meantime.

"Watch my back." Pancras used his maul to push himself to his feet and strode into the midst of the undead. With snarls and howls of fury, they turned and advanced on him.

The minotaur raised Shatterskull, and a blinding flare radiated from its head. Any undead touched by the light disintegrated into ash. Ghouls partially caught in the beam howled in anguish as their arms and legs were purified.

Pancras gestured to them. "I will clear a path. Follow the light!"

The Golden Slayer and her sister scrambled to catch up to the minotaur. Rotting corpses moaned and lunged at them. When they touched Aita's light, they crumbled into dust.

"*Kalee'steen enoch leetiké goyna!*" Azure light flooded the decrepit field as the archmage raised her staff. Scores of furry, blue boggins popped into existence around the drak and charged into the hordes of undead, yipping and snarling. The pack of boggins drew attention away from the companions as they followed in the minotaur's path.

Lord Fenwick and Scout Stonehammer followed behind Delilah. The Justicar lingered, fending off a ravenous ghoul while the dwarf's stubby legs pumped in a furious effort to catch up to the rest of the group. Gisella turned and thrust her spear into the ghoul. Unable to penetrate forged steel, its filthy nails scratched the finish on Fenwick's breastplate.

An icicle flew between Fenwick and Gisella, impaling the ghoul's head. It flopped to the ground, writing and hissing. Several other ghouls took advantage of the opportunity and fell upon their fallen kin, rending its rotten flesh with their blackened talons.

They caught up to Pancras at the base of the tower. He held Shatterskull aloft, covering as much area as possible with Aita's light. The companions crowded around him as the minotaur pointed at a banded oak door. "It's locked up tight."

Alysha examined the door. "Well maintained for a ruin. Pity. Stand back."

She leveled her staff at the door as the rest of them withdrew as close to the edge of the light as they dared. Gangs of skeletons and ghouls circled them, most now wary of the light, although many still reached toward them, rewarded with limbs that fell to dust.

The Frost Queen's staff glowed with a fierce emerald light. "*Maaxo dynami velos!*" A green bolt of arcane energy flew from her staff and impacted the door. Rattling on its hinges, it splintered.

Alysha lowered her staff and stepped aside, gesturing to the door. "Justicar, if you please?"

"Gladly." Fenwick raised his shield and raced toward the door. He threw himself into it, bursting through like a raging bull.

The companions entered the tower's interior. Deep shadows concealed the edges of the room. Delilah and Alysha illuminated their staffs, aiming them at the walls, which sparkled as though covered in gems. Gisella touched one of the glimmering spots. She noted flecks of quartz embedded in the stone reflected the mages' light.

Gisella ran her fingers along the wall, discovering the quartz fragments composed oblong carvings. "Are these glyphs? Runes of some sort?"

Alysha joined her sister while Pancras ensured Aita's protection covered the doorway. Delilah's voice filled the background as she conjured a column of whirling blades to block the way and guard it against undead that might follow.

"Gly…no, they're eyes." The Frost Queen examined the block adjacent to the one Gisella traced. "It's covered in eyes!"

The Golden Slayer recoiled, although to her hands, the surface felt like carved stone. She looked closer. Eyes of various sizes were carved onto every block Gisella viewed. Some sections contained one or two large eyes, others half-a-dozen or more smaller eyes. The hair on the back of her neck stood on end.

"Now I feel like we're being watched." Her eyes flicked to her sister.

Alysha frowned. "That's not funny."

Valora walked past the sisters and examined a depression at the bottom of the tower's spiral stairs. "Fennie, what's this? I see something."

Fenwick approached the dwarf woman. Alysha thrust her staff toward the depression. Nestled within and covered in a thick layer of dust lay a pile of bleached, curved bones. They appeared to be much like a human's ribs, however, thicker and longer. Gisella leaned over the depression alongside Valora and Fenwick. She noticed many teeth lying among the curved bones.

The Lord Justice glanced up at the others. "These aren't human bones. Maybe it's not a complete skeleton, but I'd remember encountering a creature such as this."

"If they're not walking about"—Alysha moved her staff away—"they're not important."

"Ocularus." Valora's voice was only a whisper, yet it seemed to echo off the stark walls of the tower.

"I've not heard of such creatures." Alysha's moved her staff closer to illuminate the bones.

"The elders of Korbbaddan tell tales of orb-like creatures that dwell in deep caverns beneath the mountains and refer to them as ocularuses." The dwarf shivered and stood. "Great orbs, covered in eyes, wielding powerfully destructive magic. They tell us ocularuses eat naughty dwarf children and can see in all directions even through stone or other solid structures."

Valora turned and wrapped her arms around Fenwick's leg. He knelt to comfort her. "Well, this bugger's long dead."

"Pancras's light show announced our presence." Delilah stood at the bottom of the stairs and motioned to the group. "Shall we? There can't be much to this tower. Let's put this lich in the ground so we can go home."

Gisella glanced at the doorway. The whirling blades chopped and sliced any ghoul daring enough to attempt passing through. Their howls and cries of fury formed a ghastly chorus.

"How long is that going to last?" Gisella pointed at the barrier with her spear.

"A couple of hours if I don't dismiss it." Delilah nodded at Pancras. The minotaur lowered Shatterskull, and Aita's light faded.

Gisella took the stairs. "Fenwick and I will lead the way. Pancras follows us. Then Alysha and Delilah. Valora should cover the rear."

Fenwick held her arm. "Wait. Let Valora and the archmage go first. You can still use your spear over their heads. I'll take the rear." He ushered the rest of his companions onto the stairs.

Gisella crept along behind the drak and the dwarf. Even standing a few steps behind them, she understood what Fenwick intended. Neither the dwarf nor the drak competed with the Watchmaiden's height.

Gisella moved as quietly as she was able, although between Fenwick's armor and the clip-clop of the minotaur's hooves on stone, she couldn't imagine there was anyone in Zamora who couldn't hear them approach.

The stairs widened as they spiraled up the interior of the tower's wall. Another door barred their progress. By Gisella's reckoning, they should have neared the top of the structure. She confirmed her suspicion by peering down the central shaft.

Scout Stonehammer hooked the head of her axe on the door handle. She glanced at the group? "Ready?"

Gisella raised her spear. "Do it."

The dwarf pulled down on her axe and kicked the door open. It swung on its hinges and bashed into the wall. The companions poured through the doorway.

Open to the sky, twisting spires at the top of the tower surrounded the flat roof, its surface marred only by channels, leading away from the center. A flash of lightning preceded the crack of thunder, and the sky opened up.

Icy rain brought with it a chill even though the air itself felt like a sweltering Vlorey heatwave. The droplets plinked off their metal armor and soaked into the wizards' robes. The slayer's eyes were drawn to the center of the roof. Gisella shivered as her blood ran cold.

Pulsating green and violet light spilled forth from a jagged rip in the sky and illuminated the top of the tower. In the center of the rooftop, lay the withered body of a naked woman suspended by inky tendrils stretching to the tops of the tower's spires. The coils formed nebulous shackles around her wrists and ankles as they held her, arms and legs splayed. Dark, smoky wisps swirled around her, following the contours of her body. Her head hung slack, surrounded by threads of yellowed, silver hair. A dim, ruby glow smoldered in her sunken eye sockets as she raised her head to regard the intruders.

She smiled, her sharpened teeth gleaming white against her blackened lips. "Welcome to Zamora." The Lich Queen's voice cracked like autumn leaves crunching underfoot. "I've been waiting for you."

* * *

Pancras avoided looking directly at the Lich Queen and instead focused on the fissure hanging in the sky above her. Viewing it caused familiar, unsettled feelings. The air around the gash shifted and twisted, distortions in reality caused by the tear's connection to the elemental chaos that formed Calliome. Despite fixing his attention on the chaos rift, Pancras felt a force pulling him toward the Lich Queen, not an attraction exactly, rather a compulsion to go to her. The smoky wisps crawling over her body flowed down and away from her, forming hulking, bat-winged figures as they descended. More joined them from the fissure above.

All possessed one or two canine-featured, desiccated heads. The demons towered over even the minotaur. As the beasts advanced, the bonelord's companions raised their weapons and spread out.

Lord Fenwick and Valora stayed close to each other as they advanced on a four-armed, fire-snorting dog-demon. Fenwick lunged first, a half-hearted swing to draw the demon's attention. It clawed at him, raking its talons across his shield as Valora ducked under its arm and buried her axes in the back of its knees.

Archmage Delilah and the Frost Queen double-teamed a fiery demon, wreathed in flames, attacking it with alternating blasts of ice and lightning. Although it howled as each attack slammed into it, the duo did not seem cause it significant harm.

The bonelord swung Shatterskull in an arc, smashing it on the head of a sinuous demon moving in for a low bite.

The empowered weapon seared flesh as the beast slammed into the stone rooftop. Thrashing and howling with its head trapped underneath the maul, the demon smacked Pancras's leg and sent him sprawling.

He scrambled, pulling Shatterskull along until he regained his footing. He ended up face to face with the ram-horned, four-armed demon.

It snarled and lunged.

* * *

Gisella brandished her spear as a flaming, dog-faced demon approached her. The beast snarled and swiped at her weapon, but she jerked it to the side as she thrust, catching it along the throat.

Steaming, black ichor sprayed as it roared and clutched its neck. The Golden Slayer lowered her head and rammed the beast in the chest with her helmet, knocking it off its feet.

Jumping on it, Gisella brought her full weight to bear upon her spear, impaling its torso. The demon thrashed and flung her off. She managed to keep hold of her weapon, jerking it free before she hit the rooftop and rolled.

The demon held its talons over the wound and retreated. She moved to pursue, but the flaming lash of a different towering fiery demon intercepted her, wrapping itself around her ankle. It yanked, pulling her feet out from under her.

Gisella fell and grunted. She felt the lash strike her back again and again as she crawled toward her spear. Its heat penetrated her armor. The Golden Slayer kicked her legs in the air to right herself and caught the next lash on her spear. She spun it and pulled, but the demon's iron grip held fast.

A blast of ice hit the demon's face, breaking off bits of stone-like flesh. The beast's attention turned to its new attacker. The Frost Queen, relentless in her attack, threw icy shard after icy shard at the demon until its chest quivered like a porcupine.

To Gisella's side, one of the two-headed demons kicked Valora, sending the dwarf tumbling across the roof. It rushed after her.

Leveling her spear at the foul creature, the Golden Slayer charged.

* * *

Pancras ducked the demon's claw as it swiped at his head. He thrust Shatterskull upward, ramming it into the beast's face. It howled and staggered backward as a spray of ichor rained on the minotaur.

Pancras pursued, Aita's power rending long gashes in the demon's chest as the beast clawed at the wounds. While holding the weapon against its target, Pancras noticed that each of the inky, nebulous ropes suspending the Lich Queen seemed to be anchored at the top of each connecting spire by translucent stones.

"The stones! Break the stones at the top of the spires!" he shouted to Gisella and Valora, pointing at the nearest one. The Golden Slayer nodded and hurled her spear.

The weapon sped toward its target, its steel tip shattering the crystal into a shower of knife-like shards. The tendril dissipated. The Lich Queen's left arm, released from its bindings, fell slack.

On the opposite side of the rooftop, Valora dove beneath the legs of one of the demons, hacking at its ankles as she passed. She rolled into a crouch and pitched one of her axes at the spire above her. Her weapon spun through the air, smashing the crystal just as a bolt of lightning flashed across the sky.

Her arms no longer restrained, the Lich Queen's upside-down body swung, slamming into the tower's roof. Another demon lunged at Pancras, but he saw the beast at the periphery of his vision and brought Shatterskull up just in time. The demon's hand closed around the maul. Its flesh sizzled and decorticated as energy, infused into the weapon by the goddess of death, flowed into the demon. It screamed, the sound like boulders being dragged over gravel, and released its grip.

Raising Shatterskull above his head, Pancras bounded toward the Lich Queen as she climbed to her feet. The demon spread its wings and gave chase, each step of its clawed foot shaking the tower and showering rubble from the crumbling spires.

Despite blasts of azure fire slamming into the demon from behind, it closed on Pancras and swiped low, catching the bonelord in the back of his leg. The minotaur fell, and Shatterskull flew from his hands. His calf burned like fire, and he observed raw, pink muscle twitching in the open wound.

Delilah called his name and redoubled her efforts, loosing blast after blast at the demon. Alysha joined in with the archmage. Alternating bolts of fire and ice drove the demon backward toward the edge of the rooftop.

Pancras left the beast to them and pulled himself along the roof toward his fallen weapon.

"No!"

He heard the cry a moment before a burning hand snatched him. A half-melted visage snarled and snapped. Pancras writhed and twisted in a desperate attempt to avoid the demon's jaws. It grabbed him with its other hand and bared its teeth. Its wrinkled eye, a ragged ruin, dangled from its socket where Shatterskull's power had burned it.

Pancras worked his withered arm free. He slapped and punched as the demon brought him toward its mouth, feeling his fist impact the roof of the beast's maw as it bit down.

The minotaur screamed.

Jagged teeth crushed bone and sliced through leathery flesh. Pancras's eyes bulged as the demon bit clean through his arm. He heard more shouting below him before he felt himself fall. Fenwick and Gisella slashed and stabbed the demon, driving it backward.

Stars exploded in Pancras's vision as he hit the rooftop. He struggled to breathe. Finally, he rolled over on his stomach. The Lich Queen stood near, her legs still bound by slack tethers to the remaining two spires. She stared at him, her face locked in a rictus of terror.

"Yes, come to me, Bonelord."

She reached toward him.

"Pancras!" Delilah ran toward him, skidding to a stop and crouching, intent on aiding him to his feet. He pushed her away and pointed to his weapon.

"Shatterskull!"

"Let's get you up." Delilah pulled at his robes again.

"I can end this. Go!" He reached toward the weapon, but it lay far from his hand.

Swearing, the drak archmage dove for the weapon. She scooped it up and dragged it to him.

As soon as the haft touched his hand, Pancras rolled and swung it toward the Lich Queen's head, confident she could not withstand its energy. The skull on the maul's head transformed into a screaming visage as it descended.

The Lich Queen raised her hand to shield her face and caught Shatterskull.

Pancras noted his weapon did not sear her flesh. An instant later, the world around him vanished as a flash filled his vision.

Surrounded by swirling black and violet mists, Pancras stood face to face with the withered, skeletal sorceress. Tattered threads that had once been fine linen robes clung to her body. Her spindling fingers wrapped around Shatterskull, just above his own hand.

Pancras gritted his teeth. "Get out of my mind!"

"I cannot." The Lich Queen's voice became a raspy hiss. "You are in mine. Do your job, Bonelord. Release me from this world."

Chapter 26

Delilah shielded her eyes as a flash of searing luminescence enveloped Pancras and the Lich Queen. She fell backward, scrambling to avoid an expanding field of scintillating, violet energy that surrounded them.

Blinking away the aura as her eyes reacted to the glare, she noticed the demons turn toward the amethyst bubble and charge it. They clawed and howled, their talons bouncing off the shield like pebbles thrown against a castle wall.

She ran across the roof toward Alysha. "Did you do that?"

"No, but let's not waste it." The Frost Queen raised her staff and called down a torrent of fiery hail, pelting the demons that surrounded their mistress and the minotaur. The beasts swatted at the attack, treating the hailstones as annoying flies, and continued to claw at the shield.

Alysha pointed to the rift. "We have to close that!"

The rift continued to disgorge shadowy demons, all joining their brethren in trying to claw their way to Pancras and the Lich Queen. Delilah remembered the minotaur's story about the chaos rift he and Kale dealt with near Ironkrag and committed herself to staying as far away from it as possible.

Lord Fenwick cradled Valora in his lap. The dwarf's face was covered in blood. Caressing his cheek, her hand left two crimson streaks. Delilah turned and pointed her staff at one of the spires anchoring the Lich Queen's legs.

"*Kaléste gi stoicheiaki!*"

The spire trembled. Stones shifted and pulled themselves away from the structure, forming a humanoid shape the same size as the demons. The unsupported top of the spire fell away, taking the crystal with it. The stone creature caught the crystal in its rocky hand and crushed it before lunging for the nearest beast.

"That's a neat trick." Alysha sidled up to Delilah.

She gestured to the demons. "What in the name of Selene are they doing? We're still here."

Gisella joined them, her silver armor streaked with a mixture of black ichor and blood. "They know their queen is in peril. We should strike while they're distracted."

"I'm almost spent." Delilah leaned on her staff and observed as demons clawed and lashed at the shield. The stone creature she had conjured traded punches with the one whose face Shatterskull melted, each blow sending the other reeling.

"We not going to make a dent as long as that rift keeps sending more." Alysha wiped her brow with her sleeve. "Let's close it, and then regroup."

"*Stenee pyealee… stenee pyealee…*" The Frost Queen chanted the words over and over, channeling energy into the rift. Delilah pointed her staff at the rift and followed suit. The demons clawing and flailing at the bubble surrounding the Lich Queen and Pancras paid them no mind. As they chanted and streamed arcane power into the tear, it shrank, finally vanishing under the onslaught of the combined might of the two women.

Delilah huffed and covered her eyes with her hand, giving them respite from the icy rain. "That seemed too easy."

"It's not a difficult task for two and no distractions." Alysha brushed hair out of her face. "We should prepare for the worst."

The archmage surveyed the carnage and flailing demons. "What could be worse than this?"

Her stone creature slammed its forehead into a demon, after which, her creature seized the foul beast and propelled it over the edge of the tower, pausing to regard the gap left by its creation before it sought fresh prey.

Alysha gestured toward the crowd of demons battering the shield surrounding Pancras and the Lich Queen. "He might fail at whatever he's doing in there."

"Release you?" Repeating the Lich Queen's request rendered it no less absurd. He tugged at Shatterskull. *Well, at least I have both hands in this vision.* Her grip overpowered his.

A swirling miasma of inky smoke swirled around them. It formed a column of angry black wind encircling them, but it did not touch either one. "You must. I ask, nay, beg you, Bonelord. I cannot leave on my own. You must guide me to Aita's realm."

Aita's bonelords shepherded the spirits of the dead into the next realm, particularly those who became trapped in their mortal bodies, either from disease or some other fate. The minotaur could not fathom the Lich Queen's ploy.

"You do not trust me." The ruby glow within her eyes faded slightly, and she hung her head, maintaining her death grip on Shatterskull. "Why should you? I have died twice trying to conquer this land."

"Exactly." Pancras grunted and concentrated on Aita's energy. He felt it flow through Shatterskull and into his arms. The column of dark smoke surrounding them expanded, moving farther away on all sides. When his concentration lapsed, it closed in, but it still could not reach them.

"You will never defeat Aita." That had to be her game—to challenge the Princess of the Underworld.

"Ha! That is not what I seek." Impossibly, her smile widened, splitting the thin, papery flesh of her cheek. "I know her realm is not for the likes of me. I will be damned, consigned to oblivion, or worse."

"I grew up hearing the stories. There will be no peace in death for you."

"Oblivion, non-existence, will be peaceful enough." She removed one hand from Shatterskull. Still, Pancras could not wrest control of the weapon from her. The Lich Queen cupped his chin in her icy, bony fingers.

"Hear me, Bonelord. Know that I speak the truth. When I was defeated at Badon Hill, my dominance was broken. Cursing the victors was my last, desperate act. A petty vengeance. The demons with whom I bargained for my power were not so willing to let me go, however. I was bound to them, and they kept me here, using me as a conduit to enter this world."

Her glassy-eyed gaze looked past him. "I know not for how long they have kept me like this, ravaging the life-force of my soul for their twisted passageway. I am weary."

The Lich Queen regarded Pancras once again, and their eyes met. He felt a shiver begin deep in his spine, and it spread until his whole body trembled. "They could force my spirit into one of my kin. I feel the blood of my daughter out there, fighting. They must not fall to the demons. They could make me whole again, give me flesh and power and the lust to use it. No, not my daughter's children.

"I was defeated once, and I rose for vengeance. I was defeated again after raising an army so fearsome even those born after my defeat have nightmares about it. I was a queen, terrible to behold with near-limitless power."

Her shoulders slumped, and her hand dropped away from Pancras's chin. "And now… I do not wish to endure a third defeat. The people will rise up again, as they always do. I could kill them all, but I cannot break their spirit. I would be victorious and rule over a land of the dead and a dead land. No lovers, no passion, no life."

She relaxed her grip on Shatterskull, and Pancras pulled it from her grasp.

"Show me the way to oblivion, Bonelord. Release me from this world." She stood before him, unflinching as he raised Shatterskull to strike.

Images flooded his mind, images of the demon that resided within him after defeating the bloodmaw beneath

Ironkrag. "The demon I confronted spoke of his mistress. Aita believed they acted at your behest. You must be destroyed."

"I made a pact, but I am no demon's mistress." She offered her hand to Pancras.

The minotaur, so certain the Lich Queen was the mistress to whom the demon referred, had not ever considered they served another. *Of course! All demons ultimately serve Maris, Duchess of War, Mistress of Demons, to bring strife into the world.*

"The demons misled me."

"Of course, as they misled the Princess of the Underworld." The Lich Queen's raspy chuckle mocked his erroneous conclusion. "And you have no way of knowing whether I am being truthful or not. Ask yourself this: if you truly believe I am no match for Aita's power, what harm can come from guiding me to the next realm?"

Damn it. She has a point.

Pancras allowed Aita's power to flow through Shatterskull and into him. It warmed him, and his trembling ceased. The dark clouds swirling around them expanded again.

"Very well, Bekkhildr, the Iron Witch." He took the Lich Queen's hand and guided her to the light of oblivion.

* * *

The demons surrounding Pancras and the Lich Queen raised their heads and howled. Dozens of greasy, smoky tendrils that had been hovering above when Delilah and Alysha closed the rift poured into the rooftop, racing up and over what remained of the spires and toward its center.

Gisella moved closer to her sister and adjusted the grip on her sword. "This looks bad."

"Tinian's lance! Is there no end to them?" Lord Fenwick helped Valora to her feet. The dwarf woman, unsteady, wiped blood from her eyes with the corner of her cloak. A long gash just past her hairline oozed.

Delilah and Alysha joined hands and gathered azure tendrils of arcane energy. Blood from a gash on the Frost Queen's cheek beaded and ran down her enchanted robes, and the archmage's distinctive stripes appeared muted beneath a coating of blood and gore. Their labored breathing betrayed exhaustion the Golden Slayer shared.

The inky tendrils coalesced into towering, bat-winged forms. Slavering, tooth-filled maws snapped and snarled. Twin explosions behind Gisella caused all the demons to look upward. Unable to help herself, Gisella twisted her head for a quick glance. The remaining crystal and the spire tethered to the Lich Queen exploded.

Howls of fury arose from the demons. Those that could tore at the shield surrounding Pancras with renewed vigor. The demons that couldn't turned and advanced on the companions.

Valora pushed away Fenwick's hand and held both of her axes at the ready. "My clan leader said I was a fool for coming here with you lot. He'll be happy to know he was right."

Delilah turned and winked at her. "This is not the first time I've done something foolish with a dwarf."

Fenwick beat his shield with the side of his blade. Rain bounced off his armor, and a bolt of lightning flashed across the sky. "Come on, then! The light of the Tribunal take you!" He eyed Valora, nodding to her, and charged.

The Golden Slayer raised her sword and screamed, speeding into the fray behind Lord Fenwick. Azure fire swept over their heads, searing demonic flesh. A clawed hand bearing talons larger than her sword came for Gisella, but she threw herself forward, slashing up as she dove. Hot ichor rained upon her, but the demon shrugged off her attack.

She rolled as she hit the rooftop and jerked to one side to avoid the snapping jaws of a two-headed, dog-faced demon. Gisella kicked it in the face and scrambled away.

Lord Fenwick raised his shield to block another demon's toothy bite, stabbing around its side with his sword. He sank it hilt-deep in the demon's mouth, tearing it free before it closed around his arm.

"Yaaaaaaa!" Valora's cry turned Gisella's head. The dwarf woman rode atop the two-headed dog demon, cleaving its heads with alternating blows from her axes. She swore in Dwarvish as she hacked its skulls like an angry wood cutter.

Gisella turned as a fiery, bat-winged demon landed in front of her. It threw back its head and howled as she slashed its knee. It punched her in the chest, the force of which sent her sword flying, as she slid along the rooftop.

Gasping for breath, Gisella braced herself as the demon stomped closer. Its searing talons scorched her neck as it reached toward her.

Lightning struck the demon. A peal of thunder shook Zamora as the demon growled and swatted at the charred flesh on its head. Then it convulsed. Its eyes bulged, and its flesh disintegrated.

Gisella glanced around her. All the demons convulsed, screamed, and evaporated. Their tenuous forms swirled around the roof, forming an inverted vortex that reached high into the night sky. The wind buffeted the Golden Slayer, and her cloak flapped around her head. She struggled to regain her footing, an impossible task as the wind pummeled her and the tower shook.

She heard massive detonations above her. Shards of stone pelted her from behind. As she crawled toward her sister, Gisella covered her head with her cloak. Alysha crouched near Delilah, protecting their heads as best she could.

When the shower of rock ended, all that remained was the rain. The clouds above poured their watery payload on the land, heedless of the events unfolding below. In the absence of demonic influence, the deluge became warm once again.

Gisella gazed at the sky, allowing the precipitation to cleanse the demon chill that permeated her bones. "I never thought I'd be glad for this damnable heat and rain."

Delilah slapped her hands together and laughed. "It's grand! Hey, Pancras?" She scanned the area for the minotaur. His still form lay next to a mound of ash. "Pancras!"

The companions rushed to the minotaur's side. The stump of his ruined arm was healed, albeit minus his withered forearm. His torso remained still, his fur streaked with grey, and the gash in his leg had closed.

The drak archmage knelt at his side. "No, no, no, no. Don't you die, not after all this."

Lord Fenwick took Valora's hand. "We'll leave you to your friend. Someone should check the lower level and the grounds. We should mourn away from this cursed place."

The Justicar and the dwarf headed toward the stairs. Alysha clenched her jaw and knelt alongside Delilah. Shatterskull rested beside the bonelord, its face now unadorned, indistinguishable from an ordinary weapon.

Delilah lifted his maul. "Damn it all." She turned away from the minotaur and dragged Shatterskull with her. Gisella sank to her knees at the minotaur's side and took his hand in hers.

"Thank you, my friend."

* * *

Pancras opened his eyes. He stood on a flat, stark plain of grey. The earth was hard packed, bereft of vegetation, and dispossessed of color. The sky appeared equally uniform.

So alike were the sky and the ground, he couldn't discern where the horizon ended and the sky began. The landscape felt familiar, yet he couldn't place where he'd seen it. It was as though he had visited this place before, but the details seemed just different enough now that he didn't recognize it.

Then a dot appeared. Far away, it too, seemed devoid of details. The dot grew in size. It took the shape of a robed figure, and as it approached, those features resolved into recognizable shapes—ancient robes, the curved hips and breasts of a young woman, and a skull.

The minotaur knelt before his goddess. "Aita. Another vision."

"No." She extended a porcelain-white hand and brought him to his feet. The skull transformed into the face of a raven-haired woman with eternity in her eyes. "You are with me now."

"Dead again." Pancras rubbed his arm with his withered… no, not withered. He was whole again. He marveled at his hand as he flexed it.

"Your task is complete. You shepherded a soul thought lost. Well done, Bonelord."

He glanced over his shoulder, expecting to see his friends gathered around his body. *Of course, there is nothing to see.* "At the cost of my life. My friends?"

"They live. They need not mourn you, unless you feel you need to depart the world." Aita took Pancras's hand and strode with him. He felt his hooves move, although when he tried to stop them, the sensation continued, as though they glided.

"It feels different this time. I don't remember this… place." The bonelord surveyed the area. The grey expanse appeared no different than when he opened his eyes immediately after releasing the Lich Queen.

"The Featureless Grey is where I meet all who depart Calliome, but none remember it. It feels different to you because your body clings to life, still." The goddess chuckled. "You need a bonelord."

"I have never heard of this place." Pancras was no theologian, but he was certain the name should have surfaced at some point during his studies. He found it odd that he didn't remember having forgotten his previous visits here.

"It is a realm outside of time, memory, and existence. When you have chosen, you will forget. Again."

"Everything?" Pancras eyed Aita. She gazed ahead as they walked, but he thought he perceived a nod.

"Everything that transpires here." She gestured ahead. Pancras's eyes followed her hand toward three shimmering portals, not unlike the Fae Nexus, the portal to the Fae Realm, in Drak-Anor.

"Does everyone get this choice?" Pancras had never heard any priest speak of choosing one's fate after death.

"Some do, but most do not. Even now, the Chosen of Aurora prays over your body. Aurora has heard her pleas and will grant you entry into her realm if you wish it." Aita gestured toward the left portal. It shimmered with hues of rose and lavender.

"I assume one of these portals leads to your realm?"

"Indeed." Aita gestured to the portal on the right. It shimmered deep violets and midnight blues. "You may dwell at my side for all eternity, my faithful bonelord. You will guide others to me."

Pancras's heart grew heavy. He regarded his hooves and slumped. "I… I… don't know what I was expecting."

"Whatever it is you think you will experience is nothing like what you will become. Your soul will not be bound by the constraints of time or your perceived limitations. You can do what you desire, when you desire, where you desire, although in all things, you will serve me. It is difficult to explain in this limited language you use. You will understand when you pass through the portal."

Pancras regarded the center gateway. It shimmered black, a shifting mass of nothing, like a hole in existence that was present, yet not. He sensed it would be uncomfortable to scrutinize were he alive. "And that one? The middle?"

"You have sacrificed, and you have served. Many of your dreams in life died before you had a chance to see them fulfilled." She leaned over and whispered in his ear, "We gods are not all-powerful, all-knowing."

The Princess of the Underworld straightened and gazed at the bonelord. "Perhaps you resent our meddling in your life. Perhaps you conceal a hatred for us and the life you lived. I offer you a third choice: oblivion. Pass through the center portal, and your consciousness will cease."

Aita dropped his hand and floated away. "But, if you feel you still have work, still have good to do, you need only open your eyes. As I stated, your body clings to life, although you have not emerged unscathed. Choose your eternity."

Choosing between death and life when he had no means of knowing what kind of life he would lead frustrated him. "How can I choose when I don't know what lies beyond, or even what awaits me in life now?"

The goddess of death circled him. "No one can tell you what lies beyond, Pancras. It will be what you make of it. All your regrets, all your sorrow, all your joy, all your triumphs, they will all be part of what, of who, you are. In time, you will forget your life on Calliome and become part of the fabric of existence. The choice you make now will determine if you strengthen that existence with your experiences or if you become a stain upon it."

A tear welled in Pancras's eye, but it evaporated into the dry nothingness of the Featureless Grey's reality. "I don't want to forget." The image of Orion's face lingered in the back of his mind, the sensation of his lover's tender touch. "I don't think I'm ready to leave life."

Aita approached him and placed a hand on his shoulder. "You will remember long enough to see your friends again."

"What if I choose to stay here?"

"This place will cease to exist when I depart. If you are here when I leave, you will dissipate as it does, but you will remain aware—consciousness without form. You will perceive nothing and everything at once. You will know the world, yet be unable to affect it. You will feel everything, yet you will be unable to act with regard to it. It will be a tortured existence."

It was more than Pancras expected and wholly unappealing.

"Think not too hard, my bonelord. The Great Beyond of the afterlife is a paradise or a damnation of your own making, but if you truly feel you are not ready, return to your life. You may still serve me there, if you wish. There are many who could use your help."

The idea of all the experiences he might yet know overwhelmed the minotaur. A life with Orion, watching his friends have families, seeing Delilah drag the Mages Guild kicking and screaming into a new paradigm. He didn't want to miss it.

"The time of the gods wanes, Pancras. Soon, our influence over Calliome will end. The lands beyond the sea and beyond the Western Wastes will find Andelosia once more, and together, all the peoples of the world will forge a bright, better future. Through it all, we will watch and be proud of our children."

"Proud of those who abandon you?" The minotaur gazed at his goddess. The scintillating violet hues of her portal reflected in her eyes.

"All children grow up and leave home. When the people of this world no longer need us, they will move on. We will move on." She waved her arm over her head in an arc. A sky of stars, planets, and galaxies appeared, wheeling about. Then it disappeared as though it had never existed. "There will be other worlds, other people. All those who dwell in our realms will have a hand in their creation."

Pancras turned toward the portals. The left promised an afterlife of all the pleasures Aurora so loved, many of which Pancras had never experienced, nor did he care to. Aita's Realm would be his home in due time.

He chose to live and opened his eyes.

* * *

Rain mingled with the tears on Gisella's cheeks as she knelt alongside Pancras. *What have you lost in making this sacrifice? Hopes? Dreams? Or was this your plan all along?* Her sister placed her hand on Gisella's shoulder. A smear of dust extended to where his withered hand had been. No appendage remained past his elbow.

"We should go."

Gisella brushed away Alysha's hand. "In a moment."

She clutched the seashell of Aurora at her neck. "Blessed Aurora. You teach us that sacrifice is the greatest expression of love."

Gisella stroked Pancras's cold cheek. "He followed Aita, but he deserves more than service. He sacrificed everything to rid the world of its greatest enemy. He gave of himself for others, and his efforts rewarded him with death. Guide him to a better place. He lived his life in the shadow of the underworld. Let him find peace in the light of your love."

The minotaur groaned, and his eyes fluttered open. "Giving up on me?"

"Pancras!" The scrape of a leathery foot on stone caught Gisella's attention. Archmage Delilah fell to her knees at her friend's side. "I knew you'd beat her."

Gisella regarded Delilah as the drak shivered and suppressed a sob, clearly trying to hold herself together. The

Golden Slayer wiped away her own tears and took the minotaur's hand. Warmth returned to it as she held it, the blossoming of life in a body on the brink of death.

"I will stay by your side as long as I must, Pancras."

"Me too." Delilah laid her head on his chest. He lifted her head as he pulled himself into a seated position with help from Gisella. Alysha ducked under his other arm, and the two sisters helped him to his feet.

The minotaur regarded his stump. "Well, damn. I'm losing bits of myself every time something like this happens, aren't it?"

"Life enjoys cruel jokes." Alysha wrapped her arm around his waist to steady him. "Can you tell us what happened?"

The minotaur rubbed the back of his head. "It's fuzzy. When the Lich Queen and I... joined... she"—he glanced at each of them in turn—"she wanted me to help her cross into the next life."

"What?" Alysha's jaw dropped, and she took a step backward.

Gisella put her hand on Pancras's chest. "She wanted you to help her die?"

"Wasn't she already dead?" Delilah curled her lip. "How could she die again?"

"The rift! We still have to close that rift!" Pancras looked toward the sky, but saw only clearing clouds.

"Relax." Alysha waved her hand. "We dealt with it."

"There are more where that came from, make no mistake."

"Around here?" Delilah turned her head, searching for another fissure.

"No. No, not around here, probably. In the world, I mean. Someone will have to deal with them, eventually."

"Eventually, but not today." Delilah took his remaining hand. "Tell us more about the Lich Queen."

Pancras explained how the demons bound her to this world to use as a conduit and that she had accepted her defeats and was weary, worn out, ready to depart this world and face what lay beyond. He explained that she did not want her grandchildren to fall to the demons, to become as she did.

"That pox-swilling, dust-lunged bitch deserves eternal torment. Where's the justice for all those who died at her hands?" Alysha crossed her arms, turned, and stormed away.

Delilah regarded the Frost Queen's back. "Maybe Alysha should join the Justicars."

Gisella chuckled and continued walking with them, supporting Pancras in her sister's stead. "She's just angry she was wrong about the Lich Queen's plans. She thought I was intended to be her new vessel. That's the only reason she came north when she learned I came to Vlorey."

"I'm glad she came; her assistance was invaluable. Still, I thank Hon I don't have any siblings." Pancras glanced first at Delilah and then Gisella. "Honestly, I don't know how you put up with them."

Alysha returned to assist the minotaur as he paced about the top of the tower, surveying the carnage. "Believe me, we made them pay for every mistake. Speaking of which"—she nodded at Delilah—"I still owe your brother."

"You and me both." Delilah reached up to take Pancras's withered hand, but grabbed only air. "Oh. You know, Archduke Fyodar's court wizard has a steel hand." Delilah gathered up Pancras's maul and Alysha's staff and dragged them behind her as they walked. "He seems to have full control of it. I'll bet someone could forge something like that for you. I'm sure he'd help us enchant it for you, too."

Pancras shook his head. "No, that won't do. Steel is cold, hard. Maybe some of that ebony wood they grow around here. I fancy the kind with the light-colored stripes. That would suit me, I think."

The Golden Slayer laughed. "We can't be unfashionable, can we?"

Pancras straightened up and laid his remaining hand on her shoulder. "As deputy headmaster, I have an image to maintain."

Delilah looked up at him. "You're staying, then?"

"Yes. Staying with Orion." Strong enough again to walk on his own, he released Alysha.

The Frost Queen retrieved her staff from Delilah. "With the archmage's help, I will use the moon gate to return home." She reached toward Gisella.

Gisella took her sister's hand. "I will return with you, if you'll have me."

Alysha smiled and pulled her sister into a hug. "Of course. You are most welcome, always. Grímar will be happy to see you."

"You're leaving the guild, then?" Delilah tapped on Gisella's mailed hand. "I won't stop you."

"With your permission, of course, Archmage." Gisella bowed to the drak. "If you need my help to get settled…"

"No, go with your sister. Once we've had a chance to rest up in Vlorey, I'll take you to the moon gate." Delilah tugged at her harness. "I'll need to return to Muncifer anyway. My brother, his mate, and my apprentice are still there. I'll go… back"—the drak shuddered—"where it's cold."

Alysha chuckled and held out the hem of her cloak. "Enchanted clothes. Besides, you're the archmage. If you want to move your seat to the warm climes of Vlorey, no one can stop you."

Gisella nodded. "And with the portals working, you could visit your brother any time."

"You're right, of course." Delilah shook her head. The drak regarded the two sisters and Pancras. "Let's get back to Vlorey. This place is still creepy."

"Ahem."

The three turned. Scout Stonehammer stood before them, a blood-soaked bandage around her head. "Fennie… um, Lord Blackthorne wanted me to report that all is well. All the dead are resting again, and the clouds are breaking." The dwarf woman approached them and made the sign of Anetha. "He'll be pleased you all seem no worse for the wear."

She inspected Pancras up and down. "How did you get so grey?"

The minotaur regarded his fur and chuckled. "A parting gift from the Lich Queen, I suppose."

"Speaking of whom, what about Grandmother?" Gisella gestured at the pile of dust that was once the body of the Lich Queen.

Valora put her hands on her hips. "Do you plan to keep her above your hearth?"

Gisella shook her head. "Not really."

"We will entomb her here." Alysha surveyed the rooftop. "The archmage and I will destroy the tower when we leave. Nothing will remain for misguided death cultists to find."

The sisters again eyed the pile of dust. Gisella bowed her head. "Be at peace, Grandmother."

"It doesn't seem right."

The Golden Slayer regarded her sister.

Alysha shrugged. "That someone who brought so much pain, death, and destruction to the world should have peace. She earned damnation."

Gisella didn't have an answer for her sister. She knew only what she saw on this day. "Pancras granted her salvation."

Epilogue

Although his wounds were not entirely healed, Pancras awoke each day with renewed vigor. Aita's blessing remained with him; he felt it each time he touched Shatterskull. Orion, too, was still with him, although the Justicar usually had awakened and gone to tend to his duties by the time Pancras arose.

Teaching alchemy with the use of only one arm was a skill the minotaur tried to hone, but he hoped he wouldn't have the need for it much longer. Already, a craftsman worked on creating a prosthetic forearm from a branch of striped ebony wood. Pancras chose that particular branch because it washed ashore during the storm in which he confronted the Lich Queen.

Delilah waited for him as he descended the White Tower, the bright morning sun rising later than it did when she first arrived.

"You know what today is, Pancras?"

They strode together. He nodded. "You're leaving?"

"I need to return to Muncifer. I'm going to set the other wizards and the slayers to tracking down and closing more chaos rifts. Besides, I have to make sure my brother hasn't destroyed his life completely before I even consider moving the archmage's seat to another city."

Pancras chuckled. Despite her brother's recklessness, the minotaur believed Kale would find his life's rhythm in time. *Probably faster without his sister's interference.*

"I've instructed your old headmaster there to let you use the Herald Stone whenever you want to talk to me." Delilah took his hand as they strode and gazed up at him. "You know, I thought when this mess was over, we'd all be going back to Drak-Anor, together."

"Life has a way of sweeping you to unexpected destinations. Sometimes, you find a better place in which to dwell for a while."

The archmage sighed. "You like it better here? Better than Drak-Anor?"

Pancras stopped and knelt facing Delilah. "I have something here I lacked in Drak-Anor. My life was good there, and Sarvesh was… is a good friend." He glanced at the university grounds. The leaves of the gingko trees faded from green to yellow, scattering their foliage on the earth below. "I was always an academic at heart. All those years I spent running, hiding… I can do more good here, I think."

She patted his shoulder. "See if you can find a moon gate here in the city somewhere. I meant what I said to all those students."

"I know you did. Sarvesh would be proud."

The drak's eyes glistened. "Are you?"

"I am." Pancras bowed before his archmage. "And honored. You were a wild, untamed sorceress when we first left Drak-Anor. Now"—he gestured to the buildings around them—"they all bow to you."

"I just didn't want to be bothered with dues." Delilah laughed and hugged him. He felt tears moisten his fur, but the drak's eyes dried by the time they parted.

"I'll be back, Pancras. That's a promise." Delilah waved to him as she crossed the bridge leading into the city.

He watched until she disappeared into the crowd. The minotaur wizard breathed deeply and made his way to the lecture hall, whistling a sea shanty he'd heard on the *Maiden of the High Seas*.

It was time to teach.

* * *

Alysha, Qaliah, and the Golden Slayer awaited Delilah when she arrived at the stables. The Frost Queen rubbed her eye and winked at the archmage. "I think you've got something there."

The drak wiped her eyes. "Shut up." She held her hand toward the fiendling and mounted Comet, wrapping her arms around Qaliah's waist.

Alysha and Gisella rode double on Moonsilver, the four women making their way to the tower from which Delilah and Alysha arrived. They stopped at Ravenbrier Meadery for a night of mead and song. The lad, Alfie, knew dozens of ballads. *That boy couldn't hold a tune if he tried with both hands.*

Qaliah's ebony cheeks took on a ruddy glow by her third mug of mead, and she swayed to the music. "I'm going to miss you girls, even the drak."

"Yeah?" Delilah grinned as she poured herself another mug of mead. "Come back to Muncifer; I'm sure I can find work for you at the Arcane University."

"No, thank you!" Qaliah raised her mug. "I'm done with that. I'm done with the cold. Vlorey's the place for me." She slammed her mug on the table, sloshing mead over the sides, and leaned forward.

She pointed a wobbly finger at Delilah. "Besides, there's a whole flock of young noblemen just looking for a taste of the exotic, and they are willing to pay shiny new crowns just to have me on their arm at the next ball."

Gisella shook her head as she sipped from her mug. "They're just using you, you know. They want the debutantes to see you as a threat and redouble their attentions on the young men's hearts."

"Don't care." Qaliah pointed her thumb at her chest. "Getting paid. Crowns. Gold crowns. Lots of them."

Alysha clicked her tongue and cocked her head. "She's not doing anything you're not accused of by fools every day, sister. And she doesn't even pay lip service to Aurora."

"Nobles." Gisella sneered and drained her mug. Young nobles and fools were synonyms in her experience. "True. Just take care you don't end up with a jealous knife in your ribs, Qaliah. Some of the games those men play end in blood."

Qaliah drew a dagger and promptly dropped it on the floor. "I can take care of myself." As she reached for the dagger, she fell out of her chair with a thud. The patrons of the meadery cheered and applauded. The fiendling jumped up with the dagger between her teeth and bowed with a flourish before returning to her seat.

In the morning, Delilah's head pounded, and sunlight seared her eyes with its brilliance. Its warmth intensified the pounding in her head, and she managed only to grunt good-byes to Tamera Ravenbrier and her family.

The throbbing had not improved by the time she arrived at the tower and climbed the steps ahead of Gisella and Alysha as they bade farewell to Qaliah. As she activated the moon gate, she heard the clopping of Moonsilver's hooves on the stairs.

I can't believe she's bringing the horse. The archmage set the moons, making her way around the circle with deliberate, slow steps, as she activated the runes to access the portal to Rime Frost. The gate sprang open as Gisella, Alysha, and Moonsilver reached the top.

The Golden Slayer whistled in appreciation. "So, this is ancient drak magic, eh?"

"Still working after an age. Let's see human buildings last that long." She gestured to the moon gate. "Just hold onto each other, and you'll be home in an instant."

Alysha knelt before the archmage. "Once I've settled my sister, I'll contact you and have you bring me back to Muncifer. I'll teach you all that magic you missed out on."

Delilah rubbed the base of her neck and nodded. "I'd appreciate that."

Alysha stood. "We can't have our archmage with gaps in her knowledge." She winked. "We'll be discreet, of course. In fact, I won't even come to the university if you don't need me to."

The drak offered her hand to the Frost Queen. "I can live with that."

"Good." The Frost Queen bowed, touching her forehead to the back of Delilah's hand. "It was an honor to fight beside you, Archmage. I look forward to seeing what you can do with that title."

Holding Moonsilver's reins, Gisella stepped up to the gate. She put her hand on the horse's neck and turned to Delilah. "Good luck. Selene be with you. May she keep you strong, and may Anetha give you the wisdom to wield your power with fairness and grace."

"Thanks for watching after Pancras for me." Delilah smiled at her. "He doesn't like to travel."

Gisella laughed. "I noticed."

Alysha wrapped her arm around her sister, and the three of them stepped through the gate. When the gate disappeared and the runes faded, Delilah activated them once more.

Time to go home, Deli-girl. You still need to find that dragon's treasure Manless stole.

* * *

The cold air of Rime Frost hit Gisella like a glad hand slapping her on the back. Moonsilver snorted and stomped, tossing her head and whinnying. The slayer took in a deep breath, inhaling the air of home for the first time in years.

"Good to be back?" Alysha hugged her sister.

"It is. It truly is." They led Moonsilver through the icy corridors and out to the stables. The sun hung lower in the sky in the Southern Watch than it appeared in Vlorey, and the wind blowing down from the mountains brought a bitter cold at which winters in Muncifer only hinted.

A boy clad in heavy furs took Moonsilver's reins as the women entered the stable. Gisella helped him remove the tack and harness and carried her saddlebags to the castle with her sister.

"What became of Grímar?" In all the commotion surrounding her sister's arrival in Vlorey, Gisella forgot to ask about her friend and sometimes lover.

Alysha threw back her head and laughed. "Oh, that fool. He was so terrified when he arrived with that note from Manless. I'm certain flying into a rage when I read the letter didn't help. What tales they must tell about me!"

Gisella and Alysha strode toward the living quarters on the third level, ascending a spiral staircase enclosed in one of the towers. "I confess, I'd heard so many stories, I wasn't sure myself how you would treat him."

"My first impulse was to imprison him."

"You didn't. The Frost Marten's Vaults?" A series of small cells that hung over the sea composed Rime Frost's dungeon. The back half of each cell's floor lay open to the sea. In ancient times, many prisoners flung themselves to their deaths rather than endure the harsh conditions for an extended period of time.

"Only for a day." Alysha placed her hand on her chest. "I may be the Frost Queen, but my heart is not one of ice. Besides, we all grew up together; it would be rude."

"Spare me."

Alysha chuckled. "He's around here somewhere. When I left with Yaamkyrsku, I told him to stick around through the winter, if he wanted. Despite what people think, Rime Frost is a damn sight warmer than walking to Haefstaad.

"You should hear the tales Yaamkyrsku tells of the Earth Dragon. I hope he was everything Yaamkyrsku expected. The world is changing, sister." Alysha shook her head. "A drak archmage, the Firstborne awakening…"

The Golden Slayer heard many stories during her travels about the return of Firstborne dragons but remained somewhat skeptical. Yaamkyrsku was mentor and friend to Alysha, although Gisella considered him a relic of a bygone age. *Perhaps I was too hasty in my judgment.*

"Pity Manless felt compelled to kill the Fire Dragon."

"Yes, I heard. The egg?" Gisella wouldn't have been shocked to learn that Yaamkyrsku kept it for himself.

"Safe in the claws of Terrakaptis. Yaamkyrsku contacted me; he's on his way back. I think I'll let the draks stew a bit more before letting them know." She chuckled. "I suppose he's the egg's uncle, eh? Do you think dragons observe the same familial relationships we do?"

"I wouldn't know." Gisella scratched her head as Alysha unlocked the door to her chambers. All was as she remembered it. A perpetual fire crackled in the hearth. The four-poster bed covered in fur blankets sat the far end of the room by the windows. Pine wardrobes and chests lined the walls. Reflected sunlight streamed through the stained glass which depicted a flight of dragons over craggy mountains. "Grímar stayed here? He didn't have a horse?"

"Yaamkyrsku ate his horse."

* * *

"Thank you." Kale give a silver talon to the messenger bringing yet another letter from the archduke. He stopped reading them after the third one arrived. Apparently, someone at the Arcane University told Archduke Fyodar the archmage would return to this location, so all correspondence should go to Kale. He tossed the letter upon a pile of similar envelopes in a box they set aside just for her.

"Oh, I hope she returns soon." Ori glanced up from the book he illuminated. "The archduke really wants her around when the Iron Giants come for the peace talks."

Kale turned his attention to the puzzle box he constructed. "She'll be back when she's back. That moldy old Lich Queen doesn't stand a chance against her and Pancras."

Part of him wanted to be there, but that part of his life was a memory now. His life was here, in Muncifer, and the minotaur who requested this puzzle box for his daughter's birthday paid good gold crowns for the gift. Kale bit his lip as he set the gear in place with his tweezers.

"Maris's bloody spear, that hurts!" Kali's cry broke Kale's concentration. He set down his tools. Ori regarded him, his brow crinkled. Bright daylight flooded the shop, reflecting off the snow that covered the streets of the undercity.

Sliding off his stool, Kale whooped and then raced to their bedchamber. Kali sat on a pile of linens, cradling a black-and-orange speckled egg in her arms. She smiled at him. "Glad there was just one in there."

Kale placed his hand on the still-warm egg and rested his head atop his mate's. "You should have called me. I would have helped."

She laughed. "How? Held my hand? Squeezed me until it popped out?"

Kali passed the egg to him and rolled out of their bed, dragging the soiled linens with her. She cleaned herself, still chuckling. "The real work begins now. You're going to help keep it warm and safe. Think you're up for it?"

The leathery, oblong spheroid felt heavy for its size. Kale held it up to the light, but the shell permitted no light through. "Yes, I am."

Kali approached him and wrapped her arm around his waist. They held the egg between them. "We're going to have to think of names. Boys, girls"—she tugged at one of his wings—"with those things, who knows? There might be a winged boggin in there!"

They laughed until the room trembled. Their eyes widened until Kale realized what had just occurred. The vibrations stopped, and they heard a voice call up from the cellar.

"I'm back!"

The sound of his sister's voice made Kale's heart leap. It felt as if she had been gone forever, although he knew it had not been quite that long. *Did Pancras return with her?*

Kali regarded her mate. His head turned toward the hallway, but then he faced her and smiled. "Ori can go meet her." The answers would come soon enough. "I have to take care of my family right now."

Heraldy of Andelosia

Free City of Celtangate

Free City of Ironkrag

Principality of Etrunia

Heraldy of Andelosia

Duchy of Muncifer

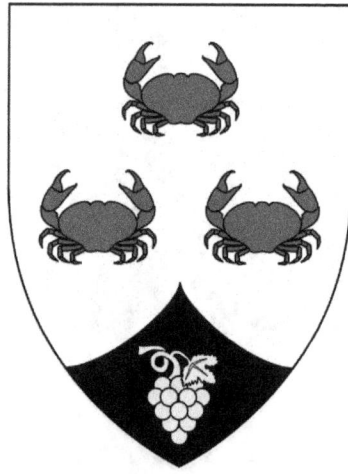

Free City of Vlorey

Arcane University

Hans Cummings
Author/Publisher

Author of the fantasy duology: The Foundation of Drak-Anor: *Wings of Twilight* and *Iron Fist of the Oroqs* as well as the Zack Jackson science fiction series, Hans Cummings published his first novel in 2011. Two of his short stories appear in Fear the Boot's Sojourn speculative fiction anthologies. He is Nuvo's Best of Indy — Best Local Author Honoree for 2014 - 2016.

Hans is a volunteer for the tabletop gaming industry ENnie Awards and maintains a gaming blog http://doctorstrangeroll.wordpress.com in addition to his writing blog http://vffpublishing.com.

Hans earned a Bachelor of Arts degree in English from Indiana University in 2006. He grew up in Indiana, Germany, and Virginia and returned to Indiana when he was 21. He currently lives in Indianapolis with his wife. Hans's hobbies include tabletop and computer gaming, cooking and smoking meat, and igniting young people's curiosity and passion for science and exploration.

Learn more about this and other works by the author at:
http://vffpublishing.com/

Use Twitter? Follow the author @hccummings